FARMLAND

AARON GUDMUNSON

The bleachers, she noted glumly but without much surprise stood empty. The snow had tapered to flurries and Susan had the grounds to herself. Well, not entirely. A figure stood in the far end zone, beside the goal post.

The last light, dying, sunk the field in shadow. Could the person at the far end be an errant player, coming to throw a few footballs before Christmas break? If so, why wasn't he? The first twinges of fear gnawed at Susie's stomach. The school would be completely deserted now, even the custodian gone for the day.

Susie glanced back at the figure and realized with horror it had drawn nearer—it hovered now on the 20-yard line. She took two stumbling steps backward. Her heels knocked against a concrete parking block and she fell over on her bottom, hard. She barely registered the pain in her tailbone. Her attention remained focused on the figure advancing across the frozen football field. It was not, she now realized, a rueful player ruminating on the results of the Devils' mediocre season.

The figure abruptly sprinted through the snow as if sensingher helplessness and desperation. It wore a heavy parka with a fur-lined hood, stained work pants, and boots of black leather. Thick gloves protected the fingers which now stretched ahead of it.

Susan shrieked, but Derby High's humble campus was as deserted as the moon. She scrambled up, her feet sliding on the icy walk, slipped again, and then the treads of her boots caught the snowpack and she jolted forward.

All she had to do was make it to the corner because she could see the steady traffic of Market Street from here—she would be able to flag down someone—and that's when a glove smelling of oil and grime closed over her face.

Copyright ©2022 by Aaron Gudmunson
ISBN 978-1-63789-818-5
Macabre Ink is an imprint of Crossroad Press Publishing
All rights reserved. No part of this book may be used or reproduced
without written permission except in the case of
brief quotations embodied in critical articles and reviews
For information address Crossroad Press at 141 Brayden Dr., Hertford, NC 27944
www.crossroadpress.com

FirstEdition

For my grandfather Knute and my grandmother Florence,
the greatest farmers I ever knew.

PRELUDE

Two hours out from the airport and they still had another thirty miles to go. She glanced at Don humming quietly behind the steering wheel, his watchful, careworn eyes scanning the roadway sprawled out before their rental car, and couldn't have been more grateful for his presence. He'd been very patient during this time. He claimed he understood because he'd experienced young love before too, but he could never fully understand. Not this.

October rain ticked on the windshield, reminding her of another autumn nearly half a century gone. Thanksgiving at the grand house on the ridge. Sneaking down to the denuded apple orchard, and climbing into the embryonic warmth of a stack of raked leaves to escape the evening chill. She remembered the feel of her hands in his, knowing in that moment they'd been completely alone in the universe. For a time nothing else mattered.

"Are you hungry?" Don asked, reeling her back to reality.

She looked around at him. "Not just yet. Let's get checked in first, okay?"

Don agreed. He usually did. "It will be fun to see some of the locales Jazzy wrote about in her book," he said.

Their daughter Jasmine had always been fascinated with her mother's tales of where she'd grown up, the scenic, rustic, lushly historic Ashford County, and had longed to learn more about the place—which she eventually did, culminating in a doctoral degree in history and a planned series of books, the first of which had been published a number of years previously via her university's press. Rachel could not be prouder of their daughter, but she only smiled at her husband's remark; seeing

Ashford County and living there were two entirely different things and Don would never know the wonder and heartache of it all.

He clicked on the radio to a classic rock station, started humming along with a Deep Purple ditty, then perhaps thought better of it, and shut it off again.

He was a good husband and they drove on in silence, the swipe of the windshield wipers the only sound. They hit the Derby Dale (known to the natives simply as Derby) town line an hour later and at the same moment the gray rain stopped, as if a curtain had been peeled back.

"My God," he said, pointing north over the harvested fields. "What is that?"

She didn't need to follow his finger to know what he meant, but she looked anyway. A rusted sign arched high into the sky, its legend spelled out in enormous globes that had intended to illuminate its message which read simply: FARMLAND.

A smile stretched across her face and a whisper of moths seemed to burst inside her belly. The arch still stood, even now, though she could tell many of the glass globes had been broken out over time, either by the elements or bored vandals. She wondered if it had ever even been lit up or if a power current had even been attached before everything fell apart, and hoped all at once that it had. In her mind she could see it lit up in full glorious splendor and her smile widened.

"That's where the apple orchard used to stand," she said. "Before someone burned it down."

BOOK I

**Apples to Apples
The Milliard Family
Autumn**

CHAPTER ONE

October, 1975.

August Milliard Sr. came to Derby, Illinois, by way of Michigan's Upper Peninsula in 1911. He brought with him that state's penchant for cultivating apples, integrating it easily enough into corn country, and for nearly a century his family's orchards had provided Ashford County enough ammunition to keep a battalion of doctors at bay. And come harvest, his farm produced enough pie and cider to feed a battalion of soldiers. The old man had gone so far as to insist that his lineage descended directly from Johnny Appleseed and even kept a portrait of the legendary American nurseryman hanging over the mantel in the great room of the family farm, though someone had yet to unearth documentation corroborating such a claim.

Milliard Farms Annual Apple Festival landed each weekend before Halloween and that year they were preparing to celebrate their 40th event. The turnout was anticipated to be nothing short of spectacular, with practically every able-bodied person in Ashford County expected to put in a cameo. Those who couldn't make it—the infirm and the elderly, mostly—could at least dream of enjoying an apple pie still warm from one of the farm's brick ovens and a jug of fresh-brewed cider steeped in mulling spices. Perhaps dare to hope a friend or neighbor kindly enough to bring them some. And someone usually did; the residents of Ashford County took care of their own.

Preparations for the event took the entire Milliard clan (and more than a few hired hands) working dawn to dusk an entire week to complete. Of course by 1975 August Sr., the festival's original patron, had been in the grave better than two decades, which left everything in the capable hands of his eldest grandson, August Milliard III—Augie to his friends.

Augie had been handling Apple Fest duties since his father, August Jr., had been struck dead by a bolt of lightning while tending to one of the orchards in the summer of '66. While this loss saddened his eldest boy deeply, Augie had taken charge with vigor. He'd secretly dreamed of being the showrunner since boyhood and now that he'd been the head honcho going on a decade, he thought (also secretly) that he'd done the best job so far.

"Where do you want this bunting, Aug?" Raymond Safford called. Ray ran the hog farm on the other side of town, down near Duck Valley. No fresher pork could be found this side of the Mississippi, and that wasn't just Augie's opinion—ask anyone in Ashford County.

"Hang it along the railing of the store, Ray," Augie called. "Facing the lot, not the field."

"You got it, buddy," Ray hollered back. He was a good guy, Ray, but not the crispest Honeygold in the bushel.

Augie stepped into the Milliard Country Store—one of the original barns his father had converted into a showpiece marketplace intended for peddling all things autumn. They made a killing this time of year selling fritters, pies, and donuts to the teeming masses. Milliard Farm's busiest stretch ran from the first of September through Halloween, and now, in the second week of October, they were just hitting their stride.

The smell of cinnamon and cider hit him playfully, like an old friend, and he inhaled deeply as he did each time he entered, a long-ingrained reflex. Jack-o-lanterns and witches adorned the walls, white-sheeted ghosts dangling from the rough-hewn rafters by lengths of kite string. Augie loved this time of year, and not just because of the tolling of the till. Festive and cozy and nostalgic, a throwback to the glory days of childhood.

The young man behind the register did not appear festive. He slouched on his stool, looking morbid and sullen, staring into a Spider-Man comic between transactions with as much enthusiasm as if it was a church hymnal. Hair too long and greasy for a teenage boy—in Augie's opinion, at any rate—touched the collar of an oil-splotched Fruit of the Loom T-shirt a size too small for his athletic frame, accentuating his biceps and pectoral muscles. At least the green nylon apron with the Milliard Farms logo covered much of the grime. The kid rang up each order with all the charisma of a sleepy sloth, concluding each transaction with a mechanical: "Thank-you-for-shopping-Milliard-Farms-Country-Store-have-a-nice-day."

Augie stepped behind the counter and whispered, "Can you at least pretend you're not a zombie during your shift, Denny?"

"I can't, Dad. This is too boring. I want to work on the Firebird." Dennis loved working on cars above all other activities in life, with playing football coming in a close second even if he did ride the bench behind Kent MacDonald, the Derby Devils' All-Conference quarterback.

"You'll have plenty of time to tinker with your toys when your work is through."

"Why can't Hannah take over? She always works short shifts."

Augie hated when Dennis whined—truthfully, he hated when any of his children did, but Denny irked him more because being eldest he ought to know better.

"Her and Tommy and the twins are working the orchard tonight. You know that. You're done in an hour anyway. Put a smile on your face, why don't you?"

"This stinks."

"Tough. If I get any customer complaints, the next time you see your car will be after graduation."

"Yes sir." The kid put on a limp smile and turned to the next customer in line, a silver-haired woman named Betsy Donahue who taught English at Ulysses S. Grant Junior High School. "Good evening, Mrs. Donahue. Did you find everything you were looking for?"

"I sure did, Denny. Your mother makes the best apple donuts I ever tasted and that's no lie," the teacher said, pulling a pinch off and setting it on her tongue to melt like a Communion wafer. She even closed her eyes in reverence.

Augie left them and pushed through the kitchen door where his wife Teresa stirred batter into a steel vat the width of an oak bole so it would be ready by the time the bakers clocked in for the early morning shift. Her customary chef's hat lay like a deflated toadstool on her head, making her all the more beautiful. Augie kissed her cheek, then dipped a finger into the mix and sucked it clean.

"Perfection, Tree," he said, using the nickname he'd given her two decades earlier which had tickled her then and had shown no signs of wearing off. "You'll have the masses swooning. Again."

"You always know what to say to get a girl giddy," Teresa said, giving the batter a good stir with a wooden spatula the size of a boat oar. Augie took his clipboard off the nail in the wall, checked over the production schedule, jotted a few changes, then replaced the board. He swatted his wife on the rump on his way through doors and she responded with a blown kiss across the space between them.

Denny seemed to have perked up some behind the counter and Augie thought at first his lecture had done the boy some good. Until, of course, he spied Rachel Safford, Ray's middle child with the honeysuckle hair, glancing over the shelf of homemade fudge. Augie sighed and stepped over to his boy.

"She's too young for you, son."

"Jeez Louise, Dad," Dennis said. Augie had startled him out of his thoughts—whatever those may have been. "I'm not into her or anything. But she turned fifteen over the summer."

"And you'll be eighteen soon enough. A man. Too old for a child."

"I already told you—I don't dig her."

"Good. Keep it that way. There are plenty of girls your age at school."

"Yeah? Like who?"

Augie shrugged, making a performance of considering. "I don't know. Lorelai Lang seems nice."

"Lorelai Lang? Dad, she's like the smartest girl in school. Not to mention the foxiest."

"You say that as if it's a bad thing."

"She's friends with Hannah. It would be weird. Plus, she'd never go for a dumb hick like me."

Augie's hand whipped out so fast it surprised even him. He gripped his son's shoulder, not hard but firm enough. "You don't ever say something like that. You hear me? If you go through life thinking you're a dumb hick, that's all you'll ever be."

"Dad, I—"

"And have you forgotten Lorelai's a farm girl too? You forget those oceans of corn her daddy grows? Who do you think helps shell come harvest? You think Grant Lang does it all himself?"

"No sir."

Augie released his son. "That's right. His girls do their share. The way I hear it, he taught the middle one—Nora is it?—to drive the combine this season."

"Nora's a tomboy," Dennis said. "She'll be running the farm by the time she's old enough to take a drink."

"Well, that may be true or it may not. My point is, Lorelai's a good girl. Got high ambitions. You could do a lot worse, son."

"Like Rachel Safford, you mean?"

Augie sniffed. "There's nothing wrong with Rachel. She's just too young for you, that's all. Put her out of your mind, you hear me?"

"Yes sir."

They looked up to find Rachel approaching the counter slowly, unwilling to intrude on the family debate, whatever its subject may be. "Hello," she said when she realized they'd finished.

"Evening," Dennis said. "Help you?"

"I'd like a dozen apple donuts, please, and a quarter pound of pumpkin fudge."

Dennis craned to see the fudge display—his sister Susan should have been there with her tongs, but naturally, like Hannah, she'd shirked her duties. Again. He opened his mouth to say something, but Augie held up a hand.

"I'll get the fudge. You box up the donuts."

When his father stepped around the counter, Dennis grinned an apology. "Sorry about that. Susie is supposed to be on fudge duty. Don't know where she's gotten off to."

Rachel smiled, displaying dazzling straight white teeth, which seemed atypical of a farm kid. Did her folks earn enough to take her to the orthodontist? Of course, the Saffords only had three kids; maybe without so many mouths to feed they were able to scrape enough together. Certainly Rachel's brothers Caleb and Samuel displayed no smiles as sterling as their sister's. It didn't matter—the feature only made her all the prettier, something Dennis found disarming.

"I saw Susie heading for the corn maze about ten minutes ago," Rachel said. She was Susan Milliard's age and the two had been fast friends since kindergarten.

"Typical," Dennis said with a sigh.

Rachel's smile vanished. "What's wrong?"

"My sisters get whatever they want," Dennis said, hating the way he sounded dangerously close to whining. "My brothers too, for that matter."

A rind of Rachel's smile returned. "It's just because you're the oldest. Your folks put the most on your shoulders, that's all." Then she reached out a hand and rested it on Dennis's. It was warm and slightly moist. The sensation was so unexpected and delightful he froze. Then he pulled his hand away under the pretense of tapping at the register.

"That's, um, that'll be three sixty-nine with tax," he said, heat climbing his cheeks. Nothing he did seemed to open the register, which only served to make the situation direr.

His father returned with the fudge in a white paper sack and handed it over. "This ruffian bothering you, Rachel?" he asked.

"Dad, jeez—"

Rachel laughed, a sound like a lullaby to Dennis's ears. "No, Mr. Milliard, but you may have to remind him how to run the register."

Finally, thankfully, the bell dinged and the drawer shot out like a busted jaw. Dennis took the crumpled bills Rachel handed over, stuffed them away, and returned the change. At least he'd gotten that right, thank God.

"Thank-you-have-a-good-night," Dennis said.

Rachel scrunched up her face which somehow, impossibly, made her more beautiful. "Um, aren't you forgetting something?"

The tips of Dennis's ears felt like they might explode. He'd given her the change and the fudge, what was he forgetting now?

"The donuts," his father said. "Don't bother, Denny, I'll get them."

When he'd gone, Dennis fumbled for words. Rachel came to his rescue.

"Hey, it's okay. I'm pretty forgetful sometimes too."

He wanted to scream at her that his forgetfulness was her fault, not his; that touching him with that lovely, warm, damp hand had stirred something in him he'd never felt. Before he could say anything, though, his father returned and handed over the box.

"You have a wonderful night, Rachel," he said. "Give my regards to your mother."

"I'll tell her, Mr. Milliard." She flashed one last smile at Dennis, then skipped out the door to where her old man's pick up stood idling in the gravel lot. Ray Safford said something to his daughter as she climbed into the cab, then turned to the store and raised a hand.

Father and son returned the hail. When only a veil of exhaust remained where they'd been parked, father again addressed son. "Okay, you can head on home to work on your car."

"Can I get a lift?"

"I'm going to be a while. Got some chores to finish. You're free to wait or walk, up to you," Then Augie pushed through the double doors leading into the kitchen. He came back just long enough to add, "You keep clear of Rachel Safford, son, you hear?"

Dennis said he did and when his father left, he watched the place where Rachel had stood as if trying to conjure her again.

CHAPTER TWO

When the old pickup rocked to a halt in the gravel drive, Rachel hopped out and helped her father unload supplies from the bed. He asked if she wanted dinner, but she politely declined.

"I knew you sneaked some of that fudge on the drive," he said, his simple crooked smile dangling to his chin.

"No, Papa, I swear," Rachel said.

"Aw, you know I won't say anything to your ma," Ray said, digging his own piece out of the bag now that his hands were free. They needed a good washing, but Ray never minded a little grit with his grub. "Why don't you go on up, do your homework?"

"Mama will have dinner on the table."

"I'll tell her you aren't feeling up to snuff."

"That's lying."

Ray Safford waved a hand in the air. "There's a difference when it comes to lies. Some of them hurt folks and some, they don't. This is one that don't."

Rachel finally allowed a fragment of the smile that so stunned Dennis Milliard to shine through. It was her mother's smile. "I'll pray for you tonight, Papa."

"You do that," he said and followed her into the house. The host of Safford hogs—all thirty-nine head, including boars, sows, barrows, and shoats—seemed to squeal a fond hello, blissfully oblivious of their numbered days.

The place smelled of chops and fresh-pressed apple sauce, but the kitchen stood empty. They found Ruth and the boys on the front room sofa, side by side, reading their Bibles. None looked up when father and daughter entered.

"Sorry we're late," Ray said. "Augie had us working overtime."

"Did he pay you?" Ruth asked, head still bowed to her scripture.

"Aw, honey, you know I don't ask for no wages. It's Apple Fest, after all. My favorite time of the year."

"Is Apple Fest any reason a man ought to *slave* for free?" Ruth asked, finally catching her spouse's gaze. "Is it any reason he ought to miss the supper his wife *slaved* over?"

"Now, Ruthie. The festival don't come but once a year."

"Dinner's in the oven. You'll want to reheat the gravy in a saucepan."

Ray heaved a sigh before tromping off to the kitchen. Rachel watched him fish a donut out of the box and stuff it into his face while he ladled potatoes and gravy onto a plate.

Rachel climbed the stairs slowly, a hand pressed to her belly. She'd told the truth about the fudge—she'd not filched any. She simply had no appetite. Hadn't for days.

Empty belly, full head, she thought. It was one of her grandmother's sayings. Well, Rachel had a full head, all right. She couldn't stop thinking about Dennis Milliard. He looked like a movie star and spoke like a snake-oil salesman. When he wasn't tripping over his own tongue, that is. She often got close to him at school just to hear him talk to his friends. She watched him practice football from the safety of the school's band room window.

What had been up with him tonight? Why had he stuttered around so much? Could it possibly be he felt something for her as well? No way—he was a senior and she a lowly freshman. It was true he didn't have a girlfriend (at least not that she knew of, though Derby boys were sometimes known for dating Murdoch girls), so was it too much to think she might have made an impression on him tonight?

She made it to the top of the stairs, but instead of going to her room she stepped into the spare bedroom the family used for storage. A headless seamstress dummy stood in the corner of the room surrounded by odds and ends that had been retired from everyday use. A table with a busted leg, an

armless threadbare chair, a tin box of skeleton keys resting atop
a scarred and stained credenza last in fashion sometime during
the Great War. Beyond this stood a door half her height which
led to an attic crawlspace. Rachel opened it, hunched inside, and
closed it behind her. The smallest of the family—even her kid
brother Samuel had outgrown her now at age 11—she was the
only one who fit well in this oft-forgotten nook of their house.
Her father, with his beer belly, could not even squeeze inside
any longer.

The crawlspace had been largely passed off as useful only
in housing spiders and mice. Rachel Safford, though, had
discovered another use for it.

Over the summer, she'd found a new book at the library and
after reading the dust jacket had checked it out and hidden it in
her backpack so her mother would not see it. *Carrie* had been
its title and it had been about a girl not much older than Rachel
who'd discovered upon getting her "monthly curse," as her
mother called it, that she had telekinetic powers. Rachel had read
it cover to cover with a flashlight right in this very crawlspace
one stormy afternoon while listening to the rain thrum on the
old wood overhead and lighting flickering through the tiny
ornamental window at the far end.

It was as if the author had plucked the idea of the title
character right out of Rachel's head. Rachel could have *been*
Carrie White. All the elements were present. The fanatical
mother. Being a relative outcast at school (most passed her off
as a grubby hick who would be nothing but a hog farmer's
daughter her whole life). Most of all, she'd gotten her curse only
a month before discovering the volume in the General Fiction
adult section. The way Rachel figured, if she bled like a woman
she ought to be able to move up from the kid's section.

The only thing she did not have in common with Carrie
was her ability to manipulate objects with her mind. In her
imagination she saw herself forcing fumbles at football games,
erupting schoolbooks out of the arms of snotty classmates,
causing Mr. Ireton's spectacles to slip off his nose in the middle
of a lecture on chemical bonding. For weeks, upon discovering
menstruation would not unleash them, she prayed God would

provide her such abilities. After two months of no response from on high, Rachel had given up.

She did, though, pray on other matters. These matters were between her and God alone, as she had no intention of confessing them to Father Scudder after Mass some Sunday. Not ever.

On her knees in the crawlspace, directly above where her mother and brothers sat in a row reading from their Bibles, Rachel clasped her hands and whispered: "Dear Father, Son, and Holy Spirit, please forgive me my impure thoughts about Dennis Milliard. I cannot stop them when they come and would not wish to even if I knew how. Also, please forgive me what I'm about to do. In Jesus' name I pray. Amen."

When she'd finished her monologue, Rachel reached into the darkness until her fingers found the contours of the battery-powered record player. She switched it on, slipped on the padded headphones, and closed her eyes.

She struggled off her blue jeans and underpants, dug around until she found the flashlight and X-Acto knife, and then held her breath.

She made the first cut across her thigh, just above her panty line, when the first dissonant chords of Zeppelin's "Kashmir" came through. The flashlight, tucked between her chin and sternum and resting on her bosom, trembled. Blood welled. She gasped in a spasm of ecstasy.

I'm so sorry, my dear God, she thought, watching the blood pool in her pubic hair, and for the first time realized how much, in the jittery yellow light, it resembled the color of ripe red apples.

CHAPTER THREE

Augie snapped off the lights and hauled the door closed behind him, ensuring all locks had been secured. He'd considered investing in an alarm system for the store, but didn't figure anyone would break in to steal apple sauce or pumpkin spice. Not in this clean little pocket of America. He removed all cash on the premises nightly and hoped the sign taped to the door saying as much would be enough to deter even the most desperate bandito. Lord knew this land had been acrawl with them in his granddaddy's day.

A stout form loped out of the trees and came up to lick his hand. "Hey, Timber." Augie scrubbed a hand through the scruff of his huskie-heeler hybrid. "Want to take a walk with me?"

Whistling, Augie bounced the zippered money bag in his palm and strode to his Ford pickup. He unlocked the door, but instead of climbing behind the wheel he tossed the bag on the bench, retrieved a battered flashlight from the floorboard, locked up, then stood looking at the orchard. It did as brisk a business as the store, with folks paying a buck a peck to pick their own fruit. Imagine that—folks paying to do labor. Augie had never gotten over his old man's ingenuity when he'd concocted that scheme.

Across a wide grassy avenue stood the outskirts of Grant Lang's remotest cornfield. Three years ago, Augie had paid Lang top dollar for five acres in order to build a corn maze. Lang, the county's leading farmer—at least since Vance Gable had dropped dead of a burst heart in 1968—had grumbled about wasting good crop for flights of fancy, but had had no trouble cashing the check in the agreed-upon amount.

"You're going to have to plant special hybrids and measure

fertilizer different," Lang had told him. "You can't just go slicing through regular feed corn and expect your maze to hold up. You got to watch for stalk rot. And you're going to want to run it by Granny before you take action."

Augie had thanked him before parting ways, already deciding he'd need to hire someone who knew about building crop mazes to deal with the planting and cutting issues; he knew nary a kernel about corn. He suspected Lang had been willing to go along with the maze plan because of a recent boom in the grain market. The Soviet Union had recently purchased an enormous amount of corn from the United States and, along with generous subsidies, the Lang clan could afford to sacrifice a few paltry acres.

As for Granny Adeline Gable, Augie didn't think she'd put up much of a fuss. Grant had been correct to suggest getting her blessing before acting, though. Every farmer got her blessing before making any major agricultural decisions. Which, of course, is exactly what cutting a maze through perfectly good crop constituted.

Now, as he picked his way through the pumpkin patch to the entrance of the maze (which had not officially opened until last Apple Fest due to the amount of work it took to get everything right), Augie glanced over his shoulder at the top of the bluff where Granny Adeline's enormous estate stood like a deity overseeing its flock. A light glowed in an upstairs window, where Augie presumed the lady of the house must stay her nights, and not for the first time thought of the Bates house in that movie *Psycho*. He imagined her up there in her antique wheelchair, a skeletal form staring out her window to survey her queendom. Perhaps she had a spyglass pressed to one ancient green eye while doing so. Perhaps even now she spotted him about to step into the very maze she'd grudgingly approved on that late summer evening in 1972. Augie resisted raising a hand in greeting, smiled at himself, and then stepped into the corn.

He'd discovered last season a nightly walk-through couldn't be helped after a couple of teens had hidden in a dead end after closing and had got up to no good. He'd be damned if any child would be conceived in his maze, by God.

Normally Augie sent Dennis on this chore, but the boy had opted to walk the mile home so he could work on the damned car he'd bought from Lloyd Avery for five hundred smackers. He had to hand it to his son—the kid knew his way around an engine. Good money in mechanics, if that's the direction Denny decided to go, though Augie had made him promise to get college educated before hauling on the coveralls and diving headfirst into a vat of Quaker State.

That got him thinking of Lorelai Lang again. He'd never admit it to anyone else, not even Tree, but the reason he pushed her so hard on Dennis was because he thought their marriage could be a catalyst for a truce with her father Grant. The Lang patriarch owned much of the land in the county, every inch and acre Granny Adeline permitted him to buy from her. Grant made no secret of resenting the Milliard orchards—he thought apple trees a waste of perfectly good farmland. Farmland that could be used for more corn and not taking advantage of ill-begotten labor.

Michael Stone, the dairy farmer from up Ashford way, had once confided in Augie that Grant didn't think of apple farming as true farming at all. "He calls it agrotourism, Augie, swear to God," Mike had said that day over drinks at Chancellor Bros. Saloon. "He said all your farm does is bring in overpaying outsiders to pick the crop for you."

Augie chuckled as he swept the beam of light along the brown stalks, looking for tears in the mesh which had been rolled along the "walls" of the maze to deter errant customers from taking an unconventional turn and getting lost. He'd walked the maze so many times he no longer needed to consult the map the aerial artist had drawn up. Starting this weekend, in honor of Halloween looming, he'd let the older kids suit up in their favorite costumes after dark and chase maze wanderers around. Of course, he'd have to advertise that the corn would become haunted after sunset so as to avoid a lawsuit for anyone with a weak heart. Lawsuits seemed to have taken the place of common sense these days, it seemed.

As Augie rounded a bend, flicking his light down a corny cul-de-sac, and still thinking of a Milliard-Lang alliance forged through marriage, Timber laid his ears flat and rumbled low in his throat.

"What is it, boy?" Augie asked, focusing the light in the direction the dog pointed. "You scent a skunk?"

Timber crouched, haunches tensed, growling louder now. Then he sprang into the darkness, snapping his long yellow teeth. Augie jogged after, sweeping the light ahead on the packed-earth path. Light rain drizzled down and he prayed it wouldn't stay long. The last thing he needed was paying customers turned away because of mucky trails. Up ahead the dog continued his savage salvo. The rain intensified, steadied, then tapered off completely. Good deal. The harm had been minimal.

Augie had made it to the halfway point, breathing hard, when he realized he no longer heard Timber. He made only cursory glances down side paths and dead ends and when he picked out the exit on a straightaway forty yards on, Augie sprinted to it. Timber waited in the open grassy area outside panting and pacing.

"What the hell got into you, boy?" Augie gasped.

The only answer he received was the great brushy tail sweeping side to side like the pendulum of a great grandfather clock. Augie stroked the dog's anvil-shaped head before ordering him to the pickup. They climbed into the cab and reversed out of the lot. At the second movement of the three-point turn, Augie hesitated long enough to fire the high beams up through the maze exit and thought he saw someone standing at the far end of the straightaway. He blinked and looked again, but saw only corn this time.

CHAPTER FOUR

Dennis Milliard lay on the oil-stained garage floor beneath the Firebird's undercarriage, working the exhaust system over with his socket wrench. Sweat stung his eyes and pasted his hair to his forehead. A corner of tongue protruded through his lips. His arm ached from holding it suspended so long, but by God he would have the exhaust running before bedtime or die trying.

WJKP had faded from Alice Cooper to a deep cut of some Pink Floyd song he didn't recognize when his father's truck rolled up beside him. The garage—or the carriage house, as his folks still called it despite it having undergone numerous renovations over the years—had been built large enough to house tractors, but only three of the four bays were occupied with any regularity—the far end for the Firebird and the adjacent space for the Ford. The Buick his mother favored took up the slot nearest the mudroom door so Teresa wouldn't have to navigate the various clutter strewn around. She didn't begrudge her husband and son their perennial mess so long as they kept it clear of the house, which she kept neat as a pin with a near religious fervor.

Dennis crawled out laughing and shoving at Timber when the old dog scooted under to lick his face. "Hey, Dad. How'd we do tonight?"

"Fair, I guess," Augie said, bouncing the money bag again. Part of his son's job was to deposit the haul from the previous night at the bank before heading to school. Until then it rested in the safe Augie kept in his upstairs den. He opened his mouth to say more, then stopped at his son's confused countenance.

"Where's Susie?" Dennis asked.

"Isn't she here?" Augie replied, unease already blooming in his belly. Then, as if a rational thought might conjure her, "It's her turn to help your mom with dinner."

"We thought she stayed behind with you at the store," Dennis said.

"She's not with me," Augie said, hustling toward the house with his son on his heels. In the kitchen he dropped the zipper bag on the breakfast bar and said to his wife: "Tree, you seen Susie?"

Teresa, stirring a pot of stew, had a thumbnail in her mouth from sampling the fare. "She's not with you?"

"Dammit all, no."

"Rachel said she saw Susie heading toward the maze," Dennis said.

"When?" his parents asked in unison.

"About, maybe, half an hour before closing time," he replied. "I was mad because she was supposed to be manning the fudge counter."

"Did you see her on the walk-through?" Teresa asked.

"What kind of question is that, Tree? Do you think I'd have left her there if I had?" he shot back. Anxiety had a way of turning him mean.

"August—"

"Everyone else accounted for?"

"Hannah's doing homework. Tommy's watching the ballgame. The twins are in the toy room."

"I'm going back to look for her," Augie said.

"I'll go with you," Dennis said.

"No, you to stay here. You're the man of the house while I'm gone. If I'm not back with Susan in half an hour, call Chief Engel at home."

"Dad—"

But August Milliard didn't wait around to argue. He took down his Winchester .30-.30 from its rack in the garage and stuffed a handful of cartridges from the box into his pocket, and jumped back into his truck. With Timber riding shotgun, he drove back to the orchard a mile down the road. Was he being paranoid? Probably. But you couldn't be too careful these days.

When they bumped back into the lot a minute later, Augie's first order of business would be searching the maze again. Someone or something had been in there with them. But if it had been Susan, Timber wouldn't have reacted as he had. The old mongrel loved all the Milliard children but favored Susie most of all. Most nights he'd wind up sleeping at the foot of her bed, to the chagrin of the twins who pleaded with the dumb animal to stay with them.

But now he saw the maze would have to wait. Every light in the store blazed bright … and he could see someone moving around in there behind the counter.

"Come on, Timber," Augie said, climbing out of the cab. He didn't have to tell the dog twice—the creature sprang past him and raced for the wide front porch of the family store.

Augie came fast behind, rifle raised, until he observed the dog's behavior. Timber ran in tight circles near the door, tail wagging as though to send it flinging into the night. He did not snarl or snap and only after Augie gained the top step did he recognize the figure near the register. His heart gave a relieved lurch and he yanked open the door.

"Susan Lynn Milliard, what in the blazes do you think you're doing?" he bellowed. Susie spun toward him, her face streaked with tears, and replaced the phone receiver on its cradle before stumbling around the counter and throwing herself into her father's arms.

At first she could manage only to stutter out one word. "D-Daddy, Daddy, D-D-Dad—"

"Calm down, Sunshine, and tell me what happened," Augie said. Timber jumped up and propped his front paws on the edge of the counter so he could lick at her elbow. She did not reject his affection. If she even felt it she gave no sign.

Only after taking a series of deep gulping breaths could the girl find the wind to speak, and when she did it came all in a gust. "Daddy, I'm sorry, I went into the maze after work and I felt tired so I found a quiet little turnaround and lay down to look up at the clouds and the sky started turning soft pink and I guess I drifted off listening to the breeze through the stalks and and and—"

"Okay, Sunshine. Okay, just calm down. Let me get you some water."

Susan shook her head. She took another shuddery breath and at last seemed to stabilize. She found it in her to stroke Timber's ears, to his delight. "I'm all right. I'm okay now, Dad."

"Tell me the rest."

"When I woke up it was almost full dark. I saw the first stars in the east and only the faintest purple in the west. I could hear Timber barking a long way off." The girl shuddered once, violently. "And then I saw something coming at me through the corn."

"What was it, Sunshine? A skunk? Timber caught the scent of something when we did our walk-through, broke away and ran—"

Susan shook her head again, her blonde hair so like her mother's flying around her head like whips. "It wasn't a skunk. Whatever I saw … it stood on two legs, Dad. It looked like a werewolf or something. And it *stank*. It stank worse than the time we found the litter of dead racoons up in Rachel's haymow."

Augie figured his daughter must have been tricked by the shadows of the imminent twilight but held his tongue. He'd hear her out. "What then, Sunshine?" he said gently.

"When I heard Timber barking way off in the distance I tried to scream for him or for you, but it was like my lungs wouldn't work, you know? Like in a bad dream when you try to scream and you can't. That's how scared I was."

"And then?" Augie prompted.

"Then I ran," Susan replied. "I didn't see the thing again … it had moved on. So I just ran. I found my way out of the maze by sheer luck because I was too scared to remember which way I'd gone and when I made it I saw you driving up the road. I tried to scream for you to stop, but you didn't hear me. So then I ran to the store and used the spare key. I tried calling over and over but the line was busy."

"I'm guessing your sister was monopolizing the phone rather than finishing her algebra," her father said in an effort to lighten the mood. It seemed to work; Susie giggled into her hand. "What do you say we get home before supper gets cold?"

"I don't think I'll have an appetite for a month," she said.

"You may not, but I'm starting to find mine again," Augie said. "Come on, kiddo, let's make tracks."

They stepped out onto the porch at the same time a black and white cruiser pulled into the lot beside the pickup and Alvin Engel stepped out. Chief of the Derby Dale Police Department and the only full-time officer on the payroll, Engel stood shy of six feet, sported a gush of loose curls beneath his trooper hat, and had a tendency to chew toothpicks to slivers. An impressive black mustache shot with first glints of silver somehow tied his face together, giving him the appearance of a wizened sage. He thumbed both ends of that mustache and then nodded a greeting at the storeowner.

"Evening, August," he said in his smoke-raspy voice. "I guess you found what you came looking for."

"Sorry, Al," Augie said. "I told Tree to give me thirty minutes before bothering you."

The chief held up a hand. "No bother. Took an early supper down at Gert's and was finishing up some homework when she called. Everything's all right, I hope?"

Augie opened his mouth say everything was fine when Susan nudged him in the belt. He looked at her. "Tell him what I saw," she whispered.

Augie cleared his throat. "Susie here had a little trouble finding her way out of the maze. Thought she saw someone looking at her through the corn."

Part of him expected Engel to laugh, but the officer merely regarded the girl with sedate eyes which betrayed nothing. "That right, Susie? Could you describe the fella if you had to?"

"I don't know that it was a man," Susan said without a hint of inhibition. "It looked like … some kind of creature. And smelled like one."

Engel's eyes widened but he still showed no sign of humor. "A creature, you say?"

She nodded emphatically. "It rose on two legs. Like an ape or something. It smelled."

"What else?" the cop asked.

"I-I don't know. I could barely make it out in the shadows of the corn, but it was there. And it *looked* at me." She shuddered again against her father.

"Well, with Halloween right around the corner I'll warrant the pranks have started early this year. Probably some punk in a costume. Tell you what. I'll put out the word, make a call to Sheriff Lisk up in Ashford too. Me 'n the boys will keep a lookout for anyone or anything suspicious. Will that do, young miss?"

Susie nodded. "Thank you, sir."

"Don't you mention it, sweetheart. You two have a good evening now," he said, then regarded Timber. "You too, Timber, you old man."

They watched as he climbed back into the cruiser, reversed, and took off up the road at a leisurely pace.

Then father, daughter, and dog got into their own vehicle and went home to dinner.

CHAPTER FIVE

The rest of the Milliard clan had crowded together in the kitchen to await word. When Augie and Susan entered, Teresa made a choked sound in her throat and rushed to wrap her arms around her second-eldest daughter. Hannah, older by two years and Susie's closest household confidant, wiped her eyes and joined the huddle. While Teresa contented herself by just squeezing her daughter to her bosom, Hannah busied herself by berating her sister.

"You idiot, what the hell did you do?"

"Language, young lady," Augie warned. "Don't you worry about what your sister did. Just be happy she's safe."

"I'd like to hear the story," Teresa said, taking on a stony countenance once her relief had burned out.

"A simple miscommunication," Augie said. "I thought she left with you and you thought she stayed to close up with me."

"You could have called," Teresa said.

"She tried," Augie said, favoring Hannah with a stern sidewise glare. "Someone had the line tied up."

Hannah's jaw worked for a moment before she blurted, "I was talking to Bonnie Lang about a homework assignment."

"Never mind," Augie said. "The important thing is everyone's safe."

The twins took turns giving their sister a squeeze around the waist, with Candace whispering, "I'm glad you're home, Sissy. I wouldn't have liked for you to be kidnapped," and Richard muttering something comprehensible only to the strange creature known as a "third grade boy."

Dennis gave her a one-armed hug and said, "Nice going, dummy. You almost gave Mom a stroke."

Only Thomas, lonely, middle-child Thomas, refrained from coming forward to greet his sister. He slouched in the doorway in true middle-school form and stared at his unabducted sibling before disappearing again into the family room to finish watching Cincinnati clobber Boston in Game 5 of the World Series.

With the excitement ebbing, Teresa made Susie finish helping her with supper. She seemed reluctant to let the girl out of her sight. Timber apparently had similar aspirations as he made a bed beneath the table and watched his favorite girl with unblinking devotion. Augie wondered if the poor mutt felt bad for being unable to locate Susie in the maze or whether he felt only relief at having her back.

With a few minutes before the meal, the man of the house stole into his den and locked the door behind him. He stepped around his wide desk, dumped down in his rollback chair, and picked up the phone. It rang only once before Chief Engel answered.

"Al, it's Augie. Listen, I just wanted to say thank you again for coming out after hours to check on Susan."

"No trouble at all, Augie. It's my job."

Augie hesitated before bringing up the real reason he'd called. He cleared his throat and said, "Look, there's nothing to that creature business, is there? It was just my girl's overactive imagination jumping at shadows, right?"

It was Chief Engel's turn to pause. In the silence, he seemed to be weighing something. "Well, the plain answer is I don't know. Mike Stone lodged a complaint with the sheriff's office. I guess something took down one of his milk cows when they were out to pasture."

"Any idea what it was?"

Engel blew out his breath into the mouthpiece. "Wolf, we figure."

"Hell, Alvin, there haven't been wolves in northern Illinois in nearly a century."

"Could be they're making a comeback."

"I doubt that."

"Yeah, well, we won't know till we have Ralph Downes check the carcass."

"Where's Ralph at?"

"He's spending hunting season up in the Northwoods of Wisconsin. Goes every year at this time."

That struck August as funny. "A game warden who hunts. Who'd have thought it?"

"Never was a good warden who didn't," Engel commented. When the call ended, Augie switched on the 13-inch black and white TV on the shelf near his desk and then kicked his feet back to watch Game 5. He didn't give a lick about either team competing this year—at least some of his roots remained in Michigan with the Tigers. He could comfortably steer clear of the age-old northern Illinois debate about the better team: Cubs or White Sox? He'd heard some of these old boys argued till they came to blows about it. Give him one team and one city when it came to his sports.

But even if his Detroit Tigers had lost 102 games that season and finished dead last in the league, watching baseball was something to do. Something to take his mind off what happened tonight.

Because whether Susie had seen a wolf or something else, he believed she'd seen *something*. Something that had set Timber off. Something unwanted on his property.

Susie came to get him for supper. She seemed all right now, no worse for wear. Weird how resilient kids could be. If only adults could bounce back the same way, forget their worries for a spell. Augie snapped off the TV and went to the table.

The twins dominated the conversation that night, seeming to have forgotten their briefly missing sister altogether. They chattered blithely about the decorations Mrs. Hulst had them make for Halloween and about which costumes they planned to choose from Sears. They went on about the trick-or-treat route they'd schemed using a map of the county they found inside the cover of the local telephone directory, which included stops in their town of Derby, then moving north to Murdoch, and concluding in Ashford.

"We do it your way, we'll have to rent a trailer to haul the candy home," Augie said.

"Two trailers," Candace corrected.

Richard said, "Yeah, two."

Teresa laughed and touched her youngest daughter's hand. "Honey, you have some gravy on your chin."

Candace plucked her napkin off her lap, missed the gravy entirely, and dropped it again. Her mother reached over and completed the mission with her thumb.

Dennis had demolished his plate and got up for seconds. Hannah prodded him. "Jeez, ape man, save some for the rest of us."

Ape man got Augie thinking again about what Susie had seen. The way she'd described it, there would have been no mistaking it for a wolf. He could only hope it had been someone in a costume having a little early Halloween fun, like the chief had suggested. The way Timber had launched away after it … it couldn't have been merely his daughter's imagination.

"Dad?"

Augie snapped his attention back to the present. "What is it, Sunshine?"

"Could you pass the beans, please?"

Augie slid the dish across to her and then sawed a hunk off his roast beef with his steak knife. "Tommy, let's hear about your day."

The boy, reticent by nature, seemed even more so tonight. He shrugged.

"What did you do in school today?"

"We learned about sex."

Teresa coughed milk into her napkin. Hannah flushed and Susie snickered. Dennis chortled and shook his head. Richard looked blank and Candace said, "What about six?"

Augie kept his cool, chewing through his meat. When he'd swallowed, he dabbed his lips with his napkin and said, "Well, that must have been quite a day."

"It wasn't," Thomas said. "It was awful."

Teresa quickly recovered. "It's natural, Tommy."

"I don't want to talk about it," the boy said, pushing his plate away. "May I be excused?"

"You go on, son. We can talk later," Augie said.

The boy rushed upstairs. His bedroom door banged shut.

"When did they start teaching little kids about … about that?" Hannah asked, her face still shining an alarming shade of scarlet.

"I learned about it when I was younger than him," Susan said, waving a dismissive hand.

Hannah, who approached the subject with a sensitivity belying her age, looked positively stricken. "From *who*?"

"Rachel showed me a book she had hid in her room," Susie said without a hint of shame.

It was Dennis's turn to choke. "Rachel *Safford*? But she's such a goodie-two-shoes."

"What's the big deal?" Candace asked. "I learned all about six when I was a baby. It comes right after five and before seven."

Augie shot his eldest son a warning look. "Never mind. This isn't polite table conversation. Susie, why don't you tell us what you've decided to be for Halloween."

Susan rolled her eyes. "Gosh, Dad, I'm too old for that baby stuff."

Augie stared at her. When had she grown up, his Susie Sunshine? God, it seemed like only last year he'd been bathing her right here in this kitchen sink, lathering her sparse blonde hair with tearless shampoo and drying her with her yellow duckling towel. Into what dark and damning funnel did all the years sink? It wouldn't be long before Richard and Candace refused to partake in the holiday.

"Well, I'm going to be a vampire princess," his youngest daughter proclaimed with an air of superiority.

"And I'll be a scarecrow," Richard said, trying to emulate his older-by-three-minutes sister.

"Like from the Wizard of Oz?" Teresa asked.

Richard shook his head, his floppy fair hair flying. "A scary one. To match Candy's vampire lady."

"Vampire *princess*, Richard," Candace corrected. Her twin was the only one she allowed to call her by a diminutive name; everyone else she insisted address her by her Christian one.

"*Princess* then, gosh," Richard said, scooping peas into his mouth.

"That's enough, you two," Teresa said. She gathered up empty plates and took them to the sink. "Hannah, why don't you do the dishes tonight."

"But it's Susie's turn," the elder daughter whined. Augie gritted his teeth.

"I want to talk to her for a few minutes in private. She'll trade you for tomorrow."

"But tomorrow it's Tommy's turn," Hannah said.

"Then she'll trade you her next day, for Pete's sake," Augie said.

Hannah grumped to the sink and ran the water while Susan followed her mother out of the room. Augie let them have their time. He'd discuss what he knew with Tree after the kids had gone to bed.

He said, "Well, Denny, what do you say we catch the last inning or so?"

His son made a face. "I hate the Reds and the Sox."

"I know but it's baseball, son. Won't be around again till spring. We'll have a long wait."

Denny agreed to forego further mechanical endeavors in favor of catching the Game 5 finale. Augie appreciated that. Plus, he wanted to spend time with Thomas if the boy could bear to show his face again tonight. Poor kid. Learning about the birds and bees could be rough stuff, especially for a sensitive boy like him.

While the rest of the family dispersed, August climbed the stairs and tapped on Tommy's door.

"I don't want to talk right now," the boy hollered.

Augie opened the door anyway. "I think it's best to get it out in the open, son."

Thomas sat on the edge of his bed, tossing a baseball between hands. His Detroit Tigers cap had been pulled low over his brow and he watched the tips of his Keds. "It's too embarrassing, Dad."

Augie took a seat beside him, gave his presence a chance to sink in. Finally he said, "May I tell you a story?"

Tommy looked up at him. "What kind of story?"

"About how I learned … what you learned today. I promise,

it's more embarrassing than anything you could possibly tell me."

"I doubt that," Thomas said, trailing off, leaving an opening for his father to begin.

"Back when I was your age, you know, when we hunted dinosaurs for dinner—"

Thomas snickered. A good sign.

"Anyway, we didn't have any sex ed classes back then. Your grandma and grandpa Milliard weren't exactly the types to sit you down and give it to you straight, either. No sir. My friend Chuck Spall and I, we were curious about girls and we knew something about them appealed to us. We just didn't know what.

"So Chuck and I, one day we're downtown and we saw a girl from our class. Edith Klein, her name was. All the boys had a crush on her because … well, because she was the only girl in our sixth grade class who had …" Augie cupped his hands to his chest. "And they were nearly as big as her head. I wondered how she didn't need a back brace just to walk around."

Thomas guffawed and hid his face in his hands.

"She saw us gawking, like we always did, and she went right into theatrical mode, like *she* always did when she caught some poor hopeless fools enchanted by her endowments."

By now Thomas had succumbed to a full-blown giggle fit. Augie had to give him a second to catch his breath.

"So she calls us over behind County Line Market and asks us if we've ever seen a girl, you know, undressed. And Chuck and I, we don't know what in the world to say. I don't think we could have said anything anyway. My tongue plain stuck to the roof of my mouth. So Edith says 'I'll let you see mine if I can see yours' and Chuck and I just sort of nod our heads as if they were on a hinge. Felt like it might clean come off, either that or explode. Edith tells us we have to go first and Chuck and I can't drop our drawers fast enough.

"We're standing there with our bottom halves bare as the day we were born and Edith just starts laughing. Chuck and I looked at each other and back at her, waiting for her turn, but she only laughs and laughs. All at once, Doc Rubek comes around the corner carrying a basket of groceries. He sees what's going on and he hollers at us to stay right where we are. Edith, she takes off like a witch on a broomstick and I figure Chuck and I might have done the same except our pants at our ankles put an end to that. Old Doc, he rounds us up and marches us back to his office where he puts on a presentation about how babies are made that I think would have bored us to tears if we weren't so horrified."

Thomas had gotten over his giggles and had sat transfixed through the rest of the story, eyes glassy with good humor. "Did Doc Rubek tell Grandma and Grandpa what you did?"

Augie shook his head, smiling through the memory. "He vowed he wouldn't spill if we swore on a Bible never to take our pants down in the presence of a lady again until we were married to one."

"Did you keep your promise?" Thomas asked.

Augie set his teeth and bonked his son lightly on the head. "That's none of your business, boy."

"Whatever happened to Edith?"

"She married a traveling salesman out of high school and they moved away. East Coast, I think."

"Did you ever get to see her … you know …"

"Also none of your business," Augie said. "Now do you want to tell me what happened today that got you in such downward state?"

Thomas's face fell. "No sir."

"If you do, I won't say a word to your mother about it. It will be just between us men."

He looked up skeptically. Augie nodded in encouragement. Finally the boy said, "I mispronounced 'vagina' when Miss Jackson called on me in class to answer a question. I got so nervous, Dad, and it just came out wrong. I said it like 'Virginia' and everybody laughed. Even Missy Byrd laughed and she's like the nicest girl in school."

Augie slung an arm around his middle boy's shoulders. "Don't you give it a second thought, sport. By tomorrow no one's even going to remember."

"You think so?"

"I know it. Now how about catching the rest of the game with Denny and me?"

"Shoot, I bet it's over by now."

"One way to find out. You with me?"

"I'm with you, Dad. Always."

Together the Milliard men went downstairs and joined Denny in the family room, sitting side-by-side-by-side on the davenport to watch the top of the ninth, which had just begun, with Boston trailing by five.

CHAPTER SIX

The rain started up again after nine, ticking chill fingers on the glass behind Augie's head. He sat up in bed, a Dick Francis paperback open in his lap, thinking the maze would have to be closed tomorrow if it didn't quit soon. Dennis would be disappointed. Teresa came in from the bathroom wearing her white nightie and cold cream.

"Everything okay with Tommy?" she asked.

"All clear."

"What was it?"

"Kid just got embarrassed in class, that's all. When did they start teaching that in school anyway?"

"Susie learned it last year, remember?"

He didn't. "I thought you told her about it. After she saw the book in Rachel's room, that is."

"Well, mostly I clarified things, answered her questions."

"I told Tommy my Doc Rubek story."

Teresa froze. "You did *not*."

"Yep. Laughed his head off."

"He's too young for that story!"

"I cleaned it up a little. I changed the name of the girl to Edith Klein. I doubt he would have found it funny if he knew you were the one who got Chucky and me to drop our pants behind County Line."

"August Milliard, you dirty birdie."

"Says the woman who made two dumb kids show off their willies in front of Doc Rubek."

She climbed in beside him and swatted his arm. "I'm a different girl now."

"I'm just glad you let me make an honest woman of you.

There's no telling what you'd've gotten yourself into if I'd let you slip away."

"You are the only man I've ever wanted."

"Sweet talker."

For a time they only lay in one another's arms and listened to the rain. It was a tranquil shower, no gusto, no flash. Augie drifted, images from the day flickering through his mind like a film reel.

Sometime later, their door opened and Susie climbed into bed with them. Augie asked what the matter was.

"I keep having nightmares," she whined. "I want to sleep with you and Mommy."

Susan hadn't used the term "Mommy" in at least five years and Augie realized the girl was still half-asleep. "Come on, Sunshine, I'll take you back to bed."

"There's someone in the rain," she said.

"There's no one in the rain," Augie said, guiding his daughter back to her bedroom. Her skin felt windburn warm through her nightgown and he wondered if she maybe wasn't coming down with something. He'd go downstairs and get the thermometer out of the medicine cabinet, maybe warm some milk for himself before bed.

"I saw him," she insisted, though it was forceless.

"You'll feel better come morning, Sunshine," Augie said, stifling a yawn against the back of his hand. Timber was not in his usual position at the foot of her bed—he must have left for warmer climes when his favorite girl departed.

Susan did not resist when he tucked her in. He opened her window an inch and closed the door behind him. He made his way downstairs, scrounged up a saucepan, and set a helping of milk over low heat. The glass bottle came from Stone Dairy Co., delivered that morning. Mike Stone did great regional business and had been looking to expand. Augie didn't figure he'd get very far if Mike kept losing cows to wolves or whatever the hell had taken down his cow.

"It's not wolves," Augie said aloud as he transferred the milk from pan to glass. "Wolves got hunted out a hundred years ago."

He almost dropped the glass when Timber abruptly fired a volley of short, sharp barks from somewhere at the back of the house. Augie hurried to shush him before the critter woke everyone up.

"Damn, boy, what is it?" he said when he found the dog scratching at the back door. Augie flipped on the rear light, illuminating the three-season room and part of the yard beyond. It couldn't quite reach all the way to the single barn where he parked the harvesters or the cornfield bordering their property, but came near enough. Nothing.

Anyone could be hiding in all that corn, Augie thought. *Anyone or anything.*

It was true. The sheer amount of corn in Ashford County staggered the imagination. He'd once seen an aerial shot of the entire 635 square miles and it had resembled a bright green sea. The Milliard orchards had been practically indistinguishable in the southwest corner of the portrait, all but swallowed by the thousands of acres of Lang stalks. Augie knew Lang would love nothing more than to take over the orchards, have the trees felled and their stumps ripped out to make way for more corn. Grant took pride in saying he "feeds the world" with his bountiful crop. He'd once made an offer—quite a generous one, in fact—to buy out Milliard Family Farms, but of course August had turned him down. Apples were his way of life and he meant to keep it that way.

Ray Safford hadn't been so fortunate. Two years back, at the start of the grain boom, Lang had engineered a deal with the hog farmer to annex the forty-odd acres he used to grow soybeans and quickly had them replaced with an experimental hybrid whose yield wound up netting Lang far more than he paid for it. Ray was left with his hogs. Maybe it was better that way—Ray Safford seemed to be a man possessed of a singular mind.

Augie shut off the light once Timber calmed. Before he went back to bed, though, he double-checked the locks on all the ground floor doors and windows. He'd completely forgotten about checking Susie's temperature.

Tommy looked like a different kid at the breakfast table the next morning. He ate his Corn Flakes through a bushel-wide smile. Every so often he would crack up. His sisters stared at him as if he'd turned green.

"I bet you did," she said, pressing him down in his chair by one shoulder. "I expect you were up half the night with laughing fits."

Dennis came in, scrounged in the fridge, and left again with a pair of apples balanced on his palm. He would be looking forward to tonight when he and his buddies got to haunt the maze in their Halloween finery.

"He needs to eat more than that," Augie said. "He's got a game tonight."

"It's not like he *plays*," Susie said. Aside from her eyes looking a little glassy, she didn't seem any worse for wear.

"You never know when the man in front of you will go down," her father said.

"I hope the man in front of him stays on his feet," Teresa said. "The idea of my son standing on that field with all those bigger boys flying at him scares me stiff."

"With our offensive line, it should," Augie said. "Got more holes in it than a screen door."

"I'll never understand what men get out of watching other men hit each other," Teresa said, spooning grapefruit out of the rind.

"Football's exciting, Mom," Hannah said. "Especially the tight pants."

"Hey," Augie said.

"Disgusting," Susan offered, pushing her plate away.

Candace said, "What?"

"Where's your brother, Candace?" Teresa asked.

"Still asleep. Couldn't wake him up for nothing today."

"Couldn't wake him for anything, you mean," Augie said. He disliked when his kids sounded ignorant even more than when they whined.

Candace said, "What?"

"Never mind," Teresa said. "Go tell him he'll be late for

school. And don't take no for an answer."

Susan said, "Dad, was I sleepwalking last night?"

"You came into our room, yes. I took you back to bed."

She gave him a funny look. "I woke up on the floor. I thought I heard Timber barking last night."

At the mention of his name, the dog picked up his head from where it had been buried snout-deep in Alpo.

"You must have slept restless, that's all. I think last night put a fright into you. You feel okay?"

"A little tired. I dreamed I saw someone standing in the rain outside, near the barn."

"So you said."

"It wasn't a dream," Richard said, shambling into the kitchen, rubbing an eye.

"Come again?" Augie said.

"I saw him too. I couldn't sleep so I decided to watch the rain, hoping for lightning. There wasn't none, but I saw the back light go on and someone standing by the barn. Then he walked into the corn."

Augie folded the paper. "There wasn't any," he said.

Richard said, "What?"

"There wasn't any lightning is what you meant to say."

"Oh."

"Who do you think it was?" Teresa asked her husband.

"Nobody," Augie said and carried his plate to the sink.

After determining the maze trails would be serviceable, he got the store opened and waited for the morning rush. He could usually expect a handful of kids on their way to school looking to score a quick fresh breakfast. One or two area business professionals, like Doctor Sidney Rubek (the son of the infamous Doc Rubek of his youth who never mentioned his father's involvement in Augie's education, if he'd ever heard the story to begin with) and Judge Farhlander would put in an appearance for a quart-jug of cider and a jar of cinnamon applesauce. Father Scudder from St. Joseph's favored pumpkin scones and took them out beneath his coat as if hiding the sin of indulgence from sight. More than one housewife would drop by to purchase a quarter pound of fudge, their guilt at the early morning sweet carefully masked by gossip and laughter.

Augie made it custom to personally greet them as he always took first shift in the showroom. Usually he did not require help, but he had a divorced former typing teacher from Murdoch High School come in to run the second register if things picked up. Mary Lou Zahn also had a talent for maximizing the aesthetic appearance of the many autumn-themed displays.

"Morning, Mary Lou," Augie said as his part-timer punched the clock and took her place behind the register.

"Morning, August," she said. "Any chance I can get those ghosts and goblins up today?"

"Matter of fact, you can," Augie said. He bent and pulled a crate full of Halloween decorations out from beneath the counter and dropped it before her. "Found it in back last night and figured you'd be able to work your magic with it."

Mary Lou glowed. She clapped her hands twice briskly, childlike. "I do so love this time of year," she said, plucking a black-clad stuffed witch from the crate. Augie watched her with a grin as she set about making ready for the holiday at hand.

Tonight he would permit his kids and their friends to don their favorite costumes and chase maze-goers around. He had reluctantly agreed to haunting the maze last season when Dennis pleaded his case like a murder-trial lawyer. Turned out to be a huge success with the younger crowd. He kept the haunted maze confined to weekend nights only and had signs clearly posted so people with children or heart conditions could avoid the terror.

It occurred to Augie that perhaps he should cancel the event this year based on Susan's experience, but he refused to allow some creep in the corn to shut it down. He'd tell Dennis to stay extra vigilant during his fun tonight and to report anything unusual straight away.

Around lunchtime, the store got so busy Teresa stepped out of the kitchen and opened the third and final register. She could barely keep the apple pies coming fast enough and most flew off the shelves still warm in the center. When they got the crowd controlled, she had a look at Mary Lou's handiwork.

"I love what you've done with all this old stuff, Mare," she said, admiring a crowd of painted wooden jack-o-lanterns leering from atop a miniature hay bale.

Mary Lou blushed. "It's always been my pride and joy, this time of year."

"I bet your house looks festive," Teresa said.

"Oh, it does, Missus." A light seemed to come on in her head. "You both should come out for coffee sometime and have a peek."

Teresa opened her mouth, but Augie answered first. "That'd be lovely, Mary Lou."

His wife gave him a look and disappeared into the kitchen. He joined her there when he found a spare moment.

"Why did you take her up on that?" Teresa asked. It wasn't that she disliked Mary Lou, it was only that the one time they'd gone to have coffee at her place—last March, it had been—the woman had dragged out a bookcase-worth of old family photo albums and had forced her guests to suffer through a four-generation personal history of the Zahn family. On that occasion, Teresa had tried several times unsuccessfully to detach herself and Augie from the proceedings, only to be thwarted consistently by their host. Mary Lou had filled them full of coffee and tales of yore, including a shockingly shameless account of her first sexual encounter ("It was with Daniel Barron, in the hayloft of his daddy's barn ... I can still remember the swallows swooping overhead and the way the straw kept scratching my back."). They'd escaped the seventh circle only when Teresa had feigned forgetting a doctor appointment for the twins.

"Mary Lou's lonely," Augie said. "Some company might cheer her up."

Teresa groaned. "Does the company have to be us?"

"We'll set a limit this time, tell her we have to go at four o'clock sharp."

She sighed. "Oh, all right. I'll go along because I love you. But if she starts talking about Daniel Barron and barn swallows again, I'll run out so fast her carpet will catch fire."

"Tree ..."

"Get out of my kitchen, Mr. Man," she said, shooing him off but not before he stole a kiss. She kissed back and lingered there. "You sure know how to make a girl feel better."

"You could say I have a special aptitude for it. Ask anyone."

"Get out before I petition Judge Fahrlander for a divorce."

Augie took the hint and stepped out the door, blowing a final kiss over his shoulder. Teresa pretended to swat it down into the pie crust she was working over.

He set a date for him and Teresa to visit Mary Lou on the first of November, when the offseason officially began. Business always peaked two or three days before Halloween, then dropped off dramatically the day after, like someone flipped a switch.

"Oh, but I wanted you to see my decorations *before* the big night," Mary Lou said.

"You'll still have them up the next day, yes?" Augie asked. "You don't take them down at midnight, do you? Maybe your pumpkin turns into a coach, like Cinderella?"

"I guess the day after will work fine. I know how busy you're expecting us to be."

"I figure we're looking at doubling our business from last year. Word's really spread about the maze—it's our star attraction now."

Mary Lou looked wistful. "I'll always prefer apple-picking in the orchards. So peaceful. And a steal. You ought to charge double what you do."

"We make up for any loss in volume," Augie said. "Just wait and see how many apple-pickers show up this weekend."

As if summoned by the conversation, the door opened and Zeb, one of the seasonal men Augie had hired on, came in. Zebulon Tuel was a good man, sharp as a darning needle, but in trouble with the drink. He'd dropped out of school and had worked odd jobs around Ashford County ever since, except for a three-year stint when he played center field for the Ashford County Alligators minor league ball club, following the late integration of the Ashford County Antelopes Negro League club. That career aspiration had fallen short when Zeb had dislocated a knee—an injury from which he'd never fully recovered. Each autumn he found work at Milliard Farms, whether maintaining the grounds, working the register, or divvying out baskets for customers. The past two years he'd assisted with maze maintenance and probably knew his way through it better than Augie did.

"It slow down out there, Zeb?" his boss asked.

"Not a soul in the trees for the time being, Mr. Milliard," he said in his full-bodied baritone, turning out pockets stuffed with crumpled dollar bills and placing them on the counter. "Our harvest thus far."

Augie set about flattening the currency into something the bank might be more inclined to accept and then slipped them into a zippered bag. A more cynical man might have insisted Zeb step out of his shoes to make sure none of the singles had made their way inside, but Augie trusted Zeb. He might be a drunk once the sun set, but he was honest as Abe Lincoln during daylight hours.

"Why don't you take the rest of the day off, Zeb? Only a couple hours till Hannah turns up for her shift. I'll hang around out there in the meantime."

"Sir, I'd like to stay on if I could," Zebulon said, doffing his wide-brimmed straw hat and turning it in his hands. He glanced at Mary Lou who paid them no more mind than a fruit fly. "I got a date tomorrow night. I'd like to take her someplace nicer'n Gert's."

Augie checked his watch. "All right. Why don't you walk the maze, check the mesh for holes. You see any, you mend them up and report to me." He didn't mention what Susie thought she'd seen the night before.

Zeb nodded, resettled his hat, and went out.

"Mary Lou, I'm going to take orchard duty for a time. It picks up again in here, give Tree a shout or call me on the walkie, okay?"

"You got it, boss," she said without looking up from the display of ghosts currently bewitching her.

Augie smiled at the back of her head then strolled out to the orchard with his lunch.

CHAPTER SEVEN

Few things came close to the peace August Milliard III felt while alone in his orchard. The trees, tall and solemn as monuments. The way the wind shuffled the leaves, the occasional thump as fruit dropped to the grass between the rows. A mourning dove's wounded warble.

The early afternoon sunlight painted dappled shadows on the rows between trees. Augie picked a trunk, sat against it, and opened his lunch pail. Teresa had packed him a hearty roast beef sandwich, Ruffles, carrot sticks, and a fresh-baked fritter for dessert. The thermos had done an able job of keeping his coffee tepid and as he sipped from the lid, he watched an apple drop across the way. Unlike Isaac Newton two centuries previous, no undiscovered scientific law made itself readily known at the sight. That was fine with Augie; he preferred a simple life, as free from conflict and complication as possible.

That very notion was soon challenged when three figures strolled through the trees. Well, two strolled, one wheeled. Augie caught sight of them and climbed to his feet, brushing crumbs from his fingers.

"Adeline," he said. "This is a pleasant surprise."

The man pushing the undisputed matron of Ashford County in her antique high-backed chair of polished oak glared him down. His companion, walking alongside, did the same. Rumor had it these guys were her sons, but Augie never bought it—from his extensive knowledge of local happenings, he'd heard all her children had fled home once they'd come of age. His father would have been able to tell him for sure had he still been alive. As it was, he (and everyone else in Ashford County) had to treat them as she called them.

"Good afternoon, August," Adeline Gable said in her ever-cool, autumn-crisp voice. She wore white gloves over her arthritis-gnarled hands, which stroked the fur of a cairn terrier asleep in her lap. The dog opened an eye to size him up before closing it again. Not, perhaps, the best choice in guard dog, but what did she need with guard dogs when she had these two goons by her side?

Augie moved to retrieve a wicker basket from the pile nearby. "Come to sample our fare?"

She fixed him with a gaze as chilly as her voice and shook her head slowly, almost sadly, side to side exactly twice. Her lips pulled into a stiff rictus and Augie could see precisely what her corpse would look like.

"When you came to me in '72 and asked if you could cut through a couple acres of corn as a means of gimmick to make an extra buck, I granted your request. I'm a proponent of free enterprise and the American Dream as anyone, so I decided as long as you'd worked out a fair deal with Grant, you could do as you pleased with the leased land."

Leased land. Granny was correct about that much, at least. The check he'd signed bearing Grant Lang's name on the payee line had not been for permanent use. Grant Lang did not sell. He bought. The amount on the check had sealed an agreement for the use of five years' time of the acreage in question and not a millisecond longer, at which time the land usage would revert to Lang. Augie did not much care for where this conversation was headed.

"That's to my recollection as well, Adeline," he said cautiously. "I was pleased to have your blessing."

"And so you've had it for the past three years," she said. "But I think it's time we allow the property to revert."

Augie blinked. "Grant and I agreed to five years. The amount I paid to use the few acres he allowed was substantial—"

"I know how much you paid and for how long," she said, her eyes locked on his. "But it would please me greatly if you accepted my request as I accepted yours three years ago."

"Has Grant said something to you? Because if he has, he knows better than to bother you with issues like this. He knows he should come to me direct."

"Grant hasn't said a word, though I know he would agree to refund a portion of your capital. On a *pro rata* basis, of course, for time unused."

Augie scratched an eyebrow with his thumbnail. The kids would be devastated. "Well, Adeline, this is a little out of left field. Would you mind telling me where your concern stems from?"

Her death rictus pulled taut at the corners a bit. "I understand we had an incident here last night."

"Oh, that? Adeline, that was nothing, that was a simple miscommunication. We found Susan and everything's just fine."

"Is that right?" Adeline asked. "I heard the police were summoned."

He silently cursed Teresa for calling Engel before the allotted time. He should have known Al would spill all to Adeline. In his mind he saw them sitting down to coffee in the Gable front parlor while the chief gave her a rundown of the occurrences that wouldn't make the Derby *Gazette*'s police blotter.

"We asked Alvin to come out as a precaution."

"It sounds like your girl spotted something undesirable in the maze."

"Truth is, we don't know what she saw. If she saw anything at all."

Adeline arched her painted-on eyebrows. "You doubt the word of your offspring?"

"She's at an imaginative age, Adeline. It was dark and she'd been dozing. It could have been nothing more than moonlight through the leaves."

"Was no moon last night, August. Cloud cover thicker'n peanut butter."

She's not even staying on topic, he thought. *She came here with this request for some other reason, not over concern for the extremely unlikely possibility of a beast on the loose.*

He said, "So you want the maze shut down for safety reasons."

"Imagine the tragedy if someone got hurt or worse," she said.

"Imagine having that on your conscience the rest of your life."

"You figure we ought to shut down all the cornfields in Ashford County?" he asked. He meant to deliver the words with a sliver of humor, but it only came out sounding pinched and bitter.

"I don't appreciate sarcasm, August."

"Well, I hope you'll grant me a night to sleep on it."

Her face tightened. When Granny Adeline wanted something, she wanted it now. She was not one who much tolerated waiting. But neither was she one to openly badger a prominent cornerstone of the local economy. "I'm only thinking of the county's best interest."

"I can appreciate that," he said.

"Very well. Good day to you," she said and her son or servant or whoever turned her chair around and trundled her away. The second man lingered a moment, his stare calcifying, before he followed his matron.

Augie watched them out of sight, then started at something moving through the trees. For a split second he was sure he'd find himself staring down some grotesque primate escaped from a traveling circus, but found only Teresa picking her way toward him.

"Augie?" she said. "What was that about?"

"Granny Adeline wants us to shut down the maze."

"What on earth for?"

"Safety reasons, she claims. She heard about Susie's story from Al."

"Why, that's ridiculous."

"Bet your sweet little butt it is," he said. "She's got ulterior motives."

"What could they possibly be?"

Augie resisted the urge to spit. "She mentioned Grant Lang's name. I'd wager tonight's register he's got something to do with it."

"Grant's a blowhard and a bully, but he knows better than most that a deal's a deal," Teresa said.

"Yeah, Grant's word is his bond, no doubt about that. That's why he sent Granny."

"Granny doesn't get *sent* anywhere," Teresa said. "She *sends* people places."

"Which only proves a theory taking root in my mind," Augie said.

"Which is?"

"They're working together. For some reason, they want that land back. Wouldn't surprise me one of them sent someone to scare us and lucked out when they found Susan in the maze. Probably meant for it to be me, but didn't count on Timber by my side."

"What do you think we should do?"

Augie chewed a thumbnail. "A deal's a deal. We keep the land through the allotted time."

"That's not going to win any points with Granny."

"Granny isn't as powerful as she was in my old man's day. We don't need to win any points with her anymore. We've got everything we need."

"So what about when the maze deal expires? That attraction brings in a lot of money."

"We'll work something out," Augie said. "Hell, what about the orchard? We could let the kids run around here."

"It wouldn't be the same and you know it."

Teresa was right. A haunted orchard would not draw nearly as well as a haunted corn maze. "Heck, by the time the lease runs out Granny might not even be with us any longer," he said with a touch more vim than he'd intended.

They spoke a while longer as the sun slanted deeper over the trees, the sound of falling apples occasionally punctuating their remarks. Ten minutes on, with still no customers appearing, they decided to head back to the store until Hannah came for her shift after school. Halfway back Mary Lou met them in the trees, her face nearly purple from the exertion of running.

"Missus, the school's on the phone. They said something's the matter with Susie."

Husband and wife bolted for the store, leaving Mary Lou in their wake. Augie beat her by a nose and snatched the phone up from where it rested on the counter. "Hello, this is August

Milliard. What's the matter with my daughter?"

Sheila Mannis, the school nurse replied, "Mr. Milliard, we think Susie's gone and gotten herself a case of the mumps."

Augie winced. "The mumps, Sheila? Are you sure?"

Behind him Teresa said, "The *mumps*?"

"I'm fairly sure. She presents all the right symptoms. You'll want to get her over to Doc Rubek for confirmation quick as you can though."

"We'll be right over," Augie said and hung up.

"It's the mumps?" Teresa said.

"That's what the nurse says."

"God, that's all we need right now. Give me the keys, I'll go get her."

"That's all right. I'll get her. Call Doc and tell him we're on our way to his office."

Teresa held out her hand. "*I'll* get her. You've never been inoculated, remember? We wouldn't want you to catch it and miss the rest of the busy season."

She had a point and a damned good one. Augie had thought the prospect of vaccinations more dangerous than the diseases themselves; he trusted modern medicine about as far as he could spit it. Plus, how could he justify shelling out two bucks a pop for a poke in the arm when every last Milliard boasted an immune system more secure than Fort Knox?

Teresa, on the other hand, had insisted on getting herself vaccinated even if her husband held his ground when it came to the kids. They didn't argue about much, but this had been about as near to open war as anything in their marriage. He hated to admit it, but he'd likely have to concede after this.

"I don't get it," he said, handing over the keys to the pickup. "I've lived on this earth forty years and have never been sicker than the sniffles."

"We'll talk about it later. You better set appointments for the other kids," Teresa said and when she left, she let the door slam behind her.

CHAPTER EIGHT

Sidney Rubek's receptionist said the doc was booked straight through to Tuesday, but suggested Augie take the kids to Wyndham Rx where the shots should be readily available for the whole family. "You'll want to keep Susie quarantined until she's better, just to be on the safe side," she advised.

An hour later Hannah came in and punched the clock, stopping to say, "Hi, Dad, how's your day?"

"Been better, sugar plum," he admitted.

"Oh, about Susie? It's all over school she got mumps," Hannah waved a hand. "She'll be okay. Susie's a fighter."

Augie wanted only to change the subject. "I'm sure you're right. You have a good day at school?"

"Aced my trig test."

Augie beamed. Finally something to be thankful for on this hellish day. "Atta girl. You inherited your grandfather's mind for figures."

"Maybe the math kind," Hannah said, she put a hand on a hip and jutted it sideways. "But I inherited Mom's figure, period."

"Get on outta here with that," Augie said, shielding his eyes theatrically. Hannah giggled and went out to the orchard. As much as he hated to admit it, his kids were growing up fast. First Tommy learning about sex in school, now Hannah flaunting her curves. Good God, he could use a drink and thought he might find one before the day ended.

Mary Lou asked if he needed her to stick around with Susan out.

"I'd be much obliged, Mary Lou," he said with true gratitude. The after-school crowd had already begun filtering into the lot, many of them headed to the maze but a good gaggle coming straight for the pumpkin fudge and apple fritters.

Augie called home during a lull to check on Susie. Teresa said the girl had been confined to her room with strict orders to stay put until otherwise notified. On last check she'd been sleeping soundly.

"How's she look?" Augie asked.

"Mumpy." ·

"Look, Tree—"

"Don't worry over it now, August. We'll work things out later."

"Well, did you at least get Doc to look her over?"

"He squeezed her in for five minutes to tell us, yep, she has the mumps. I figure we'll get a bill for a hundred bucks for that."

"If he's feeling charitable," Augie said, hoping to loosen the tension, but his wife didn't laugh.

"You need me to send Dennis down early, help around the store? I know he'll be down at dark, but I can see if he can come right after the game."

"Nah. Mare and Zeb are sticking around. Let Dennis focus on football. He's been working hard the last week or two."

When he hung up, he turned around to find Rachel Safford standing at the counter. "Hello there, Miss Safford," he said. "Come by for more of the famous Milliard pumpkin fudge?"

"No, sir. Is Dennis working today?" she said without the slightest hint of anxiety or embarrassment.

Augie cleared his throat. "I give him Fridays off. For game nights."

Some emotion, not quite concealed, flickered over her face. "Thanks anyway, Mr. Milliard," she said, turning toward the door.

"Wait a second," he called after her and she glanced over her shoulder, eyebrows at full-arch.

"He'll be working the maze tonight. After the game. I'm letting him and his friends dress up and spook people."

Rachel broke out a sweet and somehow seductive smile Augie didn't care for one bit. "Susie told me about that. I think it's fun, you letting them do stuff like that."

"Can't work 'em all the time," Augie said. "They got to have some fun too."

"Is Susie all right? I heard she left school early."

Augie sighed. "She's fine so far's I know. Mumps, I guess."

"Ouch. Tough break."

"You had 'em before?"

She shook her head. "My dad made me get a shot. My mom didn't like the idea—she thinks medicine goes against God's will." Rachel added an eye-roll for emphasis.

Augie ground his teeth. Simple man Ray Safford had been the one to insist on vaccinations, not Ruth. Sometimes the world just didn't make a damn lick of sense.

"Do you know what costume he'll be wearing?" Rachel asked.

Augie opened his mouth, then shut it again, all at once thinking of Susie's description of what she claimed to have seen in the corn. "He's going as an ape man."

"Well, if the suit fits ..." Rachel said without missing a beat and Augie had to laugh.

"I guess Denny *can* be a bit of a monkey sometimes."

She shrugged a shoulder. "His personality fits him."

For about the hundredth time that day Augie wanted to change the subject. "Your old man here?"

Rachel aimed a badly chewed fingernail out the window. "He's out taking tickets for the maze. Should I send him in?"

"No, that's just fine. He's a good man, your father." He almost added *He's loyal*, but thought that might sound too much like master and dog, a dynamic Augie secretly thought true at times. He knew Ruth Safford, Ray's wife, didn't think much of the Milliard clan and its patriarch in particular, but in true Christian form she remained at all times cordial to them. Every so often Teresa would take coffee with Ruth and always the conversation remained cool and focused. That was until Mrs. Safford began rolling out the religious rhetoric, at which time Tree would make an excuse to escape. The Milliards attended the Unitarian Church in Ashford for Christmas and Easter services, but their piety about ended there.

"Well, I'll see you around, Mr. Milliard," Rachel said,

stepping out and lingering on the porch a moment before moving toward the maze.

Dennis came in two hours later, freshly showered, carrying a paper sack. He'd come directly from the locker room. The sun had long since sunk past the ridge, just left of the Gable estate, haloing the house and outbuildings as it always did before bidding the day adieu.

"Hey, Dad."

"Hi, son. How was the game?"

"We lost, twenty-one, ten." Dennis couldn't have cared less. If he wasn't playing, he had more important things to do. Nor did he fault his family for missing many of his performances (or lack thereof); he understood the business had to come first, especially this time of year. And besides, they'd be in the stands once the busy season ended.

"Well, you'll nail 'em next time. I guess you're ready for a big night?"

Dennis rattled the bag. "I'm going to scare me some kids."

"Randy and Ted still planning on making appearances?"

His eldest son nodded, a grin spreading across his face. Augie saw a patch of peach fuzz the kid had missed shaving this morning. "Randy's dressing as a demon and Ted as a zombie."

"Scary stuff," Augie said with a grin of his own before turning all business. "Remember, though—safety first."

"I know, Dad. Jeez Louise."

"I'm serious. You see anyone in distress, you stop the show and help them out. You get me?"

"Yes, sir."

"Tell your friends, too. Remember you're representing your family and your business tonight—keep it safe and keep it professional. As professional as a gorilla man, a devil, and a brain-hungry ghoul can keep it, anyway."

Dennis laughed. "We will, Dad. And thanks for letting us try this out. I think it's going to be a big hit."

"You let your friends know where the hidden exits are, the shortcuts through the corn?"

"I'm going to show them quick before show time."

"Better hurry."

"They're here," Dennis said, watching Randy Johansen's scarred-up Pontiac pull into the lot. "See ya, Dad."

"I may stop in later, see how things are going," he called as his son retreated for the door.

"We won't hesitate to jump at you, fair warning," Dennis called over his shoulder.

He's a good kid, Augie told himself. *Good head on his shoulders. Hope he has fun tonight.*

Because after tonight the maze may no longer exist. He'd have to think on the matter, discuss it with Tree (assuming she hadn't decided to leave him following today's events).

CHAPTER NINE

Augie closed up the store at 7:00 sharp, same as always. He bounced the money bag in his hand and stepped over to the truck, marveling at the line waiting to enter the haunted maze. It must have stretched back half an acre. Screams and nervous laughter burst in increments from the corn as Dennis and his friends scared the daylights out of paying customers. Ray looked overwhelmed at the ticket booth, as if accounting for all those dollars had given him a headache. Little matter, though, as Augie spied Rachel working dutifully beside him to mitigate the rush. She was a good daughter, no doubt about it.

Hannah came up from the orchard on cue and handed over the evening's stash.

"How'd we do?" he asked, adding it to the zipper bag.

"Eighty-eight," she said.

"Not bad. I think tomorrow we'll pull double. Saturdays, they come out in droves."

"Dennis and his friends sound like they're a hit," she said, eyeing the maze entrance.

"You going to join them?"

She shook her head. "I told Kim I'd get a milkshake with her down at Gert's. Mom said it was okay. We may come back after, if we're bored enough."

Augie returned a few of the bills she'd given him. "Knock yourself out, princess."

"Thanks, Daddy," she said, dropping a kiss on his cheek.

"You need a lift?"

"Nope, Kim's waiting for me up by the road." They waved good-bye and Augie faced around again.

A group of teens lingered near the maze's exit, laughing

and smoking. He recognized one as Lorelai Lang and another as Caleb Safford, two kids who, according to Hannah's reports, never moved in the same social circles. Maybe the maze had brought them together or maybe their proximity was merely a matter of happenstance. Augie dropped the money bag on the seat, locked up, and wandered over to greet them.

"Evening," he said. "What did everyone think of our latest attraction? Scary enough for you?"

"Pretty good, Mr. Milliard," Scott Beard said. Scott played left guard on Denny's football team and had a reputation for being handy with the ladies. Augie had warned Hannah long ago to steer clear of him.

"Yeah, those guys put on a good show," Lorelai said, her black hair shining blue in the glow of the waxing gibbous moon.

"Need more monsters, though," Scott added. "Maybe tomorrow you'd let me bring my costume out and join in the fun?"

"Hell, Scotty, you don't need a costume. You're scary-looking enough," another kid Augie didn't recognize called.

"Sit on it, Finney," Scott spat, then turned again to Augie. "Sorry, Mr. Milliard. So how about it?"

"Tell you what. Show up tomorrow with your costume and if it's scary enough I'll give you an answer then. You all have a good night now," he said and headed back to the truck.

He'd tasked Dennis to close up the maze at ten o'clock sharp and have the walk-through finished by half past the hour. That gave them a few more hours of fun. He'd leave them to it. All he wanted to do was get home, check on Susie, eat supper, and see if he could mend fences with Tree.

"How is she?" he asked when he entered the kitchen.

Teresa looked up from the range where she stirred spaghetti in boiling water. "Sleeping," she said and nothing more. This tiff might be more serious than Augie had first imagined.

"I'm going to check on her."

"You most certainly are not. She's under full quarantine until next Sunday."

"Tree, I'm not going ten days without seeing my daughter."

"You will unless you let Doc give you a shot."

He sighed. "I'm taking the kids over to the drug store first thing tomorrow. I'll get one too. Okay?"

Her nostrils flared, but she nodded. "That's showing some sense."

"Good. Then can we drop the whole thing?"

"Consider it dropped." She thrust her chin at the spice rack. "Toss a pinch of oregano into the sauce, will you?"

Augie did as bid, feeling the silence build between them. He gave the sauce a stir with the wooden spoon, found it flavorful, then went to his den until she called him to eat. He wished tonight he kept a bottle stashed in his desk, but he wasn't that kind of man. Not yet, anyway.

Talk at the table remained cool except for Candace and Richard, who spoke with frank animation about their weekend plans, which included costume shopping and running around the orchard whipping rotten apples at each other. They were creatures who lived in the moment and the bigger weekend—the one after this—existed outside their perception. The Annual Apple Fest Parade & Jamboree would take place on Saturday October 25th, the perfect gear-up to the haunted holiday beyond. The prospect of next weekend proved to be the only thing to spark Tommy's interest; the boy seemed to have fallen into his funk again that not even a sexy story could save him from.

Augie felt less enthused about the parade. While it always brought a nice draw to the town of Derby—and the Milliard Country Store & Orchard by extension—it also brought with it perennial headaches. He had to hire extra help to run the store so he could ride a float with his family and wave to the masses huddled three-deep along Main and Cherry Streets. With any luck, the weather would keep mild and he could get the two hours of hell over with quick. It was the only part of Apple Fest he wished his granddad had never established.

The twins finished chattering long enough to slurp up their spaghetti and chug their milk. They asked to be excused and were granted permission. They hadn't touched their garlic bread, so Augie reached over and plucked a piece off Candace's plate. The pad of his thumb sank into the soggy bread as he brought it to his mouth—it would be a sensation locked in his mind for the rest of his life because right then the door burst open and Dennis staggered in. Blood soaked the neckline of his costume, almost the exact shade of Teresa's sauce. The ape mask was gone and his eyes rolled wildly, like a steed pushed too hard.

"Daddy?" he said, his voice small and lilting, like a toddler's. It had been pushing a decade since he'd used the diminutive form of his father's title.

Augie stood so fast his chair toppled over. "Jesus Christ, Dennis, what happened?"

"Denny?" Teresa asked as if disbelieving what her eyes relayed to her brain. She rose slowly, perhaps thinking this some tasteless early Halloween prank. Tommy and the twins gaped.

His parents reached him at the same time, pulling them against their bodies as if to protect him from the world.

"I want you to tell me exactly what happened," Augie said, holding his son by the shoulders and giving them a small shake.

"D-Dad, I-I-I—"

"Take a deep breath, son. Are you hurt?" Another shake of the shoulders, harder this time.

"God, August, can't you see he's in shock?" Teresa hissed.

Augie ignored her. "Dennis, was it the maze? Did something happen in the maze?"

His son's eyes stared without seeing. Tears formed a second shimmering lens. "It's Randy," he gasped at length. "I think Randy's dead."

"Call Alvin," Augie told his wife. "I'm heading down there."

Teresa reached for him, snagged a belt loop with one finger. "You aren't going down there, have you lost your mind?"

"Dammit, Tree, this farm's been in my family three generations. If something happened on my land, I'm going to know about it." Without giving his wife a chance to respond, Augie yanked free and stepped out into the night. The temperature had dropped ten degrees in an hour and for the first time this season his breath steamed.

He could hear the screams from the front porch. Augie

started toward the truck, realized he'd left the keys inside, and turned to retrieve them except at that moment Al Engel's cruiser screeched to a stop on the road, cherries flaring.

"Get in, Augie," the police chief called. Augie did not need to be told twice. Engel stomped the gas before the passenger door had banged closed.

"What the hell is going on, Al?" Augie asked. He tried to force his pulse to a steady pace but his heart refused to cooperate.

"That's what I aim to find out."

"Someone call you?"

"Your girl. Hannah."

Augie snapped his head around. "She okay?"

"Fine. Rattled some, but fine. Called from the store."

"She say what happened?"

Alvin inhaled. "Wasn't quite sure. Said someone got hurt in the corn. When asked to elaborate on the injury all she could tell me was it's bad."

Augie's mind flashed to the thing Susie claimed she saw first in the corn maze and then standing in the rain outside their house, the claim Richard had corroborated. He shivered, couldn't help it. Al parked in the lot and both men got out.

A crowd of gibbering, terrified teens mobbed them, all speaking at once, all tugging at the chief's coat. "Goddammit, I told Berryman to meet me here. The hell is he?" Al barked, more to himself than anyone else.

As if on cue, a second cruiser appeared up the road, lights washing everything red, and peeled into the lot to park slantwise across the entrance. Officer Nathan Berryman, a stocky kid who'd once worked summers at Milliard Farms and who hadn't made it out of his senior year (much less the police academy, Augie thought) stepped out, hitched at his belt, and said, "What've we got, boss?"

"Berry, calm these people down while I take a look. And for God's sake, keep them back."

While Berryman took over crowd control, Augie followed the chief to where a smaller group congregated near the maze's exit. "At least we don't have to go in and try to find him," Al muttered. "Thank God for small favors they got him out."

Randy Johansen lay on the fresh-mowed grass. He still wore the demon costume, the pointed tail lying like a limp lasso beside him. The mask had been removed. Alvin crouched and flicked his flashlight over the supine form. Randy's face appeared ashen, his lips cracked and brown. His throat had been wounded in some manner, and the boy had his hands clasped around it.

"Let me see, Randy," Al said gently, moving the boys hands away. An open wound followed the flesh beneath the Adam's apple.

Augie, who'd narrowly avoided the experience of 'Nam, which had desensitized many of his contemporaries (including Al Engel, who'd completed two tours in Saigon), felt his gorge rise. After a few precarious moments, he won the battle and kept his pasta in its place.

"Is he dead?" Augie asked.

"Not yet, but he might be if that ambulance don't get here quick," Al said. Turning to the crowd he asked: "Anyone see what happened here?"

Ray Safford, who'd clearly been attending to the boy based on the amount of blood covering his hands and overalls, said, "The kids who brung him out said something attacked him." With all the hogs he slaughtered, Augie didn't figure the sight of blood much bothered the man.

"What kids?" Al asked.

"Right yonder." Ray tilted his broad, bald forehead (splotched with more blood, Augie noted with revulsion) at a cluster of Dennis's classmates huddled a few yards away. Augie at once picked out Lorelai Lang, Caleb Safford, Scott Beard, and the kid named Finney whom Scott had invited to sit on it.

"Where's Ted?" Augie asked.

"Ted who?" Engel said.

"Ted Dayton. One of Dennis's friends. The three of them were running the maze tonight, dressed to scare."

"Any of you kids see Ted Dayton?" the chief called. None of them moved or bothered to speak. Al stood, snapped his fingers. "Hey, anyone see where Teddy Dayton went?"

"He ran," Caleb Safford said.

"Where to?"

Caleb raised a hand and waved eastward, toward town.

Ray, his father, looked around as if seeing his son there for the first time. "Caleb? You see exactly which way?"

His son shook his head, but said nothing else.

"Where's Rachel?" Augie asked.

Ray looked more confused than ever. "Why, she was here a few minutes ago. She was going to help us finish up."

"Dad?" Hannah called from the darkness.

"Hannah, you don't come near here," Augie said, moving to intercept her. "I want you to go into the store, lock up, and wait for me."

"What's going on, Daddy? What happened to Randy?"

"That's what we're going to figure out, sweetheart. You go on now. You don't open that door for anyone but me or Chief Engel."

Hannah hurried away. Augie watched until she got the door shut tight behind her, then came back to the crime scene.

"You still think it's wolves?" he asked and immediately regretted it. Alvin stood up straight as a stop sign.

"I sure as hell hope you aren't trying to sound pert at a time like this," he said.

"It was a serious question, Al, take it easy."

"Whatever this was, it wasn't no wolf," he said, busying himself by stanching the wound with a handkerchief from his pocket.

"Think we ought to be letting the kids stick around for the show?"

"It's dark. They can't see shit."

Augie realized he'd crossed a line with Al he'd not crossed before and decided to leave the man to his work. He stepped away and quietly shooed the mingling kids away. He went back long enough only to tap Ray on the shoulder and motion him away. Ray obliged slowly, reluctant to leave his post as first responder.

"Al, I'm going up to the shop, call Teresa, let her know what's going on."

The chief grunted something sounding like assent and

Augie gladly retreated. He found Hannah behind the main
cash register, eyes glassy and staring. She'd put on the radio
through the speakers, probably as a means of comfort, and at
the moment John Denver was thanking God he was a country
boy.

"Hannah, are you all right?" he asked.

She looked around at him as he stepped behind the counter.
"Daddy, what happened to Randy? Someone said his throat got
slit."

"Who told you that?" he asked stupidly.

"Is he going to be okay?"

"He's going to be fine, honey." He said the words, but didn't
trust them.

"Who did it to him, Dad?" Hannah asked, her voice rising
with each word. "I mean, who would hurt Randy? He's not the
smartest kid in school, but he's always been nice to me and I don't
think that's because he's Denny's friend, I think it's because—"

"Hannah, stop and listen to me. We're going to figure out
what happened to Randy, okay? Chief Engel's an outstanding
investigator. He's got an eye for detail."

"Is there someone out there, Daddy?" she asked. "Some, I
don't know, *maniac*?"

"There's no maniac, Hannah," he said and hated the next
words he spoke because they sounded so hollow. "The chief
thinks it might be wolves. Says one took down one of Mr. Stone's
milk cows."

"But the Stone farm's all the way up by Ashford."

"That's not all that far, lemon drop. Wolves can travel up to
thirty miles a day in search of food."

"Mr. Forbath says wolves won't attack people. Not unless
they're starving. And they wouldn't be starving if they got Mr.
Stone's cows."

Augie had no answer to that. He had raised no fools.

To his dying day, August Milliard could not recall precise
details of the remainder of that hellish night that set the table
for open war in Ashford County. He knew that after he tried
to console his daughter, an ambulance came to take Randall

Johansen to Ashford Memorial, a forty-minute drive north. He remembered accepting a ride home with Hannah in Nathan Berryman's car because Al had more work to do on the scene. He also remembered looking up at the Gable house on the ridge and noting its blank, black face. No light burned inside that night.

He and Teresa talked for a time when they got home, their muted feud over vaccines forgotten. She'd gotten Dennis quieted and off to bed, the poor kid unable or unwilling to talk about what he'd seen. It didn't matter. She'd already heard about what happened from Ursula Stone—funny how rural areas work like that: something happens a mile from your front door, the news travels to the other side of the county before bouncing back to you. Susie had awakened for a spell, but had conked out again after her fever had mercifully broken.

The other kids seemed no worse for wear once they learned all the pieces of their family remained intact. Teresa talked him out of returning to the scene.

"Let Al handle it," she'd argued and he'd relented, not wishing to upset their tenuous truce. Everything stayed quiet until four o'clock the next morning when Al came to tell him about the dead girl he'd found in the maze.

CHAPTER TEN

Augie hadn't been to sleep yet. Hell, he hadn't even been to bed. He'd kissed Teresa around midnight and said he'd be up soon. He'd checked in on Susie, quarantine be damned, and found her snoring lightly. Timber lay curled around himself outside her door, but he didn't try to get in when Augie opened it, though he did sniff the air.

Since then he'd been pacing in his den and sipping bourbon from the bottle. When he saw the headlights cut through the curtains and roll up the drive, he moved fast to intercept the chief before he could ring the bell and wake the whole house.

"Christ, Al, it's the middle of the night."

"We have a problem. I found a corpse in the maze."

Every cell in Augie's body seemed to lockdown. For a moment he couldn't move a muscle even to speak. Finally he managed: "Who?"

"We don't know. It's a girl, maybe high school age."

Something flashed in his mind and he said it before he could rein it back. "It wasn't Rachel Safford, was it?"

Engel gave him an unreadable look but then shook his head. "No, Rachel went home with her old man. I expect Ruth won't let any of them out of the house for near a month now. She'll keep 'em locked up like she does that little potato head they got, what's his name, Samuel?"

"Yeah, Samuel," Augie echoed, but he wasn't thinking about the Safford brood. He was thinking about everything changing after tonight. Tonight acted as a pivot and his whole world shifted around it at that precise moment; he could actually feel it happening. *I should have closed the fucking maze this morning*, he thought.

"You mind if I come in?" Engel asked. A light rain had sprung up and brought with it a chill wind. "I'd like to speak with Dennis."

Augie stood back to let the man through while saying, "I really don't want to wake Denny up, Al. Kid's been through enough today."

"It's okay, Dad. I couldn't sleep," Dennis said from the kitchen archway. He wore boxers and a white T-shirt and gripped a half-empty glass of milk in one hand. His eyes no longer looked quite so wild and his voice, thankfully, had lost that awful childlike inflection. Augie sent up a small prayer for that. He had to restrain himself from stepping over and wiping off a milk mustache on the kid's lip.

"Evening, Dennis," Engel said. "Or morning, rather. Wonder if I might ask you a few questions."

"What do you want to know, sir?"

The chief brought out a notepad and a ballpoint pen. "Could you tell me exactly what you saw in the maze, son?"

The boy took a breath. "It was dark. Ted and I were chasing a group of kids from school, making them scream. Randy, I don't know where he was. Somewhere behind us. He'd gone after these girls, I think they were from Murdoch—I recognized one of them as a cheerleader from up there.

"Well, Ted and me, we're just running along, having the time of our lives, when we hear Randy start screaming. We thought at first it was one of the girls, it sounded all high-pitched, you know? Then I hear him kind of making this choking sound, and so Teddy and me we turn around and run to him. Took us a minute to find him because we got turned around."

Engel looked up from his pad. "And what did you find when you did locate him?"

Dennis took a deep breath and wandered over to the loveseat. He set the glass on the coffee table and leaned over his knees. Engel moved to the opposite sofa, encouraging Dennis to take his time. Augie watched from the vestibule, arms crossed, mind cycling, heart thundering. *A dead girl in my maze?*

"He was sitting on the ground. His mask was off. I almost tripped over him in the dark. We could hear him breathing.

And we could see him clawing at his neck like, I don't know, like he had a sore throat, Chief."

"Then what happened?" Engel asked, pen zipping over the page. "Did he say what attacked him?"

Dennis shook his head, floppy hair flying. "We kept asking him, over and over, what happened, what happened, Randy? But he wouldn't answer. I don't think he could." Dennis paused, brought the glass of milk to his lips, then set it down again. "He'll be all right, won't he, Chief?"

"They got him up at Ashford Memorial right now. Great doctors working on him," he answered without really answering the question.

Augie cleared his throat. "Have you spoken to Randy yet?"

"He's been in surgery. The sheriff's over there now, waiting for the first chance."

"What about Ted Dayton?"

"We tracked him down at home. He didn't help much."

"Do you have any leads?"

"Working on it," Engel replied, a little coolly Augie thought. To Dennis, the cop said: "There's something else I want to tell you. It may be upsetting, but it's important."

"Somebody's dead, aren't they?" Dennis asked.

"Why would you assume that, son?" Engel said.

The boy shrugged. "That's the only thing so serious you'd have to give a warning first. Only reason why you'd be here in the middle of the night."

"We did find a body when we walked through the maze," the chief confirmed.

"Who is it?" Dennis asked.

"We were hoping you might know. Female, aged between fourteen and sixteen, close as the coroner can figure, strawberry blonde, green eyes. Wearing overalls and a plaid shirt, butterfly barrettes in her hair. You see anyone that matches that description while you were working last night?"

Dennis chewed his lip and stared hard at the coffee table. Augie sent up another prayer it wouldn't be someone from his school, a friend of his. Finally he shook his head. "Sorry, Chief Engel. That doesn't sound familiar."

Engel pursed his lips. "Thanks anyway, Dennis. You've been very helpful."

"Let me know if you need anything else," the kid said, eager to please.

"I will. You two ought to get some rest. There's liable to be some long days ahead. For now just keep doing what you're doing, go on as normal as you can," the chief said. Then he went out the door and into the weather.

Augie took Engel's advice and tried to keep things normal. After bringing in the milk delivery and the morning paper (featuring a brief blurb about the incident which said very little at all other than speculating an animal attack), he drove the healthy kids to the Wyndham Rx and had them vaccinated as promised. He got his shot too. He thought the twins might cry, but they held it together better than expected for having someone shove a needle into their skin. When it was over, he drove everyone home and tasked Dennis with making sure they got fed and no one sent themselves (or anyone else) to the hospital.

He got to the store at quarter to nine and listened to the quiet. No customers. Not a soul except for Teresa inside, spraying Windex onto the windows and wiping them until they squeaked.

"Anyone been in yet?" he asked.

She shook her head, her ponytail swinging between her shoulders. "I called Mary Lou and told her she could have the day off. How'd it go with the kids?"

"All secure against bugs. How's Susie this morning?"

"Fine. No temperature. Medicine seems to be working. I reminded her to stay in her room."

The small talk didn't work. Eventually they had to discuss the problem at hand and Teresa brought it up first and without pussyfooting around it.

"What's going to happen to us now, August?"

He looked up from where he pretended to be counting the morning till. "What do you mean?"

"Someone died on our property last night. Dennis's friend almost did too. We don't have a single customer in here two weeks before Halloween because the news has spread like syphilis all over this damned county."

"People will show up," Augie said.

"What if they don't? We have bills to pay, piling up on your desk. We have mouths to feed."

"Tree, relax. This isn't the end of the world. We may have to close the maze down, I'll concede that, but—"

"*May* have to? August, someone *died* in there. Even if we were tasteless enough to keep it open, you think anyone's going to *pay* to go in there again?"

Augie bit his lip. "You're right. The maze is going to have to go." He looked at her. "Funny timing, wouldn't you say?"

She stood there with the spray bottle against her hip like an old-fashioned gunslinger. "What on earth do you mean?"

"Yesterday Granny Adeline pays me a visit, virtually commands me to close down the maze and void the lease we have with Grant and after I refused, we have one dead and one injured on the land in question."

Teresa cocked her head. "You don't think that old woman had something to do with this, do you? Good God, August, she must be ninety years old."

"Eighty-four," Augie said.

"She can't even walk to her own mailbox."

"Nothing wrong with her brain."

"I won't stand here and entertain the idea Adeline Gable somehow orchestrated a plot to harm two innocent kids because you refused her request. She's the one who gave her blessing to build the maze in the first place."

"Convincing her wasn't any walk in the park, Tree. It took some talking."

"The point is, she did it. She knew it would be good for the local economy, an attraction like a corn maze, and she let you do it."

"Well, I'm not going to stand here and entertain the idea those kids were attacked by some wild animal. Hell, yesterday our esteemed police chief was trying to make a case for wolves coming back. *Wolves*, for God's sake."

"Maybe he's right."

"Tree, I saw that boy's wound. Wasn't an animal on earth that would've cut it so cleanly. Looked like the work of a blade, not jaws."

Teresa sighed, put her hands in the air. "I'm just trying to make sure we keep food on the table, that's all."

"We will, all right? We still have the contract with the produce company, that's our big money right there. This Apple Fest, it mainly gives us a bump before the holidays. And people will come, Tree, I'm telling you. The parade, Halloween, they'll come back." He thought of something else. "Hell, we may even get some gawkers, some thrill-seekers coming out, see if they can spot a ghost."

"Oh, August. That's just sick."

"The world is full of sick people."

They jawed on for a time, sorting things out, discussing the future, until the bell above the door dinged and they looked up at the day's first guest.

Dark circles underscored Al Engel's bleary, bloodshot eyes and two days' worth of stubble poked from his throat. He removed his hat and held it in his hands, turned it over and over as if about to deliver some particularly bad news.

"Morning, Al," Augie said, as if a friendly greeting could change what the chief was about to say.

"Not so good," Engel said. "Come by to tell you Judge Fahrlander's shutting you down."

"Already ahead of him," Augie said. "We decided we're through with the maze, after what happened and all."

"Not the maze, Augie. Your entire operation. The store, the pumpkin patch, the orchard."

"He can't do that," Teresa said. "Can he, August? He can't just order us to close down, not at this time of year, right?"

"Got the injunction right here," Engel said, sliding a sheaf of papers across the counter. Augie picked it up, set his reading glasses on his nose, and skimmed the contents while Engel proceeded: "Now this is only temporary, mind you. Only until the investigation is complete."

"When will that be?" Teresa said.

Engel sighed. "Could be two-three weeks. Could be longer. We have the Sheriff's Office assisting, but their resources are practically as limited as mine."

"Have you called the FBI on this?"

Engel threw his hands in the air. "This ain't like the movies. They won't come all the way out to the sticks over a dead kid."

"We can't shut down now," Augie said. "It's as simple as that."

"You'll have to take that up with J.F."

"I mean to."

Engel looked around. "Doesn't look like you've got any reason to stay open anyhow. Place is a ghost town."

Augie held up a hand. "Now, wait a minute. What happened last night, it's a tragedy. No two ways about it. But forcing us to close our doors? That only compounds the issue. We have kids to feed, Al, Jesus."

"My hands are tied, Augie. Not a single thing I can do about it."

"You're on our side, right? You could talk to Fahrlander."

"Look, the best course of action you can take is to hire a lawyer."

"Al, listen to me. It's Adeline. She's behind this somehow. She and her goons showed up in the orchard yesterday afternoon, threatened me."

"August—" Teresa said, a warning.

"Adeline Gable *threatened* you?" Engel said, drawing out his notepad and pen. "What'd she say?"

"She asked me to shut down the maze. Brought those two guys she has hanging around all day with to stare me down."

"What'd she say exactly?"

"Somehow she'd heard of Susie getting spooked in the maze the night before," he said, letting the words settle in the chief's mind for a moment. If Engel grasped Augie's implication, he made no sign of it. "She wanted me to close it down for safety reasons, void the lease with Grant. She said, and I quote, 'Imagine the tragedy if someone got hurt.' She made it sound all sweet, in that way she has, but there was nothing but acid in her meaning."

Engel appeared to mull this over. "I'll talk to her," he said. "You'll want to watch who you're accusing, though, Augie. You know what I mean? Be careful where you sling your words."

"Just look into it, Al. Okay? That's all I'm asking."

"We'll cover every angle. In the meantime, do your part and honor the injunction." He left them to close up alone.

After they'd placed all the pies and perishables in the walk-in refrigerator, Augie drew a sign on a sheet of paper which read CLOSED UNTIL FURTHER NOTICE - SORRY FOR THE INCONVENIENCE and hung it on the door. He hauled a sawhorse in front of the maze entrance and another to cover the exit, adding a second barrier to the police tape already covering them. Then he and Teresa got in the truck and drove home.

Augie paced the den, occasionally punching a fist into his hand. Nothing about this smelled right. Adeline's visit seemed far too convenient to be coincidence. He wanted to drive up the ridge and talk to her, but knew she wouldn't likely grant him an audience. She'd have her hired dopes make an excuse. Still, it wouldn't hurt to call. He picked up the phone and dialed her number from memory. It rang ten times before he set the receiver down.

Then he thought of something. If he couldn't speak with Adeline, he'd take a drive over to the Lang farm. He'd make it look social, but he'd see what he could glean from Grant. If he'd had any involvement in Granny's request to shut down the maze, maybe Augie could pick up on it. And if he *had* put that particular bug in Adeline's ear, there might be something to his theory about the timing of the request and the two victims in his maze.

Part of him chided himself and thought Teresa was right— controlling and manipulative as Adeline could be, she would never intentionally harm anyone, especially a couple of kids. Grant Lang wouldn't either, no matter what he thought of Milliard Farms and its owner. Or would he? Because no animal had injured Randy, of that much he was sure. He didn't know about the girl—he'd heard nothing of the condition she'd been found in, nor any suspected cause of death. He doubted Al would share that information freely.

"I'm going for a drive. Be back before lunch."

"Where are you going?" Teresa asked.

"Thought I'd pay a visit to the Lang farm, see how harvest is coming."

"August."

"I know what I'm doing, Tree." He kissed her cheek. "Back in a jiff."

He took the long way, allowing time to talk himself out of this visit. Would it be productive or would it only let Lang know Augie was on to him? The element of surprise could be a powerful ally. He felt that if Grant had any part in these recent happenings, he'd telegraph it on his face. No, this was the correct move. In any case, Augie couldn't waste the rest of the day away wearing out the carpet in his den.

The road wound through miles of browning cornstalks, those that had not yet been harvested. He knew Grant's hired men would get to them before long, plowing them down with their fleet of shiny green John Deere combines. Tin signs posted in the ditches alongside the fields announced the various hybrids of the crop like some ancient secret language: Cargill, DeKalb, Asgrow.

When the Lang farm came into view, white house with green trim, red barns standing high against a cerulean sky, situated on four acres of lush, manicured lawn, Augie nearly turned around. The idea of showing his hand, especially to one such as Grant Lang, unsettled him. But he had no choice. He needed to get a solid feel for this or he wouldn't be able to sleep.

He steered up the long gravel drive and parked in back of the house, as was custom with Lang visitors. He got out and looked around. A homemade two-tiered rabbit hutch stood against the house, all but three of the wire-mesh cubicles empty. A pair of mid-sized mongrels loped up from the barn, sniffing at his shoes. A faded pink Big Wheels lay overturned beneath the double clothesline where sheets flapped in the breeze like captured ghosts. A clutch of naked decapitated Barbie dolls lay ass-up in a tin pail beneath the ruins of a rotted-out treehouse. Horses whinnied in the barn; the Langs kept half a dozen Appaloosas which their daughters rode in regional competitions. Word had it Lorelai and Bonnie, the two eldest, were naturals.

Speaking of, Bonnie answered the door when he knocked and Augie said, "Morning, Bonnie. Your pa around?"

"Good morning, Mr. Milliard. I think he's out behind the shed." Augie touched the brim of his cap and turned toward the outbuilding she named, but she called him back. "Mr. Milliard, is it true what happened out at your place?"

His cheek twitched. "I'm afraid it is. Your sister was there. She doing okay?"

Bonnie nodded. "She didn't see anything. She feels bad for Denny."

"Denny's all right. He's tough," Augie said, remembering the way he looked when he came in the door last night.

"Tell Susie I hope she feels better. I heard about the mumps. No fun."

"Will do," he said, then escaped to the shed. He found Grant behind it, as expected. The man had his back to Augie and had a claw hammer raised overhead. He brought it down, hard and sharp, with a grunt of effort and something screamed. It flashed in Augie's mind that Grant had just murdered his youngest daughter Penny and that he had been the sole eyewitness to the crime.

"What've you got there, Grant?" he called, still a good distance off in case the man spun on him intent on murder.

Lang turned, not at all startled by the sudden intrusion, and Augie saw he held a still-kicking rabbit by the scruff in the opposite hand. "Dinner," he said, and brought the hammer down again. The rabbit quit kicking and dropped a bundle of pellets as it expired.

"Never knew rabbits made noise," Augie said, desperate to not appear rattled before Grant Lang.

"Oh, they make quite a range of noises, depending on the situation," the corn farmer said. His prematurely white hair had been tucked neatly beneath his customary FS Seed cap and his face still held much of its summer color. He flashed teeth as white and square as dice. "What, you never butchered a beast before?"

"Not one so small," Augie said.

A corner of Grant's mouth jerked. "Yeah, well, I do it back here because it upsets the girls."

"I can't imagine why."

Grant waved the hammer. Flecks of blood dotted the head. "I heard you had a bit of trouble on the land I leased you."

"You could say that," Augie replied. "Had an interesting visit with Adeline prior to it."

Grant arched his brows, feigning surprise (Augie thought). "Yeah?"

"Said you want to void the lease. May I ask why? And why you didn't come to me direct about it?"

Grant shrugged a shoulder and tossed the rabbit onto a pile of others lying on a tarp which had met the same fate. "I guess Granny jumped the gun. I was gonna call you tonight."

"Why were you discussing our agreement with Adeline in the first place?"

The corn farmer waved this off, face pinched in annoyance. "You know Ashford County etiquette as well as anyone, Augie. Our lady likes to stay in the loop."

"Maybe it's time we cut her out of it."

"You're looking for trouble with that line of thought. It's important to remember who runs the show."

"Anyway, I didn't come here to talk about Adeline. I want to know why you want to void the agreement prematurely."

"The simple answer is I want to grow feed corn on that land."

"And the complicated answer?"

Grant huffed through his teeth, half sigh, half laugh. "Complicated answer is it makes me sick to see crop wasted in such a way. People paying top dollar to traipse around on the richest damn topsoil on God's green earth."

He's jealous, Augie thought. *That's what it comes down to. He sees the maze's success and can't stand it because it's not making him any money or any fame.*

He said: "I'm willing to work with you, Grant. Civilly, man to man. So if you write me a check to cover the fifth and final season, we've got a deal."

This time Grant did laugh, a sharp sound like shrapnel exploding. "How about we just let that go, what do you say?"

"Come again?"

"The land's useless to you now, ain't it? J.F. shut it down?"

"You son of a bitch," Augie said before he could stop himself. "You *did* have something to do with those kids getting hurt out there. You set it up."

Lang brandished the hammer. "You want to watch your mouth, mister. You start making accusations, that'll come back and bite you on the ass."

Al Engel's words, echoed now from Grant Lang.

"Why'd you do it, Grant? Why'd you kill that girl, ruin that boy's life?"

Grant took two steps toward him, but Augie held his ground. "I didn't have nothing to do with that," he said. "Don't you try to pin your bad luck on me."

A man came around the opposite corner of the shed: tall, rail-thin, mop of dirty curls dangling to his shoulders. Two weeks' worth of patchy beard sprouting on his face. He used what appeared to be an ancient bayonet to carve an apple into slices, popping one into his mouth off the edge of the blood gutter. An enormous pewter Jolly Roger belt buckle hung suspended above his crotch. He said in a thick eastern European accent, "Everything is okay, boss?"

Many ethnic migrant laborers moved out from the city seeking farm work once the grain boom took off and this man was likely no different; Grant Lang hired them from time to time, especially during harvest season. Augie had taken on a few to help work the orchards, but he'd never seen this one before.

"It's fine, Kodi. We're just finishing up a spot of business," Lang said without turning. The migrant stood a moment longer, pitched the core into the grass, and vanished again.

"Take your land back," Augie said. "I sure as hell don't want it anymore, not with the blood spilled on it."

The grain farmer softened. He tossed the hammer into the grass beside the shed. "Look, Augie, I don't want to tussle. We're both men of our word. You want to keep the land until next season, it's yours. You want me to cut a check for the remainder, I'll go get my book right now." He held out a hand, speckled with blood and earth.

Augie looked at the hand, then at the man. "I don't want your land and I don't want your money. Take them with you to hell, for all I care."

Then he turned the corner and strode to his car, spinning gravel behind him as he peeled down the drive.

CHAPTER ELEVEN

Rachel dropped her Schwinn in the empty parking lot and stepped onto the porch. She tried the door but found it locked. Cupping her hands around her eyes, she peered through the window. Closed? On a weekend before Halloween? Then she spotted the sign taped to the glass: CLOSED UNTIL FURTHER NOTICE - SORRY FOR THE INCONVENIENCE.

She glanced around the empty pumpkin patch, engorged with its orange-gold bounty, and listened to the wind ripple the leaves of the orchard. Then she made her way to the maze entrance, slipped around the barrier, and moved into the corn.

Teresa fixed lunch with no real belief her husband would be back in time to eat it while it was hot. What would they do if the store stayed closed a week? Or two? How long would it take for the investigation to conclude? Why had Judge Fahrlander shut down their operation in the first place? It made no sense. The maze she could understand, but the store? The orchard? The pumpkin patch?

Something occurred to her. She would see about securing a spot at the farmer's market held each Friday in downtown Murdoch. They could haul apples and pumpkins and sell them there. It wouldn't make up what they'd lose with the store closed, not even close, but it would be better than nothing. Maybe they could even salvage a nice Christmas for the kids.

She picked up the phone and had punched in the first two digits when the doorbell rang. Teresa called out for one of the kids to answer it, but received no reply—Dennis would be in the garage working on his car and the rest of the healthy kids had scattered with a warning to stay close to the house.

She hung up and went to open the door, surprised to find Rachel Safford standing on the welcome mat. "Good morning, Rachel. I'm sorry to say Susie's still not well enough for visitors."

"Good morning, Mrs. Milliard." She worked at a thumbnail, looking bashful. "Actually, I came to see Dennis. Is he home?"

"Dennis? He's in the carriage house. You can go on out there."

"Thank you, Ma'am," Rachel said. She knew the way; she'd been friends with Susan going on ten years.

Teresa watched her walk across the lawn, thought about following, then forgot it.

Rachel found him waist deep beneath the hood of his prized Firebird. He had the radio tuned to the local station which was currently reporting on pork belly futures at the Chicago Mercantile Exchange. Rachel would have liked to time her arrival with something more dramatic, maybe the intro riffs of "Purple Haze," and even hesitated in hopes it would happen, but the announcer just kept jawing. This would have to do.

"Hey," she said.

Dennis ducked out, saw his guest, and quickly wiped grease from his hands on a semi-clean towel stuck in his belt. "Oh. Hey. Susie's still sick."

"I know. I wanted to see you."

She thought she detected a slight widening of his eyes, but he did a good job trying to stay stoic. "Me? What for?"

Rachel glanced behind her, saw they were alone. "I wanted to make sure you're okay after last night. And I want to show you something," she said.

"I'm fine," he said (untruthfully, she thought). "What do you have?"

She stepped close to him and turned out one pocket of her Levi's. In the center of her palm rested a small silver coin encrusted with grit. Dennis plucked it up. She closed her fingers over the place he'd touched her palm.

"Where did you get this?" he asked.

"I found it in the maze. Just now."

He looked at her. "You went into the maze? The cops have it

cordoned off. You could've gotten in trouble."

"You only get in trouble if you're caught," she said. "Do you know where it's from? I have no idea who the guy on the front is and can't read the language on back."

"It's Soviet, probably a ruble," he said. "See? The back says CCCP."

"How does that translate to Soviet Union?"

"Only people outside the USSR call it that. Internally, they call themselves CCCP."

"What does that mean?"

"I don't know, something Russian."

"How did it get into your corn maze?"

"Someone dropped it, I guess."

"Someone from Russia came through your maze?"

"We get all kinds of people," Dennis said.

"You get many from outside the state, much less the country? You get many from a nation we have a cold war with?"

Dennis turned the coin in his fingers. "We get migrant workers from all over, some are Russian, I guess."

This close, even with him reeking of oil, Rachel felt a little dizzy. She backed off a step. "I should go."

"Rachel?"

"I'll see you at the parade, yeah?"

"Yeah."

"Bye, Dennis," she said and ran out to the driveway. He watched her climb onto her bike and pedal away.

Augie recognized Rachel on her green Schwinn half a mile up the road and though his turn was coming on the left, he went straight and pulled up beside her.

"Need a lift?" he asked.

She braked and put a hand out to steady herself on the pickup's chassis. Even though her house stood only a mile or so up the road, she said: "Hi, Mr. Milliard. I'd love a ride."

Augie got out and lifted her bike into the bed while Rachel climbed onto the bench and waited with her hands in her lap.

"So what are you up to today?" he asked as he put the truck in gear.

"Just out for a ride. Enjoying the weather while it lasts."

"Good idea," Augie said. He glanced at her. "Are you all right after what happened last night?"

She nodded. "I'm fine. I didn't see anything."

"You disappeared for a time. Your dad was worried."

"I took a walk, that's all. To clear my head."

"That's understandable. Listen, if you need to talk about any of this, let me know."

"Thanks, Mr. Milliard. That's nice of you." She tilted her head at him. "Do you suppose they'll catch who did it?"

"Chief Engel's on it. He knows his way around an investigation."

Rachel mumbled something and looked out her window.

"Come again? Didn't catch that last."

"It's nothing," she said as they pulled into the Safford drive. "Thanks for the ride."

"Anytime, Rachel," he said, getting out and setting her bike on the gravel. She took it from him and wheeled it toward the garage. Ray spotted him from the porch and came out to talk.

"Morning, Augie," he said. "You hear anything more from Al?"

"Nothing yet."

"They figger out who the dead girl was?"

"If they did, they haven't bothered to pass it along."

Ray nodded his blocky head, looking like a chicken pecking the ground. "Well, they will."

"Let's hope so."

"Ruthie's been praying on it," Ray said, shooting a glance toward the house. "Ruthie says the Good Lord near always answers her prayers."

"Glad to have her on our side in that case," Augie said. "How's Caleb doing? He seem any worse for wear after last night?"

"Caleb? Naw, he's fine. Isn't much in this world can rattle that boy."

Which was true. Caleb Safford could very well be a psychopath from what Augie knew of him. There was something missing in that boy, you could read it in his eyes. The younger son, Samuel, may have been soft in the head but Caleb's was diamond-hard. Calculating. Observing. Full of guile. The opposite of his old man. The boy rarely spoke and when he did it came out polite as pie. Augie thought the manners were a mask he wore. He imagined Caleb the type of boy who enjoyed pulling wings off flies or beating puppies with a stick. Then again, he could be dead wrong in his judgment. Either way, Augie didn't figure it could hurt to raise the boy on Scripture.

"Glad to hear it, Ray," Augie said. "Listen, we won't need your help for a time." He explained about the court order closing down the store, the maze, and the orchard.

"Well, shoot. That ain't fair. That ain't fair one bit, Augie."

"Life isn't fair, even if it ought to be," Augie replied. "That's what my father used to say."

"Wise man, your dad."

"Well, I won't take up any more of your time. Give Ruth my best."

On the drive home, Augie had an idea. He turned around and drove north, toward Ashford. He wanted to speak with one other man before heading home. Tree might be upset he'd miss lunch, but they were facing unusual circumstances.

Rachel went directly to her attic cubby, dragged out her hidden kit, and set to work. This time Deep Purple's *Made in Japan* played through the headphones. She closed her eyes as the drums and bass picked up on "Highway Star," the rhythm sinking into her skin like some exotic lotion. Her fingers crept to the snap of her jeans as if creatures separate from her, worked them down over her hips to her ankles, panties and all. She found the X-Acto, explored her thigh for a good site, and slid the blade over the supple skin. The pain, intense and immediate, made her gasp. This time she did not use the flashlight to watch the blood pool; she wanted only to feel it slipping down her thigh like a warm red snake released.

"I love you," she whispered in the dust-choked darkness. "I love you, I love you, I love you."

CHAPTER TWELVE

Dennis did not take the coin inside to show his mother. He left it in his front pocket with the rest of the loose change he carried. He wondered how it had gotten there. It had likely lain there for years and hundreds of tromping feet had finally unearthed it.

He worked for a time installing the two-barrel carburetor until his mother called him in for lunch. By then he'd completely forgotten the Russian coin existed and that night before bed he dumped the entire handful of change into his jar, burying it. He had bigger things on his mind.

Augie made it to the Stone Dairy Farm near the topside of the county in under forty minutes—good time, considering he'd driven half the trip staring at the orange triangle on the rear of one of Grant Lang's John Deere 8630s, which appeared to be doing nothing more useful than hogging the road. He tried to see if the driver might be the man Grant had called "Kodi," but couldn't make out details with the sun glaring off the rear window. When the slow hunk of steel at last turned off onto an unnamed county road, Augie pushed the pickup to 70 and kept it there the rest of the way.

This time of day, the dairy was running full-steam. The morning milking complete, Mike Stone and his three hired hands busied themselves with other chores. The Stones relied on outside help to keep the farm afloat. Three or four (or ten) stout offspring would have been a blessing of labor, but none had come about in the course of Mike and Ursula's eleven-year marriage and it seemed at least one of the Stones must be barren.

At the moment, the man of the house appeared nowhere,

perhaps indisposed in the canning room or making space in the cooler for the day's yield. One of the hired men, Ed Hatlen, noticed Augie and ambled over.

"What say, Mr. Milliard?" he called jovially. Eddie-boy never seemed a bit daunted or discouraged by hard labor; if anything, it seemed to invigorate him. A natural laborer. A good man to have onboard.

"Afternoon, Ed. Boss man around?"

Ed tipped his straw hat back on his work-wet hair and peered around. "Figger he's probably swamping out the cooling vat. Said it got contaminated."

"Think he'll mind if I pop my head in, say hello?"

"Go on in, he'll be happy for the company," Ed said. Augie thanked him and stepped over to the barn. On the way he glimpsed the other full-time hands, Ben and Old Dad, working on the feeding trough where a fitting had come loose. He always saw these three fellows as the scarecrow, tin man, and lion from *The Wizard of Oz*. It kept him amused, at least.

"Good day, gentlemen," Augie said.

"Mr. Milliard, what brings you up this way?" Ben called, wiping his hands on his overalls. Ben Kingston was the youngest of the hands, not much older than Dennis, tall and lean but roped with muscle. He'd been forced to drop out of school when his parents died in a car wreck four years by. Mike took him on and sheltered him in the bunkhouse out back with the other guys. The young man's stout work ethic had kept him employed so far. As a Black man, Ben was far from an Ashford County rarity in 1975 as the rural territory had been a major terminus for the Underground Railroad and many of those who'd used it as a means of escape had chosen to settle in the scenic countryside. Augie never understood what all the bigoted fuss was about; every man was equal in his eyes.

Augie shook Ben's hand. "Wanted a word with the man."

Old Dad—Augie had never learned his real name, if he had one—was a Sauk Indian who'd signed on to work with Mike's grandfather since the dairy had been established in the mid-20s. He'd been working there near two decades longer than Mike Stone's bride Ursula had been alive, and was probably closer in age to Mike than she was. Old Dad had taken the younger hands under his tutelage and trained them up right. He carried an ancient pocket watch on a tarnished fob, an item the Indian claimed he'd won from a white rancher over a game of poker while the century had still been young, and which he produced often as if ticking off the remaining moments of his life. Augie thought the relic tastefully anachronistic.

"August, my boy," Old Dad said. He tugged at his ear with one gloved hand and snapped his watch closed with the other, tucking it away in his bib overalls. "A pleasure, as always."

"Go on in, Mr. Milliard," Ben said. "Cooling room, you'll find him there."

But he didn't find Mike in the cooling room. As he passed the office door, he caught him on the phone, chair swiveled around with his back to Augie.

"You heard me," he told the receiver. "I want to know exactly what she said and to who."

Augie nearly moved on to the canning room, set on leaving Mike to his privacy. It was well-known throughout the farming community his trust in his wife had slipped over the years, likely due to the age discrepancy. Mike and Ursula Stone had been forty-four and twenty-two, respectively, when they'd tied the knot eleven years ago and Mike took her naturally coquettish ways personally. The same ways which had drawn him to her in that decade past.

True, Urs *did* tend to bat her eyes at the menfolk when she thought her man had his back turned, but Augie thought it little more than harmless flirtation. She'd once blown him a kiss at a Christmas party after a few cocktails, which Augie had pretended not to see. That had been the extent of his personal experience with her.

But he thought half the reason these hands stuck around as long as they had—even Old Dad who'd once confided in Augie that his waterworks had been busted going on twenty years—was to catch a glimpse of the farmer's wife in the window. Every now and again Ed or Ben would loose a wolfish whistle when the lady of the house appeared on the porch and their boss had gone to town on errand. Ursula ate it up, pretending to ignore the men while stealing glances at them over her hippie sunglasses and wiggling her rump against the rail. All harmless, to Augie's mind. Hell, Tree still got catcalled from time to time and she'd hit forty next year, which always brought a prideful smile to his face.

Augie simply couldn't resist listening for a spell outside Mike's office, though, in case the subject happened to be his wife's fidelity (or lack thereof). Tree loved good gossip and he thought a juicy morsel might spell a way back into her good graces. He backed off a step in case Mike turned and caught him eavesdropping.

"I'm telling you, if she moved forward without my go-ahead, I'll feed her in pieces to Ray's hogs."

There followed a silence so prolonged Augie nearly retreated, but at last Mike concluded the call with a pointed expletive. Augie forced himself to count to twenty, then knocked.

"Come in," Mike called, his voice reverting to its usual calm demeanor. He hated showing an ounce of open emotion. Except, apparently, to whomever he'd been speaking with on the phone.

Augie pushed in and said, "Afternoon, Mike. This a bad time?"

Stone looked surprised to see him, but recovered quickly. He'd been fidgeting with a letter opener fashioned to look like a Medieval sword, but flipped it onto the desk blotter and stood to shake hands. "Just some damn clients who seem hell-bent on ruining my day. Say, you're about the last person I expected to see today, Augie."

"I guess you heard."

"Hell, who hasn't? I bet even deaf ol' Jerry Thom's caught wind of it by now."

"It's a damn bit of bad luck, that's for sure."

"Cops close to solving it?" Stone asked.

"If they are, it's news to me."

"Listen, you and Teresa need anything—anything at all— you let me know."

"We're going to be fine, Mike. Really." Augie paused, licked his lips. "I came by because I wanted to ask if you'd heard or seen anything."

Mike's brow furrowed. "How do you mean?"

"Anything out of the ordinary. Strangers in the area, wolf sightings. Anything like that."

The dairy farmer laughed. "Wolf sightings? No sir, not here. They were all hunted for pelts before my day. Before my dad's day, what I heard."

Wolf, we figure, Engel had told him in regard to what brought down the Stone Dairy heifer. *We*, meaning Mike and himself. The police chief had lied to him about that—Mike found the idea as absurd as Augie did. So why had Al lied? Merely to shut Augie up or … or for some other reason? Whichever, he'd failed to count on Augie to check out loose ends. Mistake.

"How's your stock?" Augie asked.

Mike seemed pleased at the subject change. "Stout as ever. Yield's up nine percent this quarter, so can't well complain."

"You lose any of late?"

"No sir, not these gals. They're healthy as they come."

"No bulls either?"

"Sent one to slaughter a couple-three weeks back. Mean fella. Couldn't gentle him, so he stocked our freezer. Urs and I are set for winter, that's no lie. The hands'll be eating sirloin till spring. We got extra, you want some." The last sentence came out dragged through a hint of Dixieland condescension, Augie thought. Mike offering the down-on-his luck guy some charity.

"We're set, thanks. And thanks for the chat, Mike. Much appreciated."

"You drove all the way up here to ask about wolves?"

"Can't a man pay a visit to his friends from time to time, shoot the breeze?"

Mike laughed again. "You bet, buddy. You stop by anytime. And you need anything, just pucker up 'n whistle."

"You know it, Mikey. Thanks a bunch," Augie said and started away. He turned again before reaching the barn door. "One last thing. You know of a man Grant hired, goes by the name Kodi?"

Mike's face pinched as if in thought. "Doesn't sound familiar," he said.

"Thanks, Mikey," Augie said again and headed for the truck.

Ben, Ed, and Old Dad had vanished from the yard as Augie made his way to the pickup, though someone else had appeared.

"Hello, August," Ursula Stone called from porch.

Augie touched the brim of his cap. "Afternoon, ma'am."

"You want to come in, have some coffee? Pot just finished brewing."

"Much as I'd like it, I can't stay, ma'am." He felt strange calling a woman younger than him such, but felt it best to keep things formal with her.

She seemed to take it in stride. "Next time, then."

"You bet," Augie said and hurried to slam the door between them. He looked through the rearview all the way down the drive, watching her watching him.

CHAPTER THIRTEEN

A week later the police still had no one in custody. They had no credible leads. No positive identification on the female victim. Engel's infrequent reports each seemed like a bigger dead end than the last. On the morning of the Apple Fest parade, Augie wore his frustration openly.

Teresa stood in the entrance of the old Derby Machine Works warehouse, which had gone out of business in 1960, and where a dozen parade floats sat ready to roll in the next ninety minutes, listening to Al Engel speaking with her husband. Both men sounded as if they'd rather be anywhere but here. She knew August despised riding in the parade and on any normal year would have happily traded it to be standing in one of their orchards. This year, though, he seemed positively demoralized. Teresa understood his position and would have felt quite similar herself had she allowed the gloom to creep over her, as he clearly had.

Judge Fahrlander—the man his cohorts and cronies referred to as J.F.—had not budged an inch on lifting the injunction against Milliard Country Store & Orchard. August had requested a formal appeal and had brought in a lawyer from Ashford to represent the family, but Fahrlander had seemed bored at the hearing. This according to her husband.

The farmer's market had brought them a little extra cash, but nothing close to what they'd lost with the closing of the store. Teresa had singlehandedly organized a yard sale, using the kids to haul junk out of basement and attic storage and set out for the best offer. The usual tussle over what to sell and what to keep ensued, which ended in Hannah sobbing over a novelty record player she hadn't used since the fourth grade and the twins begging to retain a threadbare old marionette with string so tangled it would take nothing short of a miracle to restore to functionality.

The sale brought in slightly more than $300—barely enough to scratch the surface of a typical Christmas. The next payment from the produce distributor wasn't due until early next quarter and finances were about to get tight … unless the investigation wrapped soon. She'd already asked Chief Engel if she could be of any assistance, an offer he'd politely but firmly rebuffed.

She'd spoken with August about dipping into savings to ensure no slippage in the holiday season and he'd rebuffed her as well.

"Tree," he'd said, "we agreed to once in, none out."

Which they had, years ago. She reminded him that when they'd made the agreement, they'd been flush with cash. Couldn't they just take a tiny nip so the kids wouldn't feel the deficit? He'd closed the argument by saying that if they had to go with a Norway Spruce instead of a Scotch Pine to hang the lights on, then that's the way it would have to be. He wouldn't budge an inch after that, citing only that their savings were meant strictly for college funds and retirement.

One thing he'd said in a closing argument which would have done Perry Mason proud was: "When it comes to college or Christmas presents, Tree, you're comparing apples to oranges. One cannot compete against the other."

"No, August. It's apples to apples. Sacrificing a bit of the future for a bit of the present is what we're talking about here."

But that's where the debate had ended, with August gritting his teeth and offering a firm: "We'll. Be. Fine."

Now, as she watched her husband and the police chief banter about evidence and motive and murder weapons, she noticed something curious. August no longer seemed so despondent. Now he seemed to be *enjoying* himself. He seemed to be relishing this break in the monotony of country life and all the fuss made over the dead girl and injured boy in their maze. Could that be possible? Why were men so desperate for adventure?

"Missus Milliard?" Zeb asked from behind her, making her jump. "Sorry, ma'am, didn't mean to startle you."

"It's fine, Zeb. What can I do for you?"

"They're ready for us," he said, waving a hand at an assistant to the parade grand marshal who busied herself checking off a list on a clipboard.

"Thank you, Zeb. Will you let Mr. Milliard know please?"

He tipped his hat and sauntered over to break up the meeting between her husband and the chief. Teresa climbed up onto the float and took her usual place toward the back. This year's had been decked out in crepe paper of oranges, golds, and reds to reflect the theme of *Autumn Wanderings*. The kids quit their horseplay and joined her, finding seats up front where their shining smiles would be highly visible to the masses—all but Susan who Doc Rubek had released from isolation but had strictly forbidden from participation. Teresa spent a moment getting the twins settled, then sank into her folding chair as her husband hauled himself up beside her.

"You know what he's saying now?" he whispered. "Al's saying they still can't identify the dead girl. I'm telling you, Tree, something stinks here."

"Don't start with your conspiracy theories again, August, for the love of Pete."

He didn't seem to hear. "I'm starting to doubt there even *was* a dead girl."

"Why would anyone make that up, least of all your friend Alvin? You know, your friend the *police officer*?"

"Lower your voice, Tree, Jesus," Augie said. "Now just listen a minute. A kid gets hurt in the maze, they might shut it down for the season but it wouldn't be enough to shut down our entire operation. Right? But you throw in a dead body, boom, place is unfit for business, has to be secured for a formal investigation."

"You're reaching, August."

"Maybe I am," he said. "Or maybe I'm not."

A whistle blew up ahead and a minute later the line of floats and area high school bands moved out into the sun.

The first quarter of the parade went as usual. Good turnout, thunderous applause for the veterans from four wars marching at the head of the column, woops of joy at the Derby High's marching band's rendition of "The Stars and Stripes Forever" (even if Bret McKay did drop one of his cymbals in the middle of it), and lots of waves for—and from—the Milliard clan, patrons of the Apple Fest parade for generations.

The trouble came when they rounded Main onto Cherry Street. A contingent of Randy Johansen's people and supporters had taken over the corner and greeted the Milliard float with taunts and jeers. Someone produced a bushel of rotten apples and all at once the air came alive with bruised and browning bombs. One caught Teresa square in the temple and stars exploded across her vision. A high-pitched keening overwhelmed her senses. She became dimly aware of Augie on his feet, his folding chair toppling over the edge of the float and onto the pavement, hollering at the kids to take cover, bellowing profanities at the crowd.

"Take your apples and get out of our town!" a woman screamed.

"Child killer!" someone else cried.

Teresa shook her head to clear it but that seemed only to make things worse. A shower of corn cobs came next, raining down on the family float like artillery shells. One landed in her hair, yanking loose the utilitarian braid she always wore in the parade. Hard kernels bit into her cheek, her neck, and dropped to the floor of the float like rotten teeth.

"You're finished here, Milliard," a man at the front of the crowd growled. His voice sounded suspiciously familiar, but she couldn't place it. Teresa tried to find her feet, but a second apple caught the back of her head, hard as a baseball, and she sank down into darkness.

When she came around, she heard her husband's voice first. He spoke in harsh fricatives and slithering sibilants. She tried to focus and found herself unable. It hurt to think.

"You aren't hearing me, Paul," August said. "This was a coordinated attack. In public, no less, to hurt my family. To humiliate us. Christ, just look at Teresa."

The Paul to whom he spoke would be Sheriff Paul Lisk.

Apparently, August had wearied of Chief Engel's counsel and had gone over his head.

The sheriff said, "Now, Augie, we don't know exactly what it was just yet, not till I've interviewed everyone involved."

"How many did you arrest?"

"We've taken three people into custody—"

"*Three?* They were twenty strong, Paul. Maybe thirty. They knocked my wife out cold, scared the hell out of my kids. They're already rattled after what happened in the maze. Now they're going to be terrified to stick their noses out their own front door."

Someone asked the men to quiet down. She squinted around to find Sidney Rubek at her side, his black medical bag opened. They'd brought her into his office and laid her on a sofa in the single examining room. Doc asked if she could hear him and she said yes. He shined a light in her eyes, took a peek in her ears and down her throat for good measure. "You have a mild concussion, but nothing to worry about. Stay off your feet for forty-eight hours and if symptoms persist, call me. I wouldn't mind you staying overnight at Ashford Memorial, but I know you won't."

"You're right about that, Sid," Teresa said. She allowed Doc and August to help her into a sitting position. Her husband asked if she was okay and she said, "As good as can be expected. What in creation happened?"

"We live in a county of turncoats, that's what," her husband spat. Sheriff Lisk touched his arm and Augie acquiesced. "At least Saul Scanlon promised not to print anything about it in tomorrow's paper. It's good to have friends in the press."

"Teresa, you mind if I ask you a few questions?" the sheriff asked.

"Knock yourself out. No, wait. Don't. It really stinks." No one laughed, but she hadn't expected them to. She peered blearily around. "Where are the kids?"

Augie said, "I sent them home. Told them to lock the door and don't open it for anybody."

"Is it that bad?" she asked.

"We don't know what it is right now, ma'am," Lisk said. "I'm going to be working with Chief Engel to sort through this."

"Where is he, anyway?" she asked.

Her husband shrugged. "Don't know. But I know where he wasn't—working crowd control. Didn't see a single one of his men on the scene to break up the mob. Thankfully Paul had a deputy nearby, called his boss for back up."

What was happening? Why was their world falling apart, all at once? She closed her eyes and lay back, resting, until Doc said she could go home.

CHAPTER FOURTEEN

Augie turned the absent corpse theory over in his mind. He had nary an idea why Al Engel would fabricate such a story, but until he had solid proof otherwise, he had to at least consider it a possibility.

"The question is, who benefits from shutting us down?" he asked the empty den. As he paced, he swirled an ice cube through his glass of scotch. The obvious idea, of course, would be Grant Lang, but that didn't quite wash. He wouldn't go through all the trouble, not to mention the personal risk, of maiming and murder to force the Milliards to void their contract a year prior to the agreed-upon term. It didn't make sense.

Neither did the reaction the incident had caused. Judge Fahrlander's bizarre injunction, Al's slow-burn investigation, the people who'd turned against them. Those bothered him most of all. People he'd known his entire life had turned out to bombard them with his own family-grown apples. The symbolism, at least, had not been lost on him. Now, though, he feared for his family. He would not be able to sleep peacefully until this nightmare had been resolved.

He needed to speak with Adeline Gable, and soon.

Remember, she could be in on it, his mind whispered. *She could have orchestrated the entire thing.*

That could be true, but speaking with her would clear it up. He'd be able to tell one way or the other, no doubt about it.

Augie picked up the phone and dialed her number. He got as far as the fifth digit before hanging up. No, speaking with Granny would not be a good idea. He needed to keep his cards close to his vest, not out on display. The feeling they'd entered some high-stakes poker game had lodged in his mind like a fishhook. He needed to figure out who his friends were and who they weren't.

Augie went around his desk, sat, and dug out a pencil and legal pad from the drawer above the kneehole. He made three columns, one labeled YES, one NO, and a third with a question mark. In the first column he scratched *Ray S.* In the second, *Grant L.* He hesitated before scrawling *Granny G., Al E.,* and *Mike S.* in the third. Okay, the principals had been classified, at least temporarily. Who else? Zeb and Mary Lou went into the first—loyal employees to the last. The Johansen family, once loyal customers as well as friendly acquaintances through Denny, went in the middle. He jotted *J.F.* in the third because, in all honesty, he had no idea the judge's intentions with his court order. What good did it do to close down the Apple Fest operation? And why not shut it all down, parade included? Had he done that, it would have saved the Milliards a world of pain and embarrassment.

He didn't shut down the parade because it's good for the local economy, all those out of towners coming to spend money at Derby businesses, that same quiet voice in his head advised. *Whereas the Milliard family profits not a penny from it. The parade has always been our gift to the community.*

Augie erased his last entry and moved it to the NO column. Fahrlander was not a friend, and all at once Augie decided the judge must be part of it. But what was *it*? He still had no idea why this was happening.

Teresa didn't feel like cooking, said her head still hurt, so Augie ordered pizza and the family ate together at the table for the first time in weeks. None of the usual good humor accompanying takeout appeared in evidence. The members of the Milliard clan chewed in slow, plodding thought, no one speaking more than a handful of words except the twins, who already seemed over the pelting at the parade.

Afterward, when the kids had dispersed, Augie said: "I want you to go lie down. I'm going to drive over and talk to Al. I won't be long."

Teresa did not argue. She'd only eaten half a slice before pushing her plate away. Now she kissed her husband on the cheek and made her way upstairs. Good. Augie didn't feel like another argument. He only wanted to get to the bottom of his troubles and sanitize them.

Augie drove to the brick cube on the corner of Main and Jackson which served as the Derby Village Police Department and parked in one of the four spaces beside a lone cruiser. A light burned in the lobby, but Augie found the door locked. He rapped on the glass until Nathan Berryman came and opened up.

"Mr. Milliard," he said, clearly surprised by the visitor's identity.

"Hi, Nate. Al around?"

The big boy shook his head. "Went up Ashford way to talk to the sheriff."

"About what?"

"I can't rightly say."

"Can't or won't?"

"Why, I don't know myself, Mr. Milliard." He looked sheepish. "Chief, he don't tell me much unless I need to know."

"Nate, do you know where they're keeping that girl's body?"

"The coroner's office, I expect. In the fridge?"

"I guess they would. Did they figure out who she was?"

"If they did, they kep' it to themselves."

"Need to know basis, right."

"I was awful sorry to hear what happened to you and your family today, Mr. Milliard."

"I was sorry you weren't there to stop it, Nate."

"I couldn't. Chief had me busy elsewhere."

"Yeah? Whereabouts?"

If he'd looked sheepish before, the young cop looked downright embarrassed now. "Your land, sir."

"The maze? Haven't they gone over that ground enough?"

Nathan shook his head. "Your yard."

Augie's cheeks flamed. "You were in my *yard*?"

"Yes, sir. I guess I shouldn't have told you."

"You damn well better have told me," Augie said, working to keep his temper in check. "What were you looking for?"

He shrugged a beefy shoulder. "Chief said 'anything out of the ordinary.'"

"You find anything fitting that description?"

"No, sir."

"This is getting out of hand," Augie said. Something occurred to him. "Nathan, you remember working summers for me, yeah?"

"Yes, sir," he said, brightening, relieved at the change in direction.

"I always treated you fair, didn't I? Paid your checks on time?"

"Of course, Mr. Milliard. Best job I ever had."

"Better than this one?"

Nathan's face pinched. That was a tough one. Sure, this one paid more and it certainly felt more important wearing a badge and a gun versus overalls and a straw hat, but he sported the conflict plainly on his face. "I liked the work better, that's for sure. And the people. Your family always treated me like one of their own."

"Chief Engel good to you?"

Nathan bobbed his head. "I guess so."

"He ever berate you?"

"What now?"

"Get on your case. Yell at you?"

"From time to time. Chief, he's a busy man. He don't have time for fuckups." His eyes widened. "Sorry for the language."

Augie waved this off. "Will you do something for me, Nate?"

"Sure, Mr. Milliard. Anything."

"If you hear anything fishy, anything that doesn't wash with your police sensibilities pertaining to my case, will you call me?"

A remnant of conflict returned to his face. "I don't suppose I ought to provide confidential information to a civilian. I could lose my star."

"I'm not asking you to break the law. Just put a bug in my ear if you hear anything that doesn't quite seem to fit, like a puzzle piece in the wrong box. Can I count on you for that?"

"Sure, Mr. Milliard." He sounded a little more certain now. He also sounded eager to please. "There's one thing I can tell you."

Augie waited, letting the boy take his time.

"Chief, he's been taking a lot of meetings up at the Gable place."

"I know as much. Granny likes to keep abreast of what's going on in town."

"And Mr. Lang's been joining them."

Augie looked at the young officer. "Say again?"

"Chief has me park near the house, keep watch for anyone approaching on foot or by vehicle. If I do, I'm to radio ahead, let him know."

"Why?"

Nathan shrugged again. "I guess they don't want to be disturbed."

"Any idea when they're meeting next?"

"Tomorrow night. After sundown. Always after sundown. Sometimes a third man joins them, but not always."

"This third man, what's he look like?"

"Can't really say. Never seen him up close."

"Thank you, Nate. You've been a big help."

"Say, where are you going?"

"Drive around a little, clear my head."

"Mr. Milliard? I hope everything works out for you. Your family deserves happiness."

Augie offered him a tight smile and got in his truck. He had no plans to drive around. He had one place in mind where he needed to go.

Until this night, August Milliard III had never broken a law in his life. He'd never gone drag racing out on the backroads with his buddies, never soaped a window, never filched so much as a gumball from County Line Market. He understood the ramifications of his actions and he doubted under the current climate in Ashford County Judge Fahrlander would go easy on him. So he wouldn't be caught.

Maybe if he'd not had the glass of scotch he wouldn't have considered such a foolhardy mission, but he had and he did.

The coroner's office lay behind Ashford County Jail in a squat cinderblock building painted rust brown. It stood dark at this hour, the crematory chimney smokeless. Augie had never been inside, but how complex could it be?

He drove past the Ashford County Alligators Class A minor league ballpark, shuttered and dark this time of year, parked the pickup in an alley two blocks up and walked back, glancing around to ensure no one saw him. The streets were dead, the city of Ashford quiet as a boneyard after nightfall. Larger by area and population than Murdoch and Derby combined, but still quaint and quiet, like a hamlet trapped inside a snow globe. Augie slipped up to the back door, pulling on a pair of work gloves he'd taken from the box in his truck and pulling a claw hammer from the loop in his dungarees.

The door had a simple lock, the folks in charge probably thinking who in their right mind would ever break into a morgue? Augie took a deep breath; once he proceeded there would be no going back. After another peek around, he struck the deadbolt three times, hard, bothering with neither decorum nor stealth. It gave way and he paused, listening to the breeze and nothing else. No night watchman came to investigate, no rogue ghost rushed him from within. Augie entered and eased the door shut behind him.

He clicked on his flashlight and moved from the back storage area, with its cartons of gauze and medical masks, into the building proper. He passed an autopsy room shrouded in darkness, the beam of light picking out the stainless steel table with built-in blood gutters. Augie shuddered and moved down the corridor until he found a room marked COLD STORAGE.

Inside he found six steel doors in the wall, identically square and closed tight. The girl must be in one of them, unless Andrew Chalmers had already carved her up. But Augie didn't think he had. They would want to determine identity before cause of death, at least to Augie's way of thinking.

He drew in a deep breath, heart thundering, more terrified than he thought he'd be when he set about this errand. The scotch had worn off. He'd made a mistake coming here, but here he yet stood. And more than anything, he needed to verify the girl existed so he could follow Tree's advice and give up the conspiracy theories.

He took hold of the handle of the first refrigerator door and hauled it open, quick, before he could rethink it. Cold vapor exhaled at him. The compartment lay empty. Augie went through them systematically, holding his breath any time he dragged one open. On the sixth and final door, he found himself praying though he didn't know if it was for the drawer to be vacant or occupied. Augie yanked it opened and shined the light inside.

Empty. All six, empty. There was no dead girl and never had been.

CHAPTER FIFTEEN

Susie came into the room and lay down beside her mother. Teresa stirred, then stilled. "Honey?" she asked. "You feeling okay?"

"That man's outside again. By the barn."

"Oh, sweetie, it's just a bad dream. Like Dad said."

"I saw him, Mom."

Teresa tried to sit up but her throbbing head forbade such nonsense. "Go tell your father, okay?"

"He's not here."

The first sliver of panic slid into her heart. "What do you mean, he's not here? You check the den?"

"The truck's gone, Mom. I can see the empty bay in the garage."

"What time is it?"

"Ten thirty."

Ten thirty? Where could August have gone at this hour? "Did you tell Dennis?"

"He's sleeping, won't get up. Told me to get back to bed or he'd slug me."

"Where's Timber?"

"I can't find him either."

Teresa groaned and hauled herself upright. She toed around in the dark until she found her slippers, not bothering with her bathrobe, and stepped over to the window. The yard held still in the darkness. She could make out the contours of the barn and the carriage house, but saw nothing discernible in the shadows, though, to be fair, her vision still hadn't fully evened out.

"Where did you see the man, Susan?" she asked.

"He lit a cigarette. I saw the flash of his lighter, his face glowed orange for a second."

"Could you see who it was?" Teresa asked, secretly harboring the notion that all the stress of late had caused August to take up smoking again. He hadn't smoked regularly in nine years, but perhaps it had only been him Susie had seen. He'd had lapses before and they embarrassed him.

"No, it happened too quick."

Teresa looked again, squinting, and thought she saw the wink of a cigarette in the far distance, near the corn. She made her way to Dennis's room, pleased to discover the dizziness had diminished. She knocked and opened the door.

"Dennis? Come here a minute, will you?"

Her son grunted and rolled in bed. She had to shake his shoulder to wake him. "What is it, Ma? Jeez Louise."

"There's someone outside, Dennis."

"Get Dad."

"He's not here."

This seemed to snap her son out of it, his man-of-the-house instincts locking in. He sat up. "Where is he?"

"We don't know. The truck's not in the carriage house, but it may be him outside, we can't tell."

"Let me have a look," the eldest Milliard child said. They followed him downstairs to the gun cabinet, where he selected the same .30-.30 his father favored.

"Dennis, I thought you were only going to look," Teresa said.

"I am."

"Well for Pete's sake don't shoot anyone."

"Especially Dad," Susan offered.

"I just want to scare him," Dennis said. He whistled sharply as he stepped to the door and called Timber's name. The animal did not appear. "Where's that mongrel at?"

"We don't know," Susan said.

Dennis took a deep breath, then yanked opened the back door and charged into the darkness. "If there's anyone out there who shouldn't be, you better start running," he bellowed. Then silence reigned again.

Teresa hated that they couldn't find Timber. Something had to be wrong—the dog never stayed quiet or absent this long.

A shot rang out. Teresa's heart stalled. She called her son's name twice, each moment unraveling like a loose thread, her extremities numb with terror.

Finally, an eternity later, Dennis came out of the corn. "Someone out there, for sure," he said.

"Why did you shoot? What did you see?"

"Ma, someone's trespassing on our property. I scared him off."

The other children, drawn by the report, crowded on the back porch in their pajamas and bare feet. "You kids get back in the house," Teresa ordered. To Dennis she said, "I wish I knew where in heaven your father was."

"I'm here," August called. Dennis rounded on the sound of the voice, the stock of the Winchester to his shoulder, but his mother pushed the barrel down.

"Where have you been?" Teresa demanded, simultaneously furious and relieved.

"What happened out here? Why's Denny have my gun?"

"Dad, someone's been watching the house again," his son said.

"Goddammit, that does it. I'm calling Al."

"August—" Teresa said, but her husband had already stalked passed her, confiscating his rifle from his boy along the way.

They joined him in the kitchen, his exhausted, scared family, watching as he picked up the phone. Teresa could not recall a time when she'd seen her husband's face so drawn. He looked like he'd aged five years since the disastrous parade.

"Al, it's August. Yeah, I know what time it is. I don't care, I need you out at the house." He listened. "Yes, tonight. Now. Someone's been outside, watching my family. The kids said it happened before too." He paused again and this time when he spoke again, his voice came out calmer. "Yes. Thanks, Al. Okay."

"What did he say?" Teresa asked as her husband hung up.

"He's sending Nate out to sit watch tonight."

"Nate Berryman? Al's not coming himself?"

"The man needs to sleep sometime," August said. "He's

been working this case for a week straight."

"I guess you're right," Teresa said. She looked around as if noticing the kids for the first time. "All right, everyone back to bed," she told them.

When they were alone, August said, "First thing tomorrow I'm having a floodlight installed outside on that pole. I'll be damned if we go another night with someone hiding out in the corn."

"Who do you figure it is?" she asked.

Her husband shook his head. "Christ if I know, Tree. This whole goddamned county's turned on its head in the past week. It's turned on *us*."

"Where were you, anyway? About scared me to death when I saw the time and you weren't home."

Something twitched on his face and she knew at once her husband was preparing to lie. He didn't do it often, but when he did she could read it on his face plain as newsprint. "Went up to Mike's place. I wanted to get his opinion on matters."

"Mike Stone? What could he possibly offer on our situation?"

"His family's been here longer than ours. Longer than the Langs, too. If anyone's got his ear to the ground in Ashford County, it's Mike."

"Okay, so what did he say?"

"You know what he told me? He told me he hadn't lost any cattle lately."

"So?"

"So Al lied to me. He tried to convince me a wolf attacked Randy. Said he'd heard Mike had lost one of his cows to some animal, likely a wolf. I knew it sounded like bunk from the moment he said it. Something is very wrong here. Something stinks and I mean to find out what."

Teresa sighed. "Maybe Al had his farmers mixed up. There are enough around here."

"No other dairy farmers, Tree. Mike put the last of 'em out of business a decade ago."

"So what are you going to do?"

August threw his hands in the air. "I don't know. I've got to figure something out, though. We can't go on like this. Now we've got people creeping around our land doing who knows what. I'm telling you, Tree, there's something going on. Someone knows something and they aren't speaking up about it."

"I know what you can do for starters, August. You can get some sleep."

"Who can sleep at a time like this?"

"How long have you slept in the past week, August? Ten hours? Twelve?"

August shook his head. "I can't with this mess going on."

The doorbell rang. Normally Timber would bark his head off, but now the silence seemed to bound back at them tenfold. "That'll be Nate," August said. "Where's the dog?"

"We can't find him," Teresa said.

"Great. Another mystery to solve," her husband said and went to answer the door.

Officer Berryman took a cursory look around the property with his flashlight, Augie in tow, before saying, "Really, Mr. Milliard, you ought to get some shuteye. Don't worry, I've got everything covered. You'll be safe as summer showers on my watch."

Augie thanked him as the cop settled his bulk into the cruiser parked in the drive before heading inside where he knew he wouldn't catch so much as a wink of sleep. He was pleased, though, his family had no such reservations and found them all snoring quietly when he checked. All except Susan, who sat in her bed with the table lamp switched on.

"Hey, Sunshine, everything all right?" he asked, taking a seat at the foot of the bed and overwhelmingly happy for the lift in isolation. His middle daughter still looked somewhat ill, with dark circles painted under her eyes. She crawled to him and he drew her onto his lap, the way he had when she was younger.

"I'm scared, Daddy," she said. "I want Timber."

Yes, Timber. Augie found his absence troubling. "He'll turn up, Susie. It's not like this is the first time he's run off overnight."

"Something's wrong. It's been years since he's run off."

Which was true. The last time the mongrel had been gone longer than between meals had been when he'd picked up the scent of a sick rabbit or coon and had gone gallivanting all over the countryside tracking it. He'd come back with his ruff full of burrs and a nasty gash on a hind leg.

Augie did his best to set Susan's mind at ease and at last she allowed him to tuck her in and kiss her goodnight. He poured a drink in his den, drained it, then took his Winchester and his Rayovac flashlight outside. He examined the carriage house, running the beam along the perimeter at ground level with the rifle cocked over his shoulder, then did the same with the barn.

Something Nathan had missed on his trip came into view. Augie almost missed it himself. He crouched and picked up a cigarette butt. No filter. No identifying logo to be seen other than a gilded stripe circumnavigating the paper. In his smoking days, Augie's brand had been Lucky Strike. Half a pack remained in his desk drawer, but this was not from it. That ruled out the kids, who may have stumbled upon it and experimented. In fact, it appeared to be a foreign brand.

Someone *had* been out here after all—this confirmed it. And he hadn't been home to protect his family.

"Son of a bitch, I'm coming for you," he said, staring into the corn, but had no idea to whom he spoke. How did you fight an enemy you couldn't see?

CHAPTER SIXTEEN

Augie refrained from showing the evidence to Nathan, who possessed the powers of deduction of an aphid, and he sure as hell wouldn't show it to Al, whom he now distrusted. Going forward he would work with Sheriff Lisk alone until he knew otherwise. He wouldn't allow his family to be intimidated.

Augie took up station on the sofa in the three-season porch at the back of the house, staring into the darkness. He kept watch for the spark of a lighter or the sound of someone moving through the Godforsaken corn. If he craned a bit he could make out the Gable house up on the ridge. Though no light shone, it seemed more watchful than ever now, a stern face glaring down at them.

"What are you up to, Granny?" he asked the façade of her estate. "How many webs do you have spinning up there?" He meant to find out. Tomorrow night. At the meeting Nate had hinted at.

Augie woke when dawn's first light had crept through the windows. He took the rifle inside and went to see about breakfast.

Dennis sat alone at the table, chewing through a Pop-Tart and skimming the Sports section. He'd made a pot of coffee and Augie poured a cup and picked up the front page of the *Gazette*. Nothing about the disturbance at the parade yesterday. Good. Saul had come through as he said he would. "Morning, son."

His son mumbled something through a mouthful of toaster pastry.

Augie checked the driveway through the window. Nathan's cruiser was gone. "Timber show up yet?"

"Not that I've seen."

"You okay, Denny?"

His son at last looked up from his reading. "Yeah, Dad. Fine."

"You get any sleep?"

"A little." He hesitated, licked a crumb off his top lip. "Dad, what's happening?"

"I'm working on that, son." He flipped to the police blotter and found a blurb naming three members of the Johansen family arrested for disorderly conduct and battery, but leaving the reason out. Good again. *Gazette* publisher and editor-in-chief Saul Scanlon had come through for him. No negative publicity. The Ashford County grapevine, a virile source of misinformation with deep and ancient roots would already be working against them; he didn't need the press to help it out any. Augie owed Saul one.

"If you need me to do anything, let me know."

"Right now, I just want you to help your mother look after the others."

"Are we in danger?"

"I don't know for sure. I'm counting on you to cover for me when I'm not here. Can you do that?"

"Yeah, Dad. Sure."

Augie smiled and ruffled the boy's hair. He looked like he'd grown up overnight, practically a man. This mess had gotten to everyone and Augie resented it. If it came down to something so simple and silly as a contract dispute, that should be handled between Augie and Grant, man to man—their families should be left out of it.

"I'm going to head down to the orchard for a bit, maybe tool around the store," Augie said.

"What for?"

"I can't just sit around the house all day doing nothing. I'm going to keep busy until this blows over."

"Want some company?"

"No, I want you to stay here. Hold down the fort, yeah?"

Dennis grinned, proud. "You got it, Dad."

Augie squeezed his son's shoulder, then found the keys to the truck and drove to the store.

The place felt unnatural in its desertion, like it was late February instead of late October. The orchard may as well have been haunted—he could practically see ghosts gliding among the apple trees. The barrier ribbons crisscrossing the maze entrance and exit flapped in the chill breeze. The pumpkins looked like auburn fallen stars in the patch. Augie unlocked the store and stepped inside, but couldn't think of anything to do so he went out again and locked up behind him.

For the next hour, he toured the orchard, picking up fallen apples and dropping them in a bushel basket. When he'd cleaned the place up a bit, he carried the basket back to the store and dropped it in the kitchen. For a time, he merely stared at his fallen crop, marveling not for the first time at their variety: Ruby Jon and Red Delicious, Cortland and Gala, Granny Smith and Blushing Gold. A diverse crop. Diversity, his grandfather (a devout proponent of civil rights) once told him, made the world go 'round. Not uniformity.

"Augie, my child," his namesake once told him, shortly after Jackie Robinson first donned a Brooklyn Dodgers jersey, squeezing the youth's shoulder. "Once people start waking up from this lullaby we're all born into, they'll realize it's our differences that will carve a path to prosperity. Diversity is key. Having as many choices as possible maximizes success. You know who favored uniformity? The Nazis, that's who, and how do you think that worked out for them?"

At last count, Milliard farms produced a dozen varieties of apples. Augie figured that counted as a diverse crop. Not like Grant Lang's corn: row after row after row of identical stalks, stretching as far as the eye could see, in perfect uniform lockstep.

His ruminations were cut short by something scratching at the back door. Augie knew at once who it would be and hurried to open it. Timber stood on the back stoop, fur matted, favoring a front paw. He whimpered once and limped inside, looking up at his master for validation and succor.

"Where you been, boy? We could've used your help last night," Augie said, kneeling to stroke his ruff and examine his wounded paw, which appeared to have a long but shallow wound running from the toes and up to the shoulder. "Good

God, boy, what'd you get after? Whatever it was got after you, didn't it? Hope you chewed him a new—"

But Augie stopped there. Stuck in his dog's collar and forcing it to practically strangle the poor creature, he found an ear of corn. He pulled it loose and held it up in the golden morning light filtering through the window.

On the phone with Sheriff Lisk, Augie paced until the cord had entangled him like a spider web. "I'm telling you, Paul, the son of a bitch stole my dog. He stuck a corn cob in his collar as a message to me."

Lisk did a good job of waiting patiently, hearing Augie out, before saying, "And that message would be?"

"I don't know. That he's watching me. That he can take something of mine at his whim, that he can hurt me."

"And you think Grant Lang is also responsible for the wound your dog sustained?" Lisk asked.

"I'd bet my last dollar on it."

"I'll look into it, August."

"I want that man arrested."

"I can't just arrest a man until there's evidence of a crime. It's still innocent until proven guilty in this country."

Augie forced himself to take a breath. His hands trembled and one eyelid twitched. Timber licked his paw but seemed to have calmed. He rested in the basket behind the counter reserved for him. "All right. Okay. Thanks, Paul. I'll wait to hear from you."

Augie tried to leave Timber behind while he made a walk-through of the maze, but the dog insisted on following. He limped along behind his master as a show of devotion. Or, perhaps, fear.

Man and dog made their way through the rows of corn, the former keeping an eye out for anything of note and the latter sniffing along the ground and occasionally marking his territory.

When they came to the place where Randy had been injured, the soil having absorbed most of the blood as if accepting an offering to the corn gods, Augie crouched and peered around. There had to be something the police had missed, some clue left undiscovered. Rain had washed out most of the footprints, so he hoped Al had taken plaster casts of the treads before it had, though given what he knew now Augie couldn't expect it.

He stepped over to the mesh wall, running his fingers over it, searching for anywhere it had been disturbed. Fifty feet farther on, he found it. The mesh meant to keep people from coming or going through the restricted areas of corn had been sliced clean open. The ragged edges flapped in the breeze as if taunting him. Timber took a step into the gap, nosing the air, and backed out. Had Al seen this? If so, had he even bothered to explore it?

"Come on, boy," Augie said and headed into the brown stalks. Timber refused to follow and instead waited on the trail, panting and whimpering. Augie all at once wished he'd thought to bring his rifle.

He tracked through the field a hundred yards, eyes scanning the earth in search of anything abnormal. Nothing. Only the dead cornstalks, their roots protruding from the soil like skeletal phalanges. He checked over his shoulder and found Timber shadowing him, twenty yards back as if reluctant to let his master out of his sight.

Another two hundred yards in, the corn thinned and Augie found himself standing on a dirt path running north and south before the stalks started up again ten feet on. He crouched, looking for footprints, and spotted them immediately. Boots, by the look of them—pointed toe, squared off heel, sunk deep in the mud.

"Come on, Timber. Let's find out where these prints wind up." Man and beast headed north, walled in by corn. Ten minutes later they found the cabin sitting alone on a grassy causeway that cut through the field.

CHAPTER SEVENTEEN

Susie worked her way through the mountain of homework that had accumulated during her time away from school. She worked methodically, uncomplaining, pausing only for a snack or to answer the telephone.

It had rung a lot today, people calling to check on them after the parade incident (something Susie was happy she missed—Hannah told her how awful it had been), someone from the Farm Bureau wanting to speak with her father, a saleslady peddling a diaper delivery service. Rachel had called to see how she felt and the two had chatted until Mrs. Safford had shooed her daughter off the line.

Susie's siblings had all spread to hell and gone—one of Dennis's favorite sayings—and would likely remain away until dinnertime, a Sunday tradition, while her mother rested upstairs, happy to let Susie field phone calls.

The seventh time the phone rang, she sighed and tossed her pencil aside, then got up to answer it. "Milliard residence."

A pause from the other end of the line and something that sounded like a snicker. The caller cleared his throat. "Why, hello, Milliard residence," a gruff voice said. Susie had seen plenty of detective shows and imagined a handkerchief over the mouthpiece to distort the voice. "Is the man of the house about, young lady?"

"No, sir. May I ask who's calling?"

"Where is he?"

"Working, sir."

"On the Sabbath?"

"My father doesn't take many days off."

"We'll see about that."

"I beg your pardon, sir?"

"Tell your old man I'll see him soon."

Susan, in whom manners had been ingrained since birth, asked, "Sir, do you wish to leave your name?"

The caller disconnected, the click in her ear as loud as a bullet chambered in a gun. She stared at the receiver a moment, trying to decide if she'd actually had such a strange conversation. She tapped the hook to open the line and tried to reach her father at the store, but he didn't answer. She'd be sure to tell him about it when he came home.

Dennis rode his BMX into town to catch a burger at Gert's, the friction-taped handlebars tacky in his fists. It was Hannah's turn to take the car and he hated that she could drive now. Things would be so much better once he got his Firebird fixed up (though for as much as he grumbled about his little sis taking the car, it felt pretty darn good to get on his bike again).

He knew enough to wait until the church crowd dissipated before trying to get a table or even a stool at the counter—when the flocks leave worship, they leave hungry. But now, with the clock hands standing at half past noon, he had the place mostly to himself.

"Heya, Denny, the usual?" the cook called through the window. Amos Arden had worked at Gert's since the place opened a quarter century ago, if you could believe the stories Dennis's dad told. He'd even been married to ol' Gerty for a time in the early Sixties until they realized the boss/employee dynamic didn't translate well in the bedroom. Dennis's mom got bent out of shape anytime his dad brought that nugget up, but Dennis found it hilarious. His mother had forbidden him from repeating it.

"Make it a double today, Amos. I'm starved," Dennis called back, climbing onto a stool at the counter. "Where's the boss?"

Amos made a face as he tossed hamburger patties onto the grill. "Taking another coffee break, I figure. We been open seven hours and she's already taken four breaks. You believe that?"

Dennis grinned. He believed it. Margaret Arden—she'd kept her ex-husband's name because she preferred it to her maiden name, which had been something unpronounceable and decidedly Old World—ran a tight ship with her business, but had no qualms about allowing her employees to carry it on their shoulders.

"Just the pair of you working today?" he called.

"Just me and the ol' battle axe."

"I heard that, Amos Arden," Gert said, rounding the corner from the office. "You don't watch it, you'll be tossing hay bales out at the Safford place and you can bet Ray won't pay half what I do."

Amos grumbled and flipped the burgers.

Gert stepped over to Dennis after mixing him a vanilla shake and set the sweaty glass before him. "Damn shame what happened at the parade," she said. "You folks all right?"

Dennis sighed. He'd had enough people check on them and had grown tired of fielding questions. "We're fine, Gert. Really. Thanks for asking."

"Well, you need anything, you let me know. I wouldn't serve pie as fresh as I do without your Granny Smiths."

"Thanks, Gert," Dennis said, taking a sip of his shake, grateful the proprietor hadn't pressed the issue. He only wanted the whole thing to go away, which his father promised it would in time.

While he waited, Dennis took a glance around. An elderly couple—the Castletons, who often frequented the Milliard Country Store—spoke quietly over cups of coffee, occasionally stealing glances his way. Had they been present during the onslaught at the parade? Most likely; everyone came to the Apple Fest parade. He hoped they wouldn't talk to him.

Amos hollered, "Order up!" and dinged the little silver bell even though Gert stood not two feet from him. She offered him an expletive few would dare utter on the Sabbath and picked up Dennis's plate.

"Pardon my French, Dennis," she said, sliding his food in front of him.

"I've heard worse, Ma'am," he said, grinning.

"From who?" Gert asked. "Not those Lang girls? I heard that Bonnie can be a spitfire."

Dennis had never heard so much as a slantwise word spoken from any of the Lang daughters. "No, ma'am, but the locker room can get a little rowdy."

Gert clucked her tongue and sashayed away so he could eat in peace. Over her shoulder she called: "You boys and your football. I swear, someday some poor kid's going to get his head taken off."

Dennis dug into his burger and fries, still grinning. He loved this town, even if some of its inhabitants had temporarily turned on them. At least, he hoped it was temporary—he'd heard someone tell his father their family was finished in Derby, but he couldn't imagine living anywhere else.

The door opened and a man Dennis had never seen came in. He might have been a few years older than Dennis himself, though years of hardship and toil shown plainly on his face. He wore faded jeans and a matching denim jacket. Mirrored aviator sunglasses obscured most of his face, except for a beak of a nose which had clearly been broken, probably more than once. Curls hung to his shoulders which must have stretched all the way to his Jolly Roger belt buckle when wet. He reminded Dennis of a rodent who has learned to walk upright.

The man plucked his shades off and tucked them away in the breast pocket of his jacket and had a look around. Out of all the open seats in the place, he copped the stool beside Dennis and ordered black coffee.

Gert poured him a mug and said, "Anything to eat, Mister?"

"Just the coffee for now," he said in a thick accent Dennis couldn't identify (it didn't sound like Gert's but near enough). Why had he picked this spot? Dennis fidgeted with his straw. The man did not even glance his way, but something about him signified danger.

"Can I get my check, Gert?" he called when he could no longer stand it.

"You haven't finished," Gert replied. In true Old World fashion, she took it as a personal affront when someone failed to finish a meal.

"I just remembered I have somewhere to be. If you give me a doggy bag, I'll take it with me."

Gert looked as if someone had pinched her. "You know I

don't keep those. You finish your meal, Dennis Milliard."

"You better listen to her," Arden called from the window. "Our Gerty doesn't mess around when it comes to her cuisine."

Dennis sighed and stuffed a fistful of fries into his mouth. Gert eyed him, arms crossed, until satisfied he wouldn't speak such foolishness again, then wandered away muttering.

"What's the hurry?" the hook-nosed man beside him said, still not looking anywhere but straight ahead.

Dennis swallowed. "I have chores."

"Is that right?"

"Yes sir."

"Are you fairly compensated for your labors?"

"Sir?"

"Do you get paid?"

The question took Dennis aback. He laughed. "You don't get paid for chores. Chores are just something you do because you're part of the family."

"Would you like to get paid?"

Dennis didn't know where this conversation was going, but he could always use money for the Firebird. "It depends on the work, I guess."

The man at last turned to face him, a grin spreading on his face to reveal a mouthful of teeth so white they looked painted, including a set of upper and lower incisors sharp enough to puncture flesh. "Join me at the back booth and I'll explain everything."

"I really have to be on my way," Dennis said. Even if he wanted to finish his burger, he didn't think he could. His stomach rolled uncomfortably.

The man turned away from him again, staring into his mug. "I understand. If you want to hear more, I'll be here tomorrow at five o'clock. Back booth."

"I have football practice."

"The choice is yours, of course."

Dennis set some singles down on the counter as Gert appeared nowhere in evidence (perhaps on another coffee break) and got to his feet. "I appreciate the offer, I really do. But I have commitments."

"Fair enough," the man said. "But you know where to find me if you change your mind. Or if it's changed for you."

Dennis hurried out the door. He'd made it halfway up the block before the man's last sentence struck him. What had he meant by that? He didn't know, but he would surely mention it to his father when he got home. Something else occurred to him. Could the man with the foreign accent, a stranger he'd never seen before, be the man Susie had spotted outside their home? The man Dennis himself had chased into the corn? All at once he was certain of it, and he pedaled all the faster through the blustery afternoon.

CHAPTER EIGHTEEN

Had it been stupid (and a little immature) to insist on her turn with the car even though she only had half a mile to drive while Dennis huffed the three miles into town on his bike? Probably, but Hannah Milliard couldn't help it. She'd had her driver's license less than three months and the excitement of getting behind the wheel had yet to wear off. The freedom of being mobile—that she had the power to drive anywhere in the country should the notion strike her—worked on her like a magical elixir and she quietly dreaded the day Susie would be old enough to take a turn. Hannah hoped to have a car of her own by then.

She'd driven to Lorelai's house, of course. Lori had been there the night Randy had been injured, the night the police found the girl's body in the maze. She'd also been at the parade and had been one of the first people to help the Milliards when they'd come under siege. Lorelai and Hannah had been fast friends since the fifth grade, when they'd sat beside one another in Mrs. Womack's class. Aside from Susie, Lori had been Hannah's closest confidant—especially in matters which couldn't be entrusted to her younger sister. Like Hannah's crush on Caleb Safford, for example.

After saying hello to Lori's parents, the girls slipped out to the barn and had climbed the ladder to the hayloft. In summer, the loft could get explosively hot but now, in the middle of autumn, with a cross-breeze whipping through gaps in the board siding, it made for a perfect hideaway from the rest of the world. Lorelai pulled a joint from her hip pocket and a red Bic from the other.

"Keep it away from the straw," she said after she'd exhaled and passed it to Hannah.

"You say that every time," Hannah said and took a hit.

"I say it every time because if you drop the cherry, this place would go up like a powder keg."

Hannah passed the joint back and said, "Wonder what Caleb's doing today."

"God, will you get that creep out of your head?"

"He's cute."

"Yeah, he's cute, but he's also crazy."

"Bullshit," Hannah said. "His mom's religious is all. Strict, you know?"

"Greg Ball said he saw Caleb kick a dog and break its leg."

"Greg Ball chews paint chips."

Lorelai waved smoke away as if it might be a cloud of gnats. "Either way, you should watch your step around him. Why do you think he's never had a girlfriend?"

"He went out with Tina Simonson last year."

"They went to the drive-in *one time*, H. Jeez."

"I heard they made it in the backseat while *The Godfather* played onscreen."

Lorelai made a gagging face. "All the more reason to steer clear of him, sweetheart. I heard Tina makes it with her brother and you just *know* her brother makes it with all those sheep his daddy keeps."

Hannah sighed and took another hit. "Don't you just ever want to make it with somebody, just to see what it's like?" she asked. When Lorelai answered only with a wicked grin, Hannah stared at her with wide eyes. "Lori, you *tramp*! Who'd you make it with?"

Lorelai laughed into her wrist. "I'm not supposed to tell anyone."

"You *better* tell me. You know I'd tell you. I'd call you the minute it was over." Her eyes widened even more, if that were possible. "Oh God. It's Scott Beard, isn't it?"

"Jeez, what do you think I am? I wouldn't make it with Scotty in a million years."

"*Tell* me!"

"No way. You'll tell your brother."

Hannah's brows knitted together. "Why do you care what Denny thinks?"

"This grass must be turning your brain to pudding."

Hannah was a bright girl, on track to be salutatorian of her class (right behind Lorelai, the undisputed valedictorian, who'd had Hannah beat in GPA forever), still couldn't grasp her friend's implications. It finally clicked. "Oh, *barf!* You like my *brother?*"

"He's a cutie pie and nice as a peach. I love watching him play football."

"He doesn't even *play*," Hannah said, still trying to process this new information through the veil of smoke in her brain.

"Well, I like watching him stand, then. He fills out his uniform." Lorelai was goading her now, deliberately prodding her.

"Don't date my brother, you absolute *slut.*"

"Have you ever seen his thing? How big is it?"

"I'm seriously going to puke, Lori."

Lorelai linked her arm through her friend's and pressed the joint to her lips. She made a pouty face and blew smoke toward the rafters. "Aw, don't you want to be my sister?"

Hannah mulled this, the grass still working its green magic. "I guess that wouldn't be so bad. You'd be at our table every Thanksgiving."

"Anyway, Hannah dearest, I don't plan on knocking Denny over the head and dragging him back to my cave. That's his job. I just want you to plant a seed in his ear. Can you do that for me?"

"How?"

"You're smart, you'll think of something. Just nudge him my way, that's all. I'll do the rest."

Hannah, who was indeed smart, unspooled a wicked grin. "I'll do it on one condition."

"What's that?"

"You have to tell me who you made it with."

"No way. You'll tell Denny and ruin my chances."

"Then no deal. You'll have to drag him back to your cave

on your own because I happen to know he's sweet on someone else."

Lorelai almost choked on her smoke. "Who?"

"You first."

Lorelai growled in frustration. "Oh, fine. It was Kodi."

"Who the hell is Kodi?"

Lorelai covered her face with her hands, giggling into her palms. "He's one of my dad's hired men."

"Jesus, you *are* a tramp! How old is he?"

"Twenty-four."

"You're only sixteen!"

"The age of consent in Illinois is seventeen, which I'll turn next month." As if that absolved this Kodi guy of wrongdoing.

"Lori, for the smartest kid in our class you sure can be a dope sometimes."

"Jealous?" she asked, teasing now.

"No. I've seen the men your dad hires. They're all scrappy-looking immigrants." Something occurred to her. "Oh, my. He isn't one of the Negroes, is he?"

"You don't say 'Negroes' anymore, H, *God*."

"Well, is he?"

"No, dummy, he's not Black," Lorelai said. She put on a prim smile and smoothed the seat of her jeans. "He's red. A Russian."

"A Russian?"

"As in from Russia."

"You're making it with a *Communist*?"

Lorelai rolled her eyes. "Now who's being a dope?"

"Lori, those people are killers."

"They aren't all like the way the TV makes them out. Not everyone from the Soviet Union is a red Communist, H. Kodi's a dissident who came to America to get away from Khrushchev's intimidation tactics."

"Doesn't he know Russians aren't exactly welcome in America at the moment? Especially in these parts?"

Lorelai shrugged. "Dad doesn't care about a man's background so long as he can drive a combine and fork hay, both of which Kodi does perfectly." She ran the edge of her tongue along her top lip. "He's a man of other talents as well."

Hannah made a face.

"You should try it sometime, H. I could maybe arrange it with Kodi. God, he'd eat you alive."

"Disgusting. No, thanks. You can keep your Russian. What kind of name is Kodi, anyway?"

"It's short for Kodiak. He wanted to Americanize his name, maybe help him get along a little better. Isn't that far out?"

Hannah didn't think it far out at all. She thought the whole thing dirty and unbecoming of her friend. "Give me another hit."

"Shit, this is tapped," Lorelai said. "Anyway, now it's your turn. Who's the little nympho who's caught Denny's eye and who I'll have to feed to the Safford hogs a piece at a time?"

"Funny you say that ..."

Lorelai, who remained ever-sharp despite the weed, shook her head. "No way. Not Rachel Safford? She's too young for him."

"Like you should talk."

"Oh, shut up. We're not talking about me anymore."

It was Hannah's turn to shrug. "Love's a funny thing."

"Love? No. Dennis doesn't love her. Wants to make it with her, maybe. I can see that. She's blossomed well. Her tits look quite luscious, I'll admit."

"God, can we stop talking about this?" Hannah said.

"But would he want that over this?" Lorelai pressed, raising her shirt six inches to reveal her perfect midriff—something Hannah had always envied her friend.

"I don't know. It's up to you to change his mind, I guess."

"No, it's up to you. Send him my way, sweetheart."

Truthfully, Hannah hated the idea of her brother and best friend dating now. How could she endorse it knowing what Lorelai had done with some hired hand *eight years older* than she? An *adult*, for God's sake!

You are *jealous*, her mind whispered in Lorelai's voice. *You wish it had been you making it with a hired hand, maybe right here in the loft, with the breeze blowing and barn owls hooting in the night.*

"Let's go back," Hannah said. "I need to get home."

"Already? It's barely four o'clock."

"You want me to talk to Denny or not?"

Lorelai favored her with a lingering look. "You don't think too terribly of me, do you, Hannah? Your opinion is everything to me."

"No, I don't," she lied. "I just wished maybe you'd have waited for my brother if you like him so much."

"Yeah," Lorelai said, slipping the Bic back into her pocket. "Me too."

CHAPTER NINETEEN

Thomas had been tasked with watching the twins, which sucked eggs. They'd wanted to go to Wright Park out by the water tower, which worked out just wonderfully since that was the about last place on the planet he wanted to go. But their mother, who still had a headache from the disastrous parade outing, asked him to take them since the older kids had headed for the hills.

"It's not fair," he said. "I'm not even that much older than them."

"Except when you're lobbying for a later bedtime," Teresa had said. "Go on, Tommy, it will be good for you to babysit a while."

The twins had happily jumped on their bikes and ridden for the park with Thomas pedaling behind them, glum and sullen. He couldn't wait until he was old enough to drive, like Dennis and Hannah, except by then the family probably wouldn't have enough money to own a car.

Yes, he'd overheard his folks talking about finances. They'd had to close the shop because of Denny's stupid friend getting hurt in the maze. What the store had to do with it, Tommy couldn't guess, but he figured the police must know what they were doing.

But worrying about wheels could wait. It just didn't seem like fall, like *Halloween*, without everyone in the county visiting their shop. The Milliard Country Store was an Ashford County *tradition* and wasn't that all the people in this stupid county talked about—the importance of tradition? Honestly, he thought if one major change took place in this town—like, say, the installation of its first stoplight—the whole place would collapse. Rural folk treasure the past and fear the future.

The twins reached the park with him still an eighth of a mile behind. He watched them dump their bikes in the grass and rush the jungle gym like a pair of shrieking goblins. Goblins reminded him of Halloween and he allowed himself to brighten some.

This year Tommy had decided to dress up as Ray Oyler, one-time shortstop for the Milliard clan's beloved Detroit Tigers. This would probably be the last year he'd be able to participate in trick-or-treating without catching hell at school, so he wanted to make it good. He had the uniform and everything, a Christmas gift from his parents last year.

Tommy pulled up to the park and popped his kickstand. His siblings had already made the top of the jungle gym, where Candace hung by her knees and gripping the hem of her dress so it wouldn't fall. Richard stood atop it like some conquering king, hand shading his eyes while he scanned the fields beyond the borders of his empire. These had been harvested already and the view must have been good for miles around.

"Tommy, come here, look at this," he called.

"You spot Eloise?" Thomas hollered, referring to Ashford County's resident snapping turtle who sometimes made unexpected appearances around the area. Rumor had it she was as old as the county itself and had been present at its inception. One could always tell it was her if they got close enough to spot the initials carved into her shell: F + A. No one could decipher who those initials could possibly belong to, not even Sarah Regan, Ashford's head librarian and chief local historian. The turtle would be gearing up to hibernate now, but Thomas hoped it was her because local legend held that spying old Ellie brought good luck. His family could use a dose of that about now. The last time Thomas had seen Ellie he'd gotten a Nolan Ryan card in the next pack of Topps he'd purchased, so he tended to believe that particular bit of lore.

"Ain't Eloise," Richard called while Candace sang a verse of some song she'd learned in school.

"*Not* Eloise," Thomas said.

"Huh?"

"Don't say 'ain't'."

"You sound like Daddy," Candace said, pausing mid-song.

"Yeah, like Daddy," her twin echoed. They did that a lot—so annoying.

Tommy walked up the domed structure without using his hands to show off his prowess, then scouted the place where his brother pointed among the stubble.

"You think it's a scarecrow?" Richard asked.

"No one in their right mind would put a scarecrow there," Tommy said. For reasons he couldn't identify, the blood in his veins turned to slush. "It's somebody."

"You think it's him?" Richard asked. "The guy who's been spying on us?"

Tommy squinted hard to make out any discernible features, but couldn't even tell the gender. It could be a woman standing in the field. Either way, who would do such a thing? Just stand there, unmoving?

"I don't know who it is," Tommy said. "Just mind your business and keep playing."

Candace was already one step ahead of them. She'd made for the swings and sang louder than ever while she pumped her legs: "School days, school days, dear old Golden Rule days!"

"I think it's him," Richard said.

Candace bellowed: "Reading and writing and arithmetic, taught to the tune of a hickory stick!"

"Just play, Richard."

"I can't. He scares me."

"If it was him, how would he know we'd be out here at the park?"

"Maybe he followed us."

Tommy gritted his teeth. "I'm going home unless you shut up."

Richard looked hurt. He climbed down and went to swing with his sister. Tommy watched the person in the field a moment longer, then charged down the bars and made for the merry-go-round. He toed himself around in lazy circles, listening to the twins banter. At least they spoke English now—when they'd first learned to speak they'd made up their own language only they understood and talk about *annoying*.

He tore open the pack of Topps baseball cards he'd brought with, popped the stick of chalky gum into his mouth, and chewed while taking stock of his new acquisitions. Ron Santo, White Sox, yuck. Thurman Munson, Yankees, not bad but he already had three of them—trade bait, for sure. Cecil Cooper, Red Sox, gag. Steve Stone, Cubs, *major* gag. Willie Horton, Tigers, now he was cooking.

"*Tommy*," Candace screeched, snapping his Topps trance. He stood up so fast the cards fluttered to the sand between his sneakers. The breeze caught hold and scattered them. Tommy didn't care. The man from the field—for it was a man, he now saw—had stepped into the park proper. Then he realized who it was and his heart started again.

"Hush up, Candace," he said. "It's just Old Dad."

"*Who?*" Richard cried. Both the twins remained skeptical of strangers, what with recent happenings.

Tommy had only met the Stones' hired man a handful of times, mostly on excursions to the dairy farm with his father. No one seemed to know Old Dad's true name, not even Old Dad. Tommy had asked him once what his parents called him and the elderly man had seemed to mull it over, scratching his chin before answering: "I can't say I recall much of my childhood, young man. It was a long time ago, in another time—another world, truthfully." Tommy had realized that it pained the elder hand to recall his past and wisely let the subject drop.

"Good afternoon, children," Old Dad said, coming over and lowering himself painfully into a swing. His presence here could not have looked stranger than had he stepped onto an opera stage. "Do not be alarmed, please. I came to give your father something. Would you see he gets it?"

"Of course, sir," Tommy said, extending his hand to accept whatever Old Dad had to offer. The hand fished around in an enormous overall pocket and produced a small envelope, the kind in which you'd send a sympathy card.

"Tell your father these will help him on his way. I have asked the gods to bless them. May they blossom and flourish elsewhere as they have here." Old Dad, plucked a pocket watch from his overalls, checked the time, and replaced it before lurching back into the corn stubble.

"What is it, Tommy?" Candace asked, coming up after giving Old Dad a wide berth.

"Yeah, what is it?" Richard mimicked.

Thomas opened the envelope with the ball of his thumb, peering inside. He regarded his younger siblings with naked confusion. "They're apple seeds," he said.

"Do you know what this is, Tree?" Augie demanded, shaking the envelope his son had given him. "This is a threat, clear and simple."

Her headache had cleared, though a lingering tenderness throbbed in her temples. It still hurt to think. "August, it's just a packet of seeds."

"Did you hear what he told Tommy? He asked the gods to bless them. He said he hopes they flourish elsewhere."

Teresa held up a hand. "Okay, but August—listen. Consider the source. Old Dad? What was he even doing here?"

Augie tossed his hands in the air. "How should I know? But I've known that man most of my life—he's a cryptic old mystic like something out of a Western picture, so when he does something like this it means something."

"You think that old man is threatening us."

"No, not him. Someone clearly put him up to it."

"Who? Mike? What's Mike got against us?"

"Nothing, so far's I know."

"Did you call Mike?"

"Can only get hold of Ursula. She says Mike isn't home."

"Well, Old Dad wouldn't do anyone else's bidding." She waited while her husband considered this, rubbing his chin.

"Unless someone paid him. He'll do anyone's bidding who's got cash."

Teresa groaned in annoyance.

"There's something else, Tree."

She waited, fingers pressed to her temples.

"I went out walking in the corn today, through the maze."

"You know that's been closed off pending the investigation—"

August held up a hand. "I know, but dammit, it's still our property. Did you know there's a pleasant little green causeway five hundred yards from the front of our store?"

"A causeway?"

"That's only way I can describe it. A strip of grass, maybe ten yards wide. Runs right between the corn, mowed to perfection. Know what I found at the end of it, half a mile further on?"

"I'm sure I don't."

"A shed."

"A shed?"

"A shed. Solid construction, not a crack between the boards you could slide a blade of grass through. Looks new. Door padlocked tight, tarpaper over the windows. Looks like a row of skylights on the roof. It's behind a bluff. You could see it perfectly from the leeward side, but not facing our property. I imagine positioned there intentionally, for when the fields are harvested."

"Whose do you suppose it is?" Teresa asked. She'd had no idea any such structure existed so near their property.

"I'm more concerned with what's in it."

"I'm concerned with both. Whose land is it on? Not ours?"

Her husband shook his head. "I'd lay my wager it's Lang land. I'm going up to the courthouse tomorrow morning, first thing, check the plat books. Then I'm taking a walk to the sheriff's office around the corner. I'm sure he'll be as curious to know what's inside that building as I am."

Teresa couldn't recall a time she'd seen her husband in such an agitated state as he'd been in this past week. August made it a mainstay to appear ever calm, ever in control. But she could see the cracks forming; he stomped around like a man possessed. She wanted to say she hoped he knew what he was doing, but refrained; he would feel insulted.

"Let me know how it goes," she said instead, then gently steered the conversation another direction. "Want me to start supper?"

"I'm not hungry."

"Well, I bet the kids are. I'm fixing pork chops and applesauce."

"Applesauce," her husband muttered. "Always applesauce."

"August—"

"I'm going out for a while, Tree."

"Where to?"

"Need to clear my head," he said, crushing the packet of apple seeds in his fist without realizing it.

CHAPTER TWENTY

Clearing his head meant waiting until dark. Augie got into position and watched the sun set behind the Gable house, as it had since the place had stood up there on the ridge. Over 150 years, he figured. He'd visited the place several times over the years. He'd been formally invited to dinner four or five times and had found the fare delightful even as he found the company stuffy. Adeline Gable took no nonsense and made none either. She had the sense of humor of a rabid skunk.

Now, as Augie stood inside the store his grandfather had built, he watched the ridge darken. Soon Grant Lang and Al Engel would arrive for their weekly meeting with the Queen of Ashford. What would they discuss? Would they plot the further demise of the Milliard family? Would the topic of the locked-up outbuilding nestled between two fields arise? Augie would have laid money on it.

When the sun had vanished and the Gable house stood in shadow, Augie made his move. He locked up the store and walked without hurry to a path he knew led safely up out of the valley. It would bring him unseen to the rear of the Gable property. Unless, of course, Granny Adeline had her goons on the lookout. Augie didn't think she would, though. Nathan would be stationed along the main road and no one would suspect anyone coming up from the rear where a ten-foot stone wall encircled the acre or so of back lawn she kept neatly tended.

Granny Adeline kept no pets aside from her half-blind cairn terrier, so he needn't worry about baying hounds alerting their mistress of his presence. Augie waited at the back gate, a black-painted wrought iron affair wrapped in chains and secured with a padlock. Getting over the fence wouldn't pose much of an issue; the entire Milliard clan began climbing trees practically before they could walk. There wasn't a structure in the county Augie couldn't scale.

When he'd made it to the top, he rested a moment and watched the house. No lights on in back. The place looked deserted. He wondered again at the foolishness of his actions— breaking into the Ashford County morgue last week and now the residence of the county's most prominent citizen. And for what? Because he'd grown paranoid?

It isn't paranoia and you know it, his mind scolded. *If you want to know what they're keeping from you, this is the only way.*

And it was. He saw that now. He had to do this for his family. Not just those waiting for him at home, but those waiting for him in heaven, if such a place existed. The face of his father rose in his mind like a spirit from dark water and Augie knew he had no choice but to proceed now, no matter the consequences.

The Gable back lawn could have hosted a football game with room to spare. The image of Granny in a referee's zebra stripes, whistle poking from between her weathered lips, came unbidden and Augie had to stifle a laugh. Then he envisioned Grant Lang with a clipboard on the opposing sideline, bellowing at his ragtag team composed of his hired men and his daughters, set to square off against the Milliard clan. All at once the football analogy seemed too close to home, too *real*, and he banished it from his mind.

The moon in its last quarter did not provide much light by which to navigate the lawn, but it proved enough. Augie narrowly avoided several picnic tables, their chairs resting upside down on their surfaces, the umbrellas which stood open most of the summer now folded closed and bound to their poles. He imagined Granny's goons humping these warm-weather artifacts into one of the outbuildings to wait out the winter. He also imagined the parties this yard must have hosted in its heyday—all the area farmers coming to worship at Vance and Adeline Gable's feet. Adeline would have been a rosy-cheeked housewife in those days, a headful of fire-red hair, her hips and bosom plump from childbirth, her fingers red from constant cooking and washing and mending and cleaning. Word had it she'd been a looker in her youth, if his grandfather's tales could be trusted.

Augie broke off from his reverie as he came to the door of the three-season porch. It would be locked, of course, just as the Ashford County morgue had been locked. He would have no chance of breaking in unnoticed tonight, though, so he would have to come up with another plan.

But the door opened when he tried it. No one really locked their doors in Ashford County anyway, so it didn't come as much of a surprise. Augie stepped into the cigar smell of the four-season porch and eased the door closed behind him. He crept past a hide-a-bed davenport and a coffee table loaded with back issues of *Life* and *Reader's Digest*, tempering his hope that the interior door would be similarly unsecured.

Except it was. Augie held his breath as he inched it open. Once he crossed the threshold, there would be no turning back. He hadn't been caught at the morgue and had seen nothing in the papers about a break-in, but his luck had to run out sometime. If he meant to go back, the deadline had come.

Curiosity and necessity outweighed the crime in the end. He knew Granny and Grant were in collusion against his family. They had to be. He needed to know why, but more importantly, he needed to keep his family safe. If he couldn't provide that simple measure for them, what good was he? It was Augie's *job* to keep them from harm, dammit, and he meant to execute it or die trying.

The back porch opened onto a long corridor, the floors polished wood with an Oriental rug running down the center. The walls were whitewashed plaster with stippled wainscoting and crown molding, standard farmhouse fare of a more antique era. He cocked his head, heard distant voices murmuring from the other side of the house, and got moving. He didn't want to miss anything.

Augie's limited knowledge of Adeline's house precluded the wing he currently occupied. He followed the hallway, passing closed doors on either side, to another running perpendicular to the first. He took a left on instinct.

It opened onto a parlor of sorts, laden with davenports and

loveseats that looked deep enough to drown in. A fireplace stood dark in the center of the far wall, its first lighting of the season mere weeks—perhaps days—away. Augie studied a clutch of photos resting atop the mantelpiece and recognized Adeline and her late husband Vance in many of them, riding horses, holding hands, standing on the boardwalk of some distant seaside city. His grandfather had been correct: Adeline could have been a movie star.

The parlor emptied into a short passage and Augie took it, keeping one shoulder to the wall. The voices came from up a way and around a corner. He smelled coffee and pipe smoke. The kitchen? He crept forward until he could hear the conversation but dare not peer around the jamb into the room. The risk was incredible and one Augie normally would never take—if someone rounded the corner they would walk right into him—but this was not a normal situation. It involved his family. His very reason for being.

"What will he do?" Adeline asked, her voice ancient yet powerful like a curse unearthed. "I don't want speculation, Alvin. You know him better than any of us."

Al Engel cleared his throat, a manufactured hesitation steeped in uncertainty. "I figure he'll do what any cornered animal does—he'll fight. He'll fight tooth and nail."

A measured pause, calculated. "It can't be helped."

Another voice cut in then, Grant's: "I hope you know what you're doing."

Adeline said: "Do you doubt my judgment?"

"The Milliards have been around these parts longer than you and certainly as long as me. They cannot be taken lightly. Nor underestimated."

Augie's heart thudded like a red wingless bird. He'd been correct all along—there *was* a conspiracy against the family. This confirmed it. And it went so far as to include local law enforcement. But why? Why now, out of the blue? Because of the maze? How many people had Adeline Gable bought off? Would even she stoop so low as to order the injury to Randy Johansen? And to concoct a story about a dead girl to cement the store's closing? Augie couldn't believe it.

"No one's taking this situation lightly, Grant," Al said.

"It's being handled with the utmost discretion and delicacy," Adeline agreed.

"You think traipsing out to the damned apple orchard and telling him to shut the maze down is using discretion?" Grant barked. "Might as well have just held a gun to his head. You should never have done that, Adeline, and you know it. I swear, sometimes I think you're slipping in your old age."

For one frozen moment no one spoke. When Adeline did, her voice had changed. The ice Augie heard in it chilled him, for he'd never heard her—nor any person—speak with such deadly directness. "You'll want to watch how you address me, Grant, lest you forget your place. You wouldn't want to forget your place, I can promise you that."

An uncomfortable shuffle of feet preceded Lang's apology. "I'm sorry, Adeline. Sometimes my mouth runs ahead of me."

"It brings you trouble," she said. Her voice softened again. A bit. "We must work together on our mutual problem or we won't stand a chance. Now tell me what Michael says about all this."

Al answered this time, blowing his breath out in a gust. "I have to admit, he's none too pleased you moved without giving him a heads-up."

"It couldn't be helped. No one else had made a move, so I did. As usual, if I want something done around here, I have to do it myself."

"Mike said Augie asked about Kodiak," Grant said.

"He mentioned him by name?"

"Kodi saw Augie confronting me, asked if I needed help. He's a good dog, that red fucking Russian. Pardon me, Adeline."

"I don't like it," the dowager said. "It's too close to our operation."

"You know what I don't like? I don't like that the kid got his throat cut," Al said. "Augie would've shut the maze down on his own."

"We don't know that. He seemed unreceptive to the idea when I suggested it," Adeline said.

"Well, it's shut down now," Grant said. "Just what we wanted. We can move forward."

"The excuse by which it's been shut down won't hold up much longer," Al said. "Augie's itching to open again, what with Halloween around the corner."

"Has he filed to appeal Fahrlander's ruling?" Adeline asked.

"Not that I'm aware of," Al replied. "Doesn't surprise me, though. Augie's the kind of man content with letting the wheels of justice turn so long as they aren't spinning in neutral."

"You offered him the balance of the lease?" Adeline asked Grant.

"I did. He wouldn't touch it. Called me a son of a bitch, convinced I was the one who cut the kid."

"That's exactly what we didn't want him to think," their hostess said, her voice terse.

"Let me handle that," Al said. "I'll throw him off the scent."

"What's this about the morgue being burgled?" Adeline asked. "Was it him?"

Al uttered a clipped laugh. "Who, Augie? If the man dreamed about breaking a law he'd call me from bed to confess."

"Could it be in any way connected with this case?"

"I believe it to be unrelated," Al said. "Maybe a wayward kid who jumped the gun on the holiday, looking for an early thrill."

"I hope your professional assessment is correct, Alvin," Adeline said. "What about the dog?"

"I did what you said, Adeline," Grant replied. "Don't you think the corn cob under the collar was too much?"

"It was the perfect touch," Adeline said and croaked laughter which sounded not-quite-sane and Augie wondered if the old woman had slipped a gear. "Of course his first thought would lead him to you, Grant, but August Milliard is a smart man. Smarter than any of you, at any rate. He'd second-guess the overt message, would think it too obvious to lead back to you."

"I don't know. He's pretty pissed at me, I can tell you that. I saw it in his eyes. I bet I'm the only one he's looking at."

"Well, we'll fix that, don't you worry," Adeline said.

Augie, too eager, had crept closer to the door. A shadow crossed the threshold and he drew back, sweat rolling down his ribcage. If they discovered him spying, he had a good idea no one would ever see him again—they'd shoot him and bury him beneath the oceans of corn.

Adeline's dog, the cairn terrier, ambled into the hall, nose in the air. The creature was as old in dog years as her mistress, though far more decrepit. Milky cataracts covered the eyes and its old sniffer seemed no better off. It took a few shuffling steps forward, sensing a presence but unable to identify it as friend or foe. It uttered a single creaking yap before Augie knew what he must do. He crouched and grabbed it under the belly, hauling it to his chest, and clamping the other hand around its muzzle. Then he retreated the way he'd come with as much stealth as he could muster, and by the time he reached the lawn, he'd hit a full-out sprint.

CHAPTER TWENTY-ONE

Two things happened back to back that Monday morning which reinforced in Augie's mind his decision to become a dognapper. The mail came at 11:00 sharp, as it always did, right before lunch. Teresa had gone into town on errands, claiming all trace of headache had vanished. Augie got up from his desk where he'd sat scouring the local newspaper for the third time for anything noteworthy pertaining to their situation and walked out to the mailbox.

A stack of envelopes awaited, mostly bills and circulars, routine and boring. Near the middle of the pile, though, he found two which gave him pause. The first had been addressed by hand and he knew what it contained before he'd even torn it open. Augie might have dumped it in the trash still sealed if he hadn't spotted the second item of interest resting directly beneath it.

The return address indicated that of the produce company through which Milliard Farms had been contracted since time immemorial. OPEN IMMEDIATELY had been stamped on the surface in red ink. Augie did, already knowing what it would be but praying against it with all he had.

"No," he whispered, not hearing his voice raising into the whine he so despised hearing in his children. "No, God, no ..."

But yes. It had come to his worst fear and then beyond. The produce company had terminated their contract, citing Article C, Section 2 of the agreement in which they reserve the right to sever ties with the contractor "contingent upon questionable practices engaged in by the contractor." They were using the ongoing investigation as a means of wriggling out of the agreement. Well, Augie would be damned if he'd let them—no one had been arrested, no one had even been *accused* of wrongdoing. They couldn't get away with it. They had no legal grounds. He would fight this in court, he would hire a lawyer ...

Except he wouldn't. He couldn't. And he knew it. The distributor was based outside of Ashford County, but Granny's influence had a long reach. She'd been behind cutting him off. How much had she offered the distributor? Did her pocketbook run as deep as her reach was long?

He picked up the phone and dialed the number at the bottom of the letterhead and demanded to speak with Greg Hahn, the rep the family had worked with since Augie's father had run the farm. A harried receptionist told him Farmland Distributors, Inc. no longer employed Mr. Hahn.

"Since when?" Augie demanded. True, he hadn't spoken with Greg in better than two years, their contract set to automatically renew on an annual basis unless either party wished to amend the terms. But the Milliards hadn't changed the terms of the contract with Farmland in better than a decade—and never since August III had taken over.

"I'm not authorized to provide that information, sir."

"I need to speak with whoever took his place," Augie said through gritted teeth.

"That position has been left unfilled as the company is going through alterations," the receptionist said robotically, as if reading from a script. She probably was.

"Look, let me speak to whoever is in charge."

"I'm sorry, but that person is currently unavailable. If you leave your name and number, I'd be happy to leave a message."

Augie left his information, the pulse in his throat hammering away, and demanded an immediate callback. The receptionist said his request would be relayed and then disconnected.

Fuming, Augie flicked the envelope onto his desk and snapped up the one with the familiar handwriting. It seemed to have been hand-placed in the stack of mail, a slap in the face. He tore into it and regarded the check for the remainder of what Grant Lang owed on their agreement.

"Son of a bitch," Augie growled. Lang wouldn't get away

with this. He wasn't the only one with friends in this county.

He picked up the phone and dialed Ray Safford's house, but hung up after nine rings. Ray would be afield or feeding the hogs, but he'd hoped to raise Ruth and ask her to have her husband call him back. No such luck. Maybe later he'd take a drive over to their place and have a face-to-face with Ray. Probably better than over the phone, anyway; he couldn't trust the goddamn party lines in this town. Before he went, though, he had another stop to make.

The store had a back pantry bigger than the walk-in closet in the Milliard master bedroom. Augie unlocked the store and went to it, hauling the heavy door open enough to peer inside. The dog moved quick, but he stopped the gap with his size 12 Converse before she could slip by.

"No you don't, pooch," he said. "Not yet. Not till your old lady knocks off the bullshit. Okay?"

The dog whimpered and made a second escape attempt. This time Augie shoved it back with the toe of his shoe. It rolled on its side and bounded away, scared of him now. Augie had never in his life mistreated an animal and his action stunned him. He recovered quickly, though—somehow it didn't seem near so bad knowing who the mutt belonged to. "I said no. Go eat."

He'd dumped some of Timber's kibble into a spare dish and placed a saucer of water beside it. The water was gone, but the food appeared untouched. For all he knew, the little runt had been spoiled with chopped sirloin her whole life. He pulled the empty dish through the gap and noticed a pile of scat in the center of the pantry floor.

With the water refilled, Augie stepped into the pantry with a roll of Brawny and closed the door behind him. In the newly enclosed space, the dog bared its teeth at him.

"Oh, cut it out," he commanded as he cleaned up the mess and laid down old newspaper for her to target next time. "You act like you got it bad in here. Be happy you aren't still confined to that mean old lady's lap. You've got room to run now."

But the dog didn't want room to run—it could barely turn around without knocking into something. What had he hoped to accomplish when he grabbed it? What had he been thinking?

That was it, though, wasn't it—he hadn't been thinking. If he had, he wouldn't have taken this absurd course of action. He'd sunk to their level and he hated himself for it. Just what in the hell did he think he was doing?

He'd let the dog go. That was it. He'd take it to the base of the ridge and release it into the scrub. Surely, it could find its way home.

But no. Truth was, it probably couldn't. And if no one found it, it would die in the wild. The only way to get the dog back safely would be to take it back himself. Which he would, of course, once Adeline called off this whole ridiculous situation. Once they got his contract with Farmland Distribution back. Jesus, what was he going to tell Teresa?

"I won't tell her anything," Augie said to the dog. "She doesn't have to know. I'll fix this before she learns about it."

And to fix it, he needed the dog. Just for a few days, he figured. That's all it would take to lean on Adeline.

Someone banged on the front door and Augie jumped. "Stay, pooch," he said and closed the pantry. He could hear the animal inside, scratching at the door and whimpering, but it was faint. It wouldn't carry to the front. He hoped.

Al Engel waited for him on the stoop, thumbs hooked on his gun belt. Augie composed himself, hoped he didn't look as guilty as he felt. The guilt, though, was seasoned with a heavy dose of fury at the police officer who'd been his friend going on twenty-five years and had since dumped that allegiance for that of an elderly dowager. He stuffed both emotions in a deep back pocket of his brain and opened the door.

"Al," he said. "Good morning."

"Not so good as that," the police chief said. "Jontue is missing."

Augie had no idea who Al meant. He said, "I beg your pardon?"

"Adeline Gable's dog."

Augie went cold. He tried a pinch of humor he hoped masked his emotions. "Did you put out an APB?"

"This isn't funny, Augie," Al said. "Adeline's deeply upset. Disturbed is more like it."

Oh, she's disturbed all right, Augie thought. He said, "Did the poor thing get outside somehow, make a run for the hills?"

"That animal hasn't been able to run for half a decade," Al said. He cocked his chin at Augie. "I thought if maybe she'd scooted down here into the valley you might've seen her."

Augie shook his head. "Not a whisker, I'm afraid."

"Well, if you do give me a ring, would you? Adeline's a mess without her pet."

"You got it, friend," Augie said, lightly emphasizing the last word.

Al rapped his knuckles on the jamb in an oddly aggressive gesture. "Be seeing you, Augie."

"You bet."

The police chief sauntered off to his cruiser, surveying the environment as he moved. Then he got in and drove away. Augie watched him go, then flicked his eyes toward the maze and saw the signs.

A pair of brand-new, enormous neon orange NO TRESPASSING signs had replaced the police tape, barring both the entrance and exit. He walked out to them slowly, like a man in a dream. As he neared, he could read fine print beneath the bold command: Under Penalty of Law. Violators Will Be Prosecuted.

I haven't cashed his check yet, Augie thought. *The land's still under lease until I cash the fucking check.* Then: *What in God's name are you hiding back there, Lang? What are you and Adeline cooking up that's so secret you want us gone?*

Augie pulled Grant Lang's check from his pocket, unfolded it, and read it over again. Then he tore it into scraps and tossed them upward like a magician releasing doves. The wind scattered them through the pumpkin patch. They weren't going to get away with this.

Augie dragged the signs behind the store, facing them against the back wall. When he came around front, a station wagon had pulled into the lot and a woman in a housedress and overcoat was helping her two small children out into the lot. They weren't local and likely completely unaware of the current trouble the Milliards faced.

"Hi there," she called. "Are you open?"

Augie grinned and unlocked the store. "Step right in, ma'am."

CHAPTER TWENTY-TWO

Hannah pestered Dennis for the keys to the Chevy until he turned them over with a sigh. She'd been at him since catching up with him after study hall and had actually had the gall to sit beside him at lunch, nagging all the way. He'd told her to get lost, that he needed a way to get home after practice and that she could catch a ride with Lorelai or one of her other friends.

"Maybe *you* should catch a ride with Lorelai, big brother," Hannah had said with a giggle. At the time, Dennis had only been interested in shooing her off so he could talk sports with the guys and hadn't caught her meaning.

At last, after homeroom, when she stalled him at his locker, he relented and turned the keys over. She kissed his cheek and said, "Don't worry, Den, I'll come back and pick you up after practice."

"You better," he said. "Don't leave me begging a ride."

She turned to go and gave him a look over her shoulder. "I was serious about asking Lorelai for a ride."

"What are you talking about?" Dennis asked through gritted teeth. He only wanted to get to the locker room.

"You're a lot dumber than you look," his sister said, then pushed into the Ladies' Room and left him staring at the door. Girls made no damn sense, he decided.

Like most of his classmates, the guys in the locker room had been sympathetic about the Milliards' plight. The family was well-respected in town and no one actually believed any of them had anything to do with Randy's wound. Or the dead girl. Poor Randy, who still had not returned to school and might not until after winter break, if the rumors could be trusted. Dennis had called to ask if he could see his friend, but Randy's father had hung up on him.

"Hey, Millie," Scott Beard called when he came into the locker room. For the time, they had it to themselves.

"What's up, Beard."

"You ready for Sommerville on Friday?"

"As I'll ever be. Not like I'll see the field."

"Hell you won't. They're scrubs. We'll be up thirty-five by halftime, coach'll put you in."

"A guy can hope."

Scott shut his locker and looked more squarely at his friend. "Hey, you doing all right? You know, with all this?"

"It'll pass. That's what my dad says, anyway."

"Yeah." Scott hesitated, toeing the tile with one cleat. "You seen him yet? Randy?"

Dennis shook his head. "His family hates me."

"Man, you can't think like that."

"You saw what they did at the parade," Dennis said. "Everybody saw."

There would be no denying it, so Scott didn't even try. "Hey, how's your mom?"

"She's fine. Just kind of lying low, riding it out, like we all are."

"I heard someone in Susie's class got on her case, called her names today."

Dennis snapped his head up. "Who was it?"

"Hell, I don't know. Some kid."

"Dammit, I'm going to have to kick some ass."

"Don't get in trouble over it, Millie. Jeez. It's just stupid freshman shit."

"No one messes with my sisters. You got a name, Scott, you let me know. Otherwise I'll get it out of Susie tonight after practice. Come tomorrow, I'm going to pound the little bastard into burger."

The door to the office banged open and Coach Dayton stepped into the locker room as if taking a stage cue. "There isn't going to be any practice for you, Milliard. Not tonight and not ever."

Dennis blinked. He must not have heard right. He paused

midway through strapping on his shoulder pads. "Come again, Coach?"

"You're off the team."

"What for?" Scott demanded when Dennis found himself speechless.

"I just overheard you threaten another student. You know I have a zero tolerance policy for that shit."

Dennis got his jaw working and hated the way his voice sounded, almost a whine. Hot tears formed at the corners of his eyes and he hated them even worse. "I didn't threaten anyone. I don't even know who Scott was talking about."

"It doesn't matter. You threatened physical harm to a student."

"But—"

"You also used language unbecoming of our football program."

"So did you!" Dennis screeched. Now he *was* crying. "You just said 'shit,' I heard you. Didn't he, Scott? Didn't he say it?"

Scott held perfectly still, like a wax sculpture. He didn't want to put his football career in jeopardy. Coach Dayton stalked to the door and shoved it open, waiting for the ousted second-string quarterback to depart his facility. Dennis did so on legs that held no more feeling than cords of firewood. When he passed the coach, Dayton said so only Dennis could hear: "You couldn't throw worth a shit anyway, Milliard."

The words hurt Dennis more deeply than he'd expected and he stumbled as if taking pressure from an outside linebacker. Except then something unexpected happened. His tears dried up as if an aquifer had been sealed. At the same time something else opened in him, something he hadn't even realized he contained: a volcanic rage that boiled in his belly and erupted up the chimney of his throat and out his mouth.

"How much are they paying you to fuck my family over, you son of a bitch?" he breathed. He'd heard his parents talking and knew his father at least believed someone was out to get them after what happened in the maze. He didn't know who, exactly, only that his father's words rang true enough, especially after the parade.

It was Coach Dayton's turn to reel. His face at first drained of color before flushing a hue akin to the Derby Devils' home jersey. "Get out. Get the fuck out of my locker room right now and don't come back."

A strange smile spread on Dennis Milliard's face. Standing there leering with tears still sparkling in his eyes like chips of glass, face blotchy, he resembled at that moment some strange Halloweenish creature which has emerged a few days early. "Why, Coach, you should watch your mouth. You're using language unbecoming of your precious fucking football program."

Then, without another word, Dennis left the locker room.

The buses had long since departed and a chill breeze rushed over the school grounds. Not a soul remained on campus outside of the locker room. Dennis scrubbed at his cheeks. He felt like a different person, like some hidden reservoir of poison inside him had been breached and had tainted the rest of him. He tried to tell himself being kicked off the team was a blessing in disguise. He'd have a lot more time to work on the car now, a lot more time to enjoy his favorite holiday. Think of all the time he'd wasted riding the bench. Sure, he loved the game but he could play it anytime with his siblings. Even Hannah didn't mind putting the mascara away and pulling her hair into a ponytail for a little touch football every now and again. And Thomas had the makings of a bona fide QB1 when he made it to varsity level. The kid could throw, far better than Denny could.

Unless, of course, Coach Dayton still had it out for his family by then.

Dennis stood on the curb trying to decide whether to hitch home or head toward town and maybe catch a ride with someone at Gert's. A lot of kids went there after school to sneak a malt before supper or catch a burger if their parents worked late. He thought about the stranger who'd offered him work. The man had told him to be there at five o'clock if Dennis wanted to make money. What kind of work would it be? Was the guy a new farmer hoping to get his operation off the ground? If so, good luck—the Langs, Saffords, Stones, and Milliards left little room in Ashford County for new farmers. And Adeline Gable, too, of course. The five big family farms swallowed pretty much everyone else, especially the Langs.

As if thinking that name had summoned her, Lorelai pulled up beside him in her two-year-old Mustang. "You look lost," she called through the window.

Dennis blinked at her. He wanted to smile, but felt not an ounce of happiness at the moment. "Not lost. Thinking."

"No football today?"

"I'm off the team."

Her face changed. "You're joking."

"I'm not. I really don't want to talk about it, okay?"

"Okay," she said. "Hey, do need a ride somewhere?"

"That'd be great," he said. "Can you drop me at Gert's?"

From the chem lab window, Rachel Safford watched Dennis climb into Lorelai Lang's car. She'd seen at once he hadn't been with the team when they'd jogged out onto the practice field and had left the band room to follow him like a ghost down the hall. Had he been crying? She thought he had. Why hadn't he gone to practice? Had he been kicked off the team?

When he pushed out the back door, she'd stepped into the chemistry lab and watched him standing on the curb, swiping at his face, looking as though he might be trying to decipher some particularly complex riddle. She had decided to go to him, to take his hand in hers, and offer to walk the three miles home with him. She'd leave her bike chained to the rack and pick it up tomorrow. It didn't matter how she'd get home from his house—either he could drive her or she could call her father to pick her up. Her heart surged and she moved toward the door … until she saw the Mustang pull up alongside him.

Rachel knew who owned that car. She didn't care for Lorelai Lang. Not that she hated her—Rachel didn't hate anybody because the Bible forbade it. But the person who came closest to that category would be the one who drove the '73 banana-yellow Mustang. And now she had a reason to dislike her even more. How could Susie's sister be friends with her? How could Dennis like her? Why? Why did God allow such injustice?

"You witch," she said aloud, her voice resonating off rows of beakers and test tubes stacked on shelves. "You painted jezebel."

She watched the car speed away toward town. When it vanished, Rachel slouched out to her bicycle, unhooked it, and followed the trail of dust lingering in the crisp autumn air.

When no other customers showed up, Augie locked the store and went about his business. The lady's bill had overtopped $35 and at the moment he would take anything he could get. But if no one else showed up, he couldn't afford to just sit here all day. He had things that needed doing.

He drove out to Ray's place and found him slopping the hogs in the barn. He didn't bother knocking because Ruth Safford was about the last person he wanted to see—Augie needed her religious rhetoric like he needed colon polyps.

"Ray, can I talk to you for a minute?" he hollered over the squealing swine.

The beefy farmer, who'd been engrossed in filling the troughs and speaking in terms of endearment to his beloved livestock, jumped.

"Christ on a cloud," he said, patting his heart. "I didn't hear you come up, Augie."

"Sorry about that," Augie said.

Ray laughed—he always laughed. "No need to apologize. What's on your mind?"

Augie glanced over his shoulder to ensure they still had the place to themselves. He noticed the way the brown cornstalks came right up to the Safford property, encroaching, and pushed back the unsettling thought that they might be Grant Lang's spies.

He cleared his throat. "Has anyone approached you about what happened?"

Ray Safford looked blank. "About what now?"

"The incident. At the maze."

"How do you mean, approached?"

Augie sighed. The most frustrating thing about speaking with Ray Safford was you had to be blunt. No beating around the bush. He might have been a genius when it came to farming swine, but came up short in just about everything else. "Did Grant Lang or Mike Stone come to you about it?"

Ray shook his head. "Haven't spoken to either in, hell, couple-three weeks now."

"What about Al Engel or Adeline?"

"Adeline *Gable*?" Ray asked, as if Augie could mean any other. "No sir, haven't chatted with either of them in a fair spell."

"Will you do something for me, Ray?"

"Name it, buddy."

"If any of those four come to you for any reason—any at all, it doesn't have to be about the maze—will you call me first thing?"

"You bet, Augie. What's this about?"

"I'll tell you another time. Give my best to Ruth."

"Will do," Ray said, looking more confused than ever.

On his way back to the car, Augie caught sight of the youngest Safford spawn, Samuel, standing in only a pair of Fruit of the Looms in an upstairs window. His hair stood in crazy corkscrews and his mouth was stained a melty brown which Augie prayed was chocolate. He couldn't imagine raising a handicapped child and silently thanked the universe all his kids turned out bright. God bless Ray Safford for being the man he was.

CHAPTER TWENTY-THREE

Dennis knew by the time they pulled up in front of Gert's that Lorelai would want to be invited in for a milkshake. He had better than an hour before the guy from yesterday said he'd be there, so he didn't figure it would hurt much to have some company while he waited. Getting her to leave while he and the man talked business would be the trick because Dennis had the feeling the work wouldn't be the sort he'd want to advertise. And you know what? Dennis didn't care. His world had been in the process of falling apart for better than a week now and today had put a feathered cap on it—losing football meant losing part of himself. So now he would go for broke. He'd make a play on Lorelai. If she rejected him, screw it. After today, it wouldn't even sting. But she wouldn't reject him and he knew it ... he'd finally deciphered Hannah's clues and realized this chick wanted him, bad.

Except he weathered another windfall when Lorelai said, "I'm sorry, but I've got to drop and run. I just remembered I have to do something for my dad."

"You don't have time for a shake?" Dennis asked, working to keep dejection out of his voice.

Lorelai was peering through the big plate glass window into the diner and seemed to find something inside appalling. Maybe she wasn't a fan of Monday's blue plate special.

"I really don't today," she said. "See you tomorrow, hey?"

"Yeah. Thanks for the ride. What do I owe you?" Dennis said.

She grinned. "You know the saying. Gas, grass, or ass."

Yesterday, hell an hour ago, such a proclamation from the future Derby High class of '76 valedictorian might have elicited shock from one such as Dennis Milliard, but he seemed to lack the ability to be shocked today. Instead of fumbling over his words, as he had at the register with Rachel Safford, he said coolly, "Hey, whichever you prefer."

It was Lorelai who stammered. "Uh, I ... how about a movie sometime?"

"Yeah, sure. Sounds good," Dennis said. He got out and slammed the door. Lorelai reversed and sped off toward home. It was official: he still did not understand girls. Not one bit. He'd have to talk to Hannah about what had transpired, see if she had any magical feminine insight to offer.

He opened the door and stepped into Gert's. Neither she nor Amos appeared in evidence, but the man from yesterday sat perched on a counter stool, smoking a dark brown cigarette that smelled of cloves.

"You are early," he said in that peaty accent.

"So are you," Dennis replied.

"You have no football today?"

"It got canceled." Dennis never considered the potential connection between being kicked off the team and winding up meeting up with the man who wanted to offer him a job, not even after everything was over and the bodies had been buried.

The man grinned. "Your good fortune," he said, rising and moving toward the back booth. "Please, join me."

Gert came out from her hidey hole and favored him with a scowl. "You did not finish your meal yesterday," she said. She could have been the mother of the long-haired guy; their accents were practically indistinguishable, at least to Dennis's unseasoned ear.

"Sorry, Gert. I had to go."

"I throw away perfectly good food."

"I'll tip you double today."

"Tip, tip. It's not about tip. Dennis, you are a good boy. Strong. You need to eat all your food, not throw it away."

"You sound like my mother, Gert," he said. "In fact, you could be *this* guy's mother. You sound alike." He never would have said something so pert and potentially disrespectful before today, but now he simply didn't care. People wanted to hate him? Let them.

She offered another pinched expression. "I am from Ukraine. This one, he is Soviet. Moscow, most likely, here to spread Communism."

The man's grin widened. "Madam, you pain me. I am a dissident, defected from the Motherland to *escape* Communism. And I hail from Leningrad."

"You fit right in with these American hippies then."

But the man didn't bite at her remark and seemed to dismiss the proprietor entirely. He held a hand out like a butler, inviting Dennis to proceed to the back booth. When they were seated, he said, "Allow me to introduce myself. My name is Kodiak Aristov, from the great Soviet Union as you now know. I emigrated to your wonderful land, seeking fame and fortune. You may call me Kodi if you like."

"You sought it in the wrong place, friend," Dennis said, still settling into his devil-may-give-a-shit attitude.

Kodiak turned on his gleaming grin again. "Soon enough, *comrade*. And that's where you come in."

"Yeah, let's hear about this job," Dennis said. He hoped to come off nonchalant, but the idea of work—especially covert work, as this clearly seemed to be—intrigued him. Yesterday, it hadn't. But today was a new day and he was a new Dennis.

Gert came to the table, set a glass of ice water down, and said, "You want something?"

"No thanks, Gert," Dennis said.

"This is a diner, not a meeting hall."

"Fine. I'll take a chocolate malt."

"You want more coffee?" she asked the man called Kodiak Aristov.

"Please." He waited until she'd shuffled out of earshot before saying: "Do you smoke?"

The question surprised Dennis. "No. Well, I tried it once. I found a pack in my dad's den. I didn't like it."

"I don't mean tobacco."

This surprised him even more. He glanced around and lowered his voice. "You mean grass?"

Kodiak nodded slowly as if dealing with a toddler.

"You're not a cop are you? Undercover? If you are, you have to tell me. I watch *The Rockford Files*, I know how it works."

"I'm no cop," Kodi said. "I told you what I am."

"So you're a drug dealer as well as a dissident."

He waved his hand in the air. "You make it sound so criminal."

"It *is* criminal."

Gert came back with his malt and the coffee decanter to refill Kodi's mug. "You need anything else, you let me know," she said to Dennis. It sounded as though she was offering him help instead of food.

"Thanks, Gert." When she'd gone again, he returned his gaze to Kodi. "If you're asking me to be a drug dealer, the answer is no. *Hell* no."

"You haven't heard out my proposition."

"I don't need to."

He heaved a deep sigh. "If you will not listen to me, perhaps you'll listen to my friend Benjamin." Kodi glanced around before drawing a thick wad of cash from his pocket and setting it on the table before Dennis.

Dennis picked it up cautiously as though it might have been steeped in snake venom, turned slightly toward the wall, and riffled through it. All $100 bills. There must have been fifty of them. It was the most money he'd seen in one place in his life.

"You make all this selling grass?"

"Grass and other assorted novelties." He snapped his fingers and Dennis handed the money back. Kodi made it disappear into his pocket again, smooth as a lounge magician.

Dennis knew his family might need a boost with the store closed, and he sure as hell needed money to buy parts for the Firebird. "What would I have to do?"

"That's easy. You're, what do you say in America, popular? You have friends?"

"Yeah, I have friends."

"Get them to buy our product."

"None of them really smoke. At least, I don't think they

do." Not exactly the truth though—Beard had been known to get high from time to time. He said it helped with the pain of getting hit every week on the offensive line.

"Change their minds."

"I mean, the kids at school who do smoke, they already have someone they buy from. Hell, you can drive out to some back roads around here and find it growing wild sometimes."

"Our product is better than that ditch weed. In fact, it's the best I've ever had and I've had it all over the world."

"I'll go to jail if I'm caught."

Kodi shook his head. "You're a juvenile. Clean record, no? Never been in trouble with police?"

Dennis shook his head. He'd never so much as stolen a shoelace. "You are perfect man for the job. By the time you turn eighteen, you'll know how not to get caught. I can teach you much."

Dennis licked his lips and glanced around again. Gert sat at the counter reading a magazine and sipping coffee. Amos still had not shown his face.

"How much do I stand to earn?"

"The more you sell, the more you make."

"How much to start out?"

Kodi dipped into his pocket again and came out with one of the hundreds. He slid it across the table. "Consider this an advance."

Dennis stared at it for a time, the weight of his universe balancing on the edge of a blade. At last he took it and stuffed it in his pocket. "Tell me what I have to do."

"First you tell me something. That girl who dropped you off, she is your girlfriend?"

"Who, Lorelai? No. No, she's my sister's friend."

"You have a sister?"

"I have three of them."

"Brothers?"

"Two."

"A big family, that's good. That's very good," Kodi said.

"My family stays out of this, though, okay?"

"Of course. No one knows but us. You and me. Partners."

Dennis considered that final word and decided he liked it. "Partners," he said, trying it out. It sounded even better coming from his mouth.

CHAPTER TWENTY-FOUR

Zebulon Tuel took it where he could get it. That applied to everything in his life. When Mr. Milliard had informed him of the orchard's closing, he'd picked up part-time work at the Falling Pins bowling alley where he waxed lanes and shilled shoes.

He'd also recently taken it where he could get it in the bed of Mary Lou Zahn, the other part-timer laid off after the closing. She wasn't much to look at, no sir, but all cats are gray in the dark. And she *moved* like a cat, her body fluid and nimble like she'd been around the block a few times.

Now, an hour after his shift, as Mary Lou showered and he smoked in her bed, the sheets puddled around his thighs, Zeb thought of the most recent thing he *hadn't* taken when he could get it. The long-hair had approached him at the bowling alley two days previous. Zeb hadn't seen him around before, but when the man—younger than Zeb by maybe a decade—ordered a beer, he had poured one. The guy had introduced himself as Kodi in an accent thick enough to cut with the folding knife Zeb kept in his hip pocket. A foreigner from where? Hungary? Poland? Transylvania? That last almost made the new Falling Pins counterman crack up, but he refrained. He could easily envision this young man as Dracula's protégé, what with his sharp fangs, pallid complexion, and deep accent.

"You need a better job?" the younger man had asked.

"I figure this one suits me fine," Zeb had replied.

The man named Kodi then launched into a pitch that sounded quite good to Zeb, but in the end he had refused. Sell grass to alley patrons? Mr. Mooney, the owner, would flip his bald lid at that. The foreigner had patiently explained a foolproof method by which each transaction could take place with minimal risk of detection. Zeb had followed along and had seen how it could work, but … but he couldn't go back to Ashford County. He'd done two stints for drunk and disorderly in his twenties and both had persuaded him to steer clear of legal trouble down the road.

"I understand," the stranger had commiserated, borrowing an order pad and pencil from the countertop and scribbling a local number on it. When he went to put the pencil back, a wad of hundred dollar bills fell onto the counter from his breast pocket. The man had made a show of riffling them out, pretending to count it, before making it vanish. "If you change your mind, you give me a call."

After the man had finished his beer and gone through the door beneath the glowing, fly-speckled EXIT sign, Zeb had drawn a beer for himself and swallowed it in three seasoned gulps. Mr. Mooney strictly forbade employees drinking on his dime (or while on duty), but he didn't figure the old man would find out. Zeb had the place to himself and, by dammit, he thought better when he had a cold one to let his brain stew in. It hadn't helped.

Now, as Mary Lou stepped naked into the room save for the pink towel she'd twisted over her head, her owlish eyeglasses comically steamed, he thought of that scrap of paper folded into the pocket of his overalls lying on the floor. Should he call the number? Would it be worth the risk? He studied a miniature haystack display surrounded by tiny plastic cavorting skeletons on her bureau and wished his brain would cough up an answer.

"Woolgathering, loverly?" Mary Lou asked in a sing-song lilt. Her body sagged and dragged, but Zeb didn't mind. He liked it, actually, and never mind she was old enough to be his mother. She'd certainly held no moral misgivings in seducing him.

"Trying to make up my mind on something is all."

"Need some elder perspective?"

"You're not elderly, Mary Lou."

"Well, I'm certainly not one of those spring chickens you take to bed."

He stared at her. "I don't take no one to bed."

"Then the girls of Ashford County are missing out," she said, climbing in beside him and running a hand up his thigh. His anatomy responded accordingly. "Turn out the lights, loverly."

Zeb complied and they made love again, the question that had been nagging at his mind temporarily forgotten.

By the time he walked back to the tarpaper shack he called home, all the way out on Shaker Hill Road, Zeb had made up his mind. He didn't have a home phone and he hadn't wanted to clue Mary Lou in on his intentions, but he did need to run down to the liquor store for pint of bourbon and a sixer of Iron City. They had a payphone between the front door and the Coca-Cola machine.

It had been the money which had finally persuaded him. All that money. Could he, Zebulon Tuel, finally move on from this rut in which he'd found himself this decade past? Could he earn enough to buy a respectable house, maybe up in Ashford in one of those old dignified neighborhoods behind the courthouse? Could all this ill luck finally be taking a turn? It was about time to find out.

He stepped in under the awning of American Pastime Liquors and waved at the counterman, a red-haired rosy-cheeked fellow encumbered with an enormous but soft frame whose name eluded Zeb at the moment. Brad or Brett, he thought. The fellow was a new employee and Zeb figured he'd learn his name sooner rather than later—he knew everyone else here as though they were family, especially Bernie Eisenberg, the Jewish owner. Jews beset Zeb with a kind of reticent awe, for how could anyone believe in anything other than Jesus Christ as the Lord and Savior? It staggered the mind. He hoped ol' Bern wouldn't burn in hell (the pun never failed to make him chuckle internally), but held out hope the man would one day come around. In any case, this new fellow looked anything but Jewish. Rather resembled a young St. Nick, in Zeb's estimation. For now he would think of him privately as such.

"Evening. What can I get you?" St. Nick said, cordially if

begrudgingly pausing his perusal of a well-worn copy of *Playboy*.

"Get a pint of Bonded Beam?" Zeb asked.

"You got it, my friend. What else?"

Zeb found his favored six-pack in the refrigerated section and set it on the counter. "That'll do 'er."

"Good choices," St. Nick said. "Party tonight?"

Zeb cracked up. "Yeah, party for one."

"The best way to do it," St. Nick said and Zeb cracked up again because he couldn't imagine this guy anywhere but alone in a room with a bottle and his skin mag, maybe crying as he drank alone. He paid with a portion of his nightly tips, which turned out to be more than usual since the guy with the accent had tipped him 50% instead of the customary 15 he got (if patrons bothered to tip at all—it was a crapshoot at the Falling Pins, especially with a man of color behind the counter).

Zeb took his supplies outside, set the six-pack atop the dented canopy of the phone booth, unscrewed the hooch, and took a long swallow. He felt it warm his insides and rush to his brain with that old familiar lovey-dovey rinse. All at once, as he knew it would, his confidence surged and he snapped up the receiver and dialed the number on the paper.

"Yes," the stranger—Kodi—said on the second ring.

"Hi, uh, it's Zebbo. Zebulon Tuel. From the bowling alley? I decided I'd like to hear a little more about what we discussed."

A pause. Then: "This is good, yes. Meet me at the corner of Tipton Road and Burr Valley. One hour."

"Tipton and Burr Valley? Hell, that's five miles from here. It'll take me an hour to walk there. Maybe more."

"One hour, Mr. Tuel," Kodi said. The line clicked and the dial tone buzzed in his ear like an eager bee.

"Shit," Zeb muttered. Maybe this wouldn't work out after all. He only wanted to return to his little place out on Shaker Hill, click on *Hee Haw*, and drink himself to sleep. He felt overtaxed, overworked, and oversexed.

But the money, though. *The money.* Zeb figured he could earn enough in a year, maybe two, to buy himself a house. He'd be careful. And, hell, if it got too dangerous, if ol' Al Engel started sniffing around, he'd give it up. That simple.

He took another long swallow and started walking south, toward Tipton Road.

Dennis didn't tell anyone about what had happened at school. He figured everyone would know soon enough. He likely faced a suspension for how he'd spoken to Coach Dayton, or two weeks' detention at the very least. He'd decided he wouldn't serve the penalty, whatever it happened to be. Fuck it. He'd quit school before he did. Dennis Milliard had the opportunity to make real money now. The bill burning a hole in his pocket proved it.

At dinner, he secured the use of the Buick for a few hours that night, citing a class project he needed to work on with Ted Latham. Rarely had he bald-faced lied to his parents, but he knew that would be changing permanently in the coming weeks. Now was as good a time as any to begin. His mom and dad didn't even think twice about agreeing.

"How is Ted doing?" Teresa asked. "After what happened?"

"He's good, Mom. He's doing fine. Me and him, we're going to go visit Randy soon. After Halloween, probably."

Augie didn't bother correcting his son's grammar this time. He said, "That's good, son. I'm sure Randy misses you. Any idea when he'll be coming back to school?"

Dennis shook his head. "Haven't heard yet. Chief Engel any closer to finding out who did it?"

His parents exchanged a glance they didn't mean for him to see, but he caught it. Couldn't get much past Dennis Milliard these days, no sir. "Not that we know of," his mother murmured.

"They'll catch him, though, won't they?" Dennis asked. "Chief Engel and his men will find out who did it, right?"

"We sure hope so, son," Augie said, looking down at his plate. They'd been through this before with identical results.

Dennis took his dinner utensils to the sink, then swiped the keys off the counter. "I'll be home before ten," he said.

"Nine thirty," Teresa corrected.

"Fine. See you." He had no intention of being home by then if duty dictated. He had work to do.

The place he'd been told to park was at the end of an unnamed gravel lane choked with weeds that turned off of one of the county backroads he'd rarely frequented. Dennis hadn't even known this gravel tributary existed and, in fact, seemed only to exist as an isolated access road to one of Mr. Lang's cornfields. He figured tractors the only traffic it ever saw.

The lane dead-ended with a tall barrier topped with four reflective blood-red diamonds denoting no outlet. Beyond lay nothing but dead corn and the dregs of dusk. He parked facing the barrier, switched off the engine, and sat listening to it tick as it cooled. The instructions had been to wait until dark when someone would come for him. The wait would not be long as he watched the first stars wink to life in the east.

Time ebbed on. The wind rushed through the fields, rattling what remained of the corn. It sounded the way Dennis imagined brittle bones of corpses might were they somehow suddenly reanimated. A broadsheet from an ancient newspaper edition blew by the windshield like a ghost. The car grew chilly. He considered turning on the ignition for some heat and maybe a little rock n' roll from WJKP, but he'd been explicitly instructed to keep the car off.

He didn't know what to expect and kept flicking his gaze to the rearview mirror, searching for headlights approaching from the rear. The lane stayed quiet and dark. He hunched deeper into his jacket and waited.

When the fist rapped on his window he screamed, and then nearly again when a ghastly glowing face stared in at him. It belonged, of course, to Kodi, who'd tucked a flashlight beneath his chin, transforming his countenance into a leering gargoyle.

Dennis unrolled his window. "You nearly scared the life from me."

Kodi cracked a grin. "Come along, *mal'chik*. Time is short."

Dennis got out and followed Kodi into the withered cornstalks, making sure to keep close as the man had switched off the light to make the trip. He tried to keep track of their bearing, even looking up at the stars in hopes of discerning direction but found navigation through them fruitless. Something scurried through the stalks and into the night.

Dennis didn't know how long they'd walked—it could have been a mile or it could have been three—before finally the corn receded, giving way to a grassy strip of land. He could make out the blocky shape of a building nearby and wondered where exactly they were. He'd become completely disoriented.

"Follow," Kodi ordered and Dennis did. What choice did he have now? There'd be no way of finding the car again without guidance.

In the darkness, Kodi fumbled with a padlock and a hinge squeaked. Kodi opened a door and huddled into a small vestibule barely larger than a linen closet that smelled of pine. The keys rattled again and another lock snapped and then another. A second, much more substantial door swung wide and the pungent odor of fresh marijuana wafted out.

"Inside," Kodi said. Dennis did as told and his companion closed and locked the door behind them. Dennis stood blinking around in the absolute darkness inside and then clapped hands to his eyes when quadruple rows of white fluorescents buzzed on. They weren't alone. Someone else stood swaying nearby.

When his eyes had adjusted, Dennis was shocked to find himself staring at Zebulon, his dad's hired man. "Zebbo? What are you doing here?"

"Dennis?" Zeb said, as if questioning the existence of a higher power. He was drunk, any fool could see as much, but realization dawned on his face at the same moment it did on Dennis. "You oughtn't be here, Dennis. This is no place for a kid."

"I'm not a kid," Dennis said. "And besides, my dad is your boss."

"Not anymore," Zeb said.

"You gentlemen will be working together again," Kodi cut in. "Won't that be fun?"

"Does your old man know what you're up to?" Zeb asked. "It would pull his heart out, he knew you were here."

"He doesn't know and never will," Dennis said. "I'm here to work."

"Good attitude," Kodi said. "Allow me to show you around."

He stabbed a finger at Zeb's chest. "And you—this is the last time you show up intoxicated. I will not say it again."

"Okay," Zeb said and belched into his hand. "I'm sorry about that. It's just you caught me at a bad time."

"Next time I catch you like this it will be worse, comrade," Kodi said. "Now, down to business, as you say in America."

For the next forty-five minutes, Kodiak Aristov showed them how the operation worked. Where the plants were grown (in ten-gallon plastic buckets that allowed for drainage into aluminum troughs), how much light and water they needed, what type of soil to use for optimal growth, how the temperature control and exhaust systems worked, and two dozen other aspects Dennis would forget by morning. Zeb seemed to be listening through his liquor haze and even asked a few relevant questions which hadn't occurred to Dennis.

"But all of this is background," Kodi said. "This is merely to demonstrate where the product you sell will be coming from. You will rarely, if ever, need to concern yourself with the manufacturing portion of the operation, you understand, yes? You will be our chief distributors, our field lieutenants in the trenches."

Dennis decided he liked the sound of that. Field Lieutenant Dennis Milliard, seller of premium marijuana.

Kodi led them to a pair of folding chairs and ordered them to sit. For the next hour, he instructed them on how to sell. The words to say, who to approach (and who not to), where to make the transaction, prices per ounce, how to weigh the product (they would each be provided precise scales, the settings of which should never be altered), and what to do with the cash once it had been obtained. He went into great detail about this last, instilling in them the knowledge that those in his operation strictly controlled the amount of product released and always checked it against incoming capital.

"You do not want to, how do you say, skim off the top. Not with us, comrades."

Dennis and Zeb said they understood. Zeb, for his part, appeared far less drunk than he had at first. Dennis guessed all this must be a pretty big buzzkill, and he wondered who the others in this outfit were, these faceless "we's" and "us's."

"Now for the hard part," Kodi said. "We have let you into our inner circle, comrades. We have let you see our operation, have detailed it for you down to the letter. You must never reveal to anyone what you have learned here tonight. If you are caught, you must never mention my name or the location of this building. I do not believe I need to tell you what will happen if you do."

Dennis didn't want to know. He'd seen enough movies to know what happened to rats. And their families. The thought of his parents or siblings hurt because of his actions made him nauseous.

Zeb, though, seemed quite curious about the consequences. He leaned over his knees, hands dangling between them, eyes wide. "What'll happen?" he asked without a trace of irony.

Kodi told them what would happen. He went into the fine details before dismissing them. And before he finished, Dennis's nausea got the better of him and he puked between his Timberlands. No, he would never tell a soul about this operation. Not even if he fried in hell's hottest furnace for participating in it. He was all in now.

CHAPTER TWENTY-FIVE

Dennis faced neither suspension nor detention at school. In fact, Coach Dayton had slugged him playfully on the shoulder and said he had no hard feelings and would Dennis like to be reinstated to the team? Dennis agreed, unsure what to make of the sudden amnesty, but happy to accept it. If he had to guess, Kodi's outfit had something to do with it. Just how many people were connected to this thing anyway?

On Wednesday the 29th of October, two days after his education in the makeshift greenhouse, before he'd even found the guts to approach anyone with his new trade, someone approached him. Lorelai Lang slipped up to him at his locker and said, "I heard you might have something for sale today?"

He stared her down, surprised that the valedictorian would want to smoke drugs. "Um, yeah. Sure. Meet me in the band room after school."

Lori told him she would, her eyes sparkling green as bottle glass.

When he arrived, she was already waiting for him at the podium where Mr. Albertson conducted his classes. She twirled a baton lazily between her fingers, seeming completely at ease. When it came to the actual transaction, she took control, taking the correct amount of product and providing the correct amount of recompense. She'd done this before. In fact, she seemed an old hand at this. It surprised Dennis.

"Want to toke with me?" she asked.

"I don't smoke."

Lorelai laughed. "I never knew you were so square, Dennis Milliard. Your sister happens to love grass."

He felt his cheeks redden, but recovered quickly. "It's not

that I don't like it," he lied, "it's just that I don't like cutting into my profit margin." *Hannah smoked grass?*

This seemed to impress her. "A true entrepreneur," she said. "Well, don't worry Mr. Big Shot, this one's on me."

She led him by the hand to her banana-yellow Mustang and drove him to a spot deep in the backcountry where no houses existed. They smoked together there, Lori packing a porcelain bowl with enough for each of them. Dennis, for his part, didn't do too badly on his first outing. He thought he even managed to hide his inexperience from her. Either that or she hid her knowing better from him. Either way, he found the experience delightful—he'd heard sometimes people couldn't even get high their first time. That didn't apply to him, though. After three bowls he was high as the moon and twice as dreamy.

Lorelai took a hit, held it, then leaned over and locked her lips over Dennis's, exhaling smoke as she kissed him. He took it into his lungs, shocked, sure he'd cough it back into her face. But he didn't. When she let him breathe again, he exhaled it in a long stream feeling as if part of his lifeforce went with it. His thighs trembled.

When they finished savoring the moment, Lorelai said she'd drive him home since it was Hannah's day with the car. "What's my payment?" she wanted to know.

"I already gave you grass," he said, his voice sounding to his ears as though it was bouncing around inside a balloon.

"No, no, no, huh-uh," she said. "I *bought* that. What I want to know is how you're planning to pay me for a ride home?"

He started to dig in his pocket, but she pushed his hand away. "I don't want your money."

"What do you want?" he asked, his voice unspooling into the clouds. It sounded distant, childlike.

Lorelai slipped her blouse over her head. She wore no bra. It was the first time Dennis had seen a topless woman outside of Scott Beard's father's *Playboy* magazines. He nearly fainted.

"I want your *ass*, Dennis Milliard," she said, and had dragged him into the backseat.

As the last day of October dawned, Augie still hadn't told

Teresa about the voided distribution contract and he still hadn't been able to reach anyone at their office who could help him sort out what had happened. He called a lawyer and set up a consultation so he could start proceedings on getting this mess untangled.

Neither could he reach anyone at the Stone Dairy farm other than that minx Ursula who informed him her handsome hubby had gone out of town for a spell and would he, Augie, like to come by for coffee?

Augie had politely declined and then asked if he could speak to Old Dad.

"Michael took that old injun with him on his trip," she said.

"Who's running things?"

"Oh, Ben and Ed are handling things just fine, August," she said, her voice husky. "Are you sure you don't want to stop by and—"

"I appreciate the offer, ma'am, but I really can't. Please have Mike give me a holler as soon as he's home, all right?" He didn't wait for an answer before disconnecting. He paced his den for a time, then got his jacket and went out. Morning mist crept over the fields and road; he couldn't even see the store from his driveway for the gray-white shroud covering it.

Augie had no conscious idea where he was headed until he got there. The initial plan had been to drive around the county backroads for a spell because he did his best thinking behind the wheel. He rambled everywhere on those deserted roads, plotting, scheming, assimilating, and collating the data he'd collected into one mental logbook.

It seemed his troubles began when the First Lady of Ashford County had requested he close his prize attraction at the prime of his busy season. When he'd declined to do so, someone had been severely injured in it the very next day and the police had fabricated the tale of an unidentified murdered girl to go along with it, as if the boy who suffered the trauma hadn't been a tragic enough story. Augie would bet his bank account Al Engel knew the identity of the person who'd hurt Randy if he hadn't had a hand in orchestrating it himself. Al had gone as bad as a bushel of Jonamacs left to spoil in the sun.

Judge Fahrlander had handed down the decree to close the Milliard Country Store and all its attractions until the conclusion of the investigation, without reason to do so. Obviously J.F. was part of it, perhaps even co-ringmaster. Because Augie had become convinced Adeline Gable was the driving force behind everything which had transpired over the past two weeks. She had everyone in her considerable pocketbook. Sheriff Lisk alone seemed the only authority outside of it, but he could be bought at any time. Or was Paul Lisk one of those incorruptible law men immune to the power of bribery? Had Adeline even tried or had she been warned off by someone close to Paul—Fahrlander or Al himself? Maybe the good sheriff remained a thorn in the paw of those who made up the county's seedy underbelly. Maybe they had plans to eliminate him, in which case he should be warned. Augie decided he ought to pay Paul Lisk a visit and let him know of his findings, even if it meant risking charges of trespassing.

And dognapping, he thought. *Don't forget that.*

How could he forget that? Adeline Gable seemed to have gone insane—even more than she clearly was—with her dog missing. She'd taken out ads in the local papers and even into neighboring counties. She'd had reward posters plastered all over town ($500 for the safe return of Jontue, beloved companion and friend). Augie had even heard a radio spot on WJKP following the weather in which a clearly amused DJ had read the contents of the poster over the airwaves.

Right now that little Jontue was the only ace Augie held. He hoped it would be enough to trump the hand.

But Sheriff Lisk would have to wait. Augie wanted to consult another figure of authority, one he hoped could offer a fresh perspective and perhaps some sound advice. He parked the truck in the empty lot of St. Joseph's Catholic Church, got out, and stretched.

Careful, Augie. You could be stepping into a snake pit here, he thought because, really, who could he trust anymore outside of his family and Ray Safford? The Saffords attended St. Joe's, though, and Ray had always purported Father Francis Scudder to be a fair and righteous man, but he tempered his hope in this by knowing both Granny Adeline and the Lang family also worshipped here. Did Father Scudder hold enough influence over his flock that they would leave him out of their schemes? Augie had to believe it was true, but would remain vigilant in case he sensed it was not.

The wind stirred crisp leaves around the lot as Augie approached the building. He hoped St. Joe's main man would be on site today and wasn't disappointed as he stepped into the sanctuary.

Father Scudder seemed surprised to see him, but smiled warmly. A black overcoat had been cinched beneath his clerical collar. His head, utterly devoid of hair, reflected the mid-morning light streaming through the stained glass windows.

"Good day, August," he called and hurried up the aisle between pews to shake Augie's hand. "I'm afraid I've little time to chat unless you're here to give confession."

"I thought you had to be Catholic to do that," Augie said.

"Traditionally, yes, but for my friends, I'm known to make exceptions. And I'll never turn down the chance of converting you," he said with a wink.

"I just wanted to ask you something. I won't take up much of your time, Father."

"That's good, yes, very good. I have much to prepare for tonight. I'm playing Dracula in the Jaycee's haunted house and have much to do beforehand."

"*You* celebrate Halloween?"

Father Scudder laughed from deep in the barrel of his belly. "Of course, August, of course. All Hallows Eve was originally a holyday. I don't mind mixing it up with a little secular fun every once and again. Now tell me, what's on your mind?"

"I suppose you've heard about some of the happenings going on with my family?"

He clucked his tongue. "Certainly. I'm sorry to hear it, truly."

"Have you heard any gossip about it?"

"I can't say I put much stock in the grapevine, August," he said with a wave of his hand.

"But have you?"

"What are you after specifically?"

"I want to know the identity of the girl they found on my leased land. No one seems to know anything about it. Chief Engel is keeping tight-lipped."

"I'm sure I don't know anything about the poor child."

"No one's asked you to say anything for her? Perform a service, say a prayer over her? Anything like that?"

"That's a job Pastor Stanton from the Methodists up in Ashford usually handles, on the rare instance we have an unclaimed corpse."

Augie lowered his voice. "That's what I'm worried about, Father. I have a feeling there *is* no corpse."

Father Scudder looked aghast. "Why ever should you think that?"

Careful, Augie, that voice in the back of his brain warned. "Just a hunch, Father. No one can tell me anything. There's been nothing in the paper about her. Don't you find that at all odd?"

Scudder appeared more perplexed than ever. "Why, I'm certain I read something about it in the *Gazette*. Yes, I'm quite sure of it, a squib on the second page."

"Would you still have that paper lying around?" Augie asked, knowing the answer already. And knowing instantly where Scudder's allegiance lay.

"No, I'm sorry. I never keep newspapers. Fire hazard and all."

Augie tried to smile. "Fire hazard, sure. Well, thank you for your time, Father. Enjoy the haunted house tonight."

"Thank you, Mr. Milliard. You should bring your family to Mass. I'd be overjoyed to see you all."

"I'll think it over. Good day, Father," Augie said, turning to go. In the narthex, he turned back. "Maybe I'll take a walk over to the *Gazette* office, see if Saul has a stack of back issues I could skim. You recall which issue you saw the story in?"

Scudder touched his brow with one hand, squinting up at a window depicting the Last Supper. *Good acting, Padre.* "I'm sorry, I can't say that I do."

"Thanks again. You've been a big help," Augie said, then stepped out into the chill.

He knew he had to tell Teresa about the voided contract with Farmland, but he'd wait to see what the lawyer said on Monday. In the meantime, he'd try to keep everything under control. Try to keep it together.

Augie went to the store and to the back pantry. He hauled the door open and the little runt tried to get by him again, yipping and scraping. She'd messed the floor again, nowhere near the newspapers he'd laid down.

"You're a handful, you know that?" he told the dog. "But you're my Get Out of Jail Free card. Don't worry, you'll be home safe soon enough."

The store's telephone blared from the show room and Augie hurried to it, ensuring the pantry door closed behind him.

"Milliard Country Store," he said into the mouthpiece.

"Augie, it's Al," the Derby police chief said. He sounded out of breath and more than a little pissed off. Augie at first figured he'd ask what the hell he was doing operating the store against a court order. His second thought came sharp and quick: Al knew about the dog. Either one on their own would have been bad, but Augie never would have been prepared for what Al said next.

"We've got Dennis here at the station, Augie. He's under arrest for possession of marijuana with intent to deliver."

Augie's entire respiratory system seemed to lock down. He became aware of a high whistling deep in his brain, perhaps where that little voice that often whispered advice originated.

"Augie, do you understand what I said?" Engel asked.

"No," he replied, his voice a distant echo in his ears. "No, you'll have to repeat that, Al."

The police chief did, to the letter, but Augie still didn't believe him. Not until he got down to the police department and saw for himself.

Dennis looked like a caged rabbit, sitting alone in one of DPD's two cells. He stood up when he saw his father approaching down the ammonia-smelling hall.

"Dad, I—"

"Not a word," Augie breathed, too furious to speak.

Tears stood in his eldest child's eyes and Augie noted with something approaching black, blinding rage that the boy's lower lip quivered like a toddler's. He wanted to reach through the bars and slap the stupid look off his face.

Nathan Berryman, who'd accompanied Augie, unlocked the cell, looking embarrassed. He'd told them the chief had gone out on a call right before Augie had come to bail his son out. "I'll let you two talk in private," he said before retreating.

"What on God's green earth were you thinking?" Augie asked when he thought he could speak without his voice trembling.

"Dad, please—"

"Do you have any idea what you've done? *Do* you?"

"Daddy—"

"Our name, our reputation in this town … you've put it all on the line. You've risked our entire future. Do you have any fucking clue just how bad of a hole you've put us in?" Augie demanded, knowing full well Dennis had nothing to do with any of that. That was on Augie, but by Christ it felt good to lay blame someplace else. Let someone else shoulder the burden for a spell.

"Daddy, please listen to me," Dennis said.

"No, I don't think I will. You can say whatever you want to say to Judge Fahrlander. Come on out of there and get in the truck. I paid your bail out of your college fund. You can pay me back later, after you've found a real job."

Augie marched his son up the hall and out the door, stopping only long enough to accept an envelope of personal effects from Nathan. "Have Al call me the minute he gets in, would you?"

"Sure thing, Mr. Milliard."

"On second thought, scratch that," Augie said. "You going to be manning the desk for a time?"

"I'm here till four thirty. Chief wants all hands on deck for tonight, being Halloween and all, so he's closing the shop and putting us on patrol."

"Good. I'm going to call you in fifteen minutes."

"Me?"

"Just make sure you pick up, okay?"

"Okay, Mr. Milliard."

Augie got Dennis home and sent him straight to his room. They had the place to themselves—Teresa would be busy at the farmer's market and the other kids still had three hours before school let out for the weekend.

Augie closed his den door and called Nathan. "I need you to tell me exactly what happened, Nate. Can you do that?"

"Sure, Mr. Milliard. What I know, anyway. Chief was the one who apprehended the … Dennis. I only heard what he told me."

"Let me have it."

The way Nathan explained it, Dennis had tried to sell a dime bag to a kid under the bleachers on the football field and the kid had gone inside and called the police. Nathan had taken the call himself and had radioed out to Chief Engel, who'd been on patrol. Al had driven straight over to the school and spoken with the principal, Dr. Spieth, who'd called Dennis out of class and forced him to open his locker. Inside they'd found two pounds of marijuana.

"Two *pounds*?" Augie repeated, rubbing a temple.

"That's what the report says, Mr. Milliard. Got it right here in front of me." Augie thanked him and started to hang up but Nathan caught him before he could. "Mr. Milliard? There's something else."

"What is it, Nate?" Augie said. He'd already ended this conversation, his mind turning toward his son, but what the young officer said next snapped him back to full attention.

"You know how you said you didn't think there was a girl's body in the morgue? Well, there is now."

BOOK II

**Corn to Seed
The Lang Family
Winter**

CHAPTER TWENTY-SIX

Grant Lang cast a tall shadow. He watched it probe ahead of him as he came in from the barn, having come from parking one of his John Deere combines for the rest of the season. The harvest was complete and for as many acres as he kept, Lang took pride that they'd gotten it all in by the last day of October. He could lay off three of his hired men for the winter and welcome them back next spring, should they decide to return. What would they do with their time off? That was up to them; it meant no never mind to Grant.

When he reached the porch that wrapped around half the house, Grant turned to study the barren fields which stretched as far as his eye could see. In summer, you could stand in awe of the green oceans of corn. The Ear Empire, as Grant privately thought of it, with him sitting squarely on the throne. All the other area farmers were simply the encroaching peasantry, even the larger farms like the Stones, the Saffords, and those damned Milliards. Especially the larger farms. The smaller ones like the Averys, the Bensons, and the Shooks, well they barely mattered at all and soon would be swallowed up by the lovely green sea.

Sure, Adeline Gable would—and should—be seen as the reigning queen of Ashford County, if one wished to stick with the royalty analogy, but ol' Granny would be gone before long. An heir needed to be ready to step into her place and, by God and Jesus, Grant Lang would be that heir. Hell, Adeline hadn't grown more than a vegetable patch larger than a parking space on her land in better than a decade, ever since her lowlife husband Vance had gone the way of the Edsel. Why should she get to lord over everyone? Who gave her that power?

The United States Treasury, that's who. Vance had left

his widow upwards of $6.5 million if Grant's sources could be trusted. And they could, more often than not. That sum overtopped the Lang family worth by ... well, by quite a lot. Grant meant to close that gap as soon as humanly possible. Or inhumanly possible if it came to that—and the arrow certainly seemed to be pointing in that direction.

Trouble was, Ashford County had too damned much competition. It didn't matter that he had the corn market cornered, so to speak. What mattered was that these other impostors wasted so much land on their wares ... land which could be used for corn. If Grant had it in him, he'd buy them all out and see them exiled from the county. But he didn't have it in him. His checkbook ran only so deep. Sure, he'd enjoyed a bump—quite a big one, actually—when the Soviets started buying grain by the metric ton from the U.S. heartland. But how long would that last? Who could say? Get some bleeding heart Dem in the Oval Office and watch them drop an embargo on those Red Communists. It could happen, and probably *would* before long.

None of his rivalries were personal, with the Milliards being the exception. Ray Safford and his hogs? Grant understood that. Hogs fed people. Mikey Stone and his milk cows? Absolutely viable. In fact, he considered Mike as close to an ally as anyone. But the Milliards, though. They were another story altogether.

Apples? A tidy country store? Pumpkin patches? Fucking *corn mazes*? Who the hell did August III think he was? Milliard's old man would be rolling in his grave to see such land wasted for the trifle admission the family charged. It wasn't fair and it wasn't right. That land ought to be used for raising glorious golden corn. Corn *fed* people. It *fed* livestock. Corn *fed the whole goddamned planet* and Grant Lang felt it his personal responsibility to ensure the world was *fed*. In the deepest pocket of his brain, in a part that rarely saw the light of day, Grant Lang imagined his Ear Empire solving the terrible trouble of world hunger. He would truly be hailed a king and a hero if he could only *grow more corn*.

And now winter had arrived. Grant never paid attention to what the calendar said on that front. In his mind, winter started the day after the final ear had been harvested. Fall was over and he had a long, fruitful winter ahead of him.

Grant gave his slaughtered acres a final wistful look and then turned to go inside, weary but content with yet another successful harvest, and stepped into a house where feminine aromas intermingled like a permanent cloud of comfort that overhung his land. Zucchini bread, fresh from the oven, cooling on the countertop. A flowery perfume lingering in the hall, something new his wife Dinah had tried. The smell of womanhood blanketing his house, all day, every day.

Grant and Dinah had been blessed with a battalion of daughters, that's the way he thought about it. For years, they'd weathered the inevitable question from all sides: *When are you going to have a boy?* The answer, they now knew, was never. After their little Penny was born (well, not so little now—the sweetheart had started first grade last month), the doctors had informed them Dinah's womb had had enough. She could not carry another child.

Grant had worked to make sure she took no blame on herself. After all, it wasn't her fault. It was simply nature. Dinah went on for a time about God's plan and whatnot, something Grant despised. Yes, he believed in God, just not the same one Dinah did. Not the Catholic God, in other words, who Grant thought of as a cruel and vindictive son of a bitch. If there was anything good to take away from his wife's religious aspirations, it was that she did not espouse upon it the way poor ol' Ray Safford's crazy wife did. Ruth Safford made Grant shudder anytime she opened her thin lips these days. He wondered how the hell Ray lived with it and decided having brains as soft as Ray's maybe allowed him to absorb and discard such senseless Bible babble. Or, hell, maybe Ray didn't understand any of it in the first place.

With no member of his family in immediate evidence (they knew to leave him be for a spell on the final evening of harvest; besides, the young'uns probably were chasing about upstairs preparing to trick-or-treat downtown), Grant slipped into his office and closed the door. He tossed his FS Seed cap on his desk, scrubbed both hands through his snow-white hair, then opened the bottom drawer of his desk. The bottle of Glenlivet sparkled in the overhead light. For 364 nights of the year, Lang prided himself a staunch teetotaler.

But harvest ... harvest was another beast entirely.

He pulled out the bottle and uncapped it, not bothering with a glass. He never bothered with a glass.

The first swallow slapped him in the gut and then the face. Both warmed appreciably, combatting the chill of the late October air. Grant unbuttoned his jacket and picked up the phone.

When the dialed party answered on the second ring, Grant said, "Is it done?" He listened, then said, "Good. Excellent. Talk to you tomorrow."

He hung up and drank again, wincing. Someone knocked at the door, small, timid. Alexandra or Penny. "Who is it?" he called, stuffing the bottle away. Letting others see him drink was not an option, even his wife who knew of his annual ritual but had never actually witnessed it.

"Daddy? Are you busy?" Penny. His sweet Penelope Rose.

"Come on in, sugar plum. Tell me what's on your mind."

"Are you all right? Your cheeks are all red." Their youngest daughter came in dressed as a fairy princess.

"Fine, honey. A little windburned is all."

"Can you please pin the back of my gown? It keeps slipping."

Grant sighed. "Where's your mother?"

"In the potty."

"Give it here." He worked the pin in his thick, calloused fingers and succeeded in pricking the pad of a thumb. It took effort, but he held in the curse that wanted to burble out. When he had the pin set, he turned his pretty Penny around. "There. How's that now?"

She shifted her shoulders one way and the other, then gave him a smile and a hug. "Thanks, Daddy."

"You're welcome, sugar plum. You look beautiful."

Penny offered him a gap-toothed grin and scurried off. Grant toed the door closed. This time he locked it and switched off the light.

CHAPTER TWENTY-SEVEN

An hour later he pulled up the long, looping drive of the Gable house and parked behind Engel's cruiser. The façade stared him down, as it always did, looking stern and stoic in the dusk. Grant huffed a sigh and got out, relishing the biting breeze on his face. Early winter, for sure, and a long one at that. The *Farmer's Almanac* said otherwise, but Grant Lang could tell. He was never wrong when it came to predicting winter.

Porch boards creaked beneath his boots. A single glowing jack-o-lantern leered out the front window, lit by one of Adeline's hired men. Grant let himself in and made his way to the back dining room, past paintings in gilt frames and sundry statuary. The place, as always, smelled of furniture polish and some unidentifiable spice, like a museum.

The lady of the house sat at the head of the table, per custom, flanked on her right by the Derby police chief and an empty chair on the left. Grant took it without comment. The hired men stood with their hands folded at the back of the room, looking like a pair of wax sculptures in a spook house, also customary.

"You're late," Engel told him.

"Last day of harvest is always busy," Grant said, unnecessarily, because the cop knew as much.

"We need to talk about what happens next," the chief said.

Grant ignored him and instead addressed their hostess. "Any luck with Jontue?"

Adeline shook her head. Her eyes were red-rimmed; she'd been crying—something completely alien to the matriarch of Ashford County, at least in Grant Lang's experience. "She's dead, she has to be. My little girl couldn't survive on her own in the wild."

"Now, Mother, we can't think like that," one of the men in the back said.

Adeline didn't bother acknowledging him and said, almost to herself: "She's gone and I must find means to move on."

Grant cleared his throat and took the initiative. "That's right, Adeline. We must move on. We'll always remember Jontue for the sweet soul she was, but it's time to—"

Adeline cut him off in a voice so low but full of venom that Al Engel actually leaned away from her. "Don't you dare patronize me in my own house, Grant Lang. I'll have you cut out of the business so fast your eyes will roll."

Grant said: "My apologies, Adeline. I meant no offense." He thought: *You go on and try to cut me out, old woman, and I'll see you happily into your grave before your time.*

Al Engel shot him a glance that translated into *Watch yourself, buddy.*

Grant returned one that meant: *The old witch has lost her mind.* Aloud he said: "What about Mike? Where's he at on all this?"

"Mike's gone out of town for a spell," Al said.

"Where to?" Grant more demanded than asked. He didn't like not knowing things he ought to know.

"Hunting trip," he said. "Took his Indian with."

"Old Dad? Why in creation would he take that poor creature along?"

Al shrugged. "Maybe he figures the man doesn't have much longer, decided to treat him to one last rodeo. But more likely it's because that Indian's a hell of a tracker and can sniff out game like no one's business."

Adeline sat quiet in her chair, rocking slightly, staring ahead at the door. She seemed utterly uninterested in the conversation, distracted by the loss of a creature who couldn't have but a handful of months left in this world anyhow. Grant decided it was his burden to guide the train back onto the tracks.

"What's our next step?" he asked gently, but before anyone could answer the doorbell chimed. "We still intent on moving forward with—"

One of the men came forward from his post and Adeline

said, "I told you not to light that jack-o-lantern. Now we'll have kids looking for treats all night."

"I'll send them away," the manservant said and moved to the front of the house.

Grant thought of his youngest three girls running around town, pressing buzzers and hollering *Trick or treat!* Penny the princess, Alexandra the witch, and Nora as Maleficent, in what would undoubtedly be her dress-up finale as she would transform into that most dreaded of creature come January—the teenager. Lorelai and Bonnie, his eldest, would be attending a barn dance somewhere.

When Adeline's servant returned, though, he was not alone. Someone moved in the shadows behind him. There came a small snuffling and a quick yap and Adeline reacted instantly with tears of joy and relief.

"*Jontue!*" she cried. Grant had never heard her sound so elated. "Oh, dear, sweet, friend of my heart, you've come home!"

August Milliard stepped into the room, carrying the beastly little creature in his arms, stroking her head with the ball of one thumb. "Evening, Adeline. Look who I found scratching at my back door just now."

"Wheel me over," she ordered her man, slapping the wheelchair's armrest. Augie placed the shivering dog into her mistress's lap. Adeline covered the creature's face in kisses and accepted a few in return. Grant looked away in disgust.

"It's a miracle," Adeline told her guests. "God has seen fit to protect my precious Jontue and lead her back home again. It's an outright miracle." To her servant she said: "Get my checkbook. This man is owed a reward."

Augie held up his hands. "Adeline, please. Your happiness is my reward."

He's good, Grant thought, sensing the immediate shift in power. *He's too fucking good.*

"Nonsense, August. I owe you one thousand dollars and, by all the saints in heaven, you're going to take it."

"The reward was for five hundred, Mother," the goon leaning on the back wall said.

"Well, I'm *raising* it to a *thousand*," Adeline cried. "A thousand for my darling back safe is chicken feed, Milo, do you hear me? *Chicken feed.*"

Grant stared in open wonder. They'd been conspiring for months to destroy the Milliards financially and now the one who'd dreamt it up was *giving* their target a cool grand? And Milliard, the idiot, was trying to turn it down? The world made no sense, not a lick.

"I just wanted to drop by with my bundle of good news," Augie said. "Now I really must be on my way. Evening, Adeline. Al. Grant."

He vanished as fast as he'd come.

Adeline addressed the servant named Milo. "Put that check in the mail first thing in the morning."

"Yes, Mother."

Al appeared in deeper shock than anyone. "What are you doing, Adeline? What in the name of God are you *doing*?"

"August Milliard does not deserve our mistreatment. Neither does his family. They're good people. You ruin good people, you jeopardize your place at the Good Lord's table."

"I don't believe this," Grant said. The old woman's sanity had clearly toppled over like a poorly cobbled wall.

"It took August's act of kindness for me to see the error of our ways," she said.

"Mother, you can't be serious," the other guy—not Milo—said.

"I am, Curley. Call this off, Al. See the charges against August's boy are lifted. Make sure the voided distribution contract is reinstated. I'll talk to Fahrlander and get him to rescind the court order. Everything else proceeds according to plan."

Grant dropped a fist onto the table, shivering the grand silver candelabra centerpiece. "There are too many moving parts. Once you set a machine like this in motion, there's no stopping it. It could come back on the rest of us. We need that boy's charge to stick."

"He's got a point, Adeline," Al said. "We need Milliard under our thumb and his boy's conviction is key to that. Plus, Mike will want a say—"

"You children don't seem to understand something," Adeline said, a whisper of the venom returning to her voice. She rubbed her dog's ears obsessively and the creature licked its black lips in pure poochly pleasure. "It doesn't matter *what* you want. I may be a big fish in a small pond, by Christ, but this pond is *mine* and you're my minnows, dearies. After I'm gone you can split it up anyway you like, but until that day I fucking *own* Ashford County and you boys would do best to realize it."

That day may come sooner than you think, old woman, Grant thought blackly, rising and leaving the house without another word.

Al caught up with him at their cars. "She's going to get us all cooling our heals in county."

"What are you bellyaching for, Al? You're the law. You're untouchable."

"If you think that, you're a lot dumber than I ever took you for. I was this close to getting Paul in on it."

"Sheriff Lisk is a righteous man, Al. Just like that goddamned Milliard," Grant said. He took a step closer to the Derby police chief. "We need Milliard out of our way if we're going to have any measure of success."

"We ought to get him on board, consolidate power. The four of us against Granny, hell that's an even match. Work Lisk into it, we take over."

"Mike already tried talking to Augie. That man is incorruptible, Grant, anyone knows that. And Lisk is as lazy as he is righteous. All he wants to do is sit on his ass until Ashford County voters check the ballot boxes to retain him next election. And if they don't, I imagine he's just as content to retire to the Northwoods of Wisconsin and spend his remaining days in a rowboat pulling bluegill out of the lake." Al squinted at him. "You want to move ahead still? Without Granny's backing?"

"You heard her yourself, Chief. When she's gone, we can do what we want."

"That old woman's going to live to be a hundred. Maybe a hundred and twenty."

"I'm not waiting that long. Are you?"

"If we keep moving without her say-so she'll make our lives a living hell. I don't know about you, but she's got enough dirt on me to put me away until I'm her age."

Grant snorted, hard and humorless. "I guess you should've kept your nose clean, Al, or at least made sure she didn't find out about it."

"You know well as I no one can keep secrets from Granny. That ol' spider's got her webs spun everywhere. You're not so squeaky clean yourself, Lang. Remember the Chancellor incident?"

Grant squared his shoulders and lowered his voice. "You ever bring that up again and I'll bury you so deep in my back forty it'll take archeologists a thousand years to find your fossils."

Al reached for his service pistol but stopped short of gripping the butt. "Are you *threatening* me, you son of a bitch?"

"Pull that piece and see what happens," Grant said, as calm as a clam.

"I just might."

"No, you won't. Because it would spell the end for you and you damn well know it. Now get in your car and drive home before you do any real damage to yourself. I'm not afraid to go above your head and you know I will."

"Who, Judge Fahrlander? Don't make the mistake of thinking he's your friend, Lang. He goes to the highest bidder, and we all know who that is."

Grant sighed and held up his hands in resignation. "All right. Look, this is no good. We need solidarity, not segregation."

Al's hand relaxed at his side. "You got something in mind?"

"Let's meet at your office. Even harvested, these fields have ears."

They went.

CHAPTER TWENTY-EIGHT

No one ever came all the way out to the secluded Lang farm to beg for tricks or treats. Maybe once every half a decade or so some ambitious reveler dressed as a scarecrow or pirate would drag his poor mother all the way out, but as the clock ticked over to eight o'clock, it didn't seem to be in the cards this year. Dinah had taken the little ones on their usual route through town and Lori and Bonnie had gone to the barn dance where there would be taffy-pulling, apple-bobbing (no doubt supplied from the damned Milliard orchards), and a spiked punch bowl. Grant had sternly warned them away from that particular attraction.

He had the place to himself, which suited him fine. God knew he needed time away from all that femininity. Grant held memberships in the Tigers' Club and the Tramers' Club, both of which excluded women and minorities, and used one or the other to get away when time allowed. Both clubs featured weekly card tournaments and 15-cent draft beer on the weekends for his fellow members who imbibed.

Speaking of imbibing, the last day of harvest had not yet expired and so Grant allowed himself another go at the stash in his desk drawer. As he stole nips, he reviewed the conversation held in Al's office.

The plan would move forward. It had to. They were too far in now, too invested. They'd risked too much, Grant perhaps most of all, because he had a family to provide for. Al, hell, all he had was a century-old Cape Cod with the mortgage paid down and a monthly alimony check to his ex-wife in Omaha. So they'd decided to move forward without Adeline's backing or approval. Or her knowledge. Their movements from here on out would need to remain covert. Adeline Gable may have been a frail old woman in body, but her mind remained as sharp as her pocketbook ran deep.

It had shown signs of slippage tonight, though, what with all that hubbub over a stupid fucking dog who was both incontinent and blind. He had to hand it to Augie Milliard—within two minutes he had singlehandedly swayed Adeline's mind and the son of a bitch had done so by taking a page from Grant's book. And he was going to get *paid* for it. When had Augie snatched the little bitch? How had he gotten close enough to do it?

The key would be keeping Andrew Chalmers, the coroner, on their side. He thought he and Al could convince him. Drew could be bought a lot cheaper than Fahrlander and if money didn't work, they had other methods of persuasion. The bottom line was they needed Drew to cover them about the dead girl. And as he'd been long under Adeline's employ, that might become a conflict of interests.

Grant sat alone in the dark, sipping periodically, and staring out the window at the October evening. A car swept up the county road—what the Langs had always referred to as simply "the highway"—and out of sight. A minute later it came back the other way. It was the same vehicle, Grant saw, because one headlight shone a bit dimmer than its twin. Someone trolling for him tonight? Could Milliard be out looking for a little Halloween trick?

The car pulled up on the shoulder opposite the house and the headlights went out. Grant sat forward, setting the bottle aside. Oh, this appeared to be a trick of some type for sure, Milliard or not. The house would appear completely dark from the road, completely deserted. Perhaps this was some kids from Lori's class looking to TP the house or soap the windows of the school smart girl. Well, he'd put an end to it real fast.

Without turning on lights, Grant made his way out of his office, through the dining room, and to the gun cabinet situated near the front door. He selected a Remington .12 gauge and then stood to the left of the picture window, watching the front lawn. He almost hoped it was August Milliard. They could straighten things out man to man right now.

But the figure pacing up the long yard wasn't August Milliard. It was his son.

"What in the name of our sweet Christ are you doing here?" Grant asked, his voice slow and thick like spilled syrup. The boy jumped.

"Mr. Lang, I didn't see you there."

"Care to explain why you're creeping up on a man's house in the dead of night? On this night, no less? You aiming to get shot?"

"I'm sorry, sir. I came to see if—"

Grant knew the angle he wanted to play and he played it well. "See if my daughter was home? Coming to try to sell her a little herb, are you?"

Hesitation in the darkness. "No, sir. I don't—"

"I understand you got yourself busted with a couple pounds in your locker, that right?"

"Sir, please, I—"

"I don't want you anywhere near my house or anywhere near my daughters. Any of them, you understand me? What's that you kids say these days—you *dig*? I catch you sniffing around them, next time I'll load this thing. No drug dealer is going to corrupt my babies. *Comprende, amigo?*"

"Mr. Lang, I still want to work for you."

The directness of the boy's statement, the knowledge behind it, shook Grant. Who had spilled? Who in blue *fuck* had told this whelp of his involvement in the operation? Kodi? No, the skinny bastard was too smart for that. Russian, true, but smart enough to keep his red lips buttoned on confidential business matters. Grant went through the list of people who knew and trimmed it down to one: Nathan Berryman.

The young cop wasn't supposed to have known anything at all, but he'd walked in on Grant and his boss arguing over distribution methods and Al had cut him in on it. Part of it, anyway. Enough to know Grant had bankrolled some of the startup capital. They'd left out Adeline's contributions, but dumb as Berryman looked, he was likely sharp enough to connect the dots. Grant knew Al should never have let the stupid bastard in on it. And now look. The kid who'd been set up as the fall guy—had been the fall guy until his old man returned the fucking dog—was standing on his front lawn begging for a job. Maybe this could work out to Grant's advantage, but it would mean admitting his role in things. He rolled the dice and hoped it wasn't the alcohol clouding his judgment.

"Go pull your car up behind the garage and then step into my office, young man," he said.

Dennis Milliard was still there when Dinah brought home the younger kids and got them to bed. He shifted in his seat, but Grant waved a hand at him and poured him another finger of Glenlivet.

"Don't worry. They know better than to bug me when my office door's closed. Now, I want you to understand something. I'm willing to put you to work, but you need to be more careful."

"I will, Mr. Lang."

"You were busted with a hell of a lot of Mary Jane not ten hours ago."

"But Chief Engel said he could make that go away. It won't be on my record or anything. I watched him tear up the police report. He said my case would never see the courtroom. He told me he'd fix it so it looked like I was framed and that everyone would believe it because I'm one of those 'good Milliard kids.'"

Grant stiffened. "You talked to Al?"

"Yes, sir. He's the one who told me I ought to come see you. He told me to do it tonight."

So it hadn't been Berryman after all who'd let the cat out of the bag. Grant didn't like Al taking initiative like that without consulting him first. He'd have to speak with the chief about it. It might turn out to be a stroke of genius on the cop's part, but all of this was getting too messy, too slipshod. They had to either pull it together or shut it down entirely … and shutting down was not an option. Not with how much they'd invested already.

"All right, so let's go over it one more time," Grant said. "Who do you tell about your new job?"

"No one, sir."

"No one, that's correct. Not your brothers or sisters. Not

your buddies on the football team. Not your girlfriend. And, for the love of God, not your folks."

Dennis snorted. "No, sir. They'd send me away to the military if they knew. My dad already threatened to do it."

"We're going to send you somewhere far less pleasant if they find out," Grant said over the rim of his glass. "I don't mean to sound harsh, young man, but this is deadly serious business."

The grin dropped from Dennis's face. "Yes, sir. Kodi told me the same. I'm taking this serious as a stroke."

Grant clapped Dennis on the knee and took inhuman delight in the way the boy jumped. "Good boy. Yes, I think this partnership will work out fine. You'll be able to finish restoring that car I understand you're in love with. You'll be able to take your girl out to dinner at the nicest restaurant in Ashford—in Chicago, for that matter."

"I don't have a girlfriend, sir," Dennis said, finding his smile again. Good, the kid's confidence was sky high—that's what Grant wanted to see. A confident kid. A good salesman.

"Well, you ought to get yourself one, a good-looking lad like you. Now I think we've sewn up all the particulars. I want you to wait for Kodi to contact you with further information," Grant said, rising and extending a hand. "Here, let me see you out. Partner."

The boy shook on the deal, still grinning like an oaf.

CHAPTER TWENTY-NINE

Lorelai and Bonnie came home early from the party, the clock not yet touching 9:00. They had both nipped at a bottle of vodka Jimmy Donaldson had hidden and both tiptoed to the stairs to avoid detection. Bonnie had wanted to leave on account of feeling ill—Lorelai knew her younger sister had zero tolerance for alcohol based on the two or three times they'd filched some Glenlivet from their old man's office. Lorelai had wanted to leave because Dennis Milliard had been a no-show, which had disappointed her more deeply than she thought possible. Neither had noticed his car parked behind the garage.

"Someone's in there with Dad," Lori said as they crept past the closed office door.

"I don't care," Bonnie said. "I want to go to bed. I think I'm going to throw up."

"Well don't do it down here," Lorelai said and helped Bonnie to the upstairs bathroom—the one all the girls shared (which became a battleground most school mornings).

She left the poor kid to do what she had to do and laid out both of their nightgowns. Who could her father be talking to tonight? Chief Engel? The two had been spending an awful lot of time together, if the grapevine could be trusted. What were they up to? She knew her father had a healthy dose of distrust for the law; he claimed in fifteen years no one would be able to do anything except sit at home and watch television all night—and only state-controlled channels would be allowed, like they had in Red China, especially if they voted in a Democrat in the next election.

Curiosity overcame Lorelai and she stepped quietly downstairs again, avoiding the fifth riser, which creaked. She listened at the door to her father's office—a cardinal sin in their house, but the alcohol made her bold—and found herself shocked to hear Dennis Milliard's voice answering her father's queries. What was he doing here and with her father of all people? At least it explained his absence at the dance.

She'd envisioned Dennis coming often to their house, but it would be with a bouquet of flowers, not to converse with her old man. She couldn't quite make out what they said through the thick oak, but recognized the dynamic at once: superior and subordinate.

Had her father found out about Lorelai's seduction in her car? No; Dennis would be dead and buried by now. Her father always said if he caught any boy who'd "deflowered a daughter of mine" that boy would become fertilizer come spring. Oh, she knew he didn't mean it literally … at least she thought he didn't. Said boy would be in a world of hurt, though—that much she *did* know. So it if it wasn't the sex, what could it be? She wished she could hear them.

Lorelai stepped into the shadows and made her way upstairs again. She didn't want anyone to see her down here and if her mother detected alcohol on her breath, Lori's fate would be worse than if her father did. She had much to mull over tonight and decided sleep would come far distant, if it came at all.

When Grant finally showed his newest and youngest employee out, the house had settled again. He'd heard the older girls come home first, trying to mask the fact they'd taken some booze. They thought they were sneaky, but Grant knew. He could sense it, the way an animal senses poison in a spring. He didn't begrudge them their revelry. What high school kid didn't sneak a sip from time to time? His girls couldn't be goody-goodies every day.

Grant also heard when Dinah had come in with the younger girls, so he kept Dennis occupied until his wife had gotten them all off to bed, herself included. The last thing he wanted was for his daughters to know the boy was here. He saw the way they looked at him, all of them. Lori, certainly, but last time they'd attended a Devils football game, he'd caught Bon-Bon and Alex staring at the second-stringer in his customary position on the bench. Hadn't little Penny even mentioned how handsome Candace Milliard's brother was, eliciting giggles from the lot of them? And, Christ Almighty, *Nora* had even goggled at the young athlete and Grant had long since guessed his middle daughter would wind up munching rugs once she came of age.

When the house fell silent for the night, the host ushered his guest to the door. "No one knows you were here tonight, you understand, Dennis? Deny till you die."

"Yes, Mr. Lang. I was never here."

"Good boy. Now get home and get some rest. You've got a long week ahead of you."

"Yes, sir."

Lang watched as the mismatched headlights switched on and the car rolled away. He had August Milliard now. Oh, *by Christ*, did he have him now.

The invitation arrived on November 6th. Grant read it over before handing it to Dinah.

"What do you think?" she asked after skimming it.

"I think the old bat's up to something, that's what I think."

"She hasn't much longer in this world, she can't. Maybe she just wants everyone to get together. One last hurrah. I think it's sweet."

Grant had kept his wife in the dark about his recent business expansion, of course, so she couldn't know how odd Adeline Gable's Thanksgiving invitation showing up in their mailbox was.

"Well, we're going out of town to your sister's place so we'll have to politely decline," he said.

"No, look. It's for the Sunday after. Surely Adeline realizes we'd have plans already." Dinah read the invitation again. "I wonder if the Milliards got an invitation, what with all the trouble they're going through."

"I'd place a steep wager they did," Grant said. He didn't like the idea of attending any dinner at the Gable farm, Thanksgiving or not. After what the goddamn biddy had pulled, it wouldn't make him weep if the next time he saw her it was in a casket.

"Well, in any case, I'll send our regrets in the morning."

"We should go," Dinah said.

"Why on earth would we do something foolish like that? We'll already be eating the leftovers Delia sends home with us until Christmas."

"We ought to be respectful, Grant. She's probably lonely."

Grant thought about the stupid fucking cairn terrier and heaved a sigh. "You're probably right, Di. Okay, we'll go."

In truth, this could be an enormous opportunity, a way to gauge allegiances and maybe forge new ones, depending on who'd be attending. Which, if he knew Adeline, would be every name family in the county. He imagined upward of a hundred people in attendance. Rumor had it the Gables threw dinner parties of epic proportions in their heyday. Best case scenario: a dinner party could be a good thing for him, a means of gathering intelligence, and at worst it would merely be another holiday headache. He also saw an opportunity, an opening he might not again get.

The idea grew on him over the next few weeks and by the time Sunday, November 30th arrived, Grant Lang couldn't get tucked into his suit fast enough.

CHAPTER THIRTY

The kids didn't want to go (except Alexandra, who might have only been a third of the way into her fourth-grade year but had the appetite of a varsity football player and would never look away from a turkey dinner), but Grant insisted. The invitation had been for the entire family and, by God, they'd every damn one of them go and pay respect.

They took the pickup with the kids riding in the bed as Adeline's place stood four miles south of their farm. A tray of Dinah's deviled eggs rested on the bench between the adults, carefully covered with plastic wrap. The recipe had been handed down through the generations in her family and she guarded it obsessively (the secret, for those in the know, was a dose of dill pickle juice stirred into the filling). Now, as she set a steadying hand on her precious eggs so they wouldn't slip off onto the floor, she fussed that the girls' good clothes would be covered in road dust.

"They'll be fine, my dear. Trust your old guy." Grant himself felt like clicking his heels. Today would be one of education, one of testing old waters and perhaps a few new waters. If nothing else, he looked at it as a free gourmet meal at the finest house in the county.

When they pulled in, Grant picked out the Milliard station wagon at once. It stood parked at the head of the drive, the first to arrive. Behind it rested Mike Stone's F-150, followed by five cars he didn't recognize. No sign of Al Engel or the Safford brood, but they had time yet.

Grant rushed his family up to the wrap-around porch and leaned on the bell. They heard it chime from deep in the house. A tasteful wicker wreath loaded with all the wealth of a horn o' plenty faced them down, a gentle breeze rocking it on its hook.

"Gee, this place looks like a museum," Bonnie said, fidgeting with the bow in her hair and staring around at the Ionic columns with their scrolled tops supporting the overhang.

Penny coughed into her hand and Nora appeared utterly miserable in a powder blue polka-dot frock. Lorelai looked like a member of some Old World aristocracy, going so far as to have slipped on delicate white gloves for the occasion. Alexandra merely looked hungry in her navy and white Pinafore.

Grant glanced them over. "Best behavior, girls, or you'll feel my belt across your backsides when we get home."

No one took the threat particularly seriously; they all knew in order for the belt to come off, the offense would need to be of a particularly harsh nature and the last time it had happened was in spring of '72 when Bonnie had thrown a basketball in the house which pulverized an heirloom urn.

One of the manservants, dressed in tie and tails, opened the door. He reminded Grant of Lurch from the *Addams Family* programs. He thought if the guy uttered the words *You raaang?* he might explode into mad laughter.

"Welcome," he said, sounding anything but welcoming (and thankfully nothing like Lurch). "Please follow."

The big guy led them deep into the house, past doors which stood closed against them but which Grant found familiar. He wondered, not for the first time, what secrets lay behind them.

The corridor opened into the great hall where a long table had been decked out in all the trimmings, anchored by a vast cornucopia overspilling with abundant autumnal delights. On the other side of the chamber a fire crackled on an enormous marble hearth. Grant had never seen so much as an ember on the grate, but right now the flame seemed eternal. Like some Greek torch left burning through a wide gulf of eons.

"In the parlor," the servant said with as much emotion as a haystack.

"Thank you," Grant said, patting the behemoth on one meaty shoulder. "We can find our way."

"Daddy, my neck's itching," Penny whined. Grant nearly swatted her snout, but knew it would only make her whimper.

He couldn't have whimpering here, not now. He had an impression to make.

He led his brood into the main parlor of the Gable estate (the house boasted three of them), an open atrium with slanted skylights, which allowed a clear view of the overcast November sky, and made his presence known.

"Adeline," he boomed, ignoring the looks it garnered. He threw his arms into open embrace. August Milliard milled on the periphery, he noted, Pepsi Cola in hand, speaking with Ursula Stone, and pointedly ignoring the arrival of the Langs. "We're so pleased to attend such a wonderful event."

"It wouldn't have been the same without you, Grant," Adeline said, slapping the arm of her wheelchair to instruct her man to move her closer. Her cairn terrier rested in her lap, looking dead, and Grant found himself wishing it was. Granny's hair had been curled and pinned against her scalp in waves. If the coif was meant to be stylish, such a measure eluded the Lang patriarch.

He ducked to embrace her and as he did, whispered in her ear: "There's a matter I'd hoped to speak with you about alone."

Adeline patted his shoulder and whispered in return, "Of course, Grant. Right after dinner, you may meet me in the back parlor."

Grant drew away and allowed the rest of his brood to offer their respects to their hostess while he surveyed the room. Mike Stone gave him a nod and a lift of his glass, which sported a pair of cocktail olives impaled on a toothpick—the dairyman had gotten an early start, it appeared. Grant answered him with a thrust of his chin. Larry Avery, a small-time farmer Grant had leased a handful of acres to in '71 and who wouldn't last the decade in his current situation waved heartily. Bert Spall, primarily a soy bean man, horded a plate loaded with mixed nuts, popping a fistful into his maw every few seconds and washing them down with a stein of ale. God, why had Adeline seen fit to invite the rabble?

Father Francis Scudder pumped his hand, whispering some platitude Grant promptly forgot and Sydney Rubek Jr., MD, offered to fetch him a beer, which Grant declined. The Bensons and the Shooks milled together—fitting for middling farmers as they were.

No sign of Al Engel, which suited Grant fine. He imagined the chief of police sitting in his cruiser in some turnout beyond the town limits, aiming his speed gun at holiday travelers taking a drive through scenic Ashford County. The thought made him chuckle.

August Milliard remained at the long mahogany bar which dominated the east end of the room. He sipped soda and picked at hors d'oeurves, while trying hard to ignore Grant. The rest of his clan, those spoiled rotten apple-brats, loitered at points around the room. He picked out Dennis reposed on one of the many sofas, a plate loaded with relish-tray fare balanced on his knees. The boy caught Grant's gaze and looked quickly away. He followed the rules and acted as though his boss did not exist. Good lad. And good salesman. Over the past month, the kid had hauled in the highest profit margin among the team of distributors. Much better than that Zebulon, who'd become something of a liability with his inclination to spend his wages at the local watering hole rather than on a sensible new wardrobe or perhaps a pair of shoes which weren't rotting off his feet. Ol' Zeb would bear close watching, to be sure.

A hand touched his elbow and he turned to find Teresa Milliard smiling at him. "Hello, Grant," she said.

"Teresa, it's a pleasure. Been far too long and I take the blame for that," he said, offering his own wolfish grin.

"Nonsense. We all ought to make more time to visit."

"You're correct on that count," Grant said, thinking his acting ought to garner an Academy Award. "Say, how's your girl? The one who took ill?"

"Susie's doing fine. Full recovery. A bit behind in her schoolwork, but she'll catch up. She's been staying after school to finish it."

"Now that's what I like to hear," Grant said. "None of the others got sick, I hope?" Of course, he already knew they hadn't through Dennis, but you had to keep the nice-guy façade firmly in place with these people.

"No, thank God. I insisted August take them for their shots."

"Wise woman," he said, his eyes boring into the back of her husband's skull like awls.

The Milliard matriarch said: "Listen, is Dinah around? I found a recipe for a crockpot roast I think she'll love."

"You'll find my better half speaking with the lady of the house," Grant said, cocking his finger like a pistol.

Teresa thanked him and wound her way toward the table. Another man might have taken the opportunity to admire Madame Milliard's shapely derriere, but Grant Lang wasn't like other men. Usually. The gentler sex barely warranted a whit of his time these days. He had sowed his wild oats, certainly, and had married Dinah for an equal mixture of her intelligence, her daddy's gracious dowry, and her child-bearing hips. He loved his family, but in a detached, distracted way. Grant understood the importance of descendants. He understood the need for progeny. And damned if his genes weren't destined for greatness if not now, then someplace down the road. Like the corn he grew, his superior genetics required care and cultivation. They *deserved* it.

"Ahoy, everybody!" a voice called. Grant did not need to look to know that pork-brained Ray Safford had arrived, but he did his due diligence and waved. Had Ray actually used *ahoy* by way of greeting? *Holy Jesus.*

Ray's bulk took up most of the door frame and completely blocked from view the rest of his small family. He came forward like a cork out of the bottle and let them squeeze past him. The girl led the charge, that pale tenderling, Rachel. She made for the farthest possible corner and planted herself in a folding chair there as if someone had just told her Christmas got canceled.

The elder boy came next, the gaunt and silent Caleb who Lori had reported sat alone in the high school cafeteria and only ever picked at his food; she claimed to have never actually seen him eat, like he might be some kind of vampire. Looking at him now, Grant didn't figure that assessment too far off the mark. Something about the boy raised the hairs on his neck as Grant watched him traverse the length of the room to exit into a corridor at the far end. He didn't figure Granny's goons would let him get too far into the house proper without turning him back.

Ruth Safford came last, shoveling the younger son, the idiot, before her. Samuel surely got his father's brains but was blessed with his mother's looks. For beneath that head of silky curls that stretched down clear to her slender waist, true beauty existed. If she put on lipstick and a touch of rouge, Ruth Safford was about as beautiful a woman as Grant had ever seen—the only one, truthfully, who'd ever made him look twice at another woman. He'd seen her fully made up only once, before Jesus had gotten into her, a gorgeous blushing debutante at a barn dance. He'd actually asked her to join him for a country-flavored jig 'n reel, which she'd obliged him. Afterward he'd gotten her a punch from the spiked bowl on the table and—

"Why, *hello*, Grant," Ray thundered, clapping him on the back and shattering his reverie. The pig farmer had taken off his shoddy topcoat and stood there in a white shirt with an honest-to-Christ detachable collar, the edge of which was stained yellow from perspiration. Its wearer stood pink-jowled and sweating, like one of his beasts.

"Raymond, my friend, you look the picture of sophistication today," Grant said. "I was starting to wonder if you wouldn't make it."

"Double service at St. Joe's," Ray said, glancing around conspiratorially. "Ruthie likes to go as often as possible this time of year, prepare for the Advent."

"Not a bad idea," Grant replied, thinking how much Ruth disdained being called *Ruthie*. "Better safe than sorry."

"Your attention, please," Adeline called from her space in the center of the room and Grant realized with something approaching an epiphany how spiderlike she actually looked now, a spindly old widow with all her little cooties caught in her web. He resisted the urge to shudder. "It appears as though we have a full house today and for that I am grateful. I give thanks that you all took time out of your busy schedules to share this day with a lonely old lady. Bless you all. Now, I'd like to give a brief itinerary of what I've planned, if you've got the patience to hear me out."

This was met with murmurs of affirmation and as Grant stood listening, he also observed. He watched Adeline unspool her agenda. He watched her hired men standing quietly behind her like prison guards. He watched the other farmers of the county, both big and small, as they paid full respectful attention to the Queen of Ashford. He watched his family in the various places they'd fetched up, none of them, thank God, near his new employee, the Milliard boy. Friends and foes, foes and friends.

What a tangled web we weave, he thought, *and how delicate it is beneath the winds of change.*

CHAPTER THIRTY-ONE

A fter Adeline said Grace, a surprisingly moving benediction which brought Ruth Safford to tears, Lorelai sat through dinner in a state of discomfort. She'd been relegated to one of the six card tables in orbit around the main dinner table, but unfortunately not at the one with Dennis Milliard.

He hadn't so much as spoken a word to her in the past month. Something had happened, she just didn't know what. He wouldn't even sell her grass now—she had to go to Kodi to get high. Kodi never wanted money, though. He wanted her body as payment. Jesus, she had been stupid to do it with him even once. It had been a mistake and now it seemed like she was paying for it. Had Dennis found out about her and Kodi? Had Hannah told him? Is that why he wouldn't look at her now? She should have asked before now, but Lori had held out hope the problem would self-correct. It hadn't.

She leaned toward Hannah and whispered: "What's up with your brother?"

Hannah stopped chewing her asparagus and looked around. "Who, Denny? He seems fine to me."

"He's been acting strange since Halloween."

"Sweetie, I've got news for you. He always acts strange. He's a boy, isn't he?"

Lorelai scanned the room again and this time caught Rachel Safford staring at her. "That creep is looking at me. Uck."

"Who?"

"Rachel. She makes my skin crawl. Gracie Shelton told me she saw her reading her Bible outside after lunch."

"What's wrong with that?"

"Dope, haven't you ever heard of separation of church and state?"

"I think it's sweet that she has such a personal relationship with God. Besides, Susie's pals with her. You don't think Susie would hang around with creeps, do you?"

Lorelai rolled her eyes. "I dunno. Susie's a little creepy on her own."

Hannah laughed and swatted Lori's arm. "That's mean, but you've got a point."

"Anyway, will you find out why Dennis isn't talking to me? It's driving me nuts."

"You ask him. I'm sick of being your messenger."

Lorelai sighed. "You're right. I'll corner him sometime after dinner and make him talk."

"You sound like a KGB agent."

"Zat ees correct, babushka," Lorelai said in a passable Russian accent. "I haff ways uff makeen heem tok."

Hannah giggled, then leaned close. "Just make sure those ways don't involve taking off your clothes."

It was Lorelai's turn to swat Hannah. "Don't be disgusting," she said, but thought: *Oh, H, if you only knew. Would we still be friends? Did I make the biggest mistake of my life?*

Chances were good if Dennis hadn't told anyone about their tryst in her Mustang by now he never would. He'd certainly seemed willing enough at the time, but maybe he'd changed his mind about her. Maybe she'd done something wrong. Or maybe he was ashamed of his performance—she didn't know for certain if he had been a virgin, but all signs pointed in that direction. She wanted badly to speak with him, but had spent the past three weeks mulling a way to broach it.

Well, today she'd do it. She thought she had figured a way and hoped he'd be receptive to it. Lorelai wiped her lips with her linen napkin and then dropped it over her plate, watching her one-time lover as he polished off his mashed potatoes. She still felt Rachel's gaze burning into her, but ignored it. The little freak could go fuck herself, for all Lori cared.

"I think I should ask Caleb out," Hannah said from beside her. The young man had situated himself on the floor, his plate balanced on his knees, untouched. "He's so darned cute."

"Yeah, sure, go for it," Lori said absently. She still thought Caleb Safford an even bigger freak than his younger sister, but if it would make H happy, she'd support it. But H's relationships didn't concern her at the moment. Lorelai wanted to unlock the mystery of Dennis Milliard. Part of her, in the deepest, most secret cavern of her heart, imagined them married one day. They would have a farm of their own, with horses and maybe some sheep, and a bunch of kids. Six, say. Yes, six. A nice, even number. They would spend Thanksgivings and Christmases and birthdays together and she would get to see Hannah on each and every one. A perfect life, that's how she thought about it.

But first she needed to get him to talk to her. Lorelai dug around in her purse until she found an empty Big Red wrapper and a blue Bic ballpoint. She scrawled a note on the paper side of the foil, folded it, and asked Hannah to take it to her brother.

"Take it to him yourself," Hannah said. "I'm not finished eating."

"Please? I won't ask you for another favor for as long as I live."

Hannah groaned and pushed her chair back, snatching up the wrapper and a salt cellar. "I don't suppose I get to read it?"

"Not if you're my best friend."

Hannah rolled her eyes, stepped around the main table, and dropped the wrapper in her brother's lap while pretending to deliver the salt to him. From her spot, Lori could hear him say, "Hey, we already have salt over here."

Hannah whispered something to him and his eyes widened as he nonchalantly felt around his crotch for the dropped wrapper. He unfolded it beneath the table, read its brief note, then looked directly into Lorelai's eyes. Some emotion she couldn't translate at first shone in them before he dropped his gaze to his plate. It took her only as long as it took Hannah to return to the table to determine what it had been.

Fear. Dennis Milliard was afraid.

After dinner, as fine a meal as any Grant had enjoyed in his four and a half decades on the planet, he slipped out of the dining hall with a murmured excuse and found Adeline awaiting him in the back parlor. Jontue lay snoozing in her lap.

"I hope you're not wasting both of our time," she said when he had closed the door behind him.

"I hope not either," he said. "I have something I'd like to run past you."

"I'll hear it," she said. "But if you breathe one word against Augie Milliard, I won't take it kindly. And I won't forget it."

Milliard must be a fucking genius, Grant thought. *She's eating out of his hand.*

He said, "It's got nothing to do with him." Grant spoke for ten minutes, outlining his plan to bring more money into the county and, more specifically, into Adeline Gable's purse. He wanted, starting next summer, to begin an annual event he'd dubbed Corn Fest. It would be a weeklong celebration including a small carnival, live country music acts, water balloon wars, tractor pulls, and of course lots of roasted corn on the cob.

When he finished, Adeline sat forward in her wheelchair, her insectile eyes boring into his. A light coat of sweat had broken on his brow during his exposition and he swiped it away self-consciously.

"We don't want to reach a saturation point here in our little burg. It will piss off other municipalities around Ashford to have so much ... *cheer* funneled our way. We must share. And we already have an Apple Festival," she said.

"That's the beauty of it. We'll hold it in a more centralized locale. Say, Murdoch instead of all the way down here so people can come right in off the main highway. We'll get triple the attendance than the Apple Festival ever saw. And the Apple Festival, hell, after what happened this year? Won't anyone show up ever again for it."

"It will be forgotten come next October."

"I'm not so sure, Adeline. From what I've been told, no one turned up at the Country Store after word spread about the dead girl and wounded boy. Even without the court order, no one wanted to show his face there. People are scared of it now. These bumpkins are a superstitious lot, believing in ghosts, ghouls, and boogeymen."

Adeline tapped the arm of her chair with one long, yellow nail. She fumbled her cigarette case out of a side pouch and lit a Pall Mall. "How much revenue do you suppose such an event would bring in?"

Grant spread his hands. "Potentially? Limitless. And the timing couldn't be better. If we start next summer, we can double up with the Bicentennial. Throw up some stars and stripes bunting and have the high school orchestra play 'The 1812 Overture' in the band shell? Folks'll turn out in droves." He paused, cleared his throat. "And it could provide a perfect funnel for our other business, not to mention a boost in revenue with our top salesmen working the crowds."

The dog raised its head and stared at him—or at least he thought it did; he couldn't be sure with the fur hanging over its eyes—before resettling its beastly little head in its mistress's lap. Adeline scratched its scruff absently.

"Need I remind you about the disastrous hippie concert you had a hand in setting up back in sixty-eight?"

Grant set his jaw. He knew she was only bringing that doomed event up as a power play to maintain dominance; Granny was as aware as anyone how Grant felt about hippies and their music in general. It had been Grant's cousin visiting from out of state who'd forced his hand on that matter and who'd then used the event as a template to help establish the now-famous Woodstock concert a year later in 1969, having worked out all the kinks here in the sticks.

He said, "You're not going to make me dignify that with a response, are you?"

"Are we talking the usual split on the proceeds?" Adeline asked at length.

"Naturally."

"I'll need to run it by the Murdoch village council for approval. As a formality, of course. And you'll need to submit all the proper paperwork, take it through all the right channels."

Grant relaxed. It would happen, he knew now. The old spidery witch had needed to appear reluctant at first as a means of control. Corn Fest would be the new Apple Festival and the fountain of wealth would overflow. Why hadn't he thought of it sooner?

Adeline said, "Did I ever tell you you're a genius, Grant?"

"Thank you, Adeline. I think this will work out for all interested parties."

"What about the Milliards?"

"They're free to continue their event, should people still wish to attend."

"You don't think your Corn Fest will cut into their attendance?" she asked, watching him closely now.

"I shouldn't suppose so. Corn Fest will fall a good twelve weeks before their busy season ramps up. Assuming there *is* another busy season for them."

Adeline drew on her cigarette and gusted blue smoke skyward. "Then you have my blessing."

Grant stooped and took one of her hands in his. It felt cold and papery and downright revolting, but he didn't let it outwardly disturb him. She'd agreed. Had she not, he had an envelope of powdered potassium he had planned to slip into one of her pill bottles in her master bathroom. Now he didn't have to commit murder. At least not today.

"Thank you, Adeline. You won't regret it, I assure you."

"Let's go back," she said. "I'll have dessert brought out."

CHAPTER THIRTY-TWO

B efore they served dessert, Mike Stone went out to the back terrace for a smoke. Grant needed to speak with him, so he took the opportunity to follow the dairyman out. They had the entire back lawn to themselves and Grant noticed how barren it looked with all the outdoor furniture stored away for the winter. The boughs of the firs bordering the property danced with cardinals. Wisps of clouds white as cotton scudded along the leaden sky.

Mike glanced up at him as he struck his pipe alight, balancing his whiskey tonic on the rail. During their years of acquaintance, Grant had known Stone to be a Black Label beer man and he nodded at the glass.

"Straying from the usual?"

"When the booze is free, I mix my drinks off the top shelf," Mike replied. "You talk to Al?"

"T'other day."

"He handle Augie?"

"Said he did. Much as he could, at any rate. Stopped him from sniffing around the cabin, told him it was private property. We posted some No Trespassing signs for good measure."

Mike nodded. "That's good. That's real good. His boy still working out all right?"

"Best salesman we got. He's even edging Kodi out, expanding his territory. Been taking it on the road with his football team, selling at other schools in the conference. Those teenagers, they can toke. So can Coach Dayton."

They shared a laugh, then Mike said, "What about the dead girl? Augie still nosing around that?"

"Al put him off that too, best he could. Made up some

bullshit story and Augie bought it."

"So he's not a problem anymore?" Mike asked, blowing smoke.

"Not unless he finds out his kid's dealing dope. Nearly sent the lad to boot camp after bailing him out of jail."

"Did you impress upon the boy the importance that his old man never find out?"

"Duly."

Mike nodded again. "That sets my mind at ease. And Zeb? How's he doing?"

Grant sighed. "He drinks up all his earnings, but how he spends his money isn't any business of mine. He's got the market cornered on the barflies and bowlers."

"Can't imagine that's a very big market."

"It's not, but he's trying. Chipping away. His biggest regulars are them coon cabbage farmers out near Sommerville. Augie tried to hire him back to clean up the orchard, get it ready for winter, but Zeb turned him down. The less time they spend chatting the better."

Mike grunted, noncommittal.

Grant said, "What about you? Did Old Dad deliver?"

"All aces. His man had the new product waiting."

"And this is true Indian stuff, like peyote or something?"

"Not peyote. But Grant, this stuff is going to blow our clients' minds. It hits like a shotgun blast, bam. You don't just see stars, you see other fucking galaxies. Other dimensions. Hell, you see *God*. I don't know the secret ingredient and I don't want to know."

Grant grinned. He couldn't help it. "I'll have Kodi set up a training session for our new recruits, get them up to snuff on the stuff."

The door opened and Ursula Stone stepped out, drawing a package of Vantage cigarettes one-handed from a tiny sparkling purse slung over a shoulder. Its strap ran between her breasts, accentuating them. Her other hand gripped a cocktail. The young woman's caramel-colored hair hung in loose ringlets around her shoulders and her makeup had been tartly applied. She looked less like a hippie and more like a hooker, to Grant's eye. "You boys don't mind if I join you, do you? Y'all look lonely out here."

"Sweetheart, it's cold," Mike said, eyeing her nipples poking through the fabric of her flower power dress. "You ought to go back in."

"Granny doesn't like smoking in her house." More accurately, Grant thought, she doesn't like painted young tartlets smoking in her house.

"You shouldn't call her that," Mike said. "This house has ears."

Ursula waved this away. "Old witch can't hear anyhow. What're y'all talking about out here? Looks serious."

"I was telling your happy hubby about our bountiful harvest," Grant said.

Ursula flapped the hand holding the smoke. "Boring, boring, boring. All you guys ever talk about is farming. This is a party, so let's *party*." She took a gulp of whatever indulgence the bartender had concocted her, no doubt tipping him nothing more than a blown kiss.

Ray Safford figured it a good time to stick is head out of the French doors and holler, "Hey, fellas, the pies are on!" He blinked in owlish fashion at the trio on the terrace, the clay block of his brain processing each identity individually. When he came to Ursula, he grew sheepish. "Oh, hello there, ma'am."

Ursula laughed. "See, you old coots? Here's a man who knows how to have fun," she said, striding to him and slipping an arm through his.

Ray glanced doubtfully at Mike, but when the husband made no protest, allowed Ursula to lead him back inside. Toward pie, presumably.

"If I doubted he'd blow an embolism if she slid a hand up his thigh, I'd feed him to his own swine," Mike said and both men laughed. "I had half a mind to stick her at the kids' tables, tell you what."

"Come on, buddy, let's go get some of that pie," the corn farmer said.

"We done here then?" Mike asked, sipping from his drink.

Grant waved a hand. "It's a holiday. Let's make merry. We can talk shop later."

Mike pitched his smoke into the grass, belched agreeably, and followed his business partner indoors.

Lorelai didn't stick around for dessert. She made an excuse about finding a bathroom and slipped up the corridor. She found Dennis on the back terrace, as she'd asked, and felt a relief so profound it presented as a palpable taste on her tongue. When he saw her, the brief flash of fear she'd recognized from dinner returned.

"We can't stay here," he said.

"Why not?"

"It's too open. Your father and Mr. Stone just left. I met them on the way out."

"What are you afraid of, Dennis? Is it me? Did I do something wrong?"

The fear vanished and his face softened. "Lorelai, it isn't you. Is that what you think? It's not you, I promise."

She took his hand and he let her. "Then what is it?"

"Not here," he said and grasped her slender fingers firmly. "Follow me."

He led her behind one of the outbuildings on the edge of the property. Lorelai wondered what the old lady could possibly store in these high, wide hulks. Probably nothing more than antique tractors from the days when she and her husband ran the county. But tractors didn't matter. Nothing did, except for Dennis.

She made a mistake behind the building, though. Instead of talking, she tried to kiss him and he resisted, the only boy of the half a dozen she'd kissed who ever had.

"Jesus, does my breath smell or something?" she asked after he'd pulled away.

"No," he said. "It isn't that, Lori."

"What is it, then?" she demanded, suddenly furious. "Tell me why every other boy in the county would be happy to take me into his bed and you shove me away like I'm Medusa."

She watched him mull his answers, rejecting each, before finally choosing one that sounded truthful enough. "I promised your father."

Perplexed, she said, "You promised my *father*? Why?"

"I can't tell you that, Lori. He told me to leave you alone and I promised I would."

Her anger crystalized. "So you love him more than me, is that it? You one of those AC/DC guys? You like going both ways?"

She'd meant her jeers to spark something in him, some emotion—anger, even. Something to show he had any passion in him. But he only stared at her with that wooden expression. "I'm sorry," he said. "But I promised."

"*Fuck* promises," she said. "Dennis, I like you. A lot. I think … God, I can hardly say this. I think I may even love you."

Finally something glowed in his eyes. "You love me? You *love* me? You don't even know me, Lorelai."

"How can you say that?" she asked. "I practically grew up in your house. Hannah and I have been friends since we wore diapers. How can you say I don't *know* you?"

Dennis placed a palm on the sanded planks and lowered his head. "There are things no one knows about me, things no one can ever know. It would be dangerous. It would—"

"You think I don't know?" Lorelai asked. She took his hand in hers. "You think I don't know about what goes on out in the shed beyond the corn maze?"

His head snapped up.

She uttered a short, sharp laugh. "Is that what this is all about? Of course I know what goes on out there. I'm not stupid, Dennis. I've known almost since the start. What, do you think I'd narc about my dad's little side project? You think I'm crazy?"

"How do you know?" he asked, clearly bewildered.

"I connected the dots, that's all. My father isn't as stealthy as he thinks he is and I *am* the smartest kid in school, after all."

"You won't tell him, will you? He told me never to tell." Dennis's Adam's apple bobbed. "He made it very clear no one can know."

"You think I'd rat on my own father? I don't care how he makes his money." She wrinkled her nose. "I think it's kind of cool, you know? Kind of like he's a gangster or something. Kind of like you're a gangster, too."

She slipped her hand beneath his shirt and ran it up to his chest. This time he did not pull away. "I'm not a gangster," he whispered, but she snuffed his words with a kiss. He kissed her back, with passion. They missed dessert entirely.

CHAPTER THIRTY-THREE

Grant noticed his daughter's absence along with that of the Milliard boy in his employ and he filed the information away for later use. It could be nothing. Or it could be something. He'd look into it. For now, he had bigger bears to snare.

The kids had scattered, most of them finding the Gable house's recreation room if the distant click of pool sticks proved any indication.

Father Scudder had stayed only long enough to fill his plate twice, his wine glass three times, and to offer a parting benediction, in which he managed to get his words out only slightly slurred. Doc Rubek made some excuse about a house call before making Adeline promise she'd schedule a checkup soon. The dowager said she would, but Grant doubted the veracity of her statement. Honestly, who needed doctors at her age? Adeline had wisdom enough to know the answer to that.

"Another slice of pumpkin pie, sir?" one of the rosy-cheeked maids asked as she freshened his coffee. Grant wondered not for the first time today whether Granny had raided a local brothel to find the help—there were a couple underground places in the county if you knew where to look and the ladies certainly seemed comely enough.

"Not pumpkin, love. I'll take apple this time," he replied.

"Excellent choice, sir," the girl said and glided away to fetch it. No doubt its buttery crust would be full of Milliard apples and Grant took delight in the symbolism of biting into them. He glanced across the table at Augie, who currently sat between his wife and Ray Safford, though an informal game of musical chairs had begun after the formality of dinner. Any empty seat seemed an indication for a new party to open a tête-à-tête with whomever sat adjacent. Grant himself had not moved since returning from the patio. Nor had Mike Stone, who sat with his wife on one side pointedly ignoring him in favor of Larry Avery and with Adeline herself on the other, with whom he had engaged in close conversation. He noted Nora had positioned herself near Ursula and hung on every damn one of the witchy woman's words. That might have to be addressed at some point in the future; he would hate to have sired a country daughter who not only munched rugs but transformed into a bleeding heart hippie liberal to boot.

"Isn't it nice, dear? Having everyone together?" Dinah asked, touching his arm.

"It certainly is," Grant said, covering her hand with his and hoping the lie sounded natural. With his business concluded, he'd rather be just about anywhere else and that included under the staunch gaze of Dinah's elder sister Delia, who'd despised him since they day they met.

One of Adeline's hired men approached and whispered, "Mr. Lang, you're wanted on the telephone."

"I wonder who on earth that could be?" Dinah asked.

"Probably Kodi," Grant said, tossing his napkin aside. "I asked him to call here if Ned Swanson from the Farm Bureau rang the house."

"Since when did you let Kodi into the *house* when we're not home?"

Grant didn't bother answering. He knew the caller would not be Kodi because he didn't let Kodi in the house. Ever. The hands who lived on the premises stayed in the barracks out back of the corn crib and that included the young Soviet. Especially the young Soviet.

The guy led him into a back room that may have once served as Vance Gable's den—he could see faded places on the wall where his hunting trophies had hung—but had since been converted into a less-specialized space. A vase of lilacs perched on an end table. Funny thing to spend money on, flowers for a disused room.

Grant picked up the extension and then stared at the guy until he left. "This better be good," he told the mouthpiece.

Talking about potential illegalities didn't concern him on Adeline's phone; she had a private line.

"It's not good, not one bit," Al Engel said. "The girl's gone."

For a moment Grant had no idea what girl the police chief meant. "Who?"

"The girl. The girl, goddammit. The fucking Jane Doe you wanted for the sake of continuity. She's gone."

A searing wire blinked to life behind Grant's eyes and he closed them against it. He'd instructed Kodi to find and deliver a fresh female corpse to Andrew Chalmers, another long-term employee of Adeline's and a close ally. Granny had figured out having the county coroner under your thumb offered many advantages and one of them was manipulating death records.

"Don't tell me this, Al. Don't you tell me the dead girl's gone."

"She is," the cop said simply. "Went to drag the drawer out and the body wasn't there."

Eyes still squeezed shut, Grant said, "Care to explain how such a thing is possible, Chief?"

A bloated pause. "You're not suggesting I had something to do with it. I hope, for your sake, you're not suggesting something like that."

"No, no, of course not," Grant said. "I just want you to explain how a perfectly dead body could simply vanish out of your refrigerator."

"Now hang on a minute," Engel said. "First, she wasn't in my anything. She went to county, per protocol."

"Sheriff Lisk have a look at her?"

"We have to assume."

"Why haven't they buried her yet? Been near a week since we brought her in."

"Unclaimed bodies can be stored in accordance with state law for up to six months before they're dropped at government expense. Drew has to make it look right. We probably would've been better off taking someone local, they'd've been underground three weeks ago."

"Work your lawman magic, by God. I don't like she hasn't been buried yet. This is turning messy, Al. Fix it."

"I'm working on it."

"Not hard enough. Either find that body and destroy it or make sure it's never found. Either one makes no never mind to me," Grant said and hung up.

What bothered him was that this whole thing wouldn't go away. It ought to have been a simple enough plan: a dead body in the Milliard crop should have ruined the family, but here they were, still hanging on. The injured boy should have died, but he hadn't, which forced the need to fabricate the dead girl. Kodi had fucked up, had meant to cut the kid's throat. Said he'd done the deed plenty of times back in the Motherland. It brought to mind a nagging suspicion Grant had harbored for some time: Kodi wasn't really into his role. He'd have to talk to the boy about that. He needed someone ruthless, someone bloodthirsty on their payroll. Grant thought he'd found that person in the young dissident, but maybe he'd misjudged.

Yes, this was a mess, to be sure. But not *his* mess.

Grant knew the dead girl could not be traced back to him or his young charge. Kodi had made sure of that, at least. He'd driven to Chicago's south side, to his old slum neighborhood, in the vehicle their outfit used for covert operations, and found a homeless girl, around thirteen years old, in an alleyway. It had taken only a handful of cold McDonald's fries to lure her into the car. No one had seen the abduction and he'd driven with her into the secluded woods of Murdoch, a couple dozen miles north of Derby, to do the deed. Al had been against the killing, said their interests didn't include murder, but Grant had convinced him of the necessity by laying out quite plainly what would happen if Sheriff Lisk demanded to see the corpse himself instead of entrusting its handling with Al and the coroner.

The worst part was, a body would not have even been necessary if Augie hadn't gone nosing around. Grant had a strong feeling it had been the Milliard patriarch who'd broken into the morgue that night. Of course, he couldn't prove it as no evidence had been found on the premises, but he could sense it as a horse can sense a storm hanging just over the horizon. The way Augie had been ignoring him all night confirmed it in Grant's mind. Could Milliard also be behind the bodysnatching?

Grant returned to the dining hall table where his apple pie sat congealing in a puddle of melted ice cream. It looked about as appetizing as a dead skunk on the highway. Dinah asked if everything was all right at home and he made some sound of affirmation, still staring at the tart.

"Who's up for a game?" Adeline called, snapping him out of his thoughts. It wasn't so much an interrogative as it was a declaration. Her manservant had already brought out a board game box from a cabinet and laid it on the table.

"What's *The Ungame*?" Teresa asked, tilting her head to read the cover.

"Say, I've heard of this," Ray said. "It's supposed to be a game you can't win or lose."

"Yes, that's correct, Raymond," Adeline said, removing the top with her arthritis-twisted fingers.

"That's just my kind of game," Ray said, grinning around. Ruth, his wife, kept her eyes downcast. She hadn't spoken much tonight, but Grant figured that typical of her newfound Christian nature.

"What's the point of a game you can't win?" Mike Stone asked, forking pie into his face. A fresh drink sweated nearby.

"The point is to find out something you might not have known about the other players," Adeline said. "And for as long as we've all lived in this same old county, I realized I don't know much about most of you."

What's she playing at? Grant wondered. *She's up to something, no doubt about it.*

Everyone knew better than to protest, so the area farmers crowded around the board. A few who had been out of the room as Adeline introduced it crept away so as to avoid it, perhaps in search of a television on which to watch the football game. Lucky bastards. Not that Grant cared a lick for football, but it would beat the ever-living shit out of sitting through a game one couldn't win.

Someone handed him a plain plastic token, yellow in color, to mark his progress on the board. The board itself had landing spaces marked Tell It Like It Is, Do Your Own Thing, or Hang Up! There were two stacks of cards, divided into Lighthearted or

Deep Understanding, which contained questions to ask another player. Grant already hated the game that was not a game.

"Can't we play euchre or something instead?" he said.

"Now Grant, I think you ought to honor an old lady's wishes, don't you?" Adeline asked. Then, without awaiting a reply: "There aren't enough tokens for everyone, so we'll have to play in teams. Husbands and wives together, yes?"

"Who'll your partner be?" Grant asked, hoping the reminder of her deceased husband stung. If it did, the old bitch didn't show it.

"Jontue, of course," she said, displaying her dentures in less of a smile and more of a smirk as she stroked the dog snoozing in her lap. "And we have Augie Milliard to thank for that."

Milliard, the smug bastard, held up a hand. "No thanks required. I only did what anyone would do when I found the poor creature."

Grant snapped up the die and rolled a six. "Let's play, then. High roller goes first."

CHAPTER THIRTY-FOUR

Dusk came early that day, the overcast sky lending a hand. The wind rattled the ancient, warped windows of the Gable house recreation room like ghosts seeking entrance.

"Why is that creep still staring at me?" Lorelai asked, leaning on her pool cue as though it were a sorceress's staff. Hannah looked up from where she'd been eyeing a shot into the corner pocket.

"Who, Rachel? She's not staring at you."

"She is so. She makes me feel weird."

"You're imagining things," Hannah said and fired the 5-ball into the pocket. "Now watch and weep as I run the table."

"I'm serious, H. I think she hates me."

Hannah clucked her tongue and shot the 2 into the corner. "Know what I think? You're paranoid."

Lorelai glanced at the younger girl again out of the corners of her eyes and all at once it clicked. She touched her best friend's elbow. "Oh my God. I figured it out. She likes Dennis. She's jealous."

"Now you're really dreaming," Hannah said. "She's too young for him."

"So what? All my sisters think he's a dreamboat too. God, they can barely keep their eyes off him. It's so embarrassing."

"Will you please quit talking about my brother? It's icky." Hannah mocked a shudder. "Where is the big goof, anyway?"

"I left him outside."

"You did what now?"

"We made out for a little bit behind the old lady's shed. He thought it would be a good idea to come back separately. He doesn't think my dad likes him."

"You *made out* with him? Can you be any more disgusting?"

"Come on, you know he's a cutie. You'd make out with him if he wasn't your brother."

"You're making me sick. It's your shot."

Lorelai glanced again at Rachel. "I'm going to go ask her. I want this out in the open."

"Lori, you're going to ruin the holiday. Just play the game."

"I am playing the game, just not this one. Be right back."

Hannah sighed and sat on the edge of the table to watch. Lorelai took measured steps toward where the younger girl slouched on a cream-colored davenport. "I noticed you watching us. Want to play?"

Rachel said nothing, but her upper lip twitched back slightly to reveal small, sharp teeth.

"Is something wrong?" Lorelai asked. She didn't care for that look. It made the girl appear feral.

"I don't play barroom games."

Lorelai felt her face color at the haughty tone. She put a hand on one slender hip and tossed her hair. "Too good for pool, is that it?"

"Too good for *you*," Rachel said, climbing to her feet. Then, incredibly, added: "Tramp."

Too shocked to speak, all the color that had collected in her face drained. Rachel strode out of the rec room and down the hall.

"What did she say to you?" Hannah asked. "God, you look like a ghost, Lori. Are you all right?"

"She called me a tramp."

"She didn't either."

"Yes, she did. That cornfed cunt called *me* a tramp."

"Okay. Just relax."

"I'm going to wring her neck."

"You're not going to do anything but take your next shot," Hannah said. "Who cares what some underclassman says about you?"

"I won't do it here," Lorelai said, more to herself than her friend. "No, I won't make a scene here. But that snatch has it coming."

"Lori, let it go," Hannah said, dragging her friend back to the billiard table.

"Oh, yeah. She's going to get hers when she least expects it. And don't try to talk me out of it, Hannah. I know she's Susie's friend, but I'm going to get her. See if I don't."

"Okay, okay. You're going to get her. Now will you please take your turn?"

Another voice called from across the room and both girls jumped at its abruptness. "Hey, we're playing ghost in the graveyard. You two want to come?"

They turned to see who'd spoken, but Lorelai already knew. It was the Bible bitch's psychotic brother, Caleb.

"Sure," Hannah said too quickly. "Yeah, that sounds good. Let's go, Lori."

Lorelai allowed herself to be pulled down the corridor and out back to the terrace, still too shocked to think clearly. *No one* spoke to her that way, especially not some pale-faced freshman. Rachel Safford would pay. Lorelai would see to it.

Outside the younger kids had scattered searching for whomever had been chosen as the ghost. The twins hovered near the biggest tree in the yard, which had been designated as home base, opting not to venture too far from the safe territory. A third figure lurked near them and Caleb shouted at him.

"Sammy, what in creation are you doing out here? You know Ma wants you to stay inside."

The youngest Safford child shook his head. "Doan wannu."

"I didn't ask if you wanted to, retard. I told you to git."

"You shouldn't call him that," Hannah said.

Caleb stared at her. "I'll call my own brother anything I please."

"You're an asshole," Lorelai said. "Just like your sister."

Caleb kept his same even temper he always displayed, an eerie neutrality that seemed manufactured. When he spoke he sounded as reasonable as a sermonizing preacher. "Figure you better take that back."

"I won't," Lorelai said. "You both can go home and fuck each other some more."

Caleb's face never changed. "Now look who's the asshole," he said.

"Lori, jeez, take it easy," Hannah said. To Caleb, she said, "She didn't mean that."

"Oh, she did," Caleb said. "That's okay. I forgive her."

"I don't need your forgiveness, psycho," Lorelai said, finding herself on the brink of tears. All at once she wished she were anywhere else on the planet than Adeline Gable's back lawn with everyone staring at her. Where was Dennis? Had he gone back inside? Had he walked home? She wanted nothing more than to find him and hold his hand and have him tell her everything would be all right.

Hannah started to say something, another trite attempt at intervention, but Lorelai didn't let her. Instead she turned and marched back inside. Maybe she could get Dennis's attention and they could meet in some back bedroom to talk. Maybe do a little more than talk. That would be nice.

But she found him nowhere in the house. The adults were playing some ridiculous game in the dining room. The rec room was empty, the polished console TV playing the Broncos-Chargers game to no one. Where had he gone?

"Looking for my brother?" a voice asked from behind her. Lorelai whirled and found Thomas, the middle Milliard son, lurking in the hall.

"Yes, Tommy. Have you seen him?" Already the boy had his brother's good looks. In a few years you wouldn't be able to chase the girls away with a pitchfork.

"I saw him go through the back gate a few minutes ago. He left with Rachel." Then, almost as an afterthought: "They were holding hands."

CHAPTER THIRTY-FIVE

Grant found *The Ungame* ridiculously tedious, but also found a use for it. The questions posed to the players could be mined for information. For instance, when Augie selected a card from the Deep Understanding pile during his turn, Adeline (who had appointed herself Game Master) read the question and Grant listened with great interest to the answer. It helped that most of the participants at the table were drinking steadily, something that undoubtedly loosened their lips.

The question was: What one quality do you look for most in friends?

Augie answered without hesitation and were his words a little slurred? Grant thought so. "Loyalty. Loyalty is what makes a friend. You can say dependability or anything else but if you know you can trust someone, really trust them, then you know you've found a true friend."

Grant watched Augie's eyes as the man relayed his answer and found they flicked to Ray Safford before anyone else. It was true, Augie and Ray seemed pretty companionable in recent years. It would be something to look out for in the future. It seemed Milliard had made Safford his lapdog, much as Adeline had Jontue.

"That was a wonderful answer, dear," Teresa said, rubbing her husband's shoulder before taking a sip from her Sea Breeze.

"She's right," Ursula piped in. "Loyalty is a great answer, Augie. It's what makes you and my handsome hubby such close friends, right?"

"Absolutely it is," Augie said and took another drink.

"Okay, okay, it's our turn," Ursula said, snatching up the die and casting it across the board. "'If you have complimented someone today, go to Compliment Clubhouse," she read from the space where she'd set the Stones' red token. "Oh, I compliment someone near every day, I guess. But in case I haven't, let me just say that I'm sitting among the handsomest men in the whole United States of America. And the prettiest ladies, too, of course."

"Only in America?" Grant asked and everyone laughed. Yes, the little whore was quite the coquette. He didn't know how Mike put up with it. Or why.

"Grant, Dinah, you're up," Adeline said when the hubbub died.

He rolled and counted out the spaces to his token's destination. "I guess I'll take a Deep Understanding," he said. "Let's all get to know each other, shall we? Really dig deep."

Adeline drew a card and stared into his eyes before reading: "'Make a statement about success.'"

"Good question," Grant said. "Great question, in fact. Success is what you make it. Think big, but start small. If you put your mind to it, there's nothing you can't accomplish. Success is half motivation, half execution, with a dash of luck thrown in. Dream it and then live it."

"Well said," Mike offered.

"Hear, hear," Ray added, rather absurdly.

It was pure bullshit, of course. Grant no more believed what he'd said than he believed the Good Lord Jesus Christ might suddenly swim down from the clouds and bless them all on this day of thanksgiving. Success, he knew, was what you invested, who you manipulated, and how much you got in return. Of course motivation and execution played a part, but only after you resigned yourself to knowing true success always leaves casualties in its wake. Someone always got run down on your way up. It was inevitable. It was the way of the world, like it or not. He'd lied in each of his answers because he wanted these people to know his brain like he wanted a hole in it.

When it came to the Saffords' turn, Ruth selected a card from the Lighthearted pile which read: *What really turns you off?*

"Snoring," Ray said mournfully and everyone laughed again except for Ray, who didn't seem to understand he'd made a funny.

Ruth, who'd loosened up a little after her second glass of Merlot (which had brought spots of color to her cheekbones), said, "Insincerity. When I know someone's lied to my face, well, it pretty much makes me want to have nothing to do with them again."

She said this while glancing around the room at the other players. She lingered long on Mike Stone but even longer on Grant, who had to drop his eyes. Even nearly two decades later, she knew how to get to him.

The game play went on another two rounds until someone suggested something new. Ray wanted *Monopoly* (Grant couldn't imagine the buffoon keeping track of the colored bills, much less the cardboard deeds), but when no consensus could be reached, some of the guests decided to call it a night.

The Averys and Spalls departed first and good riddance. Grant despised men who took satisfaction in mediocrity. That's why he respected Milliard even if he wanted to destroy him—at least Augie knew how to achieve and maintain affluence. Grant had had him by the balls before Adeline released him, but Augie never once considered lying down or tucking tail. He fought tooth and nail to keep his family afloat. Grant appreciated that. He'd do the same for his own family if anyone ever made the mistake of trying to ruin him.

Grant stepped over to the bar to get the hired man to pour him another club soda and found himself standing beside none other than the Milliard patriarch.

"Great party, huh?" Augie asked, gin on his breath.

"Adeline really outdid herself," Grant concurred, all the time wondering if his adversary had been behind the disappearing corpse in the Ashford County morgue.

"I want to apologize to you, Grant," Augie said. "I said some pretty foul things last time we spoke."

"No need. We both got a little hot under the collar."

Grant plucked a cigarette from an ivory case he carried in his jacket pocket and offered one to Augie. He knew the apple farmer didn't smoke, but figured a gratuitous gesture of peacemaking in order. Augie, on cue, held up a hand but pulled a silver Zippo lighter from his pocket and lit up for his rival. If

Granny wanted him to smoke outside, he figured he'd make her say it aloud.

Augie said: "Why don't you let me buy you a drink, Grant."

"Drinks here are free."

"Then you get the joke," Augie said and both men laughed. Then they shook hands and moved to opposite ends of the room.

Rachel had seen Dennis sitting alone on the back terrace and had gone to him with a mind to give him hell, but instead found him struggling against tears. He tried to hide it, but she'd seen and all the gusto had gone out of him.

"What's the matter, Dennis?" she asked and he'd taken her hand then, wordlessly drawing her toward the back gate. She had not protested, the warmth of his flesh in hers like a living heart. He seemed so different now, so much more confident than he had that day she came into the store to buy fudge. Something had changed, but she didn't know what.

They'd slipped down the ridge into the dale cupping the Milliard Farms Country Store, its windows dark now, its busy season in the books. It wasn't until they'd passed the building and the vacant pumpkin patch and the closed-off corn maze that she understood he was taking her to the orchard. Wind whistled through the branches barren of all but the last curled leaves still clinging with brittle stems to their summer homes.

Rachel realized he could show her anything short of a rotting corpse and she would find magic in it. Just being near him brought out some untapped emotion in her she could only equate somehow with the scent of lavender. It was a good feeling, one of rightness and righteousness, of hope and peace and love. This felt *correct*, their being here together now, as though the heavens had spent millennia aligning for this precise moment.

Dennis led her to a pile of leaves as high as a haystack. "I'm in charge of leaf disposal each fall," he said. "I always leave one big pile for as long as I can, until my dad makes me haul it away."

"Why?" she asked, her voice small, smaller than the pinprick which had been the universe in the innumerable eons before it exploded.

"There's no way to put it into words," he said, releasing her hand. It felt with that action like he'd untethered her, as though she might drift away without his touch. Then, incredibly, he crawled into the pile of leaves as an Eskimo might an igloo. Rachel stood in the chill wondering what to do only long enough to realize she had only one option.

She found him in what must have been the epicenter of the mountain of leaves, though the darkness was nearly complete. The smell reminded her of autumns past, a heady, earthy, entirely pleasant aroma she found intoxicating.

"What is this?" she asked, seeking his hand and finding it.

"This is my hidey hole," he said, a touch of mirth in his voice. "For a week a year, anyway."

He pulled her in close, nestling her frame against his rib cage, an arm encircling her shoulders. Just enough air penetrated the pile for them to breathe. Rachel squeezed her eyes closed against the feathery flutter of leaves and thought she could not remember a time she'd been more content in her life. Lorelai Lang no longer existed. Her family no longer existed. No school, no church, no God. Only Dennis Milliard's comforting presence, the ball of his thumb tracing patterns along the back of her hand, his even breathing in this heavenly hideaway from the universe.

This is what it must be like to be in the womb, she thought, *only better because I'm with my soulmate.*

Soulmate. It was a word she'd heard at school that someone's Flower Power mom used. It had never been a term Rachel thought would ever apply to her, but now that it had crossed her mind she realized it to be true. Dennis Milliard was her soulmate and the two of them existed in complete isolation, shielded from all else. Rachel thought she could die here, in this warm womb, and be happy so long as she did it with her soulmate.

She almost said it then. Almost told him she loved him. But no. Too soon. They had time. They had all the time in the world. Here time did not exist.

Rachel turned her head into his shoulder and inhaled, pulling the scent of the earth, the scent of decay, and the scent of

Dennis deep inside of her, into her core. As their cozy confines grew humid with their mingled breath, she at last knew the meaning of the word rapture.

CHAPTER THIRTY-SIX

They emerged an unknowable time later and for a time the spell held. They held hands, not speaking, and toured the orchard, watching the moon break through the clouds to cast its winter white glow through the branches. They might have been strolling through some enchanted forest and Rachel half-expected to catch glimpses of pixies prancing through the trees. The rest of the world existed on another plane, separate from them, and Rachel wished it would last forever. This world existed for them alone. In her mind and in her soul, she knew it always would.

"We should get back," Dennis said. "They'll be wondering what became of us."

"Let them," she replied and leaned her head on his shoulder where it felt most comfortable, as if it had been made especially for her. She wished he would kiss her, but he didn't and the moment elongated until it burst into oblivion.

"Lorelai is in love with you," she said.

"What makes you say that?"

"The way she looks at you. Anyone with a pair of eyes can see it." She hesitated before adding, "And Susie told me."

"How would she know?"

"She ... she read Hannah's diary."

Dennis clucked his tongue. "Hannah isn't going to like that."

"Don't tell her, Dennis. Please? Susie will kill me."

"I won't."

Rachel took a deep breath. "Do you love Lorelai?"

He shook his head. "No. I don't love her, Rachel."

"There's something else," Rachel said, knowing it would

ruin any chance Lorelai had with Dennis. Good. She wanted to ruin the Lang girl. You didn't get to have everything—a wealthy family, a beautiful face, a gorgeous body, and all the brains and popularity one could dream of. You didn't get to have all the boys tripping over their own toes to be with you. You just didn't. Something had to balance out along the way and Rachel would now tip the scales.

"What is it?" Dennis asked.

Rachel bit her lip lightly, thinking there was still time to change her mind, but then crossed the threshold and altered the future one word at a time. "Lorelai's been sleeping with someone named Kodi."

Dennis stopped. He stared at her. Whatever spell they'd woven together in the enchanted orchard dissipated like smoke and she already regretted speaking it aloud. "What did you say?"

"Susie read it, right there in the diary."

Rachel thought he would explode on the spot, but incredibly he relaxed. "It doesn't matter," he said. "I have no feelings for Lorelai. She can sleep with whoever she wants."

Reluctantly she let him lead her back through the trees and into their familiar reality and at last the spell *did* break, irrevocably and irretrievably, as all spells, both good and bad, one day must. They moved past the darkened store and up the ridge, out of the valley, and into the Gable back lawn where ghost in the graveyard had long since disbanded. At least they hadn't gathered a search party for them yet.

"We're going to get a whipping," Dennis said when they'd made it to the wide back doors. Warm yellow light streamed out, coloring their shoes. He plucked a leaf out of Rachel's hair.

"It was worth a hundred whippings," she said.

He smiled, and she felt something unlock in her chest. Then he took her hand again and they went inside together.

The decision to send Rachel Safford to the Catholic school behind St. Joe's was the right one, in Grant's estimation. He didn't need his top salesman getting put in stir for sexing up an underage girl. Ruth had always wanted her kids to go to

Catholic school anyhow, that much he knew, but her oaf of a husband had insisted on good ol' District 377. Raymond didn't demand much in life, but on this point he'd persisted. And he'd won, until now at least. Grant didn't know the details of that particular argument as he knew much of the inner workings of his environment (he'd long since learned to listen to that storied grapevine and had developed an almost preternatural sense for when it produced wine and when it produced vinegar), but he had a vague impression.

Ray knew things too. He might not have been sharp on all the details, but he knew someone else had fathered the elder son Caleb. Probably Rachel, too. The identity of the father—or fathers, for Ruth had been an experimentalist prior to being reborn in the blood of Christ—was a carefully guarded secret only a handful of people knew. Grant wasn't one of them, not fully, but he had his suspicions. Oh, he had his suspicions all right.

Ruth had only married Ray because he promised to raise the boy as his own and to take the secret to his grave. Ruth's folks were staunch Catholics who would have sent her to a nunnery had they learned of a child born out of wedlock. They had not approved of her choice in partner, but the two had successfully sold them a loving, affectionate union and they were pleased she'd married an established farmer with a good reputation and a better future.

Grant couldn't fault Ruth her indiscretion. He'd been young once too. They all had. Ruth had been two years behind him in the Derby school system his entire life. So had Ray. Augie and Teresa Milliard, sweethearts since middle school, had been three years behind, so Grant hadn't seen much of them through their educating years. His sweet Dinah had lived up in the neighboring Murdoch and when it came to book-smarts, few in the Midwest could call themselves Di's equal (farm-smarts was another thing entirely, but Grant didn't hold it against her). Lorelai got her knack for academics from her mother, but her shrewdness from him. No doubt about it—that girl had the best of all worlds. And, thank all things holy, he knew all five girls were his. He didn't know what he'd do if he found out otherwise, only that it would be nothing good.

But he had nothing to fear in that department. He knew Dinah's faithfulness was as iron-clad as a chastity belt. She hardly even looked at other men. Not like that hippie strumpet Mike had married. Both he and Mike had attended Ashford High, though half a generation apart. Mike liked the young ones, to be sure. Anytime he got out of town to do a little hunting, he made a point to bag more than quail. He bragged about it to his friends over weekend poker hands at the VA Hall in Murdoch, knowing full well no one would leak a whisper of it to his wife. Grant had reminded the dairyman more than once to keep clear of his daughters as they came of age, which Mike always seemed to take as a joke. It wasn't. Grant would bury Satan himself beneath his rows if he caught him trying to deflower his angels.

Each morning that early winter he watched the Safford's Crown Victoria trundle by as Ruth drove her only daughter to her new school at St. Joseph's. Kids from all over the county were enrolled there, but the entire student body couldn't have overtopped sixty. Not much chance of a pair of wayward souls meeting in secret backstage for a little monkey business— Father Scudder and his flock of nuns ran the place like an army barracks. Grant believed strict discipline shaped the best adults, but had balked at Dinah's long-ago suggestion that they send their girls to St. Joe's over Derby District 377.

"Catholic schools are for those in need of Jesus or jail," he'd said. "And since our girls will have plenty of the first and none of the second, I'm happy to let them go to public school."

He'd also argued that had it not been for Derby High School's annual Winter Enchantment dance he and Di might never have married in the first place. The dance had been part of the school's rich tradition (as were its athletic teams—Go Devils!— and its history of hiring teachers with excellent pedigrees) since the last brick had been laid in the 1940s. He'd be damned if any offspring of his missed out on it.

Plus, in Grant's estimation, *too* much God could be bad. He himself had a casually pleasant relationship with the Creator, but there came a point when Scudder's constant babble about burning bushes and pillars of salt became too much to bear. He wanted his kids to find education in school and salvation in church. The Founding Fathers had wisely kept the institutions separate.

Which brought him to the thought of boys. He saw the way his colleagues looked at him, even if no one had the balls to say it to his face. They pitied him for having no boys to raise. No one to carry on the family name. No one to take over once Grant bought the farm, as the saying went.

Well, he didn't need boys to do that. His girls would do just fine. Not Lorelai—no, his eldest was destined for something far beyond a farmer's life. She had gifts. Brains and beauty beyond what any earthly creature ought to be allotted. He imagined her leaving corn country to be a doctor in Chicago or New York. No, a surgeon. A neurosurgeon. That would suit her fine. She'd probably perform the first brain transplant. He'd leave the farm to the other girls. Nora seemed to be the front runner in terms of ability—she'd picked up sowing and reaping like a natural. She understood about soil types and hybrid crops and water tables.

The futures of his other offspring seemed less certain, but none of them would starve. All would succeed. Grant knew this because success breeds success. He didn't have a single failure gene in his body. Neither did Dinah. She'd been at the top of her class in school, but had been content to become a farmer's wife. In another time, she might have been a brain surgeon on her own. But women's lib hadn't existed in their dating days and staying home had been expected. Dinah had taken to this task wonderfully and spent time doing creative things. Painting and poetry mostly, both at which she excelled. She'd even had a couple verse pieces published in *Ideals Magazine*. Grant knew he'd lucked into his family.

He thought about watching Dennis and Rachel come into the dining room of the Gable house with their fingers locked together like a pair of toddlers. He'd watched their fathers react, Augie with alarm and Ray with admiration. Ray would welcome a Milliard-Safford union. The fool practically worshipped Augie. But Augie had nearly spilled his drink as his son stared him down in mute defiance. The subject of Rachel Safford had been discussed before, that much came immediately clear. The Milliards had departed soon after and Grant hoped the boy wouldn't be grounded long. They had a big delivery coming in before Christmas and he'd need him more than ever.

Someone tapped on his office door and he bid them come. Only when Dennis Milliard stepped inside, face ashen, did Grant realize something had gone wrong.

CHAPTER THIRTY-SEVEN

Dennis said, "Sheriff Lisk arrested Zebbo. He's got him in county right now."

Grant said, "You got a problem using the phone? I thought I told you not to come here again."

"Sir, I tried but someone was on the party line."

The goddamn party line. Right. Edna Hadsell monopolized the line most days, especially when her soaps ran through boring plot arcs. He wished the old biddy would hurry up and gasp her last.

"Does Chief Engel know?"

"I don't know, sir. Zebbo just used his one phone call to my house. Thank God I answered."

"Does your old man know he called?"

"No, sir. I told him it was Randy."

Randy. The kid who'd been hurt in the maze. Grant had all but forgotten about him. "How is Randy, anyway?" he asked, mind racing. He didn't give a good goddamn whether the kid had made a full recovery or succumbed to gangrene—the Johansens were worthless sheep farmers—but he needed to buy time to think. It was an old trick with him.

Dennis lowered his eyes. "I think he's scared of me."

"You say that like it's a bad thing."

"Randy's my friend. I don't want him to be scared of me."

"Only because you haven't learned to use the power of fear yet, son," Grant said. "It's the most powerful weapon you can possess. True fear puts any gun to shame. Remember that."

"Yes, sir."

"Did that pickle-brained darkie relate to you how much he'd told our esteemed sheriff?"

Dennis fidgeted, clearly uncomfortable with the epithet. Little bleeding heart tenderfoot still needed some seasoning, it seemed. Just wait till he had to put a man down, because that would likely be in his future if their business really got off the ground. "He hasn't told them anything."

"He say how much bail was?"

"A hundred bucks. They confiscated everything he had on him, which worked out to be a little more than an ounce."

"Thank God for small favors. Okay. I need to get in touch with Chief Engel," Grant said. "It'll have to be on him to spring the dumbshit before he flaps his gums."

"Do you think that will work, sir?"

"It by-God better," Grant said, "or else we're looking at a bunch of cooked geese and I ain't talking about Christmas dinner."

He picked up the phone and reached a finger to dial, then grunted in frustration. "Edna, would you kindly get your fat ass off the line so I can make an important call?"

He listened to the old lady's indignant squawk before she hung up, then tapped the switch hook and dialed Engel's office line. No answer. He tried the front desk and got Nathan Berryman, who told him the chief was in the field.

"Nate, I need you to radio him to contact me immediately."

"Mr. Lang, is there a crime taking place?"

"There will be if you don't call your boss."

"Sir, it's against procedure to use the radio at civilian request."

"I don't give a damn if it's against the Ten Commandments. I need to speak to Al."

"I'm happy to leave a message for when he returns to HQ."

Grant offered the officer a colorful expletive before slamming the receiver into its cradle. He looked at his young subordinate, the son of his rival. "I appreciate your coming to inform me of this unfortunate development, but I meant when I said don't come here anymore. Not for business, not for nothing. If you can't get through next time, you deal with old lady Hadsell the way you just heard me do."

"Yes, sir."

The young man turned to go, but Grant called him back. He dug out a wad of bills from his front pocket and held them out without counting them. "A Christmas bonus. Buy your mother something pretty with it."

Dennis looked at the money doubtfully. "Sir, that's too much."

"On the contrary, it isn't nearly enough. You've done fine work for our operation. There's going to be a lot more of it in the new year as we expand our enterprise. Take it, then get the hell out of here."

"Yes, sir," Dennis said, stuffing the money into his pocket. It felt as thick as a dime store paperback.

"You drive safe in that snow. I hear we're expecting six, eight inches."

Dennis didn't reply. He had already eased the door shut behind him.

Grant donned his hat and coat and drove out to Al's usual speed trap, a turnout near the town line that concealed his cruiser perfectly. The radio was tuned, as always, to a country station from up near the state line, but he snapped it off. No music now.

The turnout was empty. Grant swore. He couldn't go to the Ashford County Jail himself, nor could he send anyone closely associated with him. His first thought had been to send Kodi in there with bail, but it wouldn't take long for that to come back on Grant. He'd also considered sending Dennis—at least Zebulon had a known connection with the Milliards, so it would make sense—but scratched that idea too. Dennis coming in with bail would still raise eyebrows. And questions. Somehow he had to get Zeb out before the stupid son of a bitch spilled his stinking guts to Lisk. And then he had to get rid of him. Because it wouldn't stop there. There would be a hearing. There would be a court date. Fahrlander might be on their side, but Zeb might not draw Fahrlander. If he got that young idealistic pinko bitch who had no doubt made her way through law school on her knees, things could get ugly. They couldn't take that chance.

No, Zebulon Tuel would have to go. One way or another. The highway or the grave-way.

Grant switched on the CB mounted beneath the dash and switched to channel 8. It had been determined that if all else failed, this would be the channel through which they communicated. Only he and Al and Mike knew about it and generally 8 remained clear night and day. Every so often some hillbilly kids would be found messing around with phony handles and telling vulgar jokes, but they usually had the channel to themselves. Trouble was, using this means of communication ran the risk of eavesdroppers, much like the absurd party line.

For a time he only listened to the soft static purring through the speaker, trying to determine if 8 had company today, but heard nothing. He picked up the mic and thumbed the button. "Black Wolf, this is Bull Moose. Copy?"

He released and listened. Nothing. He tried again with identical results. Where would Al be at this time of day? Could be he'd caught wind of Zeb's misfortune and had sped full-on, lights flashing, sirens wailing, all the way up to the county seat to bounce the Negro. That would be ideal, but he highly doubted it.

He thumbed the mic again and called (without much hope), "Deerhunter, this is Bull Moose. Copy?"

No answer. He didn't expect one, with Mike likely out in the canning room this time of day. The only way he'd raise him on the radio would be if the dairyman happened to be in his office or in range of his truck, which wasn't out of the realm of possibility because of the frequent hunting trips he made to the woods outside Derby. The timing would have to be just right and at the moment it happened to be just wrong.

Grant decided to take a drive out to Stone Dairy Farm. He needed to speak to his partner and he didn't want to take the chance the line would be tied up again. In fact, he didn't want to be home at all. Not until this business was finished. He couldn't just pace around his office hoping for news—he had to take action.

Grant used the turnout to make a three-point turn and headed north.

The Stone farm held still. A cow bayed from the barn, but that was all. The sky had taken on a steely cast that hinted of snow. Neither the farmer nor any of his three hands appeared in evidence. Grant had decided to check out the canning room when the door of the farmhouse clattered open.

"Afternoon, Grant," Ursula Stone called. Grant closed his eyes and let his breath out in a slow steam before turning. The lady of the house stood bundled in a purple fur-lined parka, the hood up over her hair, dyed a comely cornsilk color today. The pair of ever-present hippie shades she'd become irrevocably associated with in his mind perched on her petite nose. Even in the overcast afternoon, the little slut had them clapped to her face.

"Hello, Mrs. Stone."

"Ursula. You know that."

"I prefer to keep things formal."

"That's your problem, see?" she said. "You're too stuffy."

"I'm not stuffy. I'm professional."

"Did you drive all the way out here to see my handsome hubby?"

"It wasn't to deliver the mail."

She laughed harder than she should have and said, "Why don't you come inside? I just brewed a pot of tea."

Tea. Of course. Not coffee. The suburban transplant still refused to do things the country way and it irked Grant something awful. "I take it Mike's away?" he said through gritted teeth.

"He took those three boys hunting this morning. I don't figure they'll be home till dinnertime," she said, running a finger along the ridge of faux fox fur at her throat.

Grant considered. It had been years since he'd had a piece of ass as young as Ursula Stone. He loved Dinah, of course, and they still made love once or twice a month, but a man occasionally had to have someone else scratch his itch.

Except for him. Not Grant.

He hadn't seriously thought about being with another woman in, oh, a decade and a half (or so he regularly insisted to himself). He could appreciate them from afar, but wouldn't crawl between the sheets with one (he claimed). The vows he and Dinah had exchanged were sacred to him.

Except when they weren't.

Grant watched the coquette sway her hips against the porch rail and felt something shift downstairs. His imagination fired a brief but potent image across his synapses. But he prized himself a practical man as well as professional, and knew screwing his partner's bride beneath his own roof and in his own bed would be bad for business. Mike had always been a powerful ally and Grant didn't see that changing anytime soon. And the little bitch would forever have leverage to hang over his head. No, best let all notions of impropriety go.

"I'd love to, Mrs. Stone, but I'd best be on my way."

Her face changed behind those ridiculous sunglasses. "But I'm scared, Grant. I swear I saw someone watching the house not fifteen minutes ago, out there by the barn."

"Probably just your imagination."

"I tell you I saw him. I see him sometimes when my husband's away."

"Well, I happen to know your husband is in possession of an impressive arsenal of premium weaponry. Arm thyself, woman."

"Hell, most of those guns outweigh me, Grant Lang. I sure could use a man around to protect me until my guy gets home." She ran a corner of pink tongue out and traced her upper lip with it.

That broke the dam. Grant glanced around the yard once more to make sure Mike's truck truly was gone, then stomped up the steps and let Ursula lead him indoors.

Zeb could wait half an hour.

CHAPTER THIRTY-EIGHT

It turned out to be both better and worse than expected. Better because he hadn't come like that in ages. Ursula Stone still had a body as lithe as a figure skater. Her belly was taut as a snare drum, her rear supple and sublime. She'd let him take her frontward, backward, and topsy-turvy.

It was worse because after the acts (there had been two consecutively, a feat he hadn't managed since his twenties), Mike Stone seemed to be everywhere. One of his jackets hung on a hook nailed to the back of the bedroom door. His bent bulldog pipe rested on its side atop the oak bureau like a dead animal, the sweet smell of tobacco hanging in the air. A wooden decoy duck with a clock set in its chest rested on the nightstand. The man who used "Deerhunter" as a CB handle might be afield in a blind with his hired men, but he might as well have been standing in the room with them. The thought made Grant realize time had grown short. Maybe too short.

"I ought to go," he said.

Ursula sighed beside him, curled one long leg over his. "Already?" she asked, tracing his nipple with a fire-red fingernail.

"I don't figure it would do us any favors to have your handsome hubby pop in about now."

She giggled as if finding the prospect funny when it was anything but. "Can I call you?" she asked.

He stared at her, aghast. "Are you out of your mind?"

"I want to see you again," she said. "I had fun."

"Think for a minute what might happen if you rang my house and Dinah or one of the girls picked up?"

"I'd pretend I was one of Lorelai's school friends," she said.

"I'm not that much older than her anyhow."

Grant nearly struck her then. He had to slide his right hand beneath a buttock to avoid it. The sound of his sweet daughter's name coming from the mouth of this whore seemed a blasphemy. When he thought he had himself under some semblance of control he rolled up on one elbow to look her fully in the face.

"I don't think I need to say this, but I'm going to because I want to make sure we're on the same page. No, scratch that. The same paragraph. The same fucking sentence, even. You're not to breathe a word of what happened in this room to anyone. Not to your husband, not to his men, not to Teresa Milliard or Ruth Safford or any other lady to whom you might make a social call. Sure as hell not to my family. Is that clear?"

Ursula studied her nails as if bored. "Aye, aye, captain."

He stared hard at her, nostrils flaring. "I want you to appreciate the gravity of the consequence your indiscretion would warrant."

She flicked her eyes his way. "What're you gonna do, give me a spanking?" she asked, deliberately rubbing a hip against his groin. He shoved it away. She was so light she slid sideways, half off the bed. Grant got up and walked around the foot toward her.

"I'm going to give you a taste of what you can expect if you feel like flapping those pretty cocksucking lips to any of your girlfriends," he said, taking her by the hips and flipping her on her belly. A snatch of poetry he'd once read to his girls recurred to him and he whispered: "Goosey gander, whither shall I wander? Upstairs, downstairs, and in my lady's chamber."

It turned out he could manage a third act, and this time she screamed when he entered her.

Grant had made sure not to leave any marks Mike might see. He didn't know how often he viewed his wife in her birthday suit these days—the man had likely lost some virility to age, if not all of it—but he hadn't taken any chances. Any damage done had been strictly internal. And psychological, of course. Psyches were fragile things, especially on the weak of mind. He thought he'd gotten through to Mrs. Stone in the end. He only hoped she'd be able to sit naturally within the next day or two.

Grant strode out past a sorry-looking Christmas tree overhung with cheap department store baubles and pushed through the back door. He took note of the dark dairy barn standing against the twilight and climbed into his truck. Mike and the boys would be back soon, probably within the hour.

He took his time heading home. No need to hurry. Before he'd left the house, after he was sure Ursula understood the price a loose tongue would fetch her, he'd raised Al on the phone in Mike's kitchen. The police chief asked to meet him later that evening at the cabin, but assured Grant all had been made right in the case of one Zebulon Tuel. Al had bounced the stupid drunk.

"The Black boy's scared, no doubt about it, but I set his mind at ease," Al had said.

"And Lisk won't press charges?"

"He might, but for now Zeb's in the clear. I played the jurisdiction card and Lisk was more than happy to pick it up. One less loser stinking up his jail. Had Zeb been carrying more than an ounce on him, though, things might have gone very different. Told him to lie low a couple weeks, stay off the sales. And stay off the sauce. The son of a bitch was drunk as a skunk when he got busted out at the Derby Speedway, trying to sneak his way into the race. That's where Lisk's deputy nabbed him."

"Might as well tell a cow to stop giving milk," Grant had said. "Look, I'll meet you at the cabin at eight o'clock. I have to go."

He'd hung up and walked straight to the truck, letting the porch door bang behind him. He hoped it had made the whore jump, was almost certain it had. He'd put a scare in her all right, along with his three loads. Smiling, he upshifted and adjusted the fly of his jeans. She hadn't been a bad lay. Not the best he'd had, but not the worst either.

Grant said Grace that evening, holding Dinah's hand in one of his and Lorelai's in the other. He closed his eyes as he chanted, trying to believe the words he spoke, and almost succeeding.

Supper went smashingly, the girls chattering on about their school days, Dinah worrying over the coming snow. He'd been lucky to sneak a shower before the table had been set in order to get the floral smell of the slut's perfume off his skin. It nearly made him gag to inhale it. But the slut had no place at his supper table and he banished her from his mind. She'd keep her trap shut. She knew better than to blab.

"Where'd you get off to today?" Dinah asked, her keen intuition perhaps detecting something unfamiliar beneath her roof.

"Oh, I took a drive up to Murdoch to see about a new drum for the combine."

"Is there something wrong with it?" she asked.

"Nothing that can't be fixed in time for next harvest."

"Not too expensive, I hope?"

"Nope. Cheap as they come."

Conversation went on this way, a little forced on his end. He had to cut it out, act natural. So he did. He laughed at his daughters' jokes. He winked at Penny when she blew him a kiss from across the table. He improvised a ghost story over dessert that made the younger girls goggle. All perfectly natural. Perfectly himself.

Afterward, he read the evening paper in his study and then told Dinah he had to go out for a bit.

"Again? You were gone all afternoon."

"I have to go see about some feed for the horses."

"Will you be gone long?"

He sniffed. "An hour, tops."

She kissed him and helped him into his coat. "We'll be here when you come home. Be careful out there if it starts to snow."

Grant waited for guilt to surge over him, but it never came. He'd suspected for years his conscience had lapsed and this dead zone apathy confirmed it. Did it bother him? He supposed it should, but it didn't. The important thing was that he still loved his family. If that emotion ever burned out of him, well, he didn't want to think of the result.

He drove out to the cabin, parking at the dead end facing the four red diamonds, in the exact spot Dennis Milliard had waited for Kodi to escort him to his destiny. The snow began on the hike to the cabin, flakes thick and white as moths melting on his face and the shoulders of his coat. He twisted the key in the padlock and hung it on its hasp, stepping into the vegetable smell within. The plants looked good. The humidity seemed right, the temperature tolerable.

Al arrived ten minutes late. "Had a drunk driver try to run on me," he said by way of excuse.

Grant had never found excuses useful. In fact, he hated them. In this case, though, he felt it best not to bring it up. "Tell me about Zeb."

The cop shrugged. "It's like I said on the phone, I don't expect it to be much trouble. Lisk is content to let me deal with him."

"What about court?"

"If it gets that far, the judge'll slap his wrist and turn him loose."

"I don't like it. He screwed up once, he'll do it again."

"What do you suggest we do about it? Cut him out?"

Grant shook his head. "What good'll that be? He knows what we do here. Sooner or later he'll get skunked and flap his gums to some barfly."

Al eyed him closely. "I'm not sure I care for the direction this conversation is headed."

"Occupational hazard. Sometimes loose ends need to be cut."

"We're not killing Zebulon Tuel." Subconsciously, or perhaps not, the cop's hand crept toward the service weapon holstered at his hip.

Grant held up his hands. "Whoa there, hoss. Who said anything about killing anyone?"

Al relaxed. A little. "What are you driving at then?"

"We send him away."

"Away? Where?"

"Anywhere but here."

"Zeb's a born and bred AC man. I don't think he's ever been out of the county. Anywhere we send him, he's going to trot right back home like a dog abandoned in the city."

This wasn't going as planned. "If you've got an idea, I'm open to hearing it."

Al heaved a sigh and fingered his nose. "This is going sour," he said, mostly to himself.

"It doesn't have to go sour," Grant said. "Mike's still fully on board and his Indian's bringing in new product. Quality product. Better than what we're growing here. Al, we have a real chance to revolutionize this industry."

The chief eyed him. "Yeah?"

Grant grinned. "This stuff is going to knock our clients on their asses. It's laced with some hallucinogenic shit."

"You got any of it here?"

"Course we do. You want a taste?"

Al unbuttoned his police-issue overcoat and slung it into a corner. "Don't mind if I do. Just a nibble, though. I still have two hours left on duty."

Grant's grin widened. "Hang tight, I'll get it."

CHAPTER THIRTY-NINE

While he toked, waiting for the high to kick in, Al burbled on about how the dead girl still had not turned up and how August Milliard must be behind it. Lisk had opened an investigation and would be posting a reward for information leading to an arrest.

August Milliard didn't concern Grant any longer. With one quick squeeze, he could strangle the apple farmer. Having his son in the brig would ruin the family. It would force them out of town because respectable Christians around these parts didn't give their business to known drug dealers. Or their families. And Derby was filled with respectable Christians. St. Joe's was practically big business—he'd seen the overflowing collection plates in Father Scudder's office on certain after-service visits. No, the natives of their little burg would rather give their hard-earned tithe to the Good Lord than to a family who'd raised a pot dealer. Drugs were the devil, to their minds.

The dead girl had been Kodi's idea and Grant had been happy to let him spearhead the mission. He hadn't wanted an actual body, but the young Russian had convinced him of its necessity. And then it had up and disappeared. Still no sign of it anywhere, a very concerning loose end. Grant hated loose ends even more than he hated excuses.

"This is some good shit," Al said through a lungful of smoke. "The colors are incredible."

Grant regarded him a long moment. "Something just occurred to me. You need to search the Milliard Country Store."

Al looked around at him, bleary-eyed. "Why?"

"They usually close up for the season the week before Thanksgiving, right? Then they take a week or two in Michigan, yeah? Snowmobiling and ice fishing and whatnot?"

It was clear the cop was having trouble keeping up. "Who?"

"The Milliards," Grant said, patiently.

"Yeah, I guess that's right."

"Only they didn't go anywhere this year."

"Money was tight, what with them out some business."

"And the dead girl disappeared the day before Thanksgiving?"

The cop's eyes rolled skyward in concentration. "Correct again."

"Search Milliard's walk-in fridge. That's where you'll find the body."

Al squinted at him as though trying to identify some strange species of plant. "I'd need a warrant."

"So have Fahrlander grant you one."

"Fahrlander's on Adeline's payroll, not ours, and you know how she feels about Augie. He might as well be the Second Coming after returning her dog."

"So we'll search it on our own."

"Augie would never steal a body and hide it on his property, for God's sake."

"He stole Adeline's dog."

"Bullshit. The little bitch got out."

"And Milliard just happened to be the one to find it and bring it back for the reward?"

The cop ground out the blunt on his boot heel and handed it back. "Augie's as straight as a signpost. I doubt he's ever stolen so much as a gumball."

"He felt cornered and got desperate. Maybe he caught wind of our meetings up at the house. Maybe he sneaked in, got an earful, saw the dog, snatched it, and ran."

"That's insane," Al said, but Grant could tell the notion had given him pause.

"Don't you remember? One of those nights the dog wandered off."

"Now that you mention it, I do," Al said. "The thing even barked once. Adeline called me direct about half an hour after we left to report it missing."

"Now how much do you suppose our pal August overheard? Enough to put us all behind bars a good chunk of years?"

"He can't prove anything."

"What concerns me more than what he heard is how he heard it. How did he find out about the meeting in the first place?"

Grant had already worked this out for himself, but wanted the cop to pull his own detective duty. He allowed the chief a few extra minutes to work through the smog in his brain, which the man did, at last. "Berry," he said.

"Bravo," Grant replied. "The kid used to work the orchards. I bet August pumped him for information."

"The little cocksucker. I'll have his star for this."

"You'll do nothing of the sort," Grant said. "You've heard the term double agent before, yes?"

Al broke into his own slow smile. "The valve turns both ways," he said, twisting the air like an invisible steering wheel.

"Exactly. See how useful our young Nathan Berryman can be to us. And for God's sake don't trust him with anything more than your Christmas list going forward. In the meantime, I want to search the fucking store."

"So search it. I won't tell if you won't."

Grant looked the cop over. "I'll need someone with me."

Al shook his head. "I can't be found illegally searching private property. They'd stick me in county."

"Look, just come stand outside the door then. I need eyes on my back."

Al licked his lips. "All right. This is probably that primo grass talking, but let's go before I change my mind."

Except they never got a chance to conduct their illegal search because when they made it back to their cars—Al had parked parallel to Grant—Nathan Berryman was going crazy trying to reach his boss via radio. Grant could hear the moron through the glass. The kid sounded like he might be suffering a brain embolism or perhaps a bout of particularly acidic diarrhea. Snow fell in skeins.

"Chief, it's me, it's Nate, do you copy? Chief Engel, please respond, it's urgent, copy?"

Al opened the cruiser's door, touched a gloved finger to his lips, and picked up the CB mic. "HQ, this is Mobile One responding. Over."

"Oh, thank God," the kid said. "Chief, we got a hell of a mess. We got a—" Berryman broke off as he tried to remember some police code or other. Unable to come up with it, he proceeded in civilian-speak. "Chief, we got a body. It's a girl, maybe thirteen or fourteen."

Grant froze, his hand halfway to the door handle.

Al stared at him through the snow, wide-eyed. "Anyone ID her?" he asked.

"No, sir, the caller doesn't know who she is. I called Scott at home, asked him to go out there until you could meet him."

"Who called it in?" Al asked, but Grant already knew. One of his family members.

"Sir, Lorelai Lang, sir," Berryman said, gasping, still on the verge of panic.

Grant's heart turned to clay. "I'm going to kill him," he said. "I'm going to kill the son of a bitch Milliard."

Al held up a hand. "Location of body?"

Berryman said, "Mr. Lang's barn, sir. In the loft, partway covered in hay."

They raced to the farm, Al in the lead with his lights strobing but sirens off. Grant wanted as little attention as possible. They roared up the gravel driveway, wipers slapping, and screeched to a stop beside Officer Scott Pernell's cruiser. Grant jumped out of the truck and ran up the walk, hauling open the screen door so fast it clattered against the wall while Al headed for the barn.

"Dinah? Lorelai? Where you at?" he hollered for no reason because his family all sat around the dinner table, quiet, shocked. His wife stood when he came in and went to him.

"It's awful, Grant," she said. "Who would do such a thing?"

He didn't answer. Instead he took his eldest daughter by the shoulders to look her in the eye. "Lori? Honey? Are you all right?"

She blinked like a camera shutter as if seeing him for the

first time. "Yes, I'm okay, Daddy. It just came as a shock, that's all."

"We'll talk about it later, okay? I'm sure Chief Engel will want to ask you some questions, but for now I want you to just relax and try to put it out of your mind."

"I'm fine, Dad. Really."

Grant wanted to ask her what the Sam Hill she was doing in the loft on a cold December eve, but figured that would come out in time. To Dinah he said, "I'm going up there."

Dinah only nodded her own absentminded nod, perhaps wondering how something like this could be happening to their perfect family.

Grant hurried out to the barn, moving around the tail of Scott Pernell's cruiser which had been parked outside the track door, and into the darkness within. A light in the loft burned and he could hear murmured conversation. His breath steamed. Slowly, like a man moving through molasses, he climbed the ladder.

The two lawmen huddled over something lying on the board floor resembling a ventriloquist's dummy. It was naked, which was to be expected having been stolen from the coroner's drawer. And it hadn't been here this morning because Grant himself had climbed into the loft for a spell.

Scott Pernell, the other Derby PD part-timer, was perhaps a step or two above Berryman, but not much of a cop. He knew how to fill out moving violations citations and could make a drunk recite the alphabet backward, but in practical policing he usually fetched up short. That was the impression Grant took, anyway, based on a few of Al's stories and with his own limited dealings with the man. On the whole, Scotty-boy would be better to have on a crime scene than Nathan—he'd have better odds of not fucking up the evidence—but Officer Pernell did not concern him at the moment. What concerned him was the dollish figure at his feet.

At first it didn't seem real. Grant had time to think it some horrible hoax perpetrated on his family. The girl's flesh looked too waxy to be authentic, too pale. He crouched for a closer look.

Al dismissed Officer Pernell with a brisk order to go home

and get rest. The young cop seemed more than happy to oblige and started away before Al called him back.

"You take any photos of the scene?"

"No, sir. Couldn't bring myself to do it."

"Not a word of this to anyone, Scott. We need to keep this quiet. Can I count on you for that?"

"Absolutely, boss. Not a word."

"I don't think I need to go into detail about what might happen if I'm disobeyed."

Scott blinked. "No, sir. You can count on me."

"Good. Go on. Get out of here."

Pernell made haste and Al didn't speak until they heard the cruiser's door slam. Finally he turned. "This her?" he asked Grant.

"We have to figure. I never laid eyes on her. Kodi took care of everything, said he knew how to do it."

"Where is he? I want a positive ID before we get her back to Drew."

The Russian appeared from the shadows as if conjured. He'd bundled up in a parka undoubtedly from the Motherland, the hood drawn over his head.

"Is this the girl?" Grant asked him.

Kodiak swiped the hood back from his brow and looked at the corpse. "It is."

"Any idea how she wound up here from the morgue?" Al asked.

Kodi shook his head. "*Nyet.*"

"You didn't see anyone come or go tonight?"

"I was in the barracks all night. I only roused when I heard the girl scream."

"Lorelai?" Grant asked.

"*Da.*"

Grant looked at the corpse again, half sticking out of the hay, a wide gash running ear to ear. He thought about his own girls huddled at the table. "You sure did a number on her."

The Russian shrugged a shoulder. "I have done worse in my country, to better people."

"I still think killing her was a bad call," Al said.

Grant was beginning to think so as well, but now it was too late. The deed was done. "Let's get her in the ground for God's sake."

"Drew still needs to ID her."

"Tell him to make something up and be done with it."

"All right, Grant. We'll get the ball rolling tomorrow, but these things take time."

"Kodi, put her in Al's car," he said. "And don't let any of my ladies see you do it."

The Russian hefted the body over one shoulder. When he'd gone, Grant said, "I'm going to make him pay, Al. I'm going to show him he can't get away with something like this."

"Don't start a war," Al warned. "We can't afford that."

Grant put a hand over his eyes, remembering the small body which had just been removed. Poor Lorelai had seen it too. She was a tough country girl, but she should not have been subjected to it. Better her than one of the others, but his baby should have been spared the sight. Yes, he was going to get August Milliard.

What if it wasn't him? a voice whispered in his mind. It had to be. Who else would have done it?

"I'm going to speak with Augie tonight," Al said. "See if I can't figure out where he's been the last twenty-four hours."

"No. I want him to get comfortable. And then I'm going to ruin him."

"You sure? Remember what Granny said."

"If she tries to get in my way, I'll ruin her ancient ass too."

CHAPTER FORTY

That night, after he'd calmed his understandably jumpy ladies and seen everyone off to bed, Grant sat alone in the darkened family room with the bottle of Glenlivet in one hand. Tonight seemed appropriate for breaking his harvest wagon rule.

The Christmas tree they'd trimmed only days before provided the only light. It had been a joyous affair, as always, everyone laughing and pointing out spots for ornaments, tossing tinsel in each other's hair. As Grant had steadied the star atop the Douglas fir, he'd been able to put his troubles out of mind. And as he lifted his precious Penny, the lone daughter in whom the possibility of Santa Claus still lived, to hang her stocking, he had known a peace and comfort he'd not felt since before marriage.

Now all seemed to be coming undone. He knew he still had time to fix it, but he'd have to hurry. And he'd need help.

For perhaps the fiftieth time since hearing the call from Berryman, Grant made a mental list of the principals involved and where they ranked. August Milliard topped the list. He would need to be dealt with in the harshest possible manner. Grant already had a scheme brewing in that regard. If Adeline Gable found out, he would deal with her as well. But dealing with her would be different than dealing with August. He was fairly sure he could slip the poison from the packet he kept in his coat pocket into her coffee or one of the medicine bottles she kept in her cabinet. Otherwise, she might slip and fall down the stairs. It was known to happen with the elderly. Of course, he'd have to work around the goons she kept on site, but they held a combined IQ in the double digits. They would pose little problem, should push (literally) come to shove.

Milliard, though, he wanted alive. He wanted the man to suffer for as long as humanly possible. The whoremonger deserved nothing less after putting Grant in this position.

He watched the Christmas lights glint in the darkness a bit longer, then got on his coat and boots and trudged out to the barracks beyond the barn. He wanted Kodi to find him another girl, only this time he wanted her alive. And local.

Susan Milliard had fully recovered from the mumps but found it nearly impossible to catch up on the homework after missing so much school. A bout with the stomach flu not long after the swelling in her cheeks subsided had done nothing to help her situation. The worst part was she'd missed a research paper on *Frankenstein*, which Mr. Dunlop had assigned before Halloween, and had to spend much of her free time reading and writing. On top of that, she still needed to finish three units from her *Practical Mathematics* text, four chapters of American History, and balance a handful of ledgers for Accounting. Add on a mild but annoying learning disability (dysgraphia) and it had taken her staying after school two days a week in the library with only old Miss Vander Haag and her cold librarian's glare as company. Susie hoped they were paying the poor woman overtime, but doubted it. Now, on the final day of school before Christmas vacation, she couldn't help but watch the clock.

It hadn't been so bad when Rachel had still been attending Derby High. But Susie's best friend had been forced to transfer to St. Joseph's Catholic School on the other side of town because her parents had gone crazy when they'd found out she liked Susie's older brother. Well, that wasn't quite right—Rachel's *mother* had gone crazy. Her father had seemed overjoyed at the prospect. It wasn't fair. People can't help who they're attracted to (even if Susie did think it a little weird her best friend found her big brother attractive).

Rachel used to wait with Susan, browsing the shelves or thumbing through *Archie* comics while her friend feverishly drafted and redrafted her *Frankenstein* paper. Now the place seemed positively empty without Rachel's calming presence.

Old Vander Haag reminded her of some witch eyeing her opportunity to snatch Susie up and take her home to boil in her cauldron. A lot of kids even called her Old Hag behind her back, so complete was her witchy image.

Sometimes Rachel would walk from St. Joe's and wait for Susie in the football bleachers. Susan had told her she didn't need to do that, but Rachel merely shrugged and said, "What else am I going to do? Go home and listen to my Deep Purple albums again?" Susan didn't know how her best friend got away with listening to what Ruth Safford undoubtedly would have labeled "devil music," but Rachel was crafty. She had a quiet cunning way about her, something Susie desperately envied and acutely admired.

Now she glanced at the clock ticking above the circulation desk while the shadows deepened over campus. She couldn't see the football field from the tall windows facing Cherry Street, but hoped to find Rachel there once she finished for the day despite the snow they'd gotten the night before. Only one more day before winter break. She could do this. Susie put her head down and scribbled in her notebook.

"Time's up, Susan," the librarian barked. Susie jumped. She'd been lost in a brilliant (in her opinion, at least) passage about *Frankenstein* as a metaphor for the Industrial Revolution. The clock stood at half past four. "Gather your things and go home."

"Well, Merry Christmas, ma'am," she said. The librarian return the sentiment in a sour vinegar voice. Susie gathered her belongings while imagining the perfect marital union between Ebenezer Scrooge and Miss Vander Haag, what kind of pillow talk they might have. She made a pit stop at her locker, dumped all her unnecessary materials, shrugged into her coat, and dragged her cable-knit cap over her ears before pushing out into the graying afternoon.

The bleachers, she noted glumly but without much surprise, stood empty. The snow had tapered to flurries and Susan had the grounds to herself. Well, not entirely. A figure stood in the far end zone, beside the goal post. Susie squinted, hoping to make out the features of Rachel Safford, but no—this figure stood much too tall for her friend's frame.

The last light, dying, sunk the field in shadow. Could the person at the far end be an errant player, coming to throw a few footballs before Christmas break? If so, why wasn't he? The first twinges of fear gnawed at Susie's stomach.

Her first thought was that she would rush back into the school and find Miss Vander Haag before the librarian could escape, but too late—the woman's ancient Chevy putted out of the lot and up Cherry Street toward the highway. The school would be completely deserted now, even the custodian gone for the day.

Susie glanced back at the figure and realized with horror it had drawn nearer—it hovered now on the 20-yard line. She took two stumbling steps backward. Her heels knocked against a concrete parking block and she fell over on her bottom, hard. She barely registered the pain in her tailbone. Her attention remained focused on the figure advancing across the frozen football field. It was not, she now realized with panic, a rueful player ruminating on the results of the Devils' mediocre season.

She scrambled to her feet, slipped, then finally hauled herself up with the aid of the post bearing the sign reserving the space for *Dr. Spieth, Principal*. Any other day of the week, students would be glad to avoid the heavy-breathing head of Derby High, but today Susie wished with all her heart he'd come charging out of the building and demand to know the meaning of this. But he'd lumbered past the library and out the door at three o'clock sharp, bundled head to toe, an early start on Christmas vacation clearly in mind.

The bottom line: No one could help her except herself.

The figure abruptly sprinted through the snow as if sensing her helplessness and desperation. It was close enough to see it wore a heavy parka with a fur-lined hood, stained work pants, and boots of black leather. Thick gloves protected the fingers which now stretched ahead of it.

Susan shrieked, knowing it would do no good. Derby High's humble campus was as deserted as the moon. She scrambled up, her feet sliding on the icy walk, slipped again, and then the treads of her boots caught the snowpack and she jolted forward.

She had time to think, *All I have to do is make it to the corner* because she could see the steady traffic of Market Street from here—she would be able to flag down someone—and that's when a glove smelling of oil and grime closed over her face. It was the smell of the thing she'd seen in the corn maze the, the thing she'd thought of as a werewolf. But it wasn't a werewolf. This was a monster of another kind.

CHAPTER FORTY-ONE

Dinah had nearly finished washing dishes when the phone rang. Normally she made one of the girls wash and another wipe, but tonight she'd allowed them to watch the Radio City Christmas Spectacular on television. The event had become something of a tradition among the girls, at least two of whom (Alexandra and Penny) dreamed of one day becoming Rockettes themselves. They seemed to have mostly gotten over the excitement of the gruesome discovery in the Lang barn and that was good. Only Alex, the second-youngest, had come in the night after complaining of bad dreams. Grant had soothed her, gotten her a drink of water, and sent her back to bed without further incident.

Dinah dried her hands on the damp dish cloth and picked up the kitchen extension, meaning to use the greeting she reserved for this time of year: *Happy holidays from the Lang residence!* but did not get a chance to speak.

"Grant, that you?" a man's voice demanded. He sounded breathless, like a winded jogger.

"I'm sorry, Grant isn't home right now," she told the caller, brows knitted together.

"Dinah, this is Al. It's imperative I get in touch with Grant immediately. Do you know when he'll be home?"

"Gosh, Al, I'm sorry but I don't. He said he wanted to run up to Murdoch and see about some tractor parts at John Deere and finish up some Christmas shopping. Left right after supper."

"John Deere in Murdoch, you say? Thanks, Di."

"Al, is something wrong?" she asked. "This doesn't have anything to do with ... what happened the other day?"

The lawman hesitated as though wrestling with a decision.

"No. Listen, if Grant gets home before I get a chance to speak with him, please tell him to wait there for me. I'll be by in an hour."

"Is this really necessary? The girls have been through a lot these past few days."

"It's absolutely one hundred percent necessary," he said and broke the connection.

Dinah poured coffee and sat at the kitchen table. What was happening? If Grant was keeping things from her, she had a right to know. The way the chief of police had sounded, the things being kept behind the scenes were indeed dire. She sipped, then pushed it away and strode to the family room archway. The girls were busy giggling over the music and the costumes, engrossed in the televised extravaganza. Good.

Dinah crept to her husband's office, easing the door closed behind her before switching on the light. She knew Grant valued his privacy and his unofficial rule was no one entered his territory without permission, but this situation warranted an exception.

Without much hope of finding anything—Grant was as meticulous as he was private—she sat at his roll top desk and began rummaging through drawers. When she reached the bottom of the third, she found something.

Grant was neither shopping for tractor parts nor Christmas shopping. He'd gone out to the cabin to meet Kodi.

"The mission was a success?" he asked the Russian.

"Of course."

"You were not seen?"

The young Ruskie did not dignify this with a verbal response; he merely cocked his head at an inquiring angle.

"And you stashed the bundle where I told you to?"

"Yes, Mr. Lang."

"You didn't harm her?"

"All is well." Something sparked in the Russian's eye that Grant didn't care for and he noticed the question wasn't directly answered. He didn't push the envelope. The young man had a dangerous—scratch that—a completely psychotic side Grant hoped to never see firsthand. He'd already seen it secondhand with the poor kid someone had stashed in the Lang loft.

Not someone, he thought. *Milliard. It was that goddamn August Milliard and now we have his daughter and let's see how the smug son of a bitch likes that quid pro quo.*

The girl would not be hurt. Scared breathless? Yes. But not hurt. Susan Milliard had become merely another token in the game between August and himself. Had he gone overboard with sinking to abduction? Maybe. But he'd learned it from his rival with the whole Jontue caper. Grant would keep the young dear stored out of sight a day or two and then instruct Kodi to turn her loose where Grant would conveniently be positioned to pick her up and bring her into Derby PD.

Had he made a mistake by not clearing it with Al first? Another maybe, but he thought the lawman would understand and accept the necessity of such action. He'd have to. Grant had given the order on impulse, not the way he liked to operate as a rule, but his fury had reached peak intensity once the discovery had been made in their barn. And by his sweet Lorelai no less.

But Lori seemed untroubled by her discovery. When asked (in the gentlest possible tones) what she'd been doing out in the hayloft in the dead of winter, she'd said only that she was getting some air. In his interrogation following the discovery, with Al present, he had gotten her reassurance the discovery of the body had not harmed her mentally.

"I've seen dead bodies before, Daddy," she'd said. He didn't think the retouched corpses of his parents and Dinah's in their funeral caskets counted, but he didn't press it.

"If you feel the need to talk to someone about this," he had said, "do not hesitate to ask. We'll get you over to see Doc Rubek, pronto."

Lorelai had agreed, but Grant did not imagine the need for her to see a doctor. His eldest was not one to be scarred by such a revelation. Any of the others, maybe. *Probably.* Especially Bonnie or Penny, who were gentler souls. But not his Lorelai. She processed reality differently than most. Calculated and detached. Clinical, even.

Even so, Grant could not abide Augie's trespass. Retaliation was automatic.

"Milliard forced my hand," he told Kodi now.

The Russian bobbed his head but said nothing. And did Grant detect the hint of a smile playing around the young man's lips?

"Something funny?" he asked.

"No, Mr. Lang."

"Good. You're on guard duty tonight. Make sure she's warm, comfortable, and fed," Grant said. He removed a roll of bills from his pocket, peeled off a small stack, and forked it over to his subordinate. "Get her something good. Not that swill Gert Arden slings."

"Yes, Mr. Lang."

"And, for the love of Christ, don't let her see your face."

"Of course not."

"And don't lay a finger on her," Grant said, raising one of his own in the air. "I read Andrew's autopsy report on that homeless girl you took from the city. It said she'd been sexually violated."

Now a grin did unspool on the Ruskie's face. "You did not specify otherwise, Mr. Lang."

"I mean it. Don't you even think about touching that child," he said.

He sent his underling off with a flap of his hand, then paced around the cabin. The product grew fantastically in these optimal conditions, but he was ready to expand into new territory. Marijuana was good, but being replaced by stronger stuff in some places. Heroine. Methamphetamines. Cocaine, in urban and suburban areas. People needed bigger, stronger, and longer escapes from their terrible realities and Grant would provide it. He needed to stay on top of the market. The sale of green plants— corn and weed—had him primed to branch out. Mike Stone's man, the old Indian with no name, had people from his tribe who could ship in the supplies to manufacture good stuff and people in the city who could receive it. But they couldn't manufacture it. Not there in the city with cops crawling everywhere. No, it needed to be mixed up out here in corn country.

He stopped, all thoughts of drug manufacture and money leaving his head. Had taking Susan been overkill? Had he overstepped? Would Milliard suspect him?

It didn't matter. It couldn't be helped now. Done is done and fun is fun, like his old man used to say.

Grant prepared to lock up and head home when someone pounded on the door. He froze, thinking August had come to confront him personally. But this building was clearly marked with No Trespassing signs any sane man would know well enough to heed. In these parts, No Trespassing was practically the Eleventh Commandment—and it always implied the trespasser could be shot on sight.

"Open the door, Mr. Lang. I know you're in there," a voice called and at first Grant thought it actually was August. It was similar, but not quite right. He hauled the door open and stared down another of his subordinates.

"I don't care for your tone, son," he told Dennis Milliard, before taking note of the boy's state: flaming cheeks, sweaty brow, wet and wild eyes. He knew, then. Of course he did. The whole town must know by now, even though it had only been ninety minutes since the abduction. When the girl hadn't arrived home promptly for her after-school milk and cookies, Milliard had probably dialed the President of the United States directly.

"Did you do it?" Dennis had the audacity to demand.

"Do what exactly?" he said, steeping his voice in gruff authority.

"Do you know where my sister is?"

"Your sister? Why, I'm certain all your dear siblings are cozied up beside the fireplace this very minute, discussing what Santy Claus might dump in their socks this year."

Playing dumb worked. He watched the boy's face collapse into a canyon of despair. Dennis hung his head and his shoulders shook. "Susie's gone. She never came home from school."

"Oh," Grant said, resting a consoling hand on the kid's trembling shoulder. "Oh, Dennis, I'm sorry to hear it." He considered. "Do you suppose ... do you suppose she just got a set of itchy feet and decided to take a powder?"

Dennis lifted his face, regarding his superior with bloodshot eyes and a sliver of hope in his voice. "Do you think that's all it is? She got sick of school and maybe ran off somewhere? I know all the make-up work drove her crazy."

"Of course, son. That's got to be it. Sometimes people simply need a breather. Have your parents been on her case?"

Dennis bobbed his head. "Dad especially. He's been hounding her to finish the work she missed. Susie's not stupid, but schoolwork gives her trouble sometimes. It's hard for her to learn from books."

"And wasn't all that missed schoolwork his fault in the first place?" Grant asked gently. "Because he refused to get her—or any of you—vaccinated?"

Something new dawned on Dennis's face. New and slightly ugly. "Yeah," he said. "Yeah, that's right."

"It's a wonder you all weren't struck down with it and forced to stay after school." He paused to let that sink in before adding: "But perhaps if you were—even one of you—someone would have been with her to talk her out of running away."

The new thing calcified in the boy's handsome features; the sudden set of his jaw gave it away. "I'll have to bring that up to my dad."

"Well, go easy on him, son," Grant said. "He must be out of his mind with worry. In the meantime, try to stay calm. I'm sure Susan will turn up soon. It's cold out there, after all."

"Thank you, Mr. Lang," Dennis said, grasping his boss's hand and giving it a single hard pump. "She's probably home already."

"I'd set my watch by it," Grant said, the lie rolling easily across his tongue like summer thunder through a valley. He walked the young man back to his mother's car which had been parked beside Grant's truck in the dead end. They shook hands again and then drove out to the highway one behind the other.

CHAPTER FORTY-TWO

Kodiak Aristov carried the steaming pie through the woods to the cabin a quarter mile into the trees. One thing he loved about America—one thing of many—was the food. How abundant it was! You merely had to step into any of a handful of establishments and for a pittance could eat yourself into a coma. The land of plenty indeed.

He told everyone he hailed from Leningrad, but that couldn't be further from the truth. Kodiak had grown up in a ramshackle village on the southwestern edge of Siberia. His father had been a farmer, but the land he'd farmed had been nothing like the bountiful richness of the soils of the American Midwest. The family fields grew mostly stunted potatoes and weeds. His father did not earn enough to survive, so Kodiak and his brothers fished and hunted. They ate anything they shot, be it bear, musk deer, or muskrat. One particularly scarce winter they survived on wild-berry garnished wolverine. You never wasted good meat.

It was never enough. He knew something had to give for the family to survive, so he'd decamped and headed west so that his portions could be rationed to his younger siblings. He joined up with a branch of Bratva, the Russian Mafia in Moscow, after proving his worth by slitting the throat of an old man reading a newspaper in broad daylight on a bench near St. Peter's Basilica. For three years he learned the ways of the street: stealing, raping, killing, dodging authority. His compadres made sure he understood what would happen if he was caught—he would find himself in some dank Kremlin cellar where masked men would start taking off his toes with garden shears and work their way north. Slowly. And they would take their time in the nether regions. Kodi never got caught. Before long he had worked his way up the ranks and had been granted his own branch to control, but around the same time the police had worked out his identity and had it plastered all over the city.

There had been no choice but to flee.

First to Leningrad, then to London, then to Chicago where he'd found work in a foundry and rented a one-room flat in the Back of the Yards neighborhood. Colored folk dominated the area, but they didn't bother him. Maybe they sensed the danger in him or maybe they merely didn't figure he was worth a second glance. He clearly had nothing of value, with his dirty long hair and his shoddy foreign clothes. If any did take a moment to speak to him, Kodiak merely acted as if he spoke no English.

In fact, Kodiak Aristov wasn't even his real name; he'd picked one of those names stupid Americans would be able to pronounce, like something out of a low-budget spy movie.

He'd stashed the Milliard girl in the woods of Murdoch, north of Derby. Mike Stone, his boss's partner, had discovered the shack on one of his hunting trips. He claimed it likely once belonged to the Frayne clan, a family of inbred hicks, who may have abandoned it when they migrated to the other side of town, near the river. In any case, it sat forgotten in a thick copse of elms and surrounded by a wall of brambles.

There wasn't much to the place, but there didn't need to be. The single room had two windows, which had been carefully covered in butcher's paper so as to obscure the glow of the ancient pot-bellied stove and the kerosene lantern turned low on the rough-hewn table. There were no chairs except the single wobble-legged ladderback Mike himself had brought from his attic. This was not a place of leisure; no poker games would ever be held beneath the half-collapsed tarpaper roof. No, this was a place of isolation. Of secrecy. It was, in fact, the place the young man calling himself Kodiak Aristov had first raped and then murdered the homeless girl from Chicago. How she had screamed for mercy before he'd drawn the bayonet across her tender throat! Screaming here did not matter, of course. She might as well have tried screaming in outer space. The only things to hear her would be the woodland creatures of the night, who would have been terrified at her shrill, broken voice.

The slow crawl of smoke up the broken chimney dissipated into the night air before it even reached the treetops. Not that he needed to worry about someone spotting the smoke and coming for a look-see. Not on a night such as this. In the coming days, if the search party for the young Derby girl widened northward, the cabin might become problematic. But Mr. Lang had made assurances they would not keep her here long. Kodi found this agreeable as losing such a strategic location would be unfavorable.

He hauled the pizza he'd purchased the final ten yards through the bramble wall (they'd cut a patch away as a makeshift gate) and up to the door, which he shoved open with one shoulder. The girl chained to the iron bed frame gave a small shriek at the intrusion and yanked her pants up. She'd been about to use the bucket he'd given her for toilet purposes.

"Do not mind me," he said. "Go about your business."

Her face, ghost-white behind a veil of tear-streaked dust, lay naked and open. "Please, sir. Please let me go. I won't tell anyone."

He kept the ski mask in place as he set about preparing her dinner. She had not seen his face, but she had heard him speak and it wouldn't take authorities long to determine his identity. He hoped Lang would let him kill her soon. He also hoped he'd let Kodi have some fun with her first—she was what these stupid Americans called "foxy." He'd had his eye on her for some time, since before she took sick. He knew his boss had ordered no harm to befall the girl, but Kodi thought he'd find a way to change his mind.

"Do your business," Kodi told her. "I promise not to peek."

"I don't have to anymore," the girl said. She looked the pizza box over.

"You are hungry, no?"

"I haven't eaten since hot lunch in school," she said.

Kodi tore the cardboard top off the box and slid half the pie over to her on it. She bent to retrieve it and wrinkled her nose.

"I don't like mushrooms," she said.

"Mushrooms should be a staple of every diet. How would

you survive in the wild without mushrooms?"

The girl seemed to relax a little. Perhaps she sensed he meant her no harm. Foolish girl. "I would eat other things. Wild berries. Walnuts. *Apples.*"

"The wilderness of your fancy is a soft one indeed, girl. Eat."

Susan picked off as many of the fungi as she could and started chewing through the cooling cheese. "How long are you going to keep me?" she asked through a mouthful.

"Until we no longer need you."

"What do you need me for?"

"No more talk. Eat."

She did, slowly, her face beautiful in the orange light of the stove. Yes, Kodi hoped Mr. Lang would authorize some fun before disposing of her. You never wasted good meat.

Lorelai's goose was cooked, and she knew it. She sat with her feet tucked beneath her on the far end of the davenport, staring at the Rockettes performing a number at the Radio City Music Hall Christmas Show without really seeing them. How could she have been so stupid to put her entire future in jeopardy? A future which figured to be a good and prosperous one, no matter where she turned up?

One hand crept to her belly as she considered the life growing there inside it. She had missed her last period, which did not mean much on its own as they did not come as regularly her sister Bonnie's or her best friend Hannah's did. She'd once gone three months without, so long she'd nearly gone to Doc Rubek's to be tested for pregnancy even though she'd not yet engaged in intercourse (raised Catholic, the idea of Virgin Birth could not be ruled out). But then the blood had come again, heavy and with a vengeance, as if to make up for lost time.

This time, though, something felt different. If pressed to describe what, exactly, she doubted she'd be able to. Lorelai felt a certain added *weight* about her, not physical, precisely, but indubitably present. Almost a spiritual presence. She wouldn't go to Doc Rubek right away; even though she knew he wouldn't say anything to her parents, things had a way of getting around town anyway. *The fields have ears,* her father often said, and while he meant it mostly humorously, it also carried some truth. Secrets didn't stay hidden long in Ashford County.

As the final credits rolled and her sisters' chatter intensified, Lorelai made her way upstairs and closed her bedroom door. As the eldest, she had been allowed a room to herself and tonight she was grateful for the privacy.

I'll go to Wyndham Rx tomorrow and buy one of those over-the-counter tests, she thought. But that would do no good, especially if Danielle Craycroft was clerking. Danielle might not be the biggest gossip in town, but she came in a close second behind Edna Hadsell. Even if she lucked out and got one of the others, the news of her covert purchase would be whispered through party lines within the hour.

Lorelai knew what she had to do and resolved to do it first thing in the morning. In the meantime, she undressed and looked at her body in the full-length mirror suspended on the back of her door. She cupped her breasts—were they fuller now? She ran her palms over her belly, seeking a rise and fancied she felt one. She stared at the thatch of hair between her legs and thought about what lay beneath it and how much trouble it could bring a person.

Why had she slept with Dennis? Why, when he clearly had no interest in her? When he seemed intent on loving the little Jesus-freak? Why, God, *why?*

God offered no answer. Instead, she fancied He sent her a better question. Why had she slept with Kodi Aristov?

CHAPTER FORTY-THREE

Six and a half miles east, the one Lorelai Lang had dubbed "the little Jesus-freak" also stood naked in her bedroom, but for an entirely different reason. She was on Day Twenty-Two of her month-long punishment. After Rachel and Dennis had come back to the Thanksgiving party holding hands, her mother Ruth had become convinced he'd "taken her purity." She'd lost her mind, forcing Rachel to change schools and forbidding her to see "that dirty boy" again while grounding her until Ruth could come up with a "just punishment" to fit her "only daughter's betrayal."

"You can't make me change schools. Dad won't let you," she had said that night after the family had driven home from the Gable party. Ray had slunk off to get Samuel ready for bed and to leave the womenfolk to their talk as such dealings bewildered him.

Ruth's eyes had blazed as a crooked leer spread across her face. "If you think that man is your father, you're as stupid as he is."

Rachel's paternity had long been a question in her mind—she carried absolutely no trace of Raymond Safford in her features—but hearing it spoken plain and true had knocked her back a step as easily as if her mother had slapped her face. Her mother had left her to stew in this new data while Ruth went to pray to God for guidance.

The next morning, God had purportedly answered with the punishment He preferred for a wanton girl.

For the entire month of December—31 days—Rachel Safford was to pay penance by standing nude on a stool in her bedroom so that "the Good Lord God and all His Heavenly Host" could see her wickedness plain. Rachel thought that if God really wanted to see her wickedness, He'd have only to peek into the attic crawlspace once or twice a week, but kept her mouth shut. She knew better than to talk back against her mother.

The first night, three weeks ago, Ruth had stood in her only daughter's room with her arms crossed.

"You want me to undress in *front* of you?" Rachel had asked.

"Darling, I'm your *mother*," had been Ruth's retort, as if that solved everything. It left no room for debate and Rachel had slowly removed every stitch of clothing. When she slid her blue jeans down, she had expected her mother to go into a fresh torrent of hysterics at the scars crisscrossing the pliant thighs. But Ruth hadn't. A slow smile had trembled to life instead.

"Oh, don't think I'm not aware of your little hobby, darling," Ruth had said. "I know about your hideaway, your blades, your devil music. I'm in possession of a great wealth of knowledge. The Good Lord keeps me in the *loop*."

Now, on the twenty-second day of her punishment, as she stood on her stool beneath the overhead lamp, staring at the blank wall before her (posters were strictly forbidden in the house, though each room was adorned with a framed rendition of the Lord's Prayer alongside a silver crucifix), with her mother sitting on the bed reading her Bible for the duration of the hour, a knock came at the door.

"Who is it?" Ruth called in a voice that forbade foolishness. She tolerated no interruption during her daughter's penance except in the most serious of matters.

"Ruthie?" her husband's voice called. "Telephone for you, dear."

"Take a message, Raymond, for Grace's sake."

"It's Father Scudder. Said it couldn't wait."

Ruth sighed and snapped her Bible closed. If anything could pull her away from duties at home, it was duties at church. She glanced her daughter over, long and appraising, and said, "Don't let me find out you've moved a so much as an eyelash, young lady. I may not be able to see it, but your Creator will."

She left the room without another word, leaving the door open an inch behind her, perhaps to let her charge know she wouldn't be completely out of earshot. Rachel stood on the stool, watching the door. She didn't mind her punishment, on the whole, and believed she at least partially deserved it. For Dennis Milliard, she would stand on a stool a thousand years.

Had she entertained impure thoughts about him? Oh, yes. On many occasions. Sometimes in her attic hideaway (now not so hidden) and sometimes while she bathed. During those moments of solitude, while she had the lone bathroom to herself, the claw foot tub filled with warm suds, Rachel Safford would let her hand creep low, to the secret spot. She would imagine her and Dennis in the leaves, isolated from the universe, from her mother, from God Himself. And in the dark, warm womb, she and her soulmate would find true love.

The door creaked. Rachel snapped back from her fancy. She kept her eyes on the door. Slowly, it eased inward, emitting a final caw from the hinges.

Caleb stood in the corridor. He took her in, his eyes flicking from her face to her breasts, to the secret place she meant to keep for Dennis. He'd seen her naked, of course, but it had been years ago, before her body had changed. She'd seen him look at her before, but had never translated it into anything other than harmless brotherly curiosity.

The way he eyed her now was not harmless. His bloodless lips, thin to begin with, parted and the edge of his tongue crept out. His nostrils flared like a coyote scenting prey. Only his eyes remained unchanged, the same dead black they'd been since boyhood.

Rachel covered herself with her hands.

"You better get," she said. "Mom will be back soon."

Caleb gave her another once-over before moving on. Rachel blinked, her face rushing with blood, and hopped down off her perch only long enough to push the door closed. Not all the way, though. She knew better than to leave it any other way than precisely as her mother had left it.

Rachel closed her eyes and tried to rid herself of the experience. She tried to imagine her and Dennis in the leaf pile, but it now it was Caleb's hand that found hers in the damp autumn musk. Hot liquid rose up her throat and she managed to keep it down only through sheer willpower until her mother came to dismiss her from that day's punishment.

Grant had a stop off to make before heading home. He urgently wanted to be with his family, but business needed tending to. He pulled up outside Zebulon Tuel's hovel and got out. The cold air smelled of woodsmoke and roast fowl (which variety, he couldn't say, but doubted very much it was turkey Marbella). A lone window had been framed in Christmas lights by way of season's greetings. He took the short walk to the ill-hung front door and banged on it.

At first there came no reply, as if the occupant might be trying to decide whether or not to answer. But even Zeb knew enough that any visitor would see the smoke crawling from the chimney.

"Whozit?" a hoarse voice called from within. Drunk already and not yet eight o'clock.

"Your employer," Grant called. "Open up."

The door gapped inward an inch. Grant noted with humor the flimsy chain bridging the gap between door and jamb that looked as though an enthusiastic toddler could snap it. A bloodshot eye appeared over the bridge of tarnished links. "Yes, Mr. Lang?"

"Aren't you going to invite me in?"

"Tell you the truth, sir, my house ain't kept up for company."

Grant thought the word *house* a bit strong in this context, but chose not to challenge it. "Zeb, we need to talk. Man to man."

"If it's about the arrest, sir, I assure you it won't happen again."

"Open the fucking door."

Zeb closed the door, slid back the delicate chain, and opened up. Grant stepped across the threshold into what turned out to indeed be the smell of fowl roasting on a spit beneath a ramshackle mantel. Grant wondered if the homeowner had gotten lucky and pegged a pigeon with his .22. A steaming pot hung beside it, some kind of stew. A warped record player spun some Motown bullshit about there ain't no sunshine when she's gone, only darkness every day. Zeb himself wore only a pair of heavily-patched trousers.

"Looks like I caught you at dinner."

"It's no bother, Mr. Lang," the salesman said, eyes downcast. And ashamed he should be. Debris decorated the floor: empty liquor bottles, filthy socks, stacks of old newspaper tied up with twine. Something that appeared to be a headless nutcracker stood atop the crumbling mantelpiece.

"I won't keep you long, Zeb," Grant said. "Only long enough to tell you that if you get arrested again, you'll be gone."

Zeb nodded at the floor. "Yes, sir. I understand. I won't make nearly as much at another job, but I understand."

Grant gripped his subordinate's shoulder like a vice until Zeb squirmed. "I don't mean you'll be out of a job, my friend. I mean you'll be out of a life. Same as your old man got. You dig me?" He concluded his discourse with the worst epithet for a person of color a white man can utter.

Zeb's head jerked up and he found his employer's eyes. Word around the woodpile had it ol' Zeb took exception to a white man openly discussing the fate his old man had suffered at the dawn of the civil rights movement, not to mention the tagged-on vulgarity. If he decided to challenge it, Grant might be in very real trouble as the other man had every conceivable physical advantage over him. But the terror he saw dancing in those drunken eyes betrayed total loss. Total resignation. He had Zeb beat, and they both knew it.

The subordinate nodded once, his lip quivering. "Yes, sir, Mr. Lang. It won't happen again."

"Good boy," Grant said, patting one stubbled cheek. "You go on and enjoy your dinner."

On his way out, Zebulon Tuel called something that might have made another man rueful of his ill-treatment, but it only served to reassure Grant Lang of the power he kept over his underlings.

"Merry Christmas, Mr. Lang. Happy New Year, too."

Grant didn't bother to return the tidings and he grinned at his windshield all the way home.

Mary Lou Zahn crept out of the shack's sole bedroom, Zeb's robe tied at her waist. She clutched the lapels closed at the throat as if trying to keep out a deep chill.

"Is he gone?" she whispered.

Zeb did not turn and he did not answer; she could read his response in the slump of his shoulders.

"I heard what he said," Mary Lou told him, touching his elbow. "You don't pay him any mind, Zeb."

"He's my boss."

"Why don't you quit?"

"Where am I going to find pay as good as this?"

"You come on back and work with me at the Country Store."

He took her hands. "You don't understand, Mare. I'm in hock with some guys. Mr. Milliard, he pays decent, but nothing like Mr. Lang does."

"What if you get busted again? What if Chief Engel can't get you out of it next time?"

Zeb let out a shuddery sigh. "I don't know."

"Let's worry about it later, okay? Let me serve you supper."

"Not hungry."

"You have to eat."

"I'd rather drink."

"Later. How about dessert first?" She slid the robe off her shoulders.

Zeb found a grin hiding in his face after all. "You got a deal, mama."

CHAPTER FORTY-FOUR

Grant knew he ought to get home and he nearly went. If he had, things might have worked out different for everyone. Might have not. Either way, he wanted to go straight home, get warm by the fire, and maybe catch the tail end of the Radio City Christmas program. Those Rockettes had some gams on them, no doubt about it.

Except instead of turning left onto the county route that would bear him homeward, he drove north. Toward Murdoch and the woods outside town. He had to make sure Susan Milliard had not been hurt.

Because the longer he mulled it over, the less he trusted Kodi. The man was insane, clearly. He and Al and Mike would have to figure a way to cut him out, and the sooner the better. The Russian had been great when the work had only been farming. But now that it had gone beyond that, Grant did not like the man's involvement. Drew's report about the sexual assault of the city girl scared him. Who would do such a thing? What kind of sick asshole would rape a *child*?

A tickle at the back of his mind arose: *What kind of sick asshole would approve of a child to be murdered?*

"That's different," he said aloud in the warm cab of his pickup. "The child had no home. No food. No future. She's better off dead. Death was a blessing."

He'd told himself the same thing time and again since giving Kodi the nod. Sometimes it helped him sleep at night, but most often it didn't. Especially since the discovery of the body in his loft. The past nights had been restless for him, plagued by nightmares of walking dolls with straw in their hair. He hoped those would pass quickly, but felt he might be disappointed in that wish.

Twenty minutes on, he found the tire tracks of the car Kodi had used and pulled to a stop in them. It pleased him to see the road vacant. That meant the Russian had returned to the barracks behind the barn. It meant he wasn't here, tormenting the poor girl.

Grant snagged a pair of ski goggles out of the glove compartment, then pulled his scarf around his face and began the long trudge through the snow. He wanted to be anywhere but here, only he had to be sure. He had to know the Milliard girl had not been molested. As soon as he ascertained that, he'd head straight home, spend the rest of the evening with his family, and then begin the plan of excising the Russian from their operation. He'd need to talk to Al and Mike. Grant guessed Al had already tried to call him at home, maybe even driven out to the farm.

"Let's make this quick," he said, his breath pluming into the night air, and picked his way through the trees.

At the start of her junior year of high school, Lorelai had predicted that within two decades nearly everyone would carry mobile telephones and could call anyone in the world at any time. Grant thought her prediction a touch ambitious—fifty years, maybe, but not twenty—but wished bitterly for one right now to save himself the snowy trek.

Some animal paced him through the trees for a time, a hungry coyote perhaps. Bears sometimes wandered this far south out of Minnesota and Wisconsin, but this companion wasn't nearly large enough. Unless it was a cub, in which case Grant would need to beware the mama. He whistled at it, called for it to show itself, but after a spell the companion split off for prey less dangerous.

The cabin appeared ahead, dark and desolate. A casual hiker would spot it and steer clear of its dilapidated walls and sagging roof. Grant made sure his scarf fully covered his face and resettled the ski goggles over his eyes, then opened the door and stepped inside.

The shack was empty. The fire in the stove had died to embers. The chain which should have shackled Susan lay slack. Grant lifted the goggles and spun in a slow circle, making sure the girl hadn't somehow freed herself and hidden away in a shadowy corner.

"You goddam Ruskie," Grant said to the empty hovel. "You better not have laid one red finger on that girl."

He ran back to the truck. If anything pursued him this time, Grant did not hear.

When he pulled into the drive, he did not bother parking near the house; he roared straight up the short turnout leading to the barracks the hired men used. As Kodi was the only one he'd kept on full-time, the young man had the place to himself—and that worried Grant mightily.

The 1951 Dodge Fargo pickup they used for covert operations (no one outside the Lang family knew of its existence; it had rested covered under a tarp for years behind the shed before Grant got the idea to use it for their marijuana outfit) sat parked outside. He realized his mistake in letting Kodi take any type of initiative. He fumbled around in the glove box for the 9mm Llama III he kept there beneath a flurry of road maps, and hoped he wouldn't have to use it.

He shouldered through the door into darkness smelling of sweat, burned food, and old leather. Even if he couldn't see, Grant knew someone else occupied the space. He could hear someone trying to keep quiet … and trying to keep someone else quiet, probably with a hand over a mouth.

The barracks hadn't been outfitted with electricity until 1960 and the man Grant had hired on the cheap held no license. Thus, no switches existed near the doors and one had to shamble eight feet into the main room and feel about for a pull string connected to a single bare bulb.

All at once he knew what needed to be done. Grant had made an enormous error and he had to correct it before it snowballed into something he could no longer contain. Now was the time. He needed to choose his words carefully, as they could be recalled on a witness stand.

"Kodiak, turn the girl loose," he called into the blackness. "We know you kidnapped her. Chief Engel is on his way here now. No one has to get hurt and no one has to go to jail. You may be deported, but that's a risk you'll have to take. Now let her go, nice and steady."

Grant could sense the confusion in the room. He took a step inside and eased the door closed behind him so he would not be silhouetted against the floodlight in the yard in case his charge had taken up a firearm. He didn't think Kodi would—the man preferred his Godforsaken bayonet, but it was better to err on the side of caution. He took a step forward, toward the bunks.

"Kodi, let's not make this difficult. Everyone knows you're the one who killed that poor girl in the corn maze. Everyone knows you hurt that boy—and if they don't, they will soon enough."

"Liar!" the Russian called, giving away his position up ahead and to the left. Near the bunk he'd claimed his first day on the job. "Don't you *lie*, Lang!"

Yes. Grant had him now. "It wasn't hard to figure out once I heard Susie went missing. I knew all about your tendencies toward young girls, so I knew to come straight here."

"You told me to!" the Russian screamed. Nearby, Susie whimpered. Grant hoped it was out of relief, but could see in his mind's eye the bayonet pressed against her jugular, gripped in a practiced fist.

"Come now, Kodi. Don't try to implicate me in this." He took a step closer, a hand splayed before him in search of the pull string. "I would never hurt a family member of a close friend."

"You told me to," the younger man called again, less certain this time.

"I told you nothing of the sort and I think young Miss Milliard knows as much." Grant found the string and tugged it. The barracks came alight in a buttery yellow glow, barely enough to read by should any of the hands ever take a hankering to it.

Yet it was more than enough to see by.

The Russian had the girl gripped around the throat. The bayonet's tip touched her flesh and a point of blood welled and spilled down to her open collar. It left a stain on the white cotton, like a rose blossom. Her blue jeans had been unbuttoned and pulled partially down her hips. Grant swallowed, then spit. He couldn't help it. Things would have been a lot worse, he figured, had he gotten here any later. Susan Milliard moaned and Grant raised the pistol.

"Put that down, comrade, or I'll carve this child like veal," the Russian said.

"If I put it down, you turn her loose," Grant said.

"You are in no position to bargain."

"Just don't hurt her."

"Place the weapon at your feet."

"You're out of your mind."

"Perhaps. Or perhaps Russian minds operate differently than Americans'. This is your final chance to surrender your firearm." Another drop of blood rolled down the pink flesh of Susie's neck beneath the tip of the bayonet. "If it is not on the floor by a five count, the girl dies. It will be a pity to kill her before I've had my fun, but it is a sacrifice I've made before. One."

"You won't get away with this," Grant said, sounding absurdly in his ears like Jack Lord in *Hawaii Five-O*. He crouched and placed the Llama on the bare concrete floor, but kept a hand on top of it.

Kodi's malevolent smile widened. "You sound like a sheriff in one of the western pictures you Americans favor. Two."

Grant knew he could not turn the weapon over. The son of a bitch would kill the girl anyway and then use the relinquished firearm to shoot Grant. He would say he found Grant in the barracks, fiddling with the girl, and shot him. But not before the farmer fatally wounded the child. It would ruin the surviving Langs and their futures would be forfeit. Especially Lorelai's, who stood to make the Dean's List every semester at any university she chose. The Russian would be named a hero.

"Mr. Lang," Susie gasped. "He slept with Lorelai."

"You shut your mouth or I'll cut out your tongue," Kodiak spat at her. The girl flinched. To Grant he said, "Three."

Grant blinked. "He what?"

Susan's eyes rolled wildly and in as much terror as she must've been in, she found a well of courage within her to speak again. "Lorelai told my sister about it."

"Is that true?" Grant asked, feeling his belly fill with

something akin to molten lead.

The Russian's grin stretched into a leer. "*Da*. We made it right here on this very bunk. She screamed my name as I pumped my seed into her. And she bled all over my—how do you Americans say it?—all over my prick." The last word came out sounding like *preek*, with an indulgent roll of the R. This last detail, the pure insolence infused within it, lit the already dangerously short fuse.

Before Grant could rethink it, he twitched the pistol up and fired twice in quick succession. The girl may have easily become an unfortunate casualty, another body to deal with, but he'd kept his hand steady enough to spare her. The reports sounded like firecrackers in the enclosed space. Susie shrieked and squirmed away as the Russian dropped sideways atop her, his body jerking like a mismanaged marionette. Grant had seen where the rounds had entered, one through the left eye and one at the corresponding nostril. The first had been the killshot, the second, insurance. He wished the red bastard hadn't died so quick. He'd have loved to have taken his time with it.

The dogs, denned up in the adjacent shed for the night, went crazy. He could hear them even over Susan, who kicked her way beneath a bunk, still shrieking, and the ringing in his ears from the gunshot reports. Grant tossed the murder weapon onto the quilt and stood processing. The shots would likely bring Dinah out to investigate because, while deer season was still in effect, rarely did hunters come near enough to their property for their shots to be heard. Grant wanted to avoid her witnessing the scene of the crime. He shoved aside all thoughts of Lorelai giving herself to the dead man. He would deal with that later; now was the time for damage control.

A seemingly limitless fountain of blood drained from the deceased Russian's head, pooling on the floor. Kodiak Aristov was not the first man Grant had killed, but he would be the first anyone else knew about, except Al. He hated that his girls would find out, that they might look at him differently going forward. He hated that it happened this close to Christmas and a shiny new Bicentennial New Year. It couldn't be helped, of course, even though his brain cycled through a hundred different stories that wouldn't implicate him. He even entertained the idea this could be covered up, that he and Al could work something out and keep it contained.

But no. Not with Susan Milliard as a living witness.

Grant kicked the leg of the bunk under which she'd hidden. "Susan, come out. We're getting out of here."

She didn't move for so long Grant thought he'd have to drag her out, but at last she wiggled free, tugging at her belt loops, and allowed him to wrap her in a clean blanket.

"You killed him," she said, a wild look in her wide eyes. Probably too deep in shock to cry.

"Are you okay?"

"My neck's cut."

"It's small. It won't need stitches."

"He hurt me."

"I know, sweetheart. He won't ever do it again. To you or anyone else. Let's get inside and call your folks." Susan allowed him to carry her out over the snow, nestling into him as they walked. Grant's heart felt like a chunk of coal unburied by a gravedigger's spade. He had much to sort out over the coming days. Much to evaluate. Much to execute.

CHAPTER FORTY-FIVE

Dinah temporarily forgot the item she'd discovered in her husband's desk when he came into the kitchen carrying the girl. His daughters had all gone to bed, but crowded together at the top of the stairs when they'd heard the gunshots. Their mother had instructed them to stay put.

"Oh my God," she said. "Is that Susan Milliard? You found her? It's all over town she went missing today."

"Get Augie on the horn, will you?"

"What happened to her?"

"It was Kodi."

Dinah put a hand to her mouth. "Did you kill him? We heard gunshots."

Grant placed the girl on the table, shivering in her quilt. "Yes. He's dead."

"Oh, dear Jesus." She clasped folded hands to her lips. "He didn't … he didn't hurt her, did he?"

Grant took a step toward the stairs and hollered at his children to get back in bed and followed it with a promise that everything was all right. When they'd scattered, he slumped into a chair and stared at the floor while Dinah placed Susan on the family room davenport. The girl's shock seemed to have deepened into a semi-catatonic state.

They stepped across the room to where the TV had been switched off and the only light came from the motley bulbs hanging on the Christmas tree. "Do the kids know she was kidnapped?" Grant asked.

"Teresa called to ask if any of the girls had seen her after school. Bonnie said she saw Susie in the library on her way out."

"Catching up on the schoolwork she missed when she was

ill," Grant mused, mostly to himself.

The item Dinah had found recurred to her, but its significance paled with what they now faced. "Did he hurt her?" she asked again.

"I don't imagine he got as far as he expected he would."

"Thank Jesus," Dinah said.

"It could have been a lot worse. I need you to call Augie now and then call Al. I'll be back."

"Where are you going?"

"To get a bandage. I figure you can patch Susie up before her father gets here."

August had not appeared as devastated as Grant had imagined. The man was one tough son of a bitch, that was for sure. He kept up a stony façade even as he carried his daughter to their truck and got her settled. Then he'd approached Grant and stuck out a hand. Aside from a couple sparkles in his eyes, Augie might as well have been sculpted of marble. Grant wondered how long it would take him to break down once he got home.

"I want to thank you, Grant," he'd said. "For finding my daughter before that monster could have done something truly terrible. Doc Rubek sedated Teresa, which was for the best. I think this just about did her in. She'll be overjoyed to learn Susie's okay."

"Get her tucked in safe and sound," Grant said. He watched the truck all the way down the drive and out of sight.

The house stayed quiet. Only Dinah remained on alert as she paced the kitchen wringing her hands.

"I never would have thought he'd do something like that," she said, pausing to fret with her toe over a scuff mark on the linoleum. "He had good references and everything."

Grant said nothing. He had lied to her about checking Kodi's background. He'd wanted a man with city connections, not a man to solely work the land. That kind of labor could be found anywhere, and cheap. Kodi had been something special. Unfortunately, he'd also been a mad dog. Grant had done right by putting the dog down.

Al arrived late after having to assist County with a traffic accident and Grant pulled the cop into the barn to get him up to speed.

"You never should have ordered that red psychopath to take Susie," Al said. "What in God's name were you thinking?"

Grant's hands curled into fists. "Augie put that girl's body in my loft. I could not let that pass."

"But, Grant, Jesus Christ. You can't go around abducting kids. We already commit a dozen felonies a day—you want them to tack another twenty-five years on your sentence?"

"I'm not going to prison," Grant said.

"You will if Augie figures out it was you behind all this."

"He won't."

"This is all coming apart," Al said, mostly to himself. "By Jesus, the seams are snapping."

"No, they're not. We've just got to keep our heads level and hold it together." Grant put a hand on the chief's shoulder. "Trust me, partner."

Al heaved a great sigh and fingered the butt of his service revolver. "We can't have any more bodies."

"We won't. And don't worry about Kodi. No one's going to miss him."

"How will you get rid of the ... him? Can't dig in this freeze."

"I have another way."

"I don't want to know."

"No," Grant said. "You don't."

CHAPTER FORTY-SIX

For the first time in her life, Dinah wished she'd gone to college. When Grant one evening eighteen years previous, upon learning she was pregnant, had promised to take care of her forever and always, she believed him. Dinah Simonds Lang may have possessed an IQ of 145, but sometimes she damned her trustfulness in her fellow human beings. She no longer trusted her husband.

After he'd shot the hired man who'd abducted the daughter of their neighbor, Dinah had not found it in her to bring up the article she'd discovered beneath the half-empty bottle of whiskey he kept in his bottom desk drawer. She held it now between her fingers, running the pad of her thumb over the lacy edge. To whom did it belong? She'd gone over and over the possibilities but had come no closer to a solution. Truthfully, it could belong to any woman, but Dinah sensed it belonged to someone close. Someone in town, most likely, and surely someone within the county. Grant rarely traveled outside his territory.

A knock sounded on her open bedroom door and she tried to stuff the brassiere beneath the counterpane, but Lorelai, standing in the doorway, had seen it.

"Mom? Is that something new?"

Dinah tried to smile and whipped up an excuse. "Your Aunt Delia sent it to me and told me to open it in private because it might be awkward come Christmas morning."

"I'm sorry. I didn't mean to sneak up on you."

"That's okay, hon. You have something on your mind?"

Lorelai tried on her own smile, but it looked lost. "Yes, actually."

"Come in. Sit down."

Her eldest did so, smoothing a wrinkle in the quilt flat with her hand. "This is hard for me to say, but you're the only person I can tell about this."

Dinah sensed a tipping point and willed it away but knew doing so would be futile. Change came, no matter how hard you fought it. Adapt or be scythed down like harvest crop. She put a hand on her daughter's arm.

"Anything, sweetheart."

"You'll be upset."

"I may be, but I won't stop loving you. You know that."

Lorelai paused, her lower lip quivering. "Mom, I think I'm pregnant."

Dinah closed her eyes. She had suspected this the moment her daughter had knocked, but hadn't allowed herself to believe it. She'd hoped it would be something trivial, like whether or not she could use the car Saturday or seeking help on a particularly tough calculus problem. But no. The queen mother of teenage troubles had at last appeared. Dinah had hoped it never would, but now here it was. History repeating, again and again.

"How sure are you?" she asked at length.

"Pretty sure."

"Who's the father?"

Lorelai cast her eyes toward the floor. She seemed on the verge of some momentous decision, probably whether or not to speak his name. Then she found her mother's eyes. Dinah had expected to see tears, but her daughter's countenance held only fierce determination.

"Dennis Milliard," she said.

This, at least, came as little surprise. She knew how her daughters watched the young man, how they giggled into their hands during football games as they studied him pacing the sideline, waiting for Coach Dayton to call his number.

"Will you marry him?" Dinah asked.

"If he'll have me."

"Haven't you told him yet?"

"You're the only one who knows." She placed a hand over her mother's. "Please don't tell Dad. He'll … overreact."

That might be in contention for understatement of the decade, Dinah thought. "You let me handle your father. There are tough choices you have to make," she told her daughter.

"I'm keeping it." For the first time, Lorelai sounded as though she might break down.

"You've already thought this through?"

"A hundred times, Mom. A thousand."

"Then the next step is to talk to Dennis. Ask to meet somewhere privately. You need to tell him in person."

"I will."

"And try to be sensitive to his feelings. He's likely going to run the gamut of them in short order. His feelings may be amplified because of what happened to Susie, so tread lightly."

"Dennis would never hurt me."

"I know he wouldn't. But you'll be adding quite a heap to his already over-balanced plate. Just use caution. And compassion."

"Thanks for listening, Mommy. I love you."

The women embraced and Dinah sent a prayer skyward, just in case. Now was the time for fortitude, not weakness. She would have to be strong for all the Lang women with what she meant to do. For what would come in the looming days.

When her daughter departed, Dinah again pulled the damning garment from beneath the quilt. She studied its fabric, flicked at the underwire with her thumbnail. She even stood before the mirror and held it to her bosom, thinking maybe it was one of hers that had somehow erroneously found its way into her husband's den. But no—it was a full cup-size too small.

Only one person came to mind who might fit the bill and Dinah found herself utterly unsurprised at the identity.

"You're going to pay for this, Grant," she whispered to her reflection.

CHAPTER FORTY-SEVEN

When she showed him the bra on Christmas Eve, with her bags packed and the rest of the house fast asleep, Grant only stared at it, his jaw working. It was all the confession Dinah needed.

"You went through my desk?" Grant asked, his voice thin as a reed.

"Don't you dare try to turn this around on me, you son of a bitch."

Grant blinked twice, hard. His wife had never in their twenty-year history taken such a tone with him, nor used such language. Rage washed over him, deeper than any he'd felt. Even when he found out about Lorelai and Kodi. It took all the restraint he possessed not to strike her.

"You had no right," he said, his breath shuddery, his knees threatening to unhinge. Everything he'd worked for all his life was coming unseamed before him; he saw it with the clarity of a medium gazing into a crystal ball. Al had been right on that count, it now seemed.

"Al called in a panic the other night. He wouldn't tell me what it was about, so I went looking," Dinah said. She tossed the brassiere at Grant, where it landed draped over one shoulder. "This is all the justification I need for my actions."

A core of acid blossomed in Grant's gut. He had to salvage this somehow. "Di, listen. I can explain."

She laughed, a high, barking sound. "You sound like an episode of *General Hospital* now. There is no explanation, Grant. I won't even humiliate you by demanding to know who it belongs to. I couldn't care less."

Bordering on panic—an emotion utterly alien to his

being—Grant nearly knelt to beg for mercy. In the end, though, he couldn't bring himself to bend knee to anyone, even if it meant losing his wife.

He said, "Let's not ruin Christmas for the girls."

"The girls will have a wonderful Christmas at Delia's."

"Di, please. Let's enjoy tomorrow morning—or at least let them enjoy it. Then, if you still feel like leaving, I won't stand in the way."

"Get out." He'd never heard her voice so full of hatred.

"Di—"

"Get the fuck out of my bedroom. Tomorrow it's yours for the rest of your life. Tonight it's mine." Grant backpedaled as if struck. He'd never heard her spout such venom. Dinah tilted her head at him while an entirely unpleasant grin split her face like a gourd. "Why don't you go spend Christmas Eve at your floozy's place?"

Defeated, he turned and stalked out of the room. He didn't make it two steps before the lock shot behind him.

Alone in his study, Grant opened the bottom drawer and retrieved the half-empty bottle of whiskey. It would be enough for tonight. How had Dinah opened this drawer? Had she found his key? No, he carried the only copy and always had. Had she made a copy at some point during their marriage? It seemed unlikely. She'd always trusted him. He must have left it unlocked. It seemed the only logical explanation.

"I'm slipping," he said aloud. "I can't afford to slip, not now."

No, he certainly could not. Not in the line of work he'd chosen. Either line—the legitimate or the other. He needed to work this out, to contain it before it spiraled out of control. He could not let Dinah take his girls away. Never in a million harvest seasons could he allow her to do that.

"I'll kill her," he said aloud, shocked at how rational it sounded. How *right*.

Grant drank. He didn't stop until the white half-moon vanished from the sky. When he woke at 9:30 Christmas morning, tipped back in his chair with a slick of spit hanging from his chin, he knew the house was empty. Dinah had taken their chickadees and flown the coop. Still, he walked room to room, head pounding like a kick drum. Once he'd confirmed himself alone, Grant stepped into the front room, turned on the record player, and sat beside the Christmas tree loaded with handmade ornaments the girls had pieced together during various school projects over the years.

For the next hour, he slowly opened the presents they'd left behind—all addressed to him—while listening to Johnny Mathis croon about winter wonderlands and chestnuts roasting on open fires.

That afternoon, Grant slept on the floor before the fireplace, a hearty blaze still crackling on the hearth, and realized he'd come awake from a knock at the door. In no mood for company, he laid low and waited for the visitor to leave. Who on God's Earth called on Christmas Day? The visitor, though, kept pounding in rhythm to the ache in Grant's head.

"All right, Christ, shut that racket up," he called. When he opened the door, he found Al standing on the porch.

"Grant, thank God. I just heard."

"Heard what?"

"Word's getting around Dinah left you. You didn't answer the phone this morning and I wanted to come check on your well-being."

"My well-being's fine, for God's sake."

"I just needed to confirm you hadn't done something rash, like throw yourself into your threshing machine."

"If I was going to off myself, I wouldn't do it that way. Wouldn't be nothing left to bury."

"What in creation happened?" Engel asked.

"Would you find it insulting if I told you it's none of your goddamned business?"

"Of course it's my business," Al said, twisting his ridiculous cop hat in his hands. "I need to make sure you're in the proper frame of mind."

"My frame of mind is in perfect working order, Al, even if my marriage ain't."

Al nodded but looked unconvinced. "Yeah. Well. If you need anything, call."

"I will," Grant said. He checked Al's eyes. "Anyone ask about the Russian?"

"Not a soul. Give it another month, no one will even remember a transient foreign farmhand, the way they tend to drift. You sure you took care of the body?"

Grant nodded. It had been a miserable task, but one he'd undertaken before. "Like he never existed."

"Listen, take care of yourself, Grant. Try to have a merry Christmas, okay?"

Grant snorted. "Oh, it'll be real merry. That's for sure."

"Say, why don't you come on over to my place? I've got a turkey in the oven and I'll be whipping up some mashed potatoes. They're from a box, not the real McCoy, but they taste about the same if you gravy 'em enough. Got no pie, but Mary Lou Zahn brought a fruit cake into the station t'other day. I took it home since no one else touched it."

Grant thought the idea of spending Christmas day with Alvin Engel about the most depressing thing he could imagine and said so. "Also, boxed spuds taste like shit. Spring for the real deal or go without."

"I'll take that under advisement as long as you promise to take care of yourself."

"I'll be fine, Al." He waved a hand. "This is … temporary."

Again the cop looked dubious, but said no more. Grant watched him drive away, then took a seat beside the dying embers and used a poker to stir them for a spell.

CHAPTER FORTY-EIGHT

Delia kept pressing her, so Dinah relented. She told her older sister exactly what she'd found and where she'd found it. The girls had gone into town to see the film *The Adventures of a Wilderness Family* with Delia's two sons, who were staggered between Lorelai and Bonnie in age.

"Did he tell you what it was doing there?" Delia asked.

"He didn't have to. The guilt showed plain on his face."

"Well, shoot, sis. Maybe it belonged to an old high school sweetheart. Some men do things like that, take trophies."

"Grant never dated anyone else in high school. It was only me."

Delia huffed in frustration. "Sis, for as goddamned brilliant as you are, you sure can be naïve sometimes."

"What do you mean?"

"If you think you were the only woman Grant ever diddled, you've been sorely misled."

This information shocked Dinah. "No, Del. You're wrong. We were each other's first and only."

Delia hesitated, choosing her words. "First, maybe. Not only."

"What on earth are you talking about?"

Her sister's face softened. "Oh, sis. I thought you knew? Near about everyone else down Derby way does, I think."

All at once Dinah didn't want to know what her sister was about to spill. Her image of her husband had already been badly tarnished. She didn't think she could stand it if it broke entirely, like a Ming vase someone bumped off a pedestal. Somehow she knew Delia's information would utterly destroy any chance of her and Grant mending the relationship they'd spent two decades cultivating. And yet, the larger part of her *needed* to know.

"Who was it?" she heard herself whisper. "Who did he sleep with? Was it Teresa Milliard? It was, wasn't it?"

"I'd heard a rumor about that a time back, but a rumor is all it was," Delia said. "She'd never be unfaithful to Augie."

"Who then?"

Delia licked her lips. "I heard once that maybe, just maybe, Grant might have had a hankering for Ruth."

This admission so blindsided Dinah she laughed. It simply couldn't be true. "Ruth *Safford*? Never in a million years, Del."

Delia tottered a hand in the air. "Part of me agrees. Part of me isn't so sure. You know how Ruth used to be."

"No, I don't. How did she used to be?" Dinah had never given much thought to students who attended other schools, aside from Grant Lang.

"She was a wild one, Ruth was. I remember being at some party once, a barn dance. Way out in the sticks. Can't recall who lived there at the moment, but it was one hell of a shindig."

Dinah waited for her sister to go on and twisted the wedding band Grant had given her all those years ago. The band which now meant less than nothing.

"Everyone was there. Grant, Ruth, Augie. Teresa. Ray Safford got so drunk he passed out in a haystack. Hell, even that Mike Stone was there with some of his buddies, even though they were all older. It was a regular hodgepodge of people."

"Where was I?" Dinah asked. She had no memory of such an event, nor that her sister had attended one.

"Where else?" Delia said. "With your nose stuck in a book, as usual."

Dinah sat back and chewed her lip. "I need a cigarette."

Delia, God bless her, didn't bother reminding her baby sis that she quit fifteen years ago. Instead, she pulled a crumpled Vantage pack from her purse and lit one for her. Dinah took it like a pro; she didn't cough once.

"It's like riding a bike," she said, exhaling blue smoke before uttering a rueful laugh.

"Di, we don't have to do this anymore. You don't have to hear about the past."

"Yes, I do. Tell me everything."

Delia sighed, clasped her hands on her apron, and told her.

Grant knew without the girls around he'd be responsible for caring for the horses. He hadn't so much as dumped a pail of oats for them since the girls had grown old enough to handle the chores themselves. And with his only full-time hand dead and gone, Grant had some labor to tend to. As if to punctuate this, one of the beasts loosed a shrill whinny.

"All right, goddammit, shut up," Grant said and picked up the telephone. With it cradled between shoulder and ear, he dialed the number of one of his part-timers and waited through a dozen rings before understanding no one would answer. Probably away for the holidays. He tried to recall the numbers of the other men he employed but found he could not. Oh, he was slipping all right.

He hauled on his coat and his cap and went out to feed the horses. An hour later, still muttering curses, he returned to the warmth of the house, but decided he'd find it considerably warmer with another bottle of whiskey. He drove into town, hoping the goddamn Jew who owned the spirits store had it in him to keep the place open on the holiday.

Lorelai did her best to calm her sisters. Even Bonnie had flipped her lid about the whole thing.

"Are Mom and Dad getting a *divorce*?" she asked, watching her sister's eyes in the rearview mirror as they drove to the movie house.

"Bon, you make it sound like the devil's work," Lorelai said. "You let Mom and Dad figure it out."

"Uncle Grant's been poking around where he shouldn't be, that's what I heard," their cousin Derek said. Roy, his younger brother by two years, snickered.

"I think you've got our fathers confused," Nora said. "Your pa left for some secretary."

"Shut up," Roy said.

"Both of you shut up," Lorelai said. She handed Bonnie a wad of bills. "Bon, you're in charge. Go in, see the picture."

"Aren't you coming?" Bonnie asked.

"I have something I need to do," she said. "I'll be back in time to pick you up and if I'm not take them out for milkshakes."

The kids got out, muttering and shoving. She waited until they bought their tickets at the box office window before reversing and driving back toward Derby.

She pulled into the Mobil station and found the phone booth beneath the sign bearing the Pegasus logo, dropped in a dime, and dialed. A few snowflakes landed on her cheeks and she brushed them away like tears. Mr. Milliard answered on the third ring and when she asked for Dennis, he told her he could be found on cleanup duty at the Country Store, following the annual complimentary brunch the family offered each Christmas Day as a gift to their little community. She thanked him and hurried back to the car.

Dennis had taken a break from sweeping the floor and had a can of Coke tipped to his lips. Lorelai watched him through the window while he stood there oblivious to the notion of how quickly, fully, and irrevocably his life was about to change.

His head snapped around when the bell above the door chimed, sounding to Lorelai's ears like a heavenly herald. She would break the news gently, which would initiate the process of cementing their lives together. Especially now that the pale little Bible-bitch was out of the picture.

"What are you doing here?" he asked, not unkindly (but also not kindly).

"Dennis," she said. "We need to talk."

CHAPTER FORTY-NINE

Grant drove by the Falling Pins and pulled into American Pastime Liquors, pleased to find them indeed open. He knew Murdoch and Ashford kept city ordinances forbidding liquor sales on religious holidays, but not Derby Dale, Illinois, Ye Olde Den of Iniquity. Ordinarily, Grant would have scoffed at any business who dared unbar their doors on Jesus' birthday, but today he decided to let it pass. The goddamn Jew would get his in the hereafter, by God.

He stepped inside and approached the counter where a stocky guy sat flicking through the pages of a girlie magazine he had tried to hide inside a month-old copy of *Newsweek*, as if doing so would hide his transgression from the eyes of the Lord.

Grant, feeling adventurous on account of a plan he'd been scheming to win Dinah back, said, "What's the most expensive whiskey in the house?"

The counterman's face gained some color at that. Maybe he worked on commission. "Sir?"

"You're not from around here, are you?"

"No, sir. Moved out from the city last summer. I wanted to try some country-quiet."

"Welcome to our little burg, my new friend," Grant said and the man brightened before actually leaning over the counter and offering his hand. Grant stared at it until the fool put it down. "Now, I asked what the most expensive whiskey you keep is."

"Well, Mr. Eisenberg keeps a couple bottles locked up in back, but they run upwards of six hundred apiece—"

"I'll take them."

The soft city boy gaped at him. "Sir?"

Grant placed his hands flat on the counter. "Good Jesus, it's a wonder Eisenberg can keep this place open with the help so unwilling or unable to ply his trade."

The counterman jerked, spouting apologies in all their various forms. "I'll get them right away, sir," he said, disappearing into the storage room. Grant realized he could rob the till of every last dime, grab a few bottles for the road, and be halfway to Milwaukee before anyone started looking for him. It was not the first time the idea of abandoning ship had occurred to him over the past twelve hours.

He stared at a poster of Clydesdales drawing a sleigh across a snowy glade when the door chimed behind him. Grant turned, wondering who in all creation would be frequenting a liquor store on Christmas Day, when he spotted the only person who made sense. He broke into a grin.

"I wondered if you might stop by today. Coincidence we're here at the same time," Grant said.

"No coincidence," Zebulon Tuel said.

Grant frowned. "Come again?"

Zeb said no more. He produced a small caliber pistol, took two towering strides, and fired twice. Grant said something even he couldn't decipher and folded like a greeting card. Zeb glanced around and then made haste into the cold.

The clerk returned with two dusty bottles, his once-ruddy face now the color of cold ash, and dropped his burden, where they smashed and seeped $1200 worth of spirits across the floor, toward where his customer lay convulsing and bleeding. Then he picked up the phone and called the police.

Dennis sat alone in his family's store. It had been a hell of a Christmas. The turnout for the brunch had been greater than ever—apparently the community had forgiven the Milliards for the corn maze debacle from a mere eight weeks before (at least long enough to stuff themselves with free food). No one threw apples and no one had trouble helping themselves to seconds, or in the case of Father Scudder, thirds. The fare remained, as always, modest—ham sandwiches, potato salad, baked beans, pie, egg nog—but oh dear God how they could put it away! He wondered why his parents had decided to keep it going this year, considering how their townspeople behaved during the Apple Festival Parade. His father had explained how people make mistakes and that they should, in most cases, be forgiven.

Mistakes. Dennis had learned all about mistakes today.

Lorelai had for some reason seen fit to drop the queen mother of all bombs on him on Christmas Day. Christmas Day, for Christ's sake. Who in God's name did she think she was, the Virgin Mary?

Oh, but he'd turned the tables on her, hadn't he? He'd let her get through her entire speech, which had startled him badly at first. But the longer she'd spoken, the more he relaxed. Because he had something on her. And when she finished, wearing openly the satisfaction that she had spun a web around him and had him where she wanted, forever and ever, he'd turned the motherfucking tables right back at her.

Dennis knew about Kodiak. Watching the color drain from her face—not to mention all her hopes about the future—had satisfied something deep inside him.

"It's not his," she insisted.

"How do you know?" he countered. To which she'd had no answer. None. Because she hadn't counted on Dennis *knowing*.

In the end, she pleaded. Begged. Actually gotten on her knees as if to pray. Told him she'd make him the happiest man in the world. That she'd tend to their children and love, honor, and obey him until her dying day. She brought up the fact that her parents were getting a divorce and how a way to salvage their relationship might be to kindle one anew, to remind them of the magic of young love. Their marriage could unite the two most powerful families in Ashford County.

That had been the last straw. Dennis ordered her off the property.

At the door, she faced him, eyes bloodshot but tearless, and told him she wasn't about to let this go. He wasn't off the hook, not by a longshot. She would prove the baby was his if it was the last thing she did on God's Earth.

Then, as he sat on an apple crate, with the broom lying across his knees, and tried to process everything, weighing whether he should join the Army, or just run away, the bell chimed again and the answer to his problem stepped through the door. Zebulon stood there, the muscles of his jaws jumping.

"Zebbo? What is it?"

"Denny, I shot him. I shot Mr. Lang."

Dennis stood, the broom clattering to the tiles. His heart clenched like a fist. "You did *what*?"

"I shot Grant Lang. I followed him and I shot him."

"Where?"

"The liquor store. He—"

"I mean where did you shoot him? What parts?"

"One in the gut, one in the head. You got to help me, Dennis."

"Why did you do it, Zebbo? Jeez Louise. *Why*?"

"He's bad, Denny. He's rotten, like an apple glutted with worms. He threatened me with what the Klan did to my pa all those years back and I can't abide it, not by that man. I just can't. A man like that, he won't stop until someone stops him. Someone had to stop him."

Dennis didn't know anything about what any Klan did to anyone's pa, but he pulled out his wallet stuffed with Christmas cash he'd found in his stocking that morning and tried to hand it over. Zeb wouldn't take it. "I have some money," he said. "What I don't have is a place to go."

"Okay," Dennis said, mind cycling through a thousand possibilities. "Okay. Is he dead?"

"I didn't stick around to take his pulse."

"Did anyone see you?"

Zeb shook his head aggressively, like a lion flaring his mane. "Not a soul."

"The clerk?"

"He was in back. I made sure. Everyone else is tucked in at home by their fires or out of town for the holidays. No one saw, I swear it."

"Okay," Dennis said again, brain churning like butter. "We have to move fast, so listen up. I only got time to say it once. And for the love of all things holy, you better hope you killed that man. If not, our lives are already worthless."

CHAPTER FIFTY

Grant Lang opened his eyes on the final afternoon of December, a sunbeam lying across his lap like a map of the heavens. Something dripped from somewhere and the smell of iodine fouled the air. His entire body felt drained, as if someone had stuck a siphon in him and sucked out his soul. The liquor store. Gunshots. Zebulon. Ashford Memorial Hospital.

He looked around, expecting Dinah to occupy the visitor's chair. Even as his eyes swung that way, his brain formed an optimistic expectation: she would have discovered what happened to him, the horrible tragedy that had befallen her husband, and she would come running to forgive him.

Only it wasn't Dinah who sat at his bedside, flicking through a limp, dog-eared copy of *Fur-Fish-Game*.

Mike Stone looked over the top of his reading glasses at Grant, his lips working the remains of a tattered toothpick. Grant thought he'd feel a stab of guilt since he'd betrayed Mike. But the guilt never came. Perhaps that particular emotional fuse had been blown out of him and pretty much figured it must have since he'd felt only the barest twinge of it when he'd bedded Di the night after his outing with Ursula. The last time he'd likely ever bed Di, he realized now.

Mike said: "Good morning, Starshine. The motherfucking earth says hello."

"Where's," Grant said, but his voice came out only as a raw scrape. He swallowed and tried again. "Where's Di?"

Mike shrugged. "She's turned them girls against you, partner."

"I need to see them."

"I'll pass it on, though I think you'll have better luck swimming to Saturn."

"The horses. My dogs."

"They're looked after."

"I need water."

Mike poured a glass from a pitcher near the bed and said nothing while Grant swallowed it.

Grant regarded him, a feeling of dread rising in his esophagus. "What is it? What happened?"

"Quite a lot, truth be told," Mike said. "I don't have much time. You're pretty tore up so I guess they figured it wouldn't hurt to let me see you in case you buy the farm. So to speak."

Grant felt tore up, all right, but he didn't care about that right now. "Did they catch him? Did they catch that melon-eating coon?"

"It *was* him, wasn't it? I knew it had to be, who the hell else would do something like that on the holiest of days?" Mike shook his head, slow and sorrowful, "No. They didn't catch ol' Zeb and I doubt they ever will. No one saw who done it. You're the only eyewitness."

Grant watched him, willing the dread to subside. It didn't. It intensified, a hot column of bile in his throat.

"You don't know how lucky you are, partner. That bullet that hit your noggin burrowed under the skin and traveled halfway around. I told the doc what saved you is you're so goddamned hard-headed." Mike leaned forward, quiet now, all business. "You're going to want to brace yourself now, okay? Someone burned the cabin flat. I'm guessing we can confirm who that someone might have been."

Grant blinked, praying Mike meant the cabin they kept in the Murdoch woods, the old Frayne clan stead. The one where they'd initially stashed Susan Milliard. He already knew otherwise.

"You heard right," Mike said. "The product. It's gone up in smoke, literally. Every last leaf and seed. It's a godsend the wind blew out over the river, otherwise every single soul in town would've been stoned out of their Yuletide minds. Al worked magic calming down your fire chief—if that's what you want to call that volunteer piece of shit."

"How do you know it was Zeb who burned it?"

Mike's eyebrows arched. "Doesn't take much to connect the dots, now that it's confirmed who attacked you. Who else would it have been? He shoots you in broad daylight on Christmas fucking morning, then the cabin goes later that day, about the time most folks would be sitting down to their turkey and trimmings, then he disappears without a trace."

"Dennis," Grant managed, his dread morphing like lava into rage. "Get Dennis here."

Mike plucked the pick from between his teeth and flicked it away. "Funny you bring him up. Dennis seems to have also flown the coop. Them boys are on the run just like Huck and Jim."

A nurse stepped in and told Mike he'd have to go. He did so, reluctantly. At the door, he gave Grant a hard, inscrutable look before vanishing down the hall.

The nurse fiddled with some equipment while informing him a doctor would see him shortly. Grant barely heard. Their operation had collapsed. All the money they had invested, all the time and sweat spent cultivating their project. All that glorious hallucinogen-laced product. All gone.

Before the doctor could visit, Grant fell again unconscious, his body wracked with shivers and spasms.

When next he woke Al Engel occupied the visitor chair, looking worried. The window behind him had darkened and Grant had no idea if it was still the same year or if the Spirit of '76 had blown in without his knowledge.

"Grant, Jesus, thank God," the chief said.

"Don't thank anyone yet," Grant said. "I feel like pulled pork."

"You don't look much better, truth be told."

"Tell me you found those boys. Tell me you got them squirreled away in lockup."

Al blew out his breath in a gust. "No. But we got some leads."

Grant closed his eyes. "Leads are about as useful as a bellyful of catgut."

"We'll get 'em, Grant."

"You better. They have some atoning to do."

"You need to worry less about atonement and more about recovering."

Grant waved this off.

Al licked his teeth. "You got anything you want me to pass on to Di?"

"Fuck that bitch," he said. He'd come to one immutable determination during his convalescence. "Fuck all those bitches."

"Come again?"

"They turned on me. They haven't even been to see me, not a one of them." He glared with purpose at the peace officer. "They're every-goddamned-one of them dead to me."

Al gaped at his partner's rage, too flabbergasted to offer rebuttal.

"I can't do shit lying in this bed," Grant said, "and we got shit that needs doing."

"You just worry about getting better," Al said. "Mike and I'll handle things until you're on your feet."

The doctor stepped into the room. "Chief, time's up."

The cop stood. "You got it, doc. Take good care of him, yeah?"

The doctor checked something off a chart and did not respond.

The calendar had indeed turned. Grant's condition seemed better, but the doctor still refused to discharge him. The damned quacks didn't seem to understand he had business to do. As it turned out, the quacks wound up keeping him in bed all the way until spring because the bullet in his gut had ruptured the wrong pipes and by mid-January sepsis had set in. It took him until mid-March to recover. By then a great many things had come to pass.

That night, before learning that the bullet had turned his guts into Spaghetti-Os, he lay staring at the ceiling and trying to piece together some semblance of a plan when his next visitor arrived, someone he never would have expected if he lived to be a thousand.

"Mr. Lang?" the voice called from the door. Grant looked over and his heart offered an abrupt, surprised lurch.

"Susan?"

The girl shuffled into the room. She looked mournfully at the floor, one fingernail stuck between her teeth like a toddler.

"Honey? Are your folks here?"

She shook her head, her straw-like hair bouncing around her shoulders in a practical ponytail. "I wanted to come alone."

"My God, how did you get all the way up here to Ashford?"

"I took the bus."

"Come in, child. Come in."

"I just wanted to stop by to … to thank you for what you did," she said, still unable to meet his eyes. Twin tears coasted down her cheeks to plink to their deaths on the cold linoleum.

"What else could I do?" Grant said, when he was able. "I couldn't let that monster hurt you. How are you feeling?"

"I'm better. My mom and dad have me talking to someone Doc Rubek recommended. A child psychologist. She's really good."

"Well, that's wonderful, Susan. I'm glad it's helping."

Susie stood swaying and Grant thought she might faint. Then she steadied and the finger dropped from her lips. She found his gaze and locked onto it. She ran forward, threw herself onto the hospital bed, and kissed him on the mouth.

The action so shocked him that he could not react until Susie's retreating, running footsteps had died in the corridor and he found it in him to release a long, shuddery breath. Her brother might have a world of shit coming to him, but Grant would never harm Susan. Small, sweet Susan. Like a ray of sunshine, that one. And he would make sure she never found out about his involvement in what had happened to her and with what her brother had coming to him.

Grant found the erection which sprouted against his hospital gown both terrifying and exhilarating, and he covered his grin with a shaky hand.

INTERLUDE

When Don got them checked into the Holiday Inn, which had the distinction of being Derby's lone place of lodging, he stood looking out the second-floor window. When he let the curtain drop, he turned and smiled.

"Pretty town," he said. "Picturesque. Like something from a movie. No wonder Jazzy devoted an entire segment of her book to it."

Rachel smiled back. "It's grown a lot since I've been here last and Derby is one of the smaller towns in the county—maybe after we leave we can drive through Murdoch, Sommerville, and Ashford. I can show you where some really creepy stuff went down back before my time."

"That sounds like a date, love. I bet this whole place attracts a lot of looky-loos. Places like this don't exist much anymore. It's tastefully anachronistic."

"I admit, it's nice to be back. But only for a short visit. There's always been something about Ashford County that feels ..." The word *haunted* was the one that didn't quite make it out of her mouth to complete the thought. Instead, she shuddered.

Don strode across the impersonal carpet and cupped her elbows. "Are you sure you're ready for this?"

She nodded. "Yeah. I think so."

He hesitated, licked his lips. "Do you ... do you still have the same feelings as you did back then?"

Rachel barked a high-pitched laugh that did not sound quite sane to her ears. "Feelings? No. God, that was a lifetime ago."

"I'm Dr. Don the Psychologist, hon, in case you've forgotten." He thumbed his glasses up on his nose. "Sometimes those types of feelings never go away."

She hugged his arm to her bosom. "Well, if you're worried, don't be. I came here with you and I intend to leave with you."

That seemed to relax him some. When he spoke next, he said, "What about your childhood friend. Susan was it? Are you ready to see her again?"

To that, Rachel found she had a harder time answering. "I suppose so, yes. I can't think of a situation that won't be awkward, though, given the circumstances. Twenty-three years ago now since we last spoke, it's been. My God, time is a slippery fish, isn't it?"

"That it is, my dear. That it is."

For a time, they only stood in silent embrace, letting memories rinse through them. Rachel couldn't speak for her husband or anyone else, but she felt the past with all five senses. The smell of autumn leaves, for instance, drew instant memories to the surface. Good memories. Perhaps her best memories. That's why she loved autumn above all seasons and probably at least partially (and maybe subconsciously) why she had chosen New England to settle after moving on from corn country. They had spectacular autumn foliage and the good memories flooded through her all the season long. Thanksgiving, likewise, had always been her favorite holiday.

"Do you suppose we ought to go?" Don asked, checking his watch.

"Not just yet," Rachel said. She and her husband had always had a healthy intimate relationship, but it had begun to flag in recent years. She'd recently read a book Jasmine had recommended called *Sex After Sixty: Everything You Need to Know*. The advice within had helped some. She decided to put it to good use for the next fifteen minutes. Then, and only then, would she be ready to go.

Don concurred.

He was a good husband.

BOOK III

**Milk to Clabber
The Stone Family
Spring**

CHAPTER FIFTY-ONE

Old habits didn't die hard. They didn't die at all, if Mike had his way. A man of tradition, one of his favorites involved a beloved breakfast the Stone family had brought with them from Dixieland when they migrated north to lick its wounds after taking a shellacking in the Civil War.

"Urs, you got my clabber ready?" he called from the dining room. The woman had slowed in recent days and it put Mike off quite a bit. Routine on a farm was essential.

His wife came in carrying a plate of the thickened, curdled milk and placed it before him. She'd done it up with baked apples this time. Not his favorite—he preferred it naked, with a drizzle of molasses—but he could forgive it today as she'd been baking apple pies for the farmer's market downtown. Mike silently lauded her thrift. Waste not, want not, as the Good Book said.

As he tucked a napkin into his collar, he mulled his dilemma. Or, rather, dilemmas. Everything had gone sour. The only thing Mike had going for him now was the dairy business. Which, admittedly, had thrived of late. More customers than ever had bought into his most recent advertising campaign, preferring to "go local" in an effort to consume the freshest possible dairy products, while rejecting the ever-expanding empire of chain grocers. And, of course, by doing so helped cling to the good ol' days of their youth. The power of tradition. Things had gotten so busy, Mike had even had to hire a full-time milkman to service the county for the first time since the summer of '69.

He'd gotten into the reefer racket as a means of staying afloat during the lull in the milk biz, and it had worked out wonderfully. Until recently. Adeline's investment had turned it into a second full-time operation and they'd needed help with distribution. Grant had insisted on hiring the Milliard kid and his darkie friend to expand their sales when their goddamn sales had been just fine. Mike should have put his foot down then, but he'd trusted his partner's judgment. Grant Lang was the most successful Ashford County farmer since Vance Gable had gone the way of the reaper—why shouldn't Mike trust him?

Then the two rookies had gotten arrested on separate occasions. That would have been the end of all of them had Chief Engel not smoothed things out with Lazy Lisk, who spent what would undoubtedly be the final term in office resting on his laurels. God praise the long arm of the law when fully atrophied.

Except now the rookies were on the run after destroying all the operation's product. Well, most of it at any rate—Mike had a few dozen keys of the good shit from Indian country stashed in the milking room behind a loose wall panel. No one knew about those, not even Old Dad who'd introduced him to it.

In a way, though, the rookies had done the operation a favor by destroying the evidence. Had they gone to Sheriff Lisk instead of burning the cabin and taking off, they might all be sitting in the piss-reek of Ashford County jail. The boys might be on the run, but they had no further ammunition with which to wound the operation. They had nothing on Grant, which meant they had nothing on Mike.

Grant and Mike, however, had plenty on them. The darkie had shot Grant and the Milliard boy had helped him escape, which made him an accomplice. Goddamn, Mike figured a Milliard to have more brains than that, but what did he know? People never failed to baffle the bejesus out of him. Anyway, the rookies could wait. That plotline would play out on its own. Either they would be caught or they wouldn't. He could only pray for the former and that he would be present to help dole out the punishment.

More pressing—and, to Mike, more personal—was his wife's withdrawal. His little wildflower was never much good for anything but serving him beer and blowjobs, but the ever-present hippie-hopeful light had gone out from her eyes.

Oh, he supposed he shouldn't complain. Urs's tits might be sagging a bit more than they had a year ago, but she hadn't sprouted any wrinkles or white hair yet, and, dear God, her snatch still squeezed the way it had at seventeen. He didn't figure that would be something she'd ever lose, at least not while he was still able to get it up. Yet that spark she'd always had, that little flirtatious flicker that drove him insane with jealousy but had always made him desire her all the more—that had gone. She hardly ever put on her flower power albums anymore. Those queers Simon & Garfunkel, the *Hair* soundtrack, that uppity cunt Carly Simon. And Mike wanted to know why.

He finished breakfast and headed to the barn, where he glimpsed Ben heading for the calving pen. He called the young man over.

"Yeah, boss?" Ben tipped his hat back on his head and swiped his brow to show the head honcho how hard he'd been at it so far, and the morning not yet gone.

"You seen Old Dad yet today?"

"He's out to the paddock, tossing straw."

"Fetch him for me, would you? Then go on and take lunch."

"Boss? It ain't but half past eight."

"You been busting your hump, Ben. Go on and take till noon for your trouble. I won't dock you none."

Ben's face lit up. "Thanks, boss. Thank you much."

"Get on out of here 'fore I change my mind. And don't forget to send the old man to me."

Ben hightailed it away, giddy for the extended break where he would undoubtedly hike into town for breakfast and maybe an early beer at Paulie's Place. Three minutes later Old Dad hobbled into the office, making good time, as always. He didn't speak; the elder rarely spoke first when he spoke at all.

"I need you to do something. For our operation."

"Our operation seems to have gone up in smoke," Old Dad said, fingering the chain to his pocket watch.

"That it has, but it's far from finished." Then Mike told his longest-tenured and most trusted hand what he wanted him to do.

CHAPTER FIFTY-TWO

After lunch, Ursula sat at her dressing table, brushing her hair and humming the tune to some old lullaby whose title she'd forgotten. It had taken days before she'd been able to sit comfortably in this most favored of her chairs, following the damage Grant Lang perpetrated upon her. Grant, she'd come to conclude, was nothing short of the devil assuming a pleasing shape. When she'd read that line from Shakespeare in senior English class back at South Elgin High, it hadn't made sense to her. It did now.

If Mike ever found out what his friend had done to her, World War III would break out right here in corn country and the number of casualties could be catastrophic.

"Urs?" her husband called and she jumped. He stepped into the room reeking of sour sweat and cow shit. She hated the way he smelled before his after-lunch shower. "I'm going to lie down for a spell. Why don't you join me?"

She knew what that meant and fumbled for a reply. "I ought to clean up the table."

There had been a time, not long ago, when he would've insisted, but those days had grown fewer of late. She prayed for the day his plumbing quit working altogether—she'd read somewhere that sometimes happened to older men. It ought to happen to *all* men, in Ursula's view, once they passed their prime.

Instead her husband just sighed in weary resignation. "Suit yourself."

She waited for his footfalls to fade down the hall toward the bathroom before finishing the chore of grooming her hair and then went down to clear the table.

The morning edition of the Ashford County *Chronicle* lay folded to the second page where Mike had left off and Ursula picked it up when a headline under the LOCAL section caught her eye: Suspect in Attempted Murder of Derby Farmer Remains at Large.

According to the article, Grant would be released from Ashford Memorial the following day and expected to make a full recovery after "allegedly being shot by another local man." It listed the prime suspect as one Zebulon Tuel and stated it was likely he'd fled the area with the aid of an accomplice, though the alleged accomplice was not named. She knew, though. All of Ashford County seemed to.

The eldest Milliard boy. The one who looked so much like his father. The one who, not long ago, she had fantasized about seducing. She wasn't but a handful of years his senior anyhow, at least in her mind. A little Mrs. Robinson action, like from that movie with the cutie pie Dustin Hoffman. Wouldn't that have driven her big strong husband mad? Clear out of his skull, which is the way she liked him, or used to. She knew she could get under his skin but, unlike the other men she'd been with, he'd never laid a hand on her. And Ursula knew he never would. It wasn't in his makeup; Mike Stone had been raised by a strong Southern father in the Catholic faith. Never had he been allowed to raise a hand to a woman.

"I catch wind you struck a lady and you'll have me to deal with," Charles Stone had been known to say more than once during his eldest son's formative years. Mike took the advice to heart because contending with his father had never been high on his list of priorities. With muscle hardened by years of farm labor and an interest in amateur boxing, Charlie Stone could lay flat anyone who crossed him and often did, piety be damned.

Mike had taken after his father and found himself in the occasional barroom brawl, using his labor-tempered muscle to best opponents (or at least he had early in their marriage; he seemed to have mellowed over the past few years, which suited Ursula fine). Many of these fights had originated with a sideways comment about Mike's young bride and often at her coquettish coaxing. The idea of men fighting over her had thrilled her to the core, but that thrill had also mellowed over time. Is this what getting old felt like, a slow draining interest in things you used to crave? If so, it sucked sour grapes.

Ursula caught sight of movement through the kitchen window and turned her head, expecting to see one of the hands amble by, perhaps hauling milk pails. But the person standing in the yard between the house and the barn was not Ed, Ben, or Old Dad. It wasn't even the milkman her husband had hired, the one who wore a ridiculous blue uniform accentuated with string tie and black-billed cap bearing the embroidered legend STONE DAIRY in red thread.

The second thought that flashed through her mind was that Grant Lang, somehow discharged early, had come back for some inexplicable reason and her heart stuttered.

But no. It was neither the milkman nor Lang. It was Ray Safford's older boy. The one people in town whispered of behind their hands. Crazy, some called him. Psycho. Late spring flurries danced around his dark hair. What was he doing all the way up here in Ashford and on her property, no less? He stood staring at her through the window, his black eyes boring into hers, and she fought an urge to rouse her husband to shoo him off.

The boy raised a hand. Ursula considered rushing to lock the door, but calmed herself. He was just a kid, a senior due to graduate this spring. If he'd come all this way, she ought to hear what he had to say. Maybe someone had been hurt. And if it turned out he had more than speaking on his mind, well, she'd be ready.

Ursula bundled into her housecoat before slipping a steak knife into the side pocket. Just in case. From upstairs, she could hear her husband snoring his way through dreamland. Then she slipped outside and stood on the porch.

"What is it, Caleb? Is everything all right?"

"I just came to look around. Quite the kingdom you've got here."

"I think you'd better go," she said through numb lips. "My husband will be up soon."

Caleb did not smirk or leer, as she expected him to. His expression never changed. Then he trudged away through the snow. She watched until he disappeared from sight before going inside to finish clearing the table.

Why had he come all the way out here? His abrupt and abnormal presence triggered a memory from a time a few years back when Mike had sent her out to his office in the barn on some errand and as she rummaged through his desk seeking whatever it had been, she had stumbled upon a photo album in the bottom drawer of a filing cabinet. Curious, she had picked it up and flipped through the pages. Mike rarely spoke about his past and she had wanted a glimpse of it.

The first few pages contained grainy black and white photographs of a severe-looking man with close cropped hair and a plump woman with kind eyes playing with a baby. Charles and Jane Stone, Mike's parents. And though the photo wasn't captioned, the baby would be her handsome hubby in his cradle days. If she and Mike ever had children, she prayed they would be as adorable as Mike had been.

As the pages turned, she watched him grow. His first day of school. Riding a bicycle down a country lane lined with poplar trees. His first Communion. A formal high school dance, in which he'd dressed in a white sport coat and tie and goodness gracious had he ever been handsome!

But as Ursula scanned each picture, she had picked up on something. Many of them contained the same young woman. A slender, dark-haired minx with wild eyes and a wicked grin, framed with long-flowing black hair down to her waist. Like a witch from a fairy tale, almost. It had taken her longer than it should have to identify her as Ruth Safford.

She had taken one photo out from behind its isinglass panel to study it up close. It appeared to have been taken at a barn dance. She could make out rough-hewn beams and plank walls. A bevy of sweaty revelers stood around a punch bowl, smiling for the camera. Augie Milliard, twenty years younger, held the delicate wrist of a woman she picked out as his one-day wife Teresa. Ursula's own husband Mike could be seen in the background, glaring down another man who had his arms around the witchy woman as if succumbing to a love spell she'd cast. That man—not much past his youth—she realized, despite a head of jet black hair in place of his current snow white, was Grant Lang. Flipping the photo over, the caption confirmed it: August M, Teresa W, Michael S, Ruth V, Grant L, Oct. '52. In 1952, Ursula would have been ten years old. Everyone pictured had attended her wedding, but seeing them in one place while she had been barely in braces at the time it had been taken, had made her feel lonely and isolated, like an outcast.

Nothing could have prepared her, though, for what she discovered two pages on. The newspaper clipping had yellowed with age, but the print was still perfectly legible.

It's a Boy!

Raymond and Ruth Safford of Derby, Ill. welcome their first bundle of joy. Caleb Michael Safford came into the world at 10:13 p.m. on June 11, 1958. Mother and baby are happy and healthy!

Baptism will be held at St. Joseph's Church on June 14. The child's Godfather is Michael Stone of Ashford and Godmother is ...

But Ursula had stopped reading then. She snapped the album shut and shoved it back into the drawer. In the intervening years, she had done her best to forget the clipping and the photos of Ruth Safford her husband kept. Mostly she had succeeded.

When Caleb had shown up, though, surveying the farm as if it might be all his one day, everything flooded back. And, good Gaia, how much he appeared to be the likeness of a young Mike Stone. She had never seen it before today, or had never allowed herself to.

So what? she thought. *So what if he is Mike's son? That was all before you had even met Mike. And he probably doesn't even know Caleb is his, if Caleb even is. And even if he does know, so what? It's probably not something Ruth and Ray want trumpeted to hell and gone.*

It meant something more, though, and she knew it. It meant that Ursula could not bear children. She was the sterile one. It meant that, even if her marriage to Mike one day ended, through divorce or death, she would never have the opportunity to bring life into this world. The idea settled her into a deep, dark despair.

Why was she even still here, out in this rural wasteland? She wished she had a way to know for sure whether her husband had sired Caleb. That would make up her mind on a great many things.

One thing, though, pleased her above all else. Spring had sprung. Spring was *her season*. The season where wildflowers blossomed, wildflowers like her. And now, as the sun climbed a bit higher and it burned a bit warmer, Ursula stone felt she could relax a bit. Felt she could *blossom* again. She'd survived another interminable Ashford County winter.

Old Dad hadn't tracked anything more complex than a ten-point buck in greater than twenty years, but he'd picked up the trail of the pair of absconders easily enough. He started at the scorched remains of the cabin where the product had been cultivated and harvested, each plant lovingly tended with painstaking care. His initial appraisal was that it had been a total loss. Except when he investigated further he found little evidence of charred vegetation within the rubble, which led him to believe much of the product had been removed from the premises prior to the destruction of the cabin.

Smart boys. They had no doubt taken it to an alternate site with the idea they could move it to finance their fugitive ways. They wouldn't dare try to sell it around here, though. If they had been wise enough to understand the value of saving the product, they would be wise enough to know they could no longer sell anywhere in the county. Which means they would have gone elsewhere. But not too far. The white boy was young still, just a green sapling not yet fully grown, and he would want to stay close to home. Despite their obvious wisdom, he doubted either would want to split from the other and that might spell their downfall. Two rabbits were more easily tracked than one and it took less than two minutes for Old Dad to pick up their trail.

They'd thought they'd be smart by heading east, through the river. Like characters in a moving picture, thinking they could fool tracking hounds by losing their scents in the running water. Well, Old Dad was one tracking hound they couldn't fool with such a method and as he stood on the west bank of the river near the levee he could clearly see the place of flattened cattails and sawgrass ten yards downstream where they'd emerged.

Old Dad was too old to go stumping through a waterway to maybe slip and hit his head on a river rock and drown, so he strolled a quarter mile upstream to where a small footbridge spanned the expanse, walked across it, and picked up on the far side where the fugitives had crossed.

He checked the brush to find out if they'd dropped anything noteworthy, anything he could take back to his boss, who craved physical evidence in most matters the way an addict craves his next fix. He found nothing of import along the bank, but a hundred paces further on into the woods, with their trail as evident to Old Dad as if it had been lit up neon pink, he discovered an errant Twinkie wrapper caught in the brush. The bit of cream filling that had clung to the inside of the wrapper was still fresh and had not yet hardened. He swiped it off with one thumb and then stuck it in his mouth. A few paces further on, he found a discarded banana peel, still yellow, and an apple core, recently browned. They'd raided mom and dad's pantry before lighting out, it appeared, and recently to boot.

Old Dad stood staring into the trees and thought he knew where the boys had gotten off to, at least temporarily. He glanced skyward, toward the setting sun, and thought he could make it there before dark—and if he could get the jump on his pair of running rabbits, he thought he'd be able to get them back to the dairy before his boss hit the hay. That would be a nice surprise and would probably garner a special bonus for the farm's longest-tenured hand. Mike Stone was a far different man than his father had been, but he shared his fair-mindedness and reason. And gratitude.

"Okay, little white rabbit and little black rabbit, I'm coming for you," the old man said aloud before checking first the loads in his old Army .38 Special and then the time on his older pocket watch before stepping into the woods. He'd made it about two dozen paces before he realized that not only was he doing the tracking, but he was also being tracked.

That was not uncommon in this cursed county. There were

things here—both flesh and spirit—that hunted people. Old Dad's ancestors had told stories about them and he had seen them many times. Usually they left you alone. Unless they needed to feed.

Old Dad moved another twenty yards into the woods and then stepped around the trunk of an enormous oak and waited, listening. Somewhere in the distance he heard the snap of a twig and then silence. Old Dad closed his eyes, counted to thirty in slow measured breaths, then continued on his way, hoping that whatever hunted these woods this day would pass him by. He didn't figure his old bones could offer much by way of sustenance. And he had a pair of rabbits to snare.

CHAPTER FIFTY-THREE

By mid-April, any hint of snow had stopped, and the first cornstalks pushed up through the freshly churned earth. Within three months they would be taller than Mike's head and, as it did every season, the green walls would make him feel like a rat in a maze all the way through harvest.

He kept up his routine. Rise early, start milking, eat breakfast, supervise the hands, eat dinner, ensure canning got underway, manage the office, finish up, eat supper, hit the hay. Sometimes he made love to his wife, but not often, and when he did, it was nothing more than ten tepid minutes both seemed happy to have over.

One new thing which had been added to his routine was waiting to hear from Old Dad. Since sending him on his errand shortly after the calendar had changed to the bicentennial year, Mike had heard nothing.

He found Old Dad's silence disturbing. He should have heard something by now, even if he'd chased those boys halfway across the country. Especially if he had. Had the geezer's ticker finally given out? Could he be lying dead in some backwoods swamp right now, reduced to nightcrawler food? The possibility could not be ruled out. The man might be a stout old warrior, but he wouldn't last forever. None of them would, hard as that was for Mike to swallow some days. He felt as strong as the herd bull they kept for breeding purposes, and he thought privately he didn't look a day over forty-five.

Breeding. When it came down to it, he knew he'd disappointed Ursula in that area. She'd wanted kids. A pair of them. Twins, if possible, like the Milliards had been blessed with. Mike had provided for her in every other capacity she could hope for except that one. Some nights he lay awake, listening to her soft bumblebee snores, and felt he'd let her down. The woman never asked for much, even if she did get under his skin with her flirtatious demeanor. But demeanor could be overlooked. He knew she'd never act on it.

Well, fairly sure, anyhow.

Ridiculous as it seemed now, not long after their marriage, Mike had gotten into his head Ursula had begun an affair with August Milliard and had spent better than four weeks covertly investigating the matter. He'd sent Old Dad to watch Milliard the way a vulture watches a dying man. Mike himself had watched his wife. Ursula flirted with the apple farmer unscrupulously, that was a fact, but he'd never found any further evidence to back his suspicions. Old Dad, as well, had come up empty and Mike had put the matter to bed, so to speak.

"That man Milliard is incorruptible," Old Dad had said in his final oral report. "He is as virtuous as your Christ himself."

Mike thought no man could be fully incorruptible, but had let the subject go. Happily, too; those four weeks of uncertainty had taken a toll on him.

Of course, the suspicions had never really gone away and he was grateful the Stone Dairy Farm existed way back in the country about as far as they could get from other human beings. Hell, Urs had shamelessly come on to both Augie *and* Grant at Adeline's Thanksgiving celebration. And Ray fucking Safford, for the love of God. He had to hand it to the menfolk, though— they never bit the bait, no matter what she flung their way. And Ray wouldn't know what to do with it even if he *had* bit. Why Ruth ever settled on marrying the village idiot, Mike would never understand. She could have done so much better, and she knew it. The only thing Ray had ever been good at was raising pigs and destroying defensive ends while playing left tackle for his beloved Derby Devils football squad.

Mike tilted back in his office chair, recalling the fun times he and Ruth had enjoyed before she'd taken her vows and become another person entirely, until Ed rapped on the open door and said, "Boss?"

"Come in, Eddie," Mike said, sitting up. He liked to maintain professionalism at all times before his subordinates. Except Old Dad, of course. He had long since dropped all pretense with the elder. "What's on your mind?"

"I think you better see what we found," Ed Hatlen said. The look on his face told tales Mike thought he'd rather not read. But the boss didn't get to avoid trouble, did he? Nope, trouble always came to the boss. It was one of the many occupational hazards bosses faced. In the next two minutes, Mike would wish like hell someone else could take the reins. But that wasn't a luxury bosses had, either.

"I saw the postman pull up, so I run down to the mailbox and found this hanging from the flag," Ben said. He held out his hand, palm upturned, and Mike's heart stalled. He stared at the item a moment before taking it.

It was Old Dad's pocket watch.

"It means they came back," Mike said. He'd taken the watch and driven to the Lang farm straight away. This development could not be spoken of over the phone.

Grant, for his part, looked like he'd aged ten years since the attempt on his life. His already-white hair had gone wispy and crows' feet edged around his eyes. He sat wrapped in an afghan Dinah had knitted and when he gripped his coffee mug, his hand shook slightly. Whether a side effect of his injury and subsequent illness or the news he'd just absorbed, Mike couldn't tell.

"Can I freshen your cup, Mr. Lang?" Jan Hempstead asked, coming into the kitchen. Grant had hired her in February to keep house during the week. God knew he couldn't keep up with anything alone and Jan, a recent widow who'd inherited a stack of debt from her dearly departed, needed a job.

At first the man of the house did not respond, his eyes glassy and distant, and the housekeeper and the guest shared a glance. Finally he blinked and smiled weakly. "Yes. Thank you, Jan."

"Mr. Stone?"

Mike declined, thinking he'd much rather have something stronger to sip on.

Grant said, "Why don't you take the rest of the day off, Jan?"

Clearly disappointed at the prospect of a truncated paycheck, she said, "I still have two loads of laundry to drag in off the line and a stack of socks in need of darning and—"

"Those can wait till morning."

Jane mumbled something about "rain tonight" and "bright and early" before donning her bonnet and heading out to her beat up old VW Rabbit. They waited until it grumbled down the gravel before resuming their talk.

"If they're still in the area, we need to take advantage of that," Mike said.

"I concur," Grant said. He got up and tottered—yes, that was the only word for it: tottered, like an old man—and snatched the kitchen extension off the wall.

Mike watched him, wondering what he had in mind. Even if he seemed frailer of body, Grant's brain seemed to be in perfect working order. "You better do the talking, Mike. It will seem more natural."

"Who'm I calling?"

"Augie. Ask him casually if he's seen his oldest boy of late. Make it sound like you're genuinely concerned, which you are. Just not for the reason you'll have him believe."

"I think I see where you're going with this," Mike said, accepting the phone.

"I'd do it myself but under the circumstances I'd guess he'd find it odd the victim of the man with whom his son conspired against was calling to find out if the boy was around."

Mike tapped the phone against his thigh. "Hell, he won't tell me if he's seen the boy."

"Of course he won't. Don't listen to his words. Listen to his tone. Listen underneath the voice. I'm going to get on the bedroom extension. Better to have two sets of ears on this, I think."

Mike waited until he heard the extension go live—it seemed to take Grant an extremely long time to go a short distance—and then he dialed.

CHAPTER FIFTY-FOUR

Augie Milliard stared at the phone in his hand a moment before setting it back on the hook.

"Hon? Who was that?" Teresa asked behind him, her voice shallow as a ravine in drought. Augie heard hope in her voice, desperate, palpable hope.

"Mike Stone," he replied, his own voice a distant echo in his ears.

"What did he want? Was it something about Dennis?"

"Not exactly," Augie replied. He faced his wife, knew his complexion would be as pale as hers, like a pail of milk. "Made small talk at first. Then asked if we'd had any word about Denny yet."

"That was nice of him," Teresa said, but her husband shook his head.

"No. That call was something else entirely."

"How do you mean?"

"I don't know, Tree. But he wanted something else." Augie bit his lip. "I think he wanted information."

Teresa clucked her tongue, the dismissive sound she had learned to pair so well with incredulity over the years. "August—" she began, but he held up one hand and lifted the receiver again with the other and listened until Wilma Beckett, the local operator, came on the line. Augie had it on good authority the woman spent most of each workday monitoring party lines, though she was known throughout the county as a reliably trustworthy keeper of secrets. In other words, the exact opposite of Edna Hadsell, the town gossip.

"Wilma, Augie Milliard."

"Good afternoon, Mr. Milliard," she said. "How may I direct your call?"

"I need a favor. Could you tell me the number that last dialed my residence?"

A confused pause. "I'm sorry, Mr. Milliard. I'm unable to provide that information."

Augie swallowed. "I understand. How's this, then. I give you the number I think it was and you simply say yes or no. Can we do that?"

"Oh, gosh. I just don't know—"

Augie rattled off the number for Grant Lang's residence and said, "You don't even need to say yes, Wilma. If I'm correct, simply wish me a good day and disconnect the call."

"Good day, Mr. Milliard," she said. The line clicked dead.

"What did you hear?" Grant asked.

"Not much. They haven't seen the boy. Nor heard from him neither."

Grant waved an impatient hand which, Mike now noted, had sprouted a small garden of liver spots across the knuckles sometime in the past three months. "What did his *tone* tell you?"

Mike shrugged a shoulder. "I think he's telling the truth."

"I think so too."

"He sounded pretty guarded. It could be he was holding something back or it could be he found me calling him out of the blue a little suspicious." Mike narrowed his eyes. "Which it was, if I may say."

"You may say whatever you damn well please, partner," Grant said, "so long as we don't let those young bugs struggle free of our web."

"We have a web?"

"Are you daft, man? This whole damned county is our web. We own this place, the two of us. We're an oligarchy, my friend. The bottom line is, you and I are two spiders who've spun one web, you in the north and me here in the south county. And we don't let bugs go unless we want to let them go."

"Unless those bugs are wasps and they sting the shit out of the spiders," Mike said.

Grant absently fingered the pink scar tissue that wrapped halfway around his head. "My point is, we are in control. This is our territory."

"I really hope them boys didn't kill my oldest hand. That man deserves a better death than that."

"I'm sure Old Dad could handle them cotton heads. If he couldn't, well, I guess it was just about his time to move on to the spirit world."

Mike stood, wiped his hands on his pants. "I'll use the usual channels, see if I can get a feeler on their position. Think like they would. They're young, stupid, scared to high Christ. It's only natural their course would swing them back this way. This is the only place they've ever known."

Grant nodded absently, his eyes gone vacant and remote again. His fingers played over that long, pink scar where the snow-white hair did not quite cover.

Mike hesitated at the door. "You forgot one very important spider," he said.

Grant snapped his eyes up.

"The very old spider who lives on yonder ridge."

Another flap of those newly aged hands. "Adeline's obsolete. She doesn't hold half the power she once did. Or thought she did."

"Still, we'll want to be careful," Mike said. "Don't ever underestimate that woman."

Then he went out into the spring sunshine and let the screen door clatter closed behind him.

CHAPTER FIFTY-FIVE

Ursula dialed, hung up, dialed again. Dust motes drowned in the late April sun streaming through the kitchen window. Cows lowed, an ever-constant sound she'd long since grown accustomed to, if not particularly fond of. Cows were disgusting beasts of burden, stupid and stinking and largely annoying. She did not eat their meat and she did not drink their milk, something her handsome hubby found bothersome but had accepted along with the rest of her liberal hippie ways.

But her handsome hubby was not home at the moment and she had time to herself.

If the crazy lady answers, I'll hang up, she thought.

She dialed. After four rings, Ray Safford answered with a jovial, "Yello?"

Ursula used her best little girl voice, which, admittedly, she did not much need to alter, and asked, "Hi, um. Is Caleb home?"

A stunned silence so pronounced followed that Ursula began to sweat. "Why *shore*," Ray said at last, then, phone muffled, hollered, "Caaa-*leb*? Phone, son!" Into the mouthpiece, he said: "Been some time since Caleb's gotten a call, especially from a girl. Say, may I ask who's calling?"

"A school friend. We have a project we're supposed to work on."

"I see," Safford said, sounding disappointed. He'd clearly been hoping his son had found a love interest. Ursula could practically see the big ol' teddy bear's pout now. Ray might not be much in the brains department, but he was kind enough, all right, and a little kindness went a long way. Ruth ought to count herself lucky to have him. She doubted he ever mistreated her. The phone clunked down and half an eternity later someone picked it up.

"Who's this?" Cautious, guarded.

"Caleb?"

"I asked who this is."

She didn't want to say her name in case Edna Hadsell or some other Nosy Nellie might be listening. "You visited me a while back? At my house?"

"Yes," he said. Sure now, confident. "What can I do for you?"

"I need to know why you came all the way out in the middle of the day."

"I told you. To have a look around," Caleb said.

Ursula said, "I think it's best if you stay away, okay? There's no reason for you to be on our land."

"Your land."

"Yes. Mine and my husband's."

"I just wanted to look. I didn't touch anything."

"Well, if you want to schedule a tour, you can call and speak with my husband next time."

"Oh, I'll be speaking to him. One of these days, he and I will have a nice, long chat," Caleb said.

"What is that supposed to mean?" she asked. Calling had been a bad idea. She should have mentioned the boy's intrusion to her husband right after she'd shooed him off their land.

"There's quite a bit I'm sure you're in the dark about. I could enlighten you, if you want. Just let me know," Caleb said.

"I'm listening," Ursula said. She had long felt as though her husband had kept much from her.

"Not over the phone," Caleb said. He told her where to meet him, if she wanted in on some truths.

When Mike got home at sunset, he noted the empty spot in the garage where Ursula's '73 VW Neptune blue Beetle usually sat parked, then got out and went into the barn. He found Ed and Ben in various states of labor.

"Hiya, boss," Ben called.

"Any of you boys happen to know where the missus got off to?"

Ed shook his head. "No sir. She pulled out about an hour ago."

"See which way she went?"

The hands shared a look. "No sir."

Mike gusted through his nose. "Keep up the good work, boys."

He stepped into his office, closed the door, and tilted back in his chair to think. Old Dad's pocket watch rested against his ribs like a tumor.

Ursula parked on an isolated side road and picked her way through the field until the young crop gave way to woodland and she moved into the trees. She hoped the kid wouldn't stand her up—she didn't know exactly what he had in mind, but if it meant pulling back the curtain on some things she'd always wondered since moving all the way out to this godforsaken corn country, she was all ears. So to speak.

The trees seemed glazed in gold in the final dying rays of sunset. The first night birds, early at their posts, trilled out their eternal melodies. A chill breeze hushed through the new leaves, shivering them on their boughs.

Now that she was out here, Ursula thought coming might have been a mistake. What if the stories were true? What if Caleb Safford was an outright psychopath, like that hotel manager in the movie who liked to stab women while they showered? What if he showed up with one of his father's butcher knives and left her in pieces out here in the woods behind the Gable house? What if he hauled her home and fed her to the hogs? No one would ever find her. She'd read hungry hogs could consume a human being in eight minutes flat, every last scrap except the teeth, which they apparently found disagreeable to their digestion.

Ursula shuddered and turned to go back to her car when a branch snapped behind her and there he stood. No knife. Hands empty and open and held up as if he could read her mind. He did not appear psychotic in the least. Quite reasonable, in fact.

Then again, the motel guy in the movie had seemed quite reasonable in the beginning too.

"Glad you came," he said.

"What did you want to tell me?" Ursula asked, cutting to the chase.

"I know the way he treats you," Caleb said. "Like one of his cows."

Ursula's face scrunched. "My husband treats me fine."

Caleb grinned, a feature which looked unsettling on his face. "Sure. If treating you like an accessory, something to be trotted out in front of his friends, is 'fine.'"

"It isn't like that," Ursula said. "If anything, I treat *him* poorly."

"Why did you come here?"

Ursula hesitated, licked her lips. "You said you could share some truths."

The boy's grin widened. "What do you want to know?"

She risked a glance at the Gable house, barely visible through the trees. A light burned on the second story and she wondered what the old woman might be scheming tonight.

Ursula watched his midnight eyes, saw only trust and goodwill in them, and said, "Is my husband ... is Mike your father?"

"Now whatever would give you that idea?" Caleb asked.

"Ashford County has ears," Ursula replied. "And I found something in his desk. Your birth announcement, naming him as your godfather. And you have his middle name. So far as I've seen over the years the two of you haven't spoken more than five words between you."

"Country folk like to keep their secrets," Caleb said. "That's why no one ever talks about them. At least not out in the open, like we are now. We live in a county full of phonies. Sometimes I think I'm the only real person here."

"I'm real," Ursula said, almost petulantly. "Now answer my question. Is he your father?"

Caleb's smirk widened. "Let's just say it's always best to trust your gut."

Ursula's heart sank. She could not recall a time when she had felt lower than she did at this moment, not even after what Grant had done to her, in those initial moments of guilt and shame. Maybe the kid was toying with her, lying to her.

"How do you know, though?" she asked, a whine edging into her voice. "How do you know for sure, one hundred percent?"

"I heard it through a reliable source who couldn't have been happier to spill the beans," he replied. "And, really, the evidence all adds up, no?"

An idea came to her then, slipping through the despair. Even if she felt poorly now, learning secrets acted as a soothing salve. It made her feel a little vindicated, a little vicious. "What about your sister?" she asked with newfound boldness.

This time Caleb barked laughter. "Oh, I found out about her too. Don't fret. Your husband's lineage stops with me. That we know of, at least."

Ursula blinked. "Ray is her father?"

"Do as I said. Trust your gut and ask that again."

She took a deep breath, released it. "Okay. Ray isn't her father. Then who is?"

"Gut. Who else do you know with a bevy of daughters?"

Ursula uttered a choked sound, put a hand to her mouth. "*Grant?*"

"Bingo, mama," Caleb said, cocking a finger at her like a pistol. "Anything else you want to know?"

CHAPTER FIFTY-SIX

Rachel sneaked out of the house at half past ten, as she had a dozen other times since being forced to switch schools. She hated St. Joe's. She hated the nuns and she hated the students. Most of all, she hated the God about which she was forced to learn. He was an abuser, an asshole, and Rachel had decided, through much careful introspection, that no such deity ruled over Earth. It simply made no sense, and the more she tried to make sense of it the less sense it made. While she attended Derby High, people had called her a Bible thumper, and that might have been accurate then, but her belief had dissolved quicker than sugar in hot tea since transferring to St. Joe's. She would have found it funny if it wasn't so celestially stupid.

Worse, though, than the Bible studies, the nuns, or losing her faith, was the way Father Scudder looked at her. It creeped her out in a major way.

Only a month left at St. Joe's and then she'd have the entire summer spread out before her like a green picnic quilt. Thank God. No, strike that. Thank whoever had designed the school system.

Rachel inched past her parents' bedroom door, always tightly closed at night (which did nothing to hinder the sound of her father lumberjacking his way through his dreams). She knew her mother would either be asleep—as unlikely as that seemed with the buzzsaw beside her—or deeply entrenched in her Bible. Either would serve Rachel's purposes.

The front door, as always, proved trickier. It squeaked. Squealed, more accurately, like a runt rooting for a sow's teat. Rachel had a suspicion her mother kept it that way to dissuade any wayward child of hers from doing precisely what Rachel had in mind now. After all, Ruth had been young once too.

Rachel eased open the door, a task which seemed as eternal as the heaven Father Scudder promised each Sunday, and finally had made enough space to slide through. One step, two steps across the porch and then her sneakers hit the grass and the cool April wind chilled her face and she had nothing but night before her. Eastwardly came the omnipresent sound of grunting swine.

Before she'd made it off the Safford land, though, a shadow crept up from the ditch and stood in her path. Rachel nearly screamed, recalling a story from her cradle days—something about a boogeyman who supposedly had once haunted their town. The slingerman, he'd been called by the old folks. Her father referenced him on occasion, usually around Halloween, and often with a visible shudder.

But the shadow before her was no boogeyman.

"Where are *you* going?" Caleb called.

Heart thundering with relief and spite, Rachel replied, "Where have *you* been?"

"Doesn't matter. I'm going to bed. Is our dear mother awake?"

Rachel shrugged in the darkness, a useless gesture to use with most people. But her older brother was not most people and Rachel, not for the first time, entertained the idea he could see in the dark. "Dunno."

"Big help you are. Sis."

"Don't snitch to her that I'm out tonight."

"Okay. But you have to show me your cans."

He really can see in the dark, she thought. To him, she said, "You're a pig."

"Not like I've never seen them before."

"I'm going. Don't tattle." She moved past him and he did not attempt to hinder her.

"See you in your dreams," he called over his shoulder. "Sis."

Rachel waited until she could no longer hear his footsteps on the gravel and then hurried on her way.

Susan Milliard lay staring at her ceiling. Her ceiling lined with precisely six and a half cracks. She'd have to tell her father about them so he could patch them. She would hate to have the whole thing collapse in on her, like her life had collapsed.

I should just let the ceiling fall on me, she thought. *It would be better than this.*

Was she being melodramatic? Yes, but she couldn't help it. Hell was no longer some distant lake of fire murmured of in church; it had come to visit her personally. That horrible foreign man had taken something from her she could never get back. He had taken what remained of her childhood. Thank God Mr. Lang had stopped him, but *oh Jesus*, the stuff that had come out of his head, where the bullets struck! Susie couldn't get it out of her mind, no matter how hard she tried to think of something nice like ponies or peonies or pineapple sundaes.

Tick. A pebble pinged off her window. Susie got up and opened it. Timber, in his usual place at the foot of the bed, sat up and woofed once.

"Come out," Rachel stage-whispered. She did not often call at this hour so Susan knew it must be something of gravity. In fact, she hadn't seen her best friend more than a handful of times since Rachel had been sent to St. Joseph's. It saddened her. It had taken her time to sort through the fact Rachel had feelings for her oldest brother, and vice versa, presumably, considering the look on the lug's face when they'd come into the Gable house last Thanksgiving. God, had that been half a year ago already? Susan had come to accept it. In fact, she had more than accepted it. To have Rachel as a sister would strengthen their bond. How many more Thanksgivings would they have to look forward to should Dennis and Rachel marry? The notion warmed her like a wood stove on a crisp December eve.

She stepped into her slippers and crept past her parents' room and outside, Timber padding along beside her. The crickets had not yet started their song this early in the year, but would before long. Susie always welcomed their dark chorus— it sounded, to her, like home.

She met her friend with a hug beneath the big elm and they

instinctively moved around the giant bole so as to be hidden from anyone who may decide to take a gander out into the night. Timber wandered off to water a neighboring tree and perhaps hope to find a lady friend.

"How are you?" Rachel asked tentatively.

"As good as I can be, I guess," Susie replied. Truthfully, she didn't know how she was. Her ordeal still weighed heavily upon her, even after her folks had made her talk to what they called a "family therapist," though she knew the true term for such was "psychiatrist." It didn't help. She could still see that awful man trudging through the snow to take her, could still feel his hard hands on her body. She supposed she always would, unless someone invented a memory eraser, like they had on some late night TV science fiction movies. One could hope.

"I came by because I found something," Rachel said, she reached into her pocket and withdrew what she'd discovered.

Susie took the envelope and scanned it. "Someone wrote you a letter?"

"Not just someone, Suze. Open it."

Susan did, carefully unfolding the letter with an unsteady hand and holding it up to read by the floodlight. At last she regarded her friend again, this time with wet eyes, and released a shuddery breath.

"It's Dennis's handwriting. Do you suppose he's really okay?"

Rachel shrugged a slender shoulder. "It would appear that way, babe."

"I guess we both should be happy, huh?"

"I don't know what you mean," Rachel said.

"Come on, Rach. Thanksgiving? You two came in looking like long-lost lovebirds."

"I know what it looked like, but it's not like that."

"Anyway, why would he leave this in your mailbox? There's no postage stamp so he delivered it personally when he knew no one would be looking."

"I didn't find it the mailbox. It was at stuck under a rock at the bottom of my bicycle basket outside St. Joe's after school."

Susan nodded. The wind gusted, trying to tug the letter

from her wayward brother out of her grip. She snatched it back and refolded it into the envelope. "I need to show this to my parents."

"That's a good idea." She laid a hand on her friend's elbow. "I hope they find him, Suze."

"Me too. At least now we know he's okay. He's not, I don't know, lying dead in a ditch somewhere."

"I have to go before my folks figure out I'm gone."

"Come by more often," Susan called softly. "I miss you."

Rachel turned, the wind making a mask of her hair. "I miss you, too, babe. Take care of yourself, okay?"

Then the shadows swallowed her and Susan Milliard stood alone in her front yard, picked out by the glow of the flood lamp.

CHAPTER FIFTY-SEVEN

The phone rang at half past three, more than an hour before Mike had his alarm set to sound. Ursula flinched beside him and muttered something about the time.

"I know what time it is, I can read a clock," Mike said, snagging the receiver from the nightstand and growling something between a greeting and a curse.

He listened for a spell, growing first cold and then hot beneath the skin. "All right. I'll be down."

"Who was that?" Ursula asked, still half-asleep.

Mike barely heard her and didn't care to answer anyway. At least not with the truth. He sat with his feet on the rug, hunched over his beer belly, and scrubbed both hands through his hair. Then he got up and stepped into his jeans.

"Mike? Who was on the phone?"

"Bobby Gray called in sick. I got to find someone to cover for him, else God forbid Edna Hadsell don't get her quart of buttermilk and pint of sour cream on time."

The lie pacified her and she fell mercifully silent. Mike finished dressing, then felt around the top shelf of the closet in the dark until he flipped open the lid of the Buster Brown box he kept buried there. He flipped back the handkerchief lining the interior and found leather-wrapped steel, which he tucked into the back of his belt. The lightweight corduroy jacket he reserved for spring weather covered the piece cleanly.

Now he was ready.

He parked in an alley a block from the breadbox that served as Derby Dale Police Department, got out, and looked around. He'd put Ed in charge of the morning operations and said he'd be back before lunch to take over. This shouldn't take long, no matter which way it wound up going. Only one way it could go, though, he figured, and it could get decidedly untidy.

The first robin song started as he made his way up the walk. Not even Gert Arden had opened her doors to early customers yet and who could blame her at this unchristly hour? A light burned in the vestibule of the PD and when Mike tried the door, found it unlocked. The meager reception area stood vacant, so he rapped on the glass closing off the office and detention areas from the lobby. Al Engel appeared and buzzed him in.

"You got 'em both?" Mike asked as they made their way down the long corridor to the twin holding cells.

"That's right. Someone called in a tip. They were holed up with Mary Lou Zahn, you believe that?"

"At this hour, I believe just about anything," Mike said as Engel produced a keyring, selected one, and opened the door to lockup.

Inside, sure as spit, sat Dennis Milliard and Zebulon Tuel, one per cell. Both gripped their heads in their hands as if trying to suppress twin hangovers, and both looked up as Mike entered the chamber. Dennis groaned. A trio of ladderback chairs had been set in the corridor between the cells.

"Grant ain't here yet?" Mike asked.

"He'll be along," Al said. He cocked a thumb at Zeb. "It takes him longer to get around these days, what with the damage this one inflicted."

"What's stopping Mary Lou from squawking to the Milliards?"

"Let's just say I gave ol' Mare the right to remain silent and she took it."

"What do you mean to do with us?" Zebulon asked.

Al said, "We mean to see justice served."

"I want a lawyer," the Milliard kid said.

The chief of police actually laughed at that. "Can I get you anything else? An apple fritter and a glass of milk, perhaps?"

"We're afforded a lawyer," Dennis said, "by the Constitution of the United States of America."

"The Constitution's been suspended until further notice," Mike said, pulling a pouch of Red Man tobacco from his jacket pocket and tucking a pinch between his lip and gum. He readjusted the jacket so it fit snug over the Smith & Wesson Airweight Model 37 seated against his spine. He considered the three chairs, and chose the one furthest from Zebulon Tuel. Couldn't trust a colored once, much less twice, and this particular colored had some reach on him. Hell, he was so tall and thin it was a wonder he couldn't just duck right through the bars. Ethiopian, Mike figured, but who the hell could tell for sure?

Chief Engel checked his watch and lit a Camel, blowing a tail of smoke into the overhead fluorescents. "I'll get us some coffee," he said and headed up toward reception.

When he'd gone, Mike regarded Zebulon. "What'd you do to my hired man?"

Zeb glanced through the bars at Dennis. Dennis said, "What hired man?"

Mike craned his head around. "Don't play stupid with me. I found his watch. You kill him?"

Dennis said, "I have no idea what you're talking about."

Zeb licked his lips. He seemed nervous, antsy. Just the way a liar behaved. "We never saw any of your men."

"Well, we'll find out for sure, won't we?" Mike asked the prisoner.

"Mr. Stone?" the Milliard boy said from behind him.

"I think it's best if none of us speak for a spell," Mike said and the boy fell silent. He was scared; Mike could smell terror coming off him like body odor. He couldn't get a read on Zebulon—the man seemed to have a lot of pent-up aggression, pacing around his cell, clenching and unclenching his hands. Yes, Mike had made the right choice in picking this chair. A desperate man was a dangerous man. He wished like hell Grant would get here so they could use whatever darkness still afforded them to their advantage. Moving bodies—dead or alive—worked better when no one could see you move them.

"Mr. Stone?" Dennis said again, his tone ever-polite, and when Mike turned his head toward him to tell him to shut his fucking cake hole, the kid hit him square on with some blunt object. He never got a chance to find out what the instrument of his unmaking turned out to be.

CHAPTER FIFTY-EIGHT

Chief Engel poured coffee into two Styrofoam cups, took them into his private office, and garnished one with a healthy dose of Jose Cuervo. He sampled a sip, found it agreeable, and replaced the bottle in his desk drawer. Then he ambled down the hall, whistling as he went. Today would be a good day, once they finished off this miserable business. Today would be a day for getting back on track.

He balanced both cups in one hand as he twisted the key in the door leading to the miniature cell block. He pushed in, opening his mouth to say something, then stopped cold.

Mike lay prone on the floor, bleeding from a head wound. From that angle, the cop couldn't tell if he was alive or dead.

"What did you—" he began, swinging his gaze to Zeb.

"Chief Engel," Dennis said from across the corridor. "Over here."

The chief regarded his other charge and felt his jaw unhinge. The coffee cups dropped from nerveless fingers to splatter across the cold linoleum. The kid had a gun trained on him. In his other hand he held one of his steel-toed boots with the toe dented as if an anvil had been dropped on it from some tremendous height. The bastard had used it on Mike—he'd wrapped the laces once around his fist and had swung it with all his might, probably six or seven times. Al could see it all too clearly in his trained investigator's brain.

The chief realized far too late he should've followed protocol and taken his prisoners' shoes away, or the laces at the very least. That's why protocols existed in the first place. He opened his mouth to say something, but the boy cut him off.

"*Shut up, Chief,*" Dennis bellowed. So loud and abrupt was

his voice that Engel actually recoiled. In a calmer tone, the boy said: "Here's what's going to happen. You're going to slowly remove your weapon and place it on the floor. You're going to come over here and unlock us. Then you're going to drive Mr. Stone to Ashford Memorial. You should have enough time to get him there before he dies."

The cop's face crumpled in fury. "You little son of a—"

Dennis thumbed the hammer back. In the tiny chamber it sounded incredibly loud.

"Now you do as I say or I'm going to put a bullet in you," Dennis said. He sounded as calm as a man ordering lunch, but Engel thought he detected a slight tremor in the kid's trigger hand.

"You boys don't know the kind of hell you just put yourself in," he said, regaining a bit of composure as he placed the revolver on the floor and unlocked the cells. "You think this is just me and Mike and Grant? This is bigger than us. All that product you burned—"

"We don't aim to stick around long enough to find out," Dennis said, stepping out of his cell and backing out of range in case Engel tried to make a grab for the gun. "We came back long enough to grab a few necessities. Then we're gone."

When Zeb had been freed, he looked the cop in the eye. "You leave Mary Lou alone. She didn't have nothing to do with this. You understand?"

Engel glanced at the gun in Dennis's hand and nodded. "Yeah. I understand." To Dennis he said, "Your father and mother are worried half to death about you, you know."

"You let me deal with them," Dennis said, edging toward the door with his friend in tow. "You deal with getting Mike's head fixed. If it can be."

"You better run far and wide, boys," Engel said. "If you're caught, the best you can hope for is twenty-to-life. At worst, you'll be buried beneath ten feet of topsoil. Either way, your lives are officially worth squat."

"I know the consequences, Chief. You—"

That's when Engel chose to go for the gun. It seemed as good a time as any and, hell, he had to try. If he failed, what did he have to live for anyway? A shattered marriage, a burnt up business, another fifteen years stopping speeders and busting kids for tipping cows before retiring a broken down veteran with a bum knee and arthritis in his fingers? No, he had to risk it. He had to try to be the hero of his own story at least once before he died.

Engel moved faster than even he expected, but it wasn't fast enough. Dennis shot him once through the throat and, as the police chief stumbled to his knees, shot him again in the head. Darkness rushed in to swallow him whole, hero be damned.

Grant could hardly comprehend the scene he beheld when he entered the police station's lockup. His business partners—his *friends*—lay on the floor, blood pooling beneath their bodies. The cells stood empty, as did Al's hip holster.

The lawman had clearly crossed over into the sweet hereafter, but Mike made a gurgling sound in his throat.

"Mike?" Grant called, kneeling beside him. "Mike, it's me. It's Grant. I'm going to get you to the hospital. You're going to be okay. You hear? I just need to make a phone call first."

Grant returned to the reception bay where the mutton-headed Nate Berryman would likely soon come to punch the clock and perch like a goddamned pelican on a pier post. Grant needed to be long gone before then. He picked up the phone in one gloved fist, pressed the button labeled Line 3 using a pen from a cup on the desk, and dialed a number from memory. It rang six interminable times before a gruff voice answered, "Gable residence."

"Put Adeline on," he said.

"Who's calling?"

"Never mind. Just put her on."

The manservant hesitated, contemplating this challenge, before acquiescing. Ninety seconds later, the lady of the house picked up and Grant explained the situation as he saw it. He listened patiently through her resistance before explaining the sinking ship they both occupied.

When the conversation ended he dialed emergency services and anonymously reported an officer down and a man in need of immediate medical treatment for blunt head trauma at Derby PD. Then he pocketed the pen, stepped to the glass doors, scanned the street to ensure its vacancy, and walked the two blocks back to his truck, not hurrying, not dallying. He drove home, thinking he'd made a clean escape without so much as a pigeon spying him.

CHAPTER FIFTY-NINE

A deline Gable hung up slowly, taking her time because arthritis had claimed her knuckles. It had been lurking for years, lingering beneath the surface of her papery skin, but had not, until lately, become unbearable. She took Bayer for the pain, but fat lot of good it did. She rested her weary hands on the shawl covering her lap and regarded Milo and Curley, not their real names, not her real sons, though they were real brothers.

"We're at war now," she said and explained what she wanted them to do and when she wanted them to do it.

Ursula heard the phone from the porch, where she'd often take her morning tea to watch the hired men work, and considered ignoring it. The hired men didn't much interest her anymore, not even Ben, upon whom she'd harbored hundreds of fantasies, but the sunrise did. Sunrises always held such beauty for her, especially now that spring had sprung and the earth and the sun drew closer to dance.

Not men. Men were all alike, she now realized. Maybe a single good one out of every thousand. Or million. Her husband included. Had he given her a good life? Sure, all things considered. But her life would have been just fine back in the suburbs, too. She'd had a good family there and plenty of suitors. It had been that something wild she'd seen in the older farmer that had made her swoon—that promise of adventure. Nothing like that old stuffy fuddy-duddy on *Green Acres* (though she did sometimes fancy herself akin to Eva Gabor). Now the adventure had gone out of their relationship. Ursula thought, not for the first time, about packing her things and moving back to Elgin. If her folks would have her, that was. Especially after what the meeting with Caleb Safford had confirmed.

Of course, a divorce would forfeit anything she might receive upon her dear husband's death, but she simply couldn't fathom another ten or—great Gaia, no!—twenty years of living with the man. It would be like a prison sentence. Did she love Mike? Part of her always would. But a larger part considered the idea of caring for him in old age—feeding him, bathing him, changing incontinence diapers—a hell beyond reckoning. The secrets he'd kept from her had been merely the feather in the cap.

"I'm coming, I'm coming," she told the braying phone, thinking it might be Mike calling to tell her he'd have to run Bobby Gray's route himself because he couldn't find a sub. It wasn't Mike on the other end of the line. She listened as someone who identified himself as a doctor from Ashford Memorial informed her that her husband had been brought in with serious head trauma.

"Will he be okay?" she heard herself ask as if from another dimension.

The doctor said it was too early to tell and that Ursula ought to come as soon as she could. She said she would and hung up. She sat on the milk can in the phone nook Mike had allowed her to paint to allay her winter blues one dreary December day years before. She put her hands to her lips, trying to keep the sounds coming through them at bay. They scared her because she couldn't tell whether she was trying to keep from crying or from laughing. Sometimes the universe hears our innermost thoughts, she understood, and sometimes it answers them.

CHAPTER SIXTY

Sheriff Lisk and a deputy came to question Ursula the day after she received the call from the hospital. They wanted to know if she had any knowledge of why her husband had been all the way down at the Derby Police Department and if he'd mentioned any prisoner he'd planned to visit there. Ursula told them the truth. She knew nothing. It wasn't her husband's habit to keep her abreast of his business. Mostly, she lamented, he seemed to keep her around for merely ornamental purposes. The deputy jotted this information in his book with a look that said he might concur with such a notion.

"Do you have any leads on who could've done this to him?" she asked, gnawing a magenta thumbnail.

The sheriff, Lazy Lisk (as Mike often called him), heaved a sigh, hitched his uniform trousers high onto his gut, and shook his head. "We'll let you know when we have something of substance, Mrs. Stone."

She thanked them and they left.

The doctors discharged Mike three weeks later, with a stack of bills and no real progress. A dent the size of a silver dollar adorned his forehead at the hairline, which seemed to have significantly receded overnight. He'd lost a chunk of motor function which doctors could not say with certainty would return. He'd also lost a good portion of his memory and could recall nothing about the day he'd sustained the injury, who had perpetrated it, or even why he'd been present at the police station. Sometimes he forgot what he was doing and would stare into space with lifeless eyes in such an unsettling way Ursula couldn't stand it. On those occasions, she would wave a hand before his face until the vacancy cleared. Once, on the fourth day of his homecoming, she'd found him urinating in the coat closet and she'd had to lead him to the bathroom in order to clean him up and remind him of the proper place to dispense of waste.

This is exactly what having a child would have been like, she often thought. She'd wanted children, sure, but not like this. She hadn't signed on to mind a man old enough to be her father. She thought again about how she did not possess the means or desire to do this for the rest of his life. Or the rest of hers.

Who'd done this to him? She thought she knew and planned to confront him on it as soon as she found the time. But she would need to be careful. It wouldn't do to be discovered conversing with Caleb Safford. Too many questions would arise. Word would spread. Ashford County, after all, had ears.

Her husband talked in his sleep now. Every night, it seemed, he would mutter something or other, often unintelligible babbling. Sometimes he moaned. Others he screamed. Usually he called out for his mother, but other times he uttered phrases which Ursula found meaningless.

"The watch. Those damn boys put the watch in there," seemed to be Mike's favorite. What watch? Probably some fragmented memory from his childhood. It didn't matter. What mattered is that when Mike talked in his sleep, Ursula got quietly out of bed and tiptoed to the front room davenport in hopes of salvaging some measure of sleep.

On the morning of the fourth week of Mike's discharge from the hospital, she found him standing in the kitchen wearing only a stained pair of Fruit of the Looms and a single sock. He gripped a glass bottle of milk in on hand bearing the Stone Family Dairy label on one side.

"Mike? Hon?" she called gently.

He turned toward the sound of her voice and Ursula saw something she'd never seen in her married life: tears trembled in her husband's eyes. As she watched, first one than another spilled over and trailed down his gray face. What he said slushed her blood.

"Who am I?" he asked. "Who are you? Please, can't you help me?"

He peed himself then, the trickle flowing down his leg to splatter on the faded linoleum.

It was that moment—that precise instant, which would remain frozen in Ursula's head for the rest of her life—that she knew her husband had to die.

And the sooner the better.

CHAPTER SIXTY-ONE

She dwelled on it daily, mulling ways in which it could be done cleanly and without arousing suspicion, before ultimately rejecting each in turn. Ursula might be many things, but a murderess was not among them. Someone else, then? Who could do such a thing and why would they do it for her? And for what price?

Night after sleepless night, Ursula paced the kitchen while her damaged husband snored and peed in bed. Often she muttered to herself as she wrung her hands, working the large diamond of her wedding band, turning it over and over around her finger. Again and again her mind returned to Caleb Safford.

"Not like this," she whispered to the empty kitchen. "No, not like this."

A cow lowed in the distance and Ursula realized with a start dawn had come. Time had slipped away from her like the spirit of a long-lost love.

Right on time, she watched as Ed strode up from the yard with Ben close behind to begin the milking. They'd worked diligently since Mike had "taken ill," as Ben called it, but they'd informed her they would need extra help or risk the farm "falling behind," as Ed put it. She had told them she'd look for help, but still had not gotten around to it. She had this other chore to finish first.

But how?

And who?

Ursula made three calls that morning. The first was to her parents' house in Elgin, a far western Chicago suburb. She hadn't spoken to her parents in nearly a decade, a decision she'd stood by that entire duration except for recently. In her haste to escape their staunch, civilized, puritanical confines, she had left behind a great many material items from her past. One of them happened to be her diary, the thought of which anyone else reading would have sent her into panic mode, but that blind panic had abated over the years until she realized she didn't care if her parents chose to publish it. Her past was her past; she no longer needed it and no longer felt attached to it in most fundamental ways.

But there was one thing she needed from within that ancient leather-bound tome she'd received for her eighth birthday and had proceeded to fill with her innermost secrets: the contact information for a particular young man she'd once had the luxury of knowing. The young man who'd been her first love and first lover. Her parents never knew of their secret trysts as teenagers, but they undoubtedly suspected as young Ursula had plastered his name on just about every conceivable surface in her room: Bryan Lee Denham. The last she'd known of Bryan, he'd lit out for Texas in 1965 with the hopes of starting a hippie commune. Her friends Daisy and Gayle, also admirers of Bryan, had reportedly followed him south. Last she'd heard, anyway. A spark of some deep-seeded emotion (jealousy, she knew, though she refused to name it) ignited in her belly as she waited through six interminable rings.

Finally someone answered in a severe female voice. Not her mother's. At least, not the way she remembered her mother's voice sounding from a decade previous.

"Hello, I'm trying to reach Burt or Simone Lathrop," she said, mind racing as to whom she might be speaking with and coming up empty.

"Who's calling?"

"This is their daughter, Ursula."

A long, considering pause. "Mr. and Mrs. Lathrop have no daughter," the austere woman—perhaps a live-in maid; in her mind she saw Alice from *The Brady Bunch* with a set of devil horns growing out of her bouffant hair—said before hanging up.

Mr. and Mrs. Lathrop have no daughter. The words stung her deeper than she could have dreamed and tears pricked her eyes. There would be no returning home again, then. Not ever. That bridge had gone up in flames at some point during her marriage and she wondered when that tipping point might have come. The second missed Thanksgiving? The sixth lapsed Father's Day card? It didn't matter, she knew. It was over and done. Part of her had known it would be and now that it had been confirmed a little walled up part of her collapsed in relief.

That didn't allay the fact that she still needed Bryan Denham's information. She sat on the painted milk can positioned beneath the kitchen phone and tapped her teeth with a violet fingernail. Then she dialed the operator and requested to be put through to Daisy's parents' residence, also in Elgin, three blocks over from her former home.

This time when the phone was answered, Ursula knew it was her friend's mother immediately, the voice sunny and steeped in nostalgia. It hadn't changed a bit since she'd heard it last, at her senior graduation, and the warmth invited Ursula to identify herself.

"Ursula Lathrop?" Daisy's mother said. "My gracious, how have you been?"

Ursula endured a bit of small talk catch up, which felt good and natural after the shutdown she'd received calling her own former home, but then asked the question she needed an answer to. "Martha, can you tell me how to reach Daisy? There's something I've been needing to ask her."

Daisy's mother Martha grew somber. "Why, I can give you the last known number I have for Daze, but I can't guarantee you'll reach her there. It's got to be ten years old at least."

Ursula's heart fell. "You haven't heard from her?"

"Goodness, no. Not since her father forbid her from leaving with that charlatan in saint's clothing. I couldn't stop him from disowning her no matter how I tried."

"Gosh, I'm sorry to hear that," Ursula said through numbing lips. "Well, if it's not too much trouble, I'd like to see about getting in touch with her. I miss her something awful."

Martha made a show of scraping around through catch-all drawers and index cards undoubtedly still tacked to the cork board Daisy's family had kept fastened to the wall near the fridge. Finally she came back on the line, her sinuses troubled, and rattled off a phone number with an unfamiliar area code. Texas, no doubt. Somewhere near Abilene.

"I hope this helps, Urs, honey," Martha said. "And if you get ahold of my Daisy, would you ask her to give me a call please?"

Ursula, fighting back her own tears for a past long lost to history, promised she would. Then she said good-bye, tapped the switch hook, and dialed the number she'd scratched on the palm of her hand with a blue Bic ballpoint.

CHAPTER SIXTY-TWO

Mike wandered the eroded caverns of his ruined brain. The place he inhabited seemed vast and foggy, indefinable. Gray, everywhere. Gray on top of gray and underneath of it. He didn't know where he was or why—only that he shouldn't be.

For one thing, his father often accompanied his wanderings and Charlie Stone had been dead two decades come August. Charlie appeared as he had when Mike was around ten years old: conservative blond haircut, kind eyes, hard face—younger by years than Mike was now. The last time he'd seen his father, the old man had been gray, worn, and withered as a cornstalk at harvest. This rejuvenated version of him raised Mike's spirits in this desolate place.

"What happened to me, Papa?" he often ask this vision of his father because he'd forgotten he'd asked it already before. Always the answer came the same way.

"You're in a place you oughtn't be, son. It's a place between places, where folks oughtn't linger."

This did not frighten Mike as much as he would have suspected, and he took the answer in stride. "Will I have to stay much longer?"

"I don't think so, boy. Not if the Good Lord shows mercy." He waved a hand at the wasteland surrounding them. "This here? This is the true hell. Moving on, you'll find, is much better."

"Will Urs make do without me?" he asked and discovered himself genuinely concerned about her in a way he hadn't felt in years. He *did* love her, not just the idea of her. That's why her flirtatious ways still galled him so. He simply hadn't allowed himself to believe it and now he had no chance to rectify the many ways he'd wronged her. No, he'd never laid a finger on her—his old man had seen to that—but he had hurt her in other ways, he now understood, perhaps even in ways she didn't know or understand. Why could he only now see the error of his ways? How was that fair?

"Your wife will get on fine, son." His father seemed to consider, then added: "Better even, maybe."

A sorrow greater than any he'd known overwhelmed Mike and if he'd been able to weep in a place like this, he surely would have.

"I wasn't no good for her, Papa."

"You did your best. No one's perfect, Mikey."

Mike whipped his head side to side like a defiant, petulant toddler. "No, I wasn't. I was a terrible husband. I may have never beat on her, you taught me better'n that, but I didn't treat her the way she deserved, like a May Queen from one of those hippie revivals she's always on about. Hell, I didn't even give her no kids she always wanted."

At this, her father held silent and looked away into the surrounding colorlessness.

"Papa, I hope I see you again," Mike said. "You know, on the other side."

His father gave him a companionable if somewhat pitying smile. "I hope you do too, Mikey."

Then his father faded into the mist, leaving his son alone to wander in misery.

Ursula's third and final call that rainy spring morning yielded the greatest results yet. When she dialed the number Daisy's mother had provided, it rang ten times before anyone picked up and when someone finally did, the voice was so smoke-choked she couldn't determine gender through the green smog. She identified herself and asked to speak with Daisy Humphries.

"Daisy *who*, man?" the voice asked. A male. Stoned out of his mind for sure. Something Ursula wished she could be right now, though she knew her husband would never allow marijuana in the house. She tried to imagine Mike taking a hit off a joint and stifled a giggle against the back of her hand. The old fuddy-duddy would freak out if he knew he was even in the same room as a bag of reefer.

"Daisy Humphries," Ursula repeated. "She came there about ten years ago with our friend Gayle Delmonico?"

The guy on the other end hit the blunt again. She could hear him hold it in his lungs and didn't begrudge him the time waste. Finally he released the breath, coughed a bit, then said, "Oh, mean Indigo and Saffron? From, like, Chicago, man? Yeah, they're here. Which one you want to talk to?"

Ursula laughed aloud. Indigo and Saffron were the nicknames her friends had chosen in high school if they ever moved to a commune. They each hated their given names, though Ursula had always loved her own.

"Either one," she said, feeling the first true joy she could remember in forever. "Indigo first, please, if she's available."

The guy muttered a choked "far out, man" and the phone clattered down. Ursula waited an interminable time. If Mike could see the long-distance phone bill she was racking up, he'd come undone. But she doubted bills—phone or otherwise— would ever concern her handsome hubby again. Finally the phone was picked up and she recognized Daisy's voice right away.

"Copacabana, Indigo speaking," she deadpanned. High as a kite. Ursula loved it and teased her introduction.

"Indigo, this is Lucille Ball, *dahling*," she said in her best comedienne interpretation. "I was wondering if you'd care to make a guest appearance on *The Lucy Show*?"

But Daisy—Indigo—wasn't fooled for a second, stoned to the gills or not. "*Ursula?*" she squealed through the earpiece so loud Mrs. Stone had to yank it away from her head, still grinning. "*Ursula Lathrop?* Oh my God, Saffron, get your sweet heinie over here, it's Urs!"

Ursula endured a volley of girl-shriek before both of her old friends were jamming the line with bubble gum conversation. If pressed to remember the lioness's share years later, Ursula would have been unable. But what she did remember of that long, long-distance conversation was the most important part— her friends advised her that should she ever decide to leave that cursed corn country and join their commune (Saffron: "not *just* a commune, Ursie baby, it's so much *more* than that"), she would always be welcome. They even offered to send her money for a bus ticket to Abilene, which Ursula declined.

At some point she asked if Bryan was busy, to which Saffron replied that Bryan—aka Eagle Eye—was *always* busy, but they'd tell him she called.

When the conversation finally ended, Mrs. Stone, still smiling, replaced the receiver on the hook and sat on her milk can with her feet drawn up and her wrists on her knees. She couldn't stop smiling. She couldn't stop scheming. She couldn't stop daydreaming about joining her friends' in their west-central Texas commune.

And she'd already picked out a nickname for herself: Spring. What could be more fitting?

CHAPTER SIXTY-THREE

One evening while Mike had fallen blessedly asleep on the davenport in front of a *Gunsmoke* rerun Ursula had taken her knitting (knitting! Like some ancient schoolmarm! When had she gotten so icky-old-fashioned?) into the other room to think. She knew she could not live like this much longer. If she did, she would lose her mind. She considered, for about the thousandth time in a week, packing a few things in a satchel and heading south. She thought she had access to Mike's bank accounts.

He'd set her up with an account of her own years ago into which he deposited a monthly allowance she was free to spend as she pleased. He'd grunt in annoyance when she came back from town with a new "hippie sundress," as he called them, or bellbottoms embroidered with flowers, or another pair of oversized sunglasses to add to the countless others in her collection. Her allowance money never went far, lasting usually less than half the month before running dry.

But Mike's accounts, though … that's where the real money rested. She didn't know exactly how much Stone Dairy Farm might be worth, but it had to be substantial. Why, just last year hadn't he purchased brand-new milking machines? And hadn't he given his three main men handsome Christmas bonuses? He had; she recalled Ed saying he might just take a trip to Acapulco with it. Mike Stone might as well have been made of money. But how could she get to it? She hadn't a clue as to where he kept his passbooks—probably locked away in a hidden safe somewhere—and didn't think she'd be able to get anyone at the bank to give her a second look if she tried to make a withdrawal.

Except. Except she was his *wife*. And he was currently

mentally incapacitated with a prognosis that did not exactly inspire hope of an imminent revival. Couldn't she, as his next of kin—his only kin, truth be told—couldn't she make withdrawals on his behalf? Wasn't that a law? She was sure she'd seen it on an episode of *Perry Mason*. It would be a matter to look into. If she could score even a fraction of Mike Stone's net worth, Ursula could make a clean getaway and no one would have to die.

She set her knitting aside and went to the telephone nook in the kitchen, planting herself on the decorated milk can. She dragged the county-wide White Pages directory from the shelf beside the phone and flipped to F, running one turquoise-tinted fingernail down the list of names until she found the one she wanted.

The phone rang three times before someone picked up on the other end and said, "Fahrlander residence."

Ursula swallowed. She knew her husband and Judge Fahrlander had many close dealings, both in business and personally. She said, "Is the judge in, please?"

"Who's calling?"

Her mind spun. "A … a client, I guess."

The woman on the other end of the line said, "You'll have to be more specific."

"I'm a friend."

"A friend or a client?" The woman's voice had adopted an edge.

"My husband is a friend of his."

"Ma'am, if you don't provide a name I'm sorry to say I'll have to hang up. I'm quite busy elsewhere today."

Ursula had not wanted to give a name over the phone, but realized now she had little choice. "I'm Ursula Stone, Mike's wife. Please tell the judge it's urgent."

"One moment please."

After what seemed an interminable interval, the line clicked as an extension elsewhere in the house picked up and Judge James Fahrlander's low rumble of a voice—the one he used to send criminals to their destiny—said, "Mrs. Stone? How good to hear from you. Has Mike shown improvement?"

"No, he hasn't," she said, trying to ignore the fire in her belly. "I—I have a legal question."

"Then I suggest you consult an attorney."

"Sir, I can't afford an attorney ... unless I can access my husband's bank accounts. And the bills are piling up on his desk. The hired men need their pay. Part of the fence needs mended. You see why I called you, sir?"

A considering pause in which Ursula imagined Judge Fahrlander sitting tipped back in a leather-upholstered chair in a dark-paneled den smelling of pipe tobacco and plum brandy, tucked into a smoking jacket and a pair of red puffy slippers. When he spoke, he sounded as if he might be treading carefully on this subject.

"Are you his power of attorney?"

"His what?"

"Have you ever, over the course of your marriage, signed documents in concert with your husband?"

Ursula thought back. "Yes, several. I cosigned on a few things for the farm and—"

"I suggest you review the files Mike keeps in his office and search for power of attorney paperwork. Whoever's signature appears at the bottom alongside his has the ability to access his accounts in the event he cannot."

Hope bloomed in Ursula for the first time in as long as she could recall. In a dim chamber of her mind, she thought she remembered such a document. She would ransack the office until she found it.

"Thank you, sir, you've been a big—"

"Good evening, Mrs. Stone. Give my best to Mike."

The phone clicked dead in her ear.

CHAPTER SIXTY-FOUR

Mike had always kept his office in as meticulous condition as he did the rest of the farm. Cleanliness was one of his quirks. Stepping into his inner sanctum, one never would have guessed it existed on a cow farm; it could've been in any downtown Chicago skyscraper and looked right at home.

It took Ursula all of five minutes to find the documents she sought. The filing cabinets weren't even locked as she had feared they might be; the last thing she wanted to do was go digging around in search of the right key. She flipped through the rows of folders neatly labeled in Mike's even hand, such things as *Bank Acct's, Mar'g Lice., Med. Rec's, Ins. Policy's, Payrole,* until she came to one that read *P.O.A* and flipped it open. The first sheet heading read: ILLINOIS STATUTORY SHORT FORM POWER OF ATTORNEY FOR PROPERTY.

"Yes," she whispered. "Oh, yes, baby, here we *go.*"

A quick scan of the document got her heart thudding. According to it, Mike's Power of Attorney (a glimpse at the signature confirmed it was indeed her, thank Gaia, and the date read 5/29/1965, nearly eleven years ago—no wonder she didn't remember signing!) had control of, among other things, real estate and financial institution transactions, business operations, stocks and bonds, and contents of a safety deposit box located at First Union Bank in Ashford.

Ursula turned to go, still skimming, then stopped and returned to the cabinet. She collected the financial files, patted them into a neat stack, then left the office.

Out of the grayish hell, Mike heard his mother call his name. She called out to him that breakfast would be served in five minutes and she wanted him at the table. They were expecting thunderstorms that day and she wanted him to have something hot in his belly for the long walk to school. From somewhere far distant came the insane discordant jangle of circus calliope music.

As if conjured by a wizard, his childhood kitchen appeared around him, with its worn wooden floor and its ancient, scarred table with the one wobbly leg. While his mother remained absent, he did find a plate of clabber waiting for him on the red woven placemat he recalled from his youth, and he sat down to eat.

Seated across the table, strangely enough, was Ursula. No, that wasn't right. It wasn't his Ursula, but one this place—this waste—had fabricated. She had somehow taken the place of his mother, Jane.

"Make sure you eat it all, Michael," the odd amalgamation of his mother and his wife coaxed. "It's going to storm today and you'll need your strength crossing through the fields."

Mike forked off a bite of his favorite breakfast food and stuck it in his mouth. It tasted like nothing. Bland as sand. He chewed and swallowed anyway, not wishing to disappoint the woman across the table from him.

"It's good," he lied and ate another slice.

"It won't always be this way, Michael," the woman said. "Things will get better, I promise."

"That's what Papa says."

"Your papa is right."

"I sure hope so," he said with a sigh and helped himself to another forkful. The familiarity of eating made him feel better, even if the fare tasted less than nothing. "I know I done wrong in life, but I'm not perfect."

"No one is, honey," the woman said.

Mike finished his clabber and set the fork atop the plate, dabbing his lips with his napkin. He glanced across the table but discovered he had it now to himself. Soon the kitchen melted into the gray, leaving the table, and his plate, and his fork for a moment before they, too, dissolved into mist.

"I sure am sorry," he told no one as he wandered off into nowhere.

CHAPTER SIXTY-FIVE

Ursula met Ed and Ben halfway through the milking room where they toiled with broom and mop, respectively, finishing up the day's chores.

"Evening, ma'am," Ed said, leaning on the broom handle.

Ben touched the brim of his hat and mumbled, "Ma'am."

"Good evening, fellas," Ursula said, wishing for a hasty escape. She didn't want her husband's hands to see her with anything from his office. No such luck. Ed and Ben set their tools aside and strode up to her, each on a side. Now unease mingled with the guilt of discovery.

"Miss Ursula, we're a week behind in pay," Ed said.

"We need to eat too, you know," Ben added.

"I'm sorry, boys," she said. "It's been a hard month, what with my husband laid up like he is. I'm still trying to find my way around his office. How about I cut your checks first thing in the morning, how would that be?"

"But it's quittin' time on Friday," Ed said. "Me and Ben was wanting to head down Murdoch way, catch us a drink at Chancellor Brothers."

"Tell you what. Let me run up to the house and get my wallet. I've got some cash I could loan you?" She added: "Interest free, of course," before regretting it.

"Tell *you* what," Ben said. "I know where the boss keeps his payroll checks. How's about we show you where, give you our timecards, and you can sign the checks?"

Ursula relented. "I suppose you fellas are owed your paychecks. You did the work, after all."

The men followed her to the office and Ben pointed out which desk drawer held the check binder.

"It's locked," she said, giving he handle a few good tugs to illustrate. "How about I give you boys some cash to play with until I figure out where my husband keeps the key."

Ed toed the door shut. "How 'bout you pay us another way?" he said.

"We see the way you look at us," Ben said, coming around the desk.

Ursula froze, file folders clutched to her chest. "I don't think I like this joke, boys," she said, praying that's what this was. It had to be.

"We ain't boys," Ben said, unbuckling his belt.

"Yeah. We'll show you," Ed remarked calmly as if reporting nothing beyond an interesting cloud formation overhead.

Ursula glanced around, looking for anything to use as a weapon. She'd already endured one brutal assault and would be damned if she'd endure two more. The men advanced, their faces humorless and dead. Hungry. Her eyes flashed across the surface of her husband's desk and focused on what she needed—a vintage letter opener fashioned to look like a medieval broadsword. She fumbled it up, dropped it between her feet, bent to grab it off the floor, and then brandished it at her would-be assailants.

"Don't you come near me, you hear?" she said, shocked at the venom in her voice. It didn't sound like her at all. It reminded her of that movie that Mike had taken her to a few years back, the one about the little girl possessed by the devil.

Ben and Ed stopped and their hands moved from their flies to midair. "Now, now. No need for that," Ed said.

"We just want what you want," Ben said in a perfectly reasonable tone, as if they'd all agreed to play the same song on the 8-track.

"What I want is for you both to get out of my way so I can go tend to my husband. Remember him? Your *boss*?"

Her words seemed to hold more sway than the makeshift weapon in her hand. Both men paused and looked at one another. Finally Ben said, "The way I hear it, he might not be our boss much longer. This place can't run without him, and I hear he got his clock cleaned but good."

Ed added, "How many days we got till you hand us our walking papers, Missus? We seen the files you got there. How many days till you sell the farm to some hoity-toity like that Grant Lang? He's been itching to get his fingers on this place a long time, if you believe the grapevine."

Fine, Ursula thought. *Just keep them talking. Keep them talking long enough and you can figure your way out of this.*

"I'm not selling the farm," she said. "You guys have jobs as long as you want them, but I'm asking—asking *nicely*—for you to stop this foolishness. Just stop. What you're thinking of is a serious crime and so help me God I will go straight to Sheriff Lisk unless you back off."

The men looked at one another again, then Ed relaxed and a sunny grin opened on his face. "Hell, we didn't mean nothing, Mrs. Stone."

Ben took the cue and took a long step back. "Yeah. Yeah, that's right. We was just playing, that's all."

Ursula kept the letter opener poised. For each step the men retreated, she took another forward. The power had shifted and they all knew it. By the time they'd reached the milking room door, both men hung their heads.

"We're awful sorry, ma'am," Ed said, refusing to meet her gaze. His lips trembled when he spoke. "We really didn't mean nothing by it, honest Injun."

"Go on and finish up for the day and I'll have checks taped to the door for you."

They scurried off into the nether regions of the barn. Ursula watched them go, then stepped back into her husband's office, locked the door, and sat down at his desk to collect herself. When she had, she checked the hands' timecards, wrote out two checks (both from the personal account she shared with her husband), signed them in her name, and taped them to the door as promised. Then she gathered up the folders and hurried to the house.

CHAPTER SIXTY-SIX

U rsula locked the door, dumped the load on the kitchen table, and went to check on her husband. When she got to the front room, though, she found the davenport vacant, the duvet thrown aside. The TV now played an old *Have Gun—Will Travel* episode which depicted Paladin harassing a cattle rustler.

"Mike?" she called, the dregs of adrenaline making her voice tremble. "Mike, honey?"

No answer.

Ursula moved room to room, looking for her damaged husband, the paperwork all but forgotten. She found him in the bathtub, at first certain he'd killed himself, and felt a bubble of some unidentified emotion swell in her. But no blood stained the tub and she detected a pulse beating in his throat.

"Honey, let's get you to bed, okay?" she said, knowing she'd be unable to lift him alone. He resisted at first, muttering something incomprehensible under his breath, before pushing up from the tub and leaning on her all the way to the master bedroom where he allowed her to tuck him in. She watched him snore for a time in the darkening room, twisting the wedding band on her finger. Remembering how she had invited Mike's closest friend into their bed. Great Gaia, what had she been thinking? Stupid, the whole thing. Finally she went downstairs to review the files she'd pilfered from his office.

They appeared in perfect order and she thought she'd be able to access his accounts without trouble. The ones she knew of, anyway. Mike likely had hidden funds—he was nothing if not cautious, even around her. The relief she felt at knowing she could do this all while he still drew breath made her head spin. He wouldn't have to die after all and she would probably be able to set up round-the-clock care for him before making her great escape. Heading to Texas to meet up with her old friends was sounding better and better.

The phone rang forty minutes later and Ursula found to her surprise that Judge Fahrlander had called her back. "How may I help you, sir?" she asked.

"You can start by ceasing and desisting your inquiries into your husband's financial affairs," the judge shocked her by saying. It sounded as if he'd made it pretty well deep into the hypothetical bottle of plum brandy, if the slur in his voice proved any indication.

"Excuse me?"

"Excuse me, *Your Honor*," the booming and not quite steady voice corrected. "You will address me with *respect*."

For a moment Ursula found herself so taken aback she couldn't speak. A hot pulse beat in her temple. When she found her voice, she said, "No, I don't believe I will address you with respect."

"*What* did you say to me?" the judge bellowed. "*What?*"

Ursula thought such a situation as this would send her into a blind panic, to be spoken to as such by a man of high authority, but instead she found the opposite true. A quiet confidence blossomed in her core and she found herself on the verge of laughter. "Not only will I no longer address you with respect, but I also cordially invite you to eat shit."

She hung up, a giggle bubbling up behind her lips, and stared at the phone as if willing it to ring again. It didn't. It had felt good—no, amazingly *groovy*—to tell that son of a bitch off. Just who the hell did Judge Fahrlander think he was, trying to order her away from what was rightfully hers? Oh, she knew he and Mike went way back, since well before she'd come into the picture, but *she* had married Mike. Fahrlander hadn't. In sickness and in health, for richer or poorer, till death do us part. Both she and Mike had spoken those words at the altar that day so many years ago and if she had to honor them, then so did he.

Till death do us part, dear husband, she thought again, then returned to the kitchen to finish reviewing the paperwork.

CHAPTER SIXTY-SEVEN

Caring for her husband soon became a virtual impossibility. He had started to decline the first week of May, but now seemed to be in total freefall. He never made it to the bathroom any longer, and she had to spend nearly fifteen minutes changing him each time he soiled himself. Mealtimes seemed to have lost all meaning for Mike and he sat through each of them drooling and staring into space while Ursula chided him like a toddler to finish everything on his plate.

"If you don't scrape it clean, Michael Stone, you will *not* get any dessert tonight," she'd holler at him. Sometimes it worked. Mostly it didn't, and by the middle of June he'd lost an alarming amount of weight.

She'd gotten a doctor from town to come out and see him since she had no possible way of getting him to the clinic—she lacked the strength required to get him to and from the car and couldn't bring herself to seek the farmhands to assist her. The doc, a new fellow in town, recommended hiring a part-time nurse if Ursula could spare the expense.

"From the look of the place," the man said, peering out at the numerous outbuildings kept in fastidious repair, "money ought not be an object."

Ursula wanted to explain she didn't quite know how to get at their money, but found herself too embarrassed to admit such. Oh, she'd looked into it in the intervening days since she'd told drunken Judge Fahrlander off, but no one seemed able to help her. The vice presidents of both First Union Bank & Loan in Ashford and Old Third Bank in Murdoch—the institutions in which her husband had stashed the majority of their wealth—had been unwilling to allow her access to the funds on the grounds of "discrepancies in the POA paperwork" and both recommended consulting an attorney on how best to resolve the issues. Both men's monologues sounded scripted, their wording practically identical, and she suspected Fahrlander had given each an earful about what they should tell a certain little Mrs. Michael Stone should she come creeping around her man's hard-earned money. She'd formed a theory over the years that all the successful men in this pocket of the world had formed a kind of secret brotherhood intent on watching out for each other's interests. A secret society, almost. A patriarchy for certain.

She had, in fact, consulted an attorney on Thursday. She'd driven into town in the blue Beetle Mike had bought her, leaving him to his own devices. Part of her hoped viciously, upon returning home, that she would find him lying at the bottom of the staircase with a broken neck. She hadn't, of course, and her dialogue with the attorney had only served to deepen the disappointment she'd felt at discovering him still very much alive and with a freshly-loaded adult diaper to boot.

The attorney advised her, succinctly and without a shred of compassion, after reviewing the Power of Attorney paperwork, that in order for Ursula to access any of the Stone accounts—except, of course, their joint account which she had practically tapped out—she would have to wait for her husband to pass.

Mike Stone's Last Will and Testament appeared, the lawyer said, in perfect order—naming her as the sole beneficiary. Thank Gaia for that, at least.

As she drove home, Ursula realized that, perhaps worst of all, she hadn't even taken the time to make a flower wreath this spring. Spring was her season. She lived for spring. All the long Midwest winter, as she remained trapped inside the dusty, musty farmhouse, she longed for spring. Green grasses, blooming flowers, the burbling of the brook, and birdsong. But flowers took precedence. She was, after all, a flower child. Always had been, always would be.

Instead of driving home, with the information she'd been forced to process over the past days still floating around in her head like lost ghosts, Ursula made a left onto an unpaved county road and took it to a small meadow she knew. A place untouched by all the terrible corn that walled in the county come summertime. A rectangle of unspoiled prairie smack-dab in the center of all this damnable farmland.

She made several trips each spring to the patch of meadowland to gather flowers for making wreaths. Mike allowed her these reprieves because he knew how much she enjoyed watching spring bloom around her. He knew she had never been nor would ever be a farm girl. She let off the accelerator so begin slowing and thought of her friends Daisy and Gayle—oops, Indigo and Saffron—cutting up at the commune in Texas, no doubt sharing the myriad enjoyments of Bryan "Eagle Eye" Denham as she once had.

Ursula sighed and parked on the shoulder and stepped into her little meadow wonderland, the rueful smile due to having missed out on much of the spring flowering slipping slowly from her face. Something was wrong here; something had happened. She could sense it long before she saw. And when she saw it, she had to clap both hands over her mouth to keep from screaming.

CHAPTER SIXTY-EIGHT

Ursula's parents had warned her repeatedly about what awaited her if she chose to leave their suburban sanctuary for "that damned farm boy." All sorts of hazards existed "out in the boondocks" against which a cultured (translation: sheltered) city mouse would have no means of defense. Inbred hillbillies! Wild animals! Hell, her father had explained, there were reports of savage Indians still lurking out in corn country.

She'd listened with an air of defiance and nonchalance, though the warnings *had* rattled her some. None had startled her more, though, than her mother's insistence that Satanic cults congregated in the dark corners of rural areas. They lurked in the shadows, awaiting unsuspecting victims to kidnap and sacrifice to their twisted overlord.

Of course, in the years she'd been married to Mike, Ursula had never actually seen any evidence to support her parents' fervent claims—until now. What she saw appalled her on a level previously unknown to her. That someone could do something so atrocious shocked the very fundamentality of her essence.

The boar had been slaughtered on site. That much was clear. Blood painted the long grasses and flower petals. Entrails blue and shiny as pewter overhung the branches of the elms bordering the meadow, their surfaces acrawl with swarming flies. The carcass itself had been flayed from throat to groin; the head and testicles had been removed and appeared nowhere in evidence.

Ursula took a stumbling backward step and nearly screamed when a tree limb touched her shoulder like the bony fingers of Death himself. She raced to the Beetle and experienced a moment of blind panic when she couldn't find the keys, only to realize they still dangled from the ignition. Her head snapped around, trying to survey three hundred and sixty degrees of her environment in case those who'd perpetrated such a heinous act might decide swine hadn't been a worthy enough sacrifice to their devil and required the flesh of a higher station. But the meadow remained as serene as ever, except for the horror lying at its center.

Mike walked alone in the gray wastes. Occasionally he would hear sounds familiar to him: morning birdsong, a snatch of dialogue from an old western on TV, his wife calling his name, a few bars of calliope music from a traveling circus he'd attended long ago in boyhood. Sometimes shapes resolved themselves nearby, nothing more than shadows in the mist. No one discernible. His father had not visited in what felt like ages.

One late night—at least it felt late to him; time had no meaning here beyond what his perception told him—he heard the squeal of a hog. It seemed to echo at him from everywhere, and it took him back to the days of his youth when his folks let him keep a piglet from the Safford farm as a pet. His father had warned against it, that nothing good could come of it, and on that count he had been right. The pig, which he had named Snort, had gotten loose of its pen one night and wandered out into the wilds. They found its carcass a week later, eaten mostly down to the bone.

Mike had sobbed for a week over the loss, but never requested a replacement and never kept another pet. Animals were for milk or slaughter only.

The squeal came again, though it sounded nothing the way his Snort had. It sounded ready for the slaughter or perhaps ready to eat. Those two sounds a hog makes are sometimes hard to distinguish.

Then, right beside him, Ruth Safford stepped out of the mist. She wore a forlorn look upon her face and though her lips moved, Mike made out nothing she spoke.

"What is it, Ruth?" he asked. "Is something the matter?"

Ruth continued her ventriloquist act before reaching out

to touch his face with a hand carrying all the substance of a cobweb.

I'll see you soon, she mouthed. *I'll bring help.*

"What does that mean, Ruth, what help?" he asked, but she had already faded again into the gray.

CHAPTER SIXTY-NINE

She meant to call the Sheriff's Department as soon as she got in the door, but discovered a pair of unlikely visitors sitting on the front porch, awaiting her return. She composed herself before exiting the vehicle, not sure whether to divulge her grisly find to them or save it for the sheriff. She selected the latter at the last moment.

"Good afternoon, Mrs. Safford," Ursula said. "What brings you up this way?"

Ruth Safford stood from the wrought iron porch chair in which she'd made herself at home and took a stiff step forward. Her face looked pained today, though that was not much different than most other days, in Ursula's admittedly limited experience with the woman. Her son Caleb sat on the porch swing, rocking methodically. He watched Ursula intensely, the way a cat studies a goldfish through aquarium glass, until she had to look away.

"I'm sorry to bother you," Ruth said. "But I was hoping to see Mike."

Ursula found Ruth's request odd and wholly inappropriate and if nothing else convinced her of Caleb's paternity, this did.

"I'm sorry, Mrs. Safford, but Mike is unwell," Ursula said, wringing her hands to hide the fact they still shook from the discovery at the meadow. "I'd be happy to pass along your well-wishes."

"Please," Ruth said, taking another step forward. "There's a rumor running around town he might not ... might not be with us much longer."

Ursula opened her mouth to resist, then closed it again. Maybe Ruth was right. Maybe Mike didn't have much time left.

She hadn't fully decided yet. It would play better if she let a few of his friends see him before he passed.

"Of course," she said. "I'm sorry. Please, come in."

The Saffords followed her inside and she asked them to wait in the kitchen while she tended to her husband. She wanted to get this over with so she could report the slaughtered animal to the authorities. The idea of it lying there soiling what she had always considered to be her secret meadow made her stomach roll.

She found Mike reclined on the davenport, jaw agape, and for perhaps the hundredth time she wondered if he'd died in his sleep. Then he loosed a strangled snore and she shook him gently awake and wiped a slick of spittle off his chin.

"Mike, honey? You have visitors. Ruth and Caleb Safford. Can you step into the kitchen with me?"

Somewhat miraculously, Mike seemed to come around. He uttered something unintelligible, which Ursula took as affirmation and together they made their way to the kitchen and got him settled in his chair. When Ruth saw him, she pressed her fingers to her lips and her eyes glistened.

"I'll give you a few minutes," Ursula said. The boy stood staring at the man seated before him, his face inscrutable.

Ursula gave them privacy and went into the front room to call the police.

CHAPTER SEVENTY

The Sheriff's Office promised to send a deputy to check out the meadow, but said it was likely nothing more than a prank pulled by a bunch of high school kids.

"The hoodlums that come out of the public school system these days may well be the end of us," the desk sergeant mourned. "I read a book last year about these kids who kill a pig and spill the blood on a poor girl at her high school prom. With trash like that in the hands of our youth, no wonder their heads are filled with guts and gore. The worst part? I heard they're even making it into a *moving picture*. You believe that? My Lord, what is this world coming to?"

Ursula said, "As long as you don't think it's devil worshippers or something. Someone told me they may congregate out here."

The desk sergeant laughed. "Ma'am, we're in God's country here. Devil worshippers would be stupid to step foot among us. All the same, I'll send a car to have a look. You have a blessed day, now."

The line dropped and Ursula hung up. Teenagers who killed animals for fun? She didn't buy it. Either times had changed drastically in the handful of years since she'd bid her own youth adieu or the slaughtered swine was part of something larger … and more terrifying than a mere high school prank. Why leave the carcass in a secluded meadow if it was meant to be a prank? Why not drop it on the school lawn or hang it from a church steeple? In any case, she'd recovered from her shock and now wished only to move on to thinking about how she would handle her husband.

Cool wind. A waterfall, someplace distant. Sharp birdsong. White bulbous clouds with leaden underbellies scudding by overhead. Something other than all this damned gray; that's what Mike longed for.

And that's what he got. Only for a moment, but that was fine by him. Anything to break up these gray, murky wastes.

"Thank you," he whispered to the benefactor of this relief, whoever that may be. Maybe God. Maybe not. "Thank you, thank you."

Then his reprieve vanished and he was left alone in the misty valleys of his ruined mind.

CHAPTER SEVENTY-ONE

The scene in the kitchen upon her return so took her by surprise that Ursula was rendered momentarily speechless. Ruth had Mike's head between her hands and her cheek laid atop his thinning hair in an almost motherly gesture. Then she kissed the top of his head and wiped her eyes.

"I'm sorry to be a bother, Mrs. Stone," she told Ursula. Then, to her son, "Come along, Caleb."

But Caleb lingered a moment after the screen door banged at his mother's departure. "I could do it for you, if you want," he said.

The rationality in his tone chilled her to the marrow because she knew what he meant. "Do what?" she asked anyway, through numbing lips.

Caleb thrust his chin at Mike. "I could put him at peace."

"No," she said. "God, no."

"It would make your life easier, that's plain enough to see."

"I want you to go," she whispered. "Please don't contact me again."

Caleb's thin lips spread into a goblin's leer. "You know how to find me if you change your mind," he said, then reached out and patted Mike's cheek. "So long, Pops."

He went out into the June afternoon and got into the car beside his mother.

Ursula fretted around the kitchen long after she'd gotten Mike put to bed. This, by far, had been one of the strangest days of her life. She needed to talk to someone about it, but had no one. No close confidant she could turn to. Imagine that—better than a decade in this county and she'd made no friends. Always the outsider, the outcast. The silly hippie chick. More than ever she wished she'd followed her instinct and joined Daisy and Gayle at the commune in Texas. She wondered what her life might have been like if she'd made better choices.

Once night had fallen, she went upstairs to watch Mike sleep, twisting the wedding band in hard semi-circles. Was she a terrible person because she wished her husband would die? She'd never been the religious type, rejecting the patriarchy of Christianity in favor of loving Mother Earth, Gaia. But sometimes she felt the guilt of a Catholic. Oh, why wouldn't he just go on and leave her in peace? Gaia (or Whoever) had seen her unfit to properly equip her for motherhood so why had she now been thrust into this abysmal motherhood role? It made no sense. None whatsoever.

And it wasn't fair.

She thought about what Caleb had said. That he would put Mike at peace, if she wished. Maybe he had killed before. Maybe he'd been behind the terrible attacks at the Milliard maze last autumn. Ursula did not read the papers as fastidiously as her husband, but she hadn't heard of the police apprehending anyone in connection with the crime and surely in a place as tight-knit as Ashford County she would have.

"How would he do it?" she whispered, unaware she'd spoken aloud. "Could he do it painlessly?"

No. No. She could not entertain the notion even a moment longer. Ursula Stone might not believe in God, but neither did she believe in murder. It was not the place of a man to take another man's life. Or the place of a woman.

She paced the hallway outside the master bedroom, twisting her ring, and as she faced about for another lap, heard her husband moan in his sleep.

CHAPTER SEVENTY-TWO

On the final night of spring, with the crickets and cicadas in full song, Ursula Stone spent her last dollar. She had an ocean of cash in her husband's name, but no way to access it. A green sea behind impenetrable walls of fiduciary law and the obstructionism of Judge Fahrlander, her husband's crony, who clearly meant to keep Mike's wealth intact in the event he made a full recovery. This latter infuriated her to no end and, in a fit of rage and despair, picked up the phone and dialed his number.

After several minutes of jostling and jousting with the same woman who'd answered last time, his wife or maid, no doubt, she at last got Fahrlander on the line. His tone sounded tinged with honey, sticky and sweet. And more of that perceived plum brandy.

"Mrs. Stone," he said. "How are things in your neck of the woods?"

"Terrible, since you ask," she said. "Mike's not getting better and I no longer have the means to care for him."

"Oh, that's too *bad*. I'm sorry to hear it, *truly*."

"No thanks to you."

"Surely you've straightened out any lingering financial issues by *now*?"

"Surely I have not. It seems no one is willing to help me."

"Why, I'm sure that's none of *my* concern, Mrs. Stone."

Her fury spiked. "Do you understand that my husband, your business associate in whatever underhanded operation you're pulling, is going to die without financial means by which to care for him?"

"That's going a bit far, I'd say."

"Do you further realize that should he die, all his money goes to me?"

Silence from the far end of the phone. She had gotten his attention. She imagined him again in that dark-paneled den, tucked into his stupid smoking jacket with his slippered feet up on his oak desk, the hand holding the glass pausing halfway to his lips.

"Every last red cent," Ursula continued, seized by a fierce satisfaction. "I took your advice and had his paperwork reviewed. The lawyer found several discrepancies and inconsistencies in the Power of Attorney paperwork, yes. But he found nothing wrong in Mike's Last Will and Testament. Not one word out of place or misused. If Mike dies, I'll only have to wait until the probate period passes and then everything he owns belongs to me. How's that grab you, Mr. Judgey?"

When Fahrlander found his voice, it came through the earpiece dripping with venom. "Now you listen to me, you meddling little hippie *bitch*. You better pray your husband lives to ripe old age, do you understand me? Because if anything happens to him—"

Ursula wavered between fear and fury. She knew how connected men like the Judge were. Men like her husband. She thought of Grant Lang and how even if she'd reported his violation of her body, he would have walked free. She knew it. All her shame would be left on the courtroom floor, laid bare for all to see and he would walk free. That's how wealthy men were. Their privilege knew no bounds. And when they all worked together, when they all watched each other's backs, they became an unstoppable force. An immovable patriarchy.

Ursula mustered her confidence and said: "That sounds like a threat, Judge Fahrlander. That's what it sounds like to me. And I just so happen to have a witness monitoring this call on our extension. So I would say *you* better pray I decide not to take matters further."

Another stunned silence before the judge barked a sharp laugh. "I don't care if you have a hundred witnesses listening to this conversation. You know as well as I no jury in the county would convict me based on what I said over the phone. Hell, no cop would even dare to knock on my door over it, not even that goody-two-shoes sleepy-eyed sheriff of ours. You've got no case, missy, so you better just watch your tone with me."

It was Ursula's turn to laugh. "Who said anything about taking you to court, Your Honor? I said I'd take matters *further.*"

She slammed the phone so hard into its cradle the bell chimed crisply. The extension in the front hall was similarly mistreated and her guest came around the corner into the kitchen.

"Should we begin?" he asked, dark eyes glistening.

Ursula drew a shuddering breath, knowing now there could be no going back. "Yes, Caleb. We should. Make it quick, please. He may not have been perfect, but he deserves it to be quick and painless. And he deserves better than this hell he's been living in. He deserves *dignity.*"

Caleb Safford's face grew solemn. "On my honor," he said and then opened door to the master bedroom.

CHAPTER SEVENTY-THREE

Charles Stone stepped out of the gray hellish waste and Mike had never been so glad to see him.

"Someone's coming for you, son," he said. "In fact, he's already here."

"I suppose I should be afraid, but I'm not," Mike said. "I'm ready to go."

"I know you are. He knows it too."

"Who is he?"

"It doesn't matter, Mikey."

Mike picked up his chin, looked his father in the eye. "I want to know, Papa. I *need* to know."

"Can't you just take solace the Good Lord has seen fit to call you home? You won't have to stay here, in these dusklands any longer."

"Yes, Papa. Of course. But, please. I ought to know who will spell my unmaking."

His father peered off into the grayness as if scouting some distant invisible horizon. "I think you do know who it is, son."

Mike swallowed and nodded. "I guess it makes sense. I guess it's the right way."

"There ain't no right way, Mikey, but some are better than others. Some are more appropriate."

"How long have I got?"

"Not long."

"Will it hurt, Papa?"

Charlie shook his head. "No. And that's more than most any soul can pray for, I promise you that."

A loneliness unmatched in Mike's experience swept over him. "I hope I see you, Papa. On the other side. I hope you're there to greet me, and take me by the hand. Like when I was a little boy and you took me to the circus and showed me the clowns and the mermaid and the magic show."

"I hope so too, son. I hope so too."

Mike opened his mouth to say some final farewell and that's when the darkness swallowed him whole.

CHAPTER SEVENTY-FOUR

The footsteps came down the hall, measured and deliberate. Caleb rounded the corner into the kitchen where Ursula waited with her palms pressed to the tabletop. When she stood, their outlines remained in the condensation from her skin before evaporating into oblivion.

"It's over," Caleb said. "He's free. And so are you."

A giddy relief shuddered through her, followed by a wave of guilt so strong it was nearly crippling. "Did he … did he suffer?"

Caleb shook his head evenly, as if it rested atop a spindle. "He was suffering far more by being alive. He's at rest now. We did him a favor tonight."

He started toward the door, but Ursula called him back. "Why?" she asked. "Why did you want to do this for me?"

Caleb offered a lopsided grin which never came close to touching his eyes. It was the leer of a psychopath and all at once Ursula knew he would wind up some kind of mass murderer if someone didn't stop him.

"Because," he said, "he was my father. And he was our hell."

He stepped out the door, eased it shut behind him, and headed out into the cool breeze of the last evening of spring.

CHAPTER SEVENTY-FIVE

Ursula stood over the body of her husband, hands clasped. She considered praying, but didn't figure it would do much good—for him or for her.

He looked so natural reposed on the bed, so like he had before the injury. She even checked his breath to make sure the job had been properly done. It had.

"I'm sorry," she said. They weren't the words she sought because they weren't exactly true, but they were the closest she could muster. Maybe later, with time and distance, she could find the proper eulogy for her departed husband.

When she felt an appropriate amount of time had passed, she went downstairs with the intention of calling the police to report discovering her husband's body. She rifled through the words she wanted to use, testing them, and finally found the ones she wanted. Then she worked up some tears, but stopped when she realized someone else was in the house.

The kitchen lay ahead, sunk in darkness, but she could sense someone in there, watching. The wind gusted outside, ushering in summer, and cattle lowed from the barn.

"Who's there?" she called, terrified Ben and Ed had come to finish what they'd started those weeks ago. Or Judge Fahrlander, drunk and hoping to intimidate her. Or, worst of all, Grant Lang. She shuddered. "Whoever it is, I'm warning you. I just called the police. Mike's dead. They're on their way to pick him up."

The presence in the kitchen stirred. She could hear feet padding softly over the worn linoleum in a poor attempt at stealth. Ragged breathing like a kid in a rubber Halloween mask followed and Ursula knew she had to run, but found herself rooted in place like she sometimes did in her worst nightmares.

Her voice box similarly had gone into lockdown.

Then the smell hit her and everything unhinged. It was an organic smell familiar to her, but only recently, and it took only the span of half a second to identify where she'd last smelled it. In the meadow. The decapitated, disemboweled, castrated boar.

She became aware only dimly that a keening like a tea kettle at boil came from her throat, a satire of a scream. Mike would save her. Mike, her overprotective but oft-neglectful husband, would come sweeping down the hall with one of his hunting rifles to his shoulder and blast the intruder's head clean off.

But no. Mike would never protect anyone again.

The footsteps shuffled nearer, the labored breathing intensified, and soon the invader would step into the dim light of the corridor. If the carcass of the boar somehow came shambling toward her, she knew her mind would pulp like an apple in a cider press. The boar didn't come, though. At least not its body.

The figure who stepped out from the shadowed kitchen wore a yellow raincoat and red galoshes like something out of a kid's cartoon. These barely registered with Ursula Stone, though, because she was fixated on the face of a monster. The boar's head leered at her over the yellow plastic collar of the coat, its blackened tongue lolling foolishly between stunted teeth. Holes had been bored through flesh and bone to allow its wearer to see clearly. If the odor of dead flesh was potent outside, it must have been utterly overwhelming from within. Incredibly, the thing wore a pink bow pinned between the pointed ears as if to suggest it had come at the invitation of a formal dinner party. The very human hands grasped an ax and the deadly cleaving head dripped bright blood onto the hardwood floor.

Ursula at last found her voice and shrieked, peal after peal, into that last night of spring.

BOOK IV

**Swine to Slaughter
The Safford Family
Summer**

CHAPTER SEVENTY-SIX

Scott Pernell pushed through the batwing doors of Chancellor Bros. Saloon and copped a stool. The bar stood smack-dab right between Derby and Murdoch, so both towns tended to claim it (or not, if the claimant happened to be invested in a religious denomination that frowned upon the drink). The barkeep, a sturdy man with a bald head and a black beard hanging to the middle of his chest ambled over, polishing a beer stein. Royce and Martin Chancellor had both been dead for years, but Oswald Triplett had bought the place from Royce's widow and often ran the place on his own to cut down on paying out wages. He kept a couple part-timers on the payroll, but tonight he had the place to himself.

"Evening, Officer Pernell," he said. "The usual?"

Pernell shook his head. "Make it a double tonight, Ozzie."

Oswald plucked a toothpick out of his breast pocket and stuck it between his teeth and poured Jack into a glass. "Bad day?"

Pernell shot the whiskey, winced, and replaced the glass on the bar. Oswald refilled it without prompting. "I can't take it no more, Oz."

"The job?" Oswald asked, but he knew that's what Pernell meant.

"Mayor Simonson made me acting Chief of Police and I can't take it." He snorted humorlessly and licked his teeth. "A place this small, a shit splat town like this? Hell, I took the job here because I thought the most action I'd ever see were kids smoking grass and the occasional speedster on the highway."

This stuff interested Oswald to no end. Half the reason he'd wanted to open a bar was to listen to gossip and help it along down the grapevine. "Something happen?" he asked nonchalantly, hoping not to overplay his hand.

Pernell opened his mouth, closed it again, shook his head.

"Anything to do with that mess they found up in Ashford?" Oswald asked, knowing he was pushing it but not caring.

Pernell's eyes bulged. "Don't even get me started on that, good God. I may have my problems here, but you couldn't pay me enough to be Sheriff Lisk right now. I'd quit outright and fuck the two week notice."

"Is it true what I'm hearing around town? Some folks got whacked up to the Stone place?"

Acting Chief Pernell tapped the rim of his glass and Oswald refilled it. The cop took it, then leaned over the bar like a conspirator. "Two hired men were found hacked to pieces in the milking barn. An ax, most likely."

"Jesus Christ," Oswald said, feigning fear. In truth, if any psycho son of a bitch chose to grace his establishment with that kind of craziness, Ozzie kept a sawed-off .12 gauge beneath the bar. See how much ax-hacking he could do with his brains blown all over the plate glass. "They catch the man who did it?"

Pernell rubbed his jaw. "Way I hear it, it may not even be a man. The only eyewitness, Mrs. Stone, well, she says it was—" He snorted humorlessly. "—she says it looked like some kind of monster."

This time when Oswald refilled the cop's glass, he filled another for himself. First rule of Chancellor Bros. Saloon was no drinking during operating hours. This, though, called for an exception. They drank. And as boss, he could play the "do as I say, not as I do card" as frequently as he damn well wished. Having lived in Ashford County his entire life, he had heard more than a few local monster stories in his time.

"A monster?" he echoed.

"Part man, part animal," Pernell said. "And apparently it was headed south, according to Mrs. Stone's statement. Struck right damn out across the fields on foot."

"Coming this way," Oswald mused.

"This way," Pernell confirmed.

Both men took another shot apiece. "She happen to say why it didn't hack her up too?"

Pernell shook his head, blew his breath out in a gust. "Not an inkling. She did confirm, though, it had nothing to do with Mike's death. I guess he'd passed on a little better than half an hour before the alleged monster put in its cameo."

Oswald never put much stock in spiritual possession stories, especially after he'd seen that movie about the girl and the priests, but he wondered if maybe the ghost of Mike Stone hadn't collaborated with some ungodly creature to wreak revenge on those hired men who'd undoubtedly had their way with his wife more than once. Something like that seemed all too abruptly a very real possibility.

The door opened and Ray Safford shuffled in. His cheeks flamed and his eyes leaked. This hadn't been his first liquor stop. He took the stool beside Pernell and ordered a whiskey and a beer.

Pernell seemed to take the appearance of the town clown as a way to blow off steam. He clapped the big man amiably on one beefy shoulder and asked him how the pig life was treating him.

"To be honest, not so great," he said. "Someone stole one of my boars."

Pernell and Ozzie exchanged a glance. "Only one?" the cop asked.

Ray nodded glumly and chugged beer. "Just the one."

"You call it in?"

Ray shook his head. "I ain't had the heart to do it, not since … not since your boss got kilt."

Personally, Pernell only gave a damn about his boss's death in as much as it affected him directly. Al Engel had been about as genuine and classy as a Hostess fruit pie. Also wrapped up in some type of dirty business, Pernell had no doubt. He thought if Mayor Simonson didn't hire on a new police chief soon, he'd be tendering his resignation before Independence Day. Maybe he'd find another line of work, like bartending. Ozzie seemed to have a good gig going here.

"If you want, I'd be happy to file a report, Ray," Pernell said.

"Maybe tomorrow. Tonight alls I want to do is have a few drinks before heading home."

"Speaking of your boss," Ozzie said, "you figure out what happened with him and Stone?"

Pernell heaved another sigh as if the entire mass of the Milky Way rested on his shoulders. "Best I can figure it, Al and Mike had some kind of disagreement. Al knocked Mike over the head, thought he was unconscious. Then Mike came around and shot Al. The bullets we found in Al matched a model of firearm registered to Mike. We ain't recovered the firearm, though, which is problematic in and of itself, meaning there must have, at some point, been a third party present. This can further be confirmed by the fact a male caller summoned an ambulance for Mr. Stone. Why they were in the cell block together at all is a complete and utter mystery the mayor is expecting me to unravel. And you boys may not have noticed, but I'm not exactly the Sherlock Holmes type."

Ray opened his mouth to reply, but Nate Berryman burst through the batwing doors, face red as clay.

"Scott, thank God," he said.

Pernell's heart kicked into overdrive. The monster that had taken out the Stones' hired men had made it to Derby and was currently slicing and dicing his way through the villagers. "What is it, Nate?"

Berryman gulped three enormous breaths before he could speak. "It's the Milliards. Their orchard is burning."

CHAPTER SEVENTY-SEVEN

They could see the smoke two miles away, casting a veil across the face of the moon and obscuring the stars. Ray rumbled along behind the pair of police cruisers to the orchard behind the Milliard Country Store. He pulled up short of the cider house and jumped out of his Chevy pickup with tears standing in his eyes. The flames had already consumed the entire orchard, new apples and all, and had dropped to a smolder. The smell reminded him of Christmas at his grandparents' ranch, when his grandmother would roast apples on the hearth.

"Where the hell's the fire department?" Scott Pernell screamed at Berryman.

Berryman said, "I called them half an hour ago. Ain't no one showed up yet."

"Where's Augie at? I figured he'd be out here with his family on bucket brigade duty."

Ray came up beside him. "They're on vacation. Michigan."

Pernell said, "Jesus Honeypot Christ, fine time for that." To Berryman, he said, "Berry, get on the horn and find out where in God's name the fire department's at. Not that there's much point now—them trees are beyond saving. Just want to make sure the fire don't jump on their store, too."

"I got keys to the store," Ray said, pulling a thick ring from his pocket. "I guess I better see if I can't reach Augie by phone."

"You know where they're staying at?" Pernell asked. He didn't figure Ray Safford knew his own address, much less the accommodation arrangements of the Milliard family.

"Yeah," Ray said. "Augie left me all the information in case … in case anything bad happened while they were out of town."

"Well, I figure this qualifies," Pernell said.

Berryman hustled back. "Got hold of Jimmy Donnelly's wife. Said the captain took the boys out drinking tonight up in Murdoch. They're all drunk as skunks."

"*All* of them?" Pernell spat. "What the hell was Jimmy thinking?"

Berryman said, "Chief, she told me Jimmy got a call a few hours ago. She didn't know who it was, but the caller told him he and the boys could take the night off."

"*What?*"

"What she said, Chief."

Pernell ground his teeth. He really wished Berry would quit calling him that. "Only person who'd have authority to do that would be the mayor."

"There ain't been any fires of note around here in ages," Berryman said. "Maybe Mayor Simonson thought the boys could use a break."

"Their whole damn career is a break," Pernell said and spat again.

The lodge operator put Ray through to the right cabin and he waited through a dozen rings before hanging up. He called back and asked the operator to leave word with August Milliard III to call him as soon as he got the message and stressed its urgency. Then he stood behind the counter in the small store and looked around. The busy time of year would be upon them before they knew it. Only this year would be different. There would be no Apple Fest. Maybe not next year either. Maybe never. Ray sat down on the stool beside the register and began to cry.

CHAPTER SEVENTY-EIGHT

He looked up when the bells above the door chimed, swiping at his eyes, expecting Acting Chief Pernell to come looking for him. The person who came through the door, though, was the last one he expected to see.

"Rachel?" he asked. "Sweetheart, what are you doing here?"

"Dad, what happened?" she asked, tears trembling on the edges of her own eyes. "What happened to the orchard?"

"It's just terrible, ain't it? Looks like someone torched it."

"Why would someone do such a thing?"

Ray shook his head, words failing him entirely at the heinousness of the crime. When he found his voice again, he said, "How'd you hear about this, hon?"

"It's all over town. Edna Hadsell's telling everyone who'll listen."

"You ought not concern yourself with the likes of this. You ought to get on back home."

"I can't, Dad. Not until I can talk to Susie."

Ray waved a hand at the phone. "I just tried their lodge. No answer."

Rachel sat down beside the man she knew as her father and picked up one of his huge hands in both of hers. "They'll catch who did this, won't they? They can't get away with this, right?"

Ray thought it over. He didn't know how well Acting Chief Pernell would be at handling a case like this. The young man still seemed pretty raw. And, by the look of his face in the bar, he seemed pretty desperate. "I'm sure the police will do everything in their power to figure it out," he said.

"I hope so," Rachel said.

The phone rang. Ray jumped, then snatched it off the wall.

"Augie, that you?" he barked, nervous, unready to deliver the news.

But the voice on the other end of the line did not belong to Augie Milliard. It came through muffled and scratchy, like the speaker suffered from a sore throat. In fact, he couldn't even tell if it belonged to a male or female.

"Raymond Safford, this is your one and only warning. Remove yourself from this situation immediately or you will be removed. You see nothing, you know nothing. If we determine you are not in compliance, you will be made to suffer. And so will your daughter."

The line clicked dead and Ray stared at the receiver as if it might start leaking poison vapors.

"Dad? Who was that?" Rachel asked.

Ray blinked and looked at her. "No one," he said. "Wrong number."

CHAPTER SEVENTY-NINE

Things happened quickly after that. In the intervening years, as Rachel pieced events together, she would come to understand that the moment her father answered the telephone in the Milliard Country Store the true avalanche began.

At roughly the same time her father was replacing the phone on the hook behind the counter, the phone at the Safford residence rang.

Ruth answered and was surprised to find herself speaking to Augie Milliard, who seemed out of breath and out of sorts.

"Ruth, it's Augie. Ray around?"

"I'm afraid he stepped out," Ruth replied, not at all afraid about it.

"He asked me to return his call. He said it was important."

"Well then he called you from somewhere else. He isn't home." Ruth could have easily reported what the rumor mill had been churning that night about burning apple trees, but she believed gossip the devil's work. She believed the Lord would clue Augie in on current events in His own way and in His own time, and sooner rather than later.

"Thanks, Ruth. I'll try again later."

But Ruth hadn't finished with him yet. "How's your little family getaway?" she asked.

"It's going well, thanks."

"Even without your eldest?" she asked. "Isn't he still on the run?"

"We've been in contact with Dennis," Augie said in a tight voice. "He's fine."

"Is that right?" Ruth asked. "Do the police know you've been in contact with him?"

Augie, whom Ruth had never known to lose his cool, seemed perilously close to it now. "I'm not sure how my son's case concerns you, Ruth."

"Oh, so you haven't heard about what happened up at the Stones' farm?"

A confused pause. "No, what happened up there?"

Ruth didn't consider what she was about to say gossip. More like current events. "Mike's dead. So are his hired men."

Total bewilderment seeped through the line and Ruth relished it. "Dead? How?"

"Mike succumbed to his injuries, I'm told," she said, leaving out her suspicion that Dennis had been behind the attack that had taken her one-time lover. She didn't feel bad for Mike, for he was with the Good Lord now. He had been relieved of this hell on earth, this cursed farmland. She would miss him, sure, but they hadn't been alone in a room together in nearly twenty years, long before she'd become born again.

"And the hired men?" Augie asked.

"Someone killed them. Mike's wife, that strumpet Ursula, claimed she saw the devil in the house not long before the bodies were discovered." Ursula had actually claimed to have seen a half-man, half-pig in her kitchen, but a little embellishment never hurt anyone.

"Jesus," Augie said.

"No, not Jesus," Ruth replied. "If Ursula had kept Jesus in her life, maybe all of this could have been avoided."

"But Ursula's okay? She's not hurt?"

"Oh, I imagine such a shock has hurt her deeply," Ruth said, and prayed it to be true.

Samuel shuffled into the room, his face smeared with something red. Raspberry preserves, no doubt. Ruth had canned a dozen jars last fall and it had quickly become the boy's favorite treat. Sometimes he ate it by the fistful when she'd turned her back for moment.

"August, I need to let you go. I'll have Raymond call you if I see him before I retire for the night."

She cut off his thank you by hanging up, then drew her youngest child to her, digging for a handkerchief in her handbag.

CHAPTER EIGHTY

When Ray finally got ahold of Augie and broke the news, his good friend thought he was putting him on at first. Only Ray rarely put people on—he didn't feel he knew enough jokes to do it proper and he always felt a little guilty about making someone laugh at themselves. When he finally convinced Augie of the truth, the apple farmer said he'd drive right back and asked Ray to meet him at the Country Store the following morning around six o'clock. Ray showed up half an hour early to have a look around at the still-smoking orchard.

Jimmy Donnelly and the Derby Volunteer Fire Department had finally shown up sometime around dawn, still drunk, but by then both the Murdoch and Ashford FDs had responded and put the worst of the flames to rest. Ray stood at the edge of the orchard and stared at the stumps of trees jutting up from the ground like stubbed-out cigars. Who could have done something like this?

Whoever it was who called you last night, he thought. But who could that have been? Someone who knew he'd stepped into the store. Someone who knew he'd be the one calling Augie to report the news. This was too big for him, too much. He hoped Augie would be on time. Augie would know what to do.

But dare he mention the menacing caller to anyone? He didn't want his family put in danger; aside from the farm, they were all he had in the world and he would set fire to his own homestead, which had been the Safford's property for five generations, if it meant keeping them safe.

Crickets struck up their timeless tune. A warm wind stirred ashes and something shone from the ground in the waning light of summer's first full day. The longest day of the year. Ray bent to examine the thing on the ground.

It was a Zippo cigarette lighter, partially tarnished with soot and still warm from the fire. Augie's Zippo. Could someone have stolen his lighter and done the deed with it, leaving it behind as evidence to frame the (now former) apple farmer? Could Augie have returned early and set the fire himself, maybe dropped his lighter in the dark by mistake? Why would he?

When Augie pulled up forty minutes later, Ray was still examining what would undoubtedly turn out to be the instrument which had caused the blaze. He slid it into his pocket for the time being—some deep-seated instinct in him told him to withhold the discovery for now and Ray had learned that when that voice spoke, which was rarely, he did best to listen. Augie stepped out of the truck.

"Oh my God. Oh my dear God in heaven," he said, surveying the destruction.

Fresh, genuine tears burst at the corners of Ray's eyes. "Augie, I'm so sorry. I know what these trees meant to your family."

When Augie found his voice, he said: "Insurance will cover the loss. I'm more concerned about who did this and why."

"But the trees—they'll take years to grow back," Ray protested.

"I don't care about the trees," Augie said. "There are other trees, other places. Other lines of work I've been interested in exploring. I care about who did this so I can find them and eliminate them. Whoever it is—they're a blight that needs to be blotted out."

"Augie, Jesus, listen to yourself—" Ray began but Augie turned and seized his shoulder hard enough to hurt.

"Did you tell anyone I was coming back?" he asked.

"No, I did just like you said."

"And did you tell anyone you got ahold of me to tell me about the orchard?"

"Not a soul. Why, Augie? Why did you want me to keep this a secret?"

"Because you're the only one who bothered to call me. No one else—not someone from the police department, not someone from the sheriff's office, not Grant Lang or Adeline Gable. Hell, not even Old Lady Hadsell. I even talked to Ruthie and she dummied right up about it. The lodge phone lines should have been flooded with everyone vying to be the first to spill the beans."

"Well, they probably didn't know where you was staying," Ray said.

"It wasn't a secret," Augie said. "Nothing in this godforsaken county is a secret, except for those who run this place." He pointed to the mansion on the hill. "Starting with her."

"You tell Teresa about this?"

"I told her, but not the kids. I didn't want to ruin their fun. Especially Suze. She needed to get away from this place for a spell. They all did."

"What do you mean to do?" Ray asked.

"I've got an idea that's been percolating on the drive home. I'm going to need your help, Ray."

Those words resonated with Ray, always had. He liked feeling important, especially to Augie. "Sure, Augie. Anything."

"I need to speak with your daughter."

"You need to speak with Rachel? What for?"

"Because she knows where Dennis is and I need to talk to my son."

CHAPTER EIGHTY-ONE

Augie followed Ray back to the Safford farm and the two men met at the back door. The smell of hog manure hung thick in the warm air. They could hear a few of the animals rooting around the troughs. A couple of them squealed at one another before falling silent again.

"You better wait out here, Augie," Ray said. "I'll get Rachel, though I don't know how she'd know where Denny is. Why don't you go on out by the barn and we'll be out directly."

Augie nodded and stepped away into the shadows while Ray entered the house. He said hello to his wife, who smiled tightly in return without looking up from her Bible, then went upstairs and tapped lightly on his daughter's door.

"Rachel? You in there?"

The door opened a sliver and one beautiful sea-green eye appeared. She got her eyes from her mother, that much could not be disputed. "Yeah, Dad?"

"Could you come outside a minute?"

She did not protest or ask why and they went out the back door together. Ruth asked where they were going, but Ray had been prepared for the query.

"Want to show her Debra's belly. Old sow is ready to bust just about any day now," he called, then hurried his daughter through the door before further discourse could ensue. Fibbing made him as uncomfortable as pranking.

They found Augie just inside the doorway to the livestock barn. Rachel's breath caught. "Mr. Milliard?"

"Hi, Rachel," he said. "I need to speak with Dennis."

Ray said, "Why do you think she'd know where—"

Augie put a hand up. "Ray, I'm afraid I haven't been fully

truthful with you. For the past few weeks, since Denny's been hiding out, Rachel's been my go-between. He trusts her. And so do I." He shifted his weight. "Now I know my boy and I know he doesn't want to put his family or himself at risk until we can get this whole mess sorted out, so up until now I was content with having a mediator. But with this thing with the orchard, I need to see him now more than ever—no more passing notes. I need you to tell me where he is."

Rachel bit her lip and studied the toes of her shoes. She scratched her chin with one badly chewed nail; if she'd been allowed to use polish, it would have been chipped mostly away. She opened her mouth to say something but a voice called out from the dark.

"It's okay, Rachel," Dennis Milliard said. "You don't have to cover for me anymore. It's okay."

"Denny?" Augie called. His eldest son toed down the ladder from the hayloft and stepped to the edge of the white glare from the floodlight seeping in from the yard.

"Hi, Dad," he said and even in the dimness Ray could see the boy had lost ten pounds. Maybe fifteen. His hair stood in filthy screws and grime streaked his face.

Augie pulled his son into an embrace and kissed the top of his head. "Thank God. Thank God you're all right."

"I'm fine, Dad. Rachel's made sure I'm seen after."

"You got Zeb up there with you?"

Dennis shook his head. "Zeb's living out somewhere in the woods. Thought it safer if we split up." His eyes filled with tears. "Dad, I didn't mean for any of this to happen."

"I know you didn't. I know, son."

"They were going to kill us, Dad."

Ray sensed more than saw his old friend's posture stiffen. He held the boy out at arm's length. "Who was?"

The young man's lip trembled. "Chief Engel. Mike Stone. Grant Lang. I didn't mean to hurt Mike that bad, honest. And the chief ... Dad, I had no choice. He was going to gun us down."

Augie blinked. "Oh. Oh my God. That was *you*?"

The boy nodded miserably. "Dad, I'm sorry. I'm sorry you have to hear it like this, but I didn't want to put it in writing. It was self-defense. They had us locked up and wouldn't let us call you. They think we killed Old Dad. They were going to take us out somewhere and bury us. The chief and Mike, they talked about it. They *laughed* about it."

"We're going to work this out, all of it," Augie said. He addressed the Saffords. "For now, I'll ask both of you to keep what you just heard to yourselves. Can I count on you to do that?"

Ray nodded. "Of course, Augie. A hunnert percent."

"Rachel?"

The girl nodded in an exact imitation of her father, though her eyes never left Dennis's face. "Yes, Mr. Milliard. Not a word."

A hog—perhaps the pregnant Debra herself—snorted in the darkness, sounding practically like laughter.

CHAPTER EIGHTY-TWO

Augie thanked his hosts and said he'd be in touch with Ray soon.

"For now, I'm taking Dennis home, fixing him a meal, and get him a night's sleep in his own bed." He looked at Ray. "You think Scotty Pernell will come sniffing around?"

Ray shrugged a hock of a shoulder. "I doubt it. He seems pretty burnt out on this job already and it ain't been but a month since he got it."

"That's good. What's better is at this point the only charge they've got on Denny is abetting a fugitive. They know Zeb shot Grant but no one except us knows who clubbed Mike and shot Al."

"There's something you ought to know," Ray said, staring at his boots.

"What is it?"

"Rachel, you go on in the house," Ray said.

She went, giving Dennis a long last look. When she had gone, Ray breathed deep.

"Mike died last night. In his sleep, I hear." He glanced at Dennis. "Then someone took an ax to his hired men while they slept in the barracks."

"I know," Augie said again. "Ruth saw fit to inform me of that but not a word about my trees."

"I didn't do that," Dennis said, backing up a step.

"No one said you did, son," Augie said.

"I don't want that pinned on me too."

"No one's pinning anything on you."

"They'll try," he said. "Or they'll blame it on Zeb."

"Zeb didn't have any reason to want to harm those men and

neither do you," his father said.

"It doesn't matter," Dennis said. "I know how these things work. I've seen it on *Perry Mason*. I've read *To Kill a Mockingbird*."

"Dennis, we're a family in good standing in this county. Our name is respected. If it ever came down to a court case—which is highly unlikely, especially for you—we have a name everyone knows."

"Zeb doesn't." The boy's eyes glowed in fierce defiance.

"Look, Zeb's a family friend. He always will be. But the truth is, he pulled the trigger on Grant Lang, not you."

"I shot Chief Engel," Dennis said, "and I can't get it out of my mind. All the blood. Dad, I can't stop seeing it. And now Mike's dead too because of what I did to him? I'm a murderer, Dad. A *murderer*. Zebbo isn't, Mr. Lang didn't die. I am. Nothing in the world will ever change that."

Augie reached to put a hand on his son's shoulder, but the boy drew back another step. "Dennis, you said it yourself. What you did, it was self-defense. It was you or them. A jury will understand if it comes to that."

Dennis stepped backward again and this time the shadows swallowed him. *"You* don't understand, Dad. There isn't ever going to be a trial. You think they're going to believe what I did was in self-defense? Killing the chief of police and an upstanding member of Ashford County?"

Ray stood by, quietly digesting the scene unfolding in his barn. A hog squealed again. Behind them, unseen, Eloise the snapping turtle crawled across the lawn and vanished into the surrounding corn.

Augie kept his tone of quiet reason. "No one knows anything right now. Right now the only person who can place you at the scene of the crime is Zebulon Tuel and he's not going to say a word."

Ray nodded. "Yeah, that's right. I heard Scotty Pernell over at Chancellor's talking about his theory that both those guys got in an argument and kilt each other."

"You see?" Augie said. "Dennis, come home with me. We'll work this out. It will be okay. Trust me, okay? Trust your old man."

"I can't go home, Dad," the boy whispered. "No one else may know what I did, but I do. No one else has to live with it."

The boy rushed down the cracked concrete aisle between the hog pens, toward the back access door. When Augie reached to snap on the overhead lamps, the men found themselves looking at an empty barn.

CHAPTER EIGHTY-THREE

"I won't ever see him again," Augie said. The slump of his shoulders betrayed his despair.

"Don't say that, Augie," Ray replied, alarmed. He'd never seen his closest friend exude anything but quiet confidence and strong leadership. "Of course you'll see him again. He'll get in touch with Rachel when he's feeling comfortable again."

"I don't know. Maybe you're right. The thought of him living like a fugitive kills me."

Ray fingered the Zippo lighter he'd found near the incinerated orchard. "What about the apple trees? Any idea who'd've done something like that?"

Augie looked around. "Oh, I've got a pretty good idea."

"Who?"

"Who would have cause? Who would benefit from our pain?"

"Grant Lang," Ray said as understanding dawned.

"Grant may have known about it, but he wouldn't be caught dead anywhere near something like that. He'll also have an airtight alibi if the law ever gets around to asking him about it. Think closer to home."

Ray churned this in his mind a minute. Then his eyes widened. "You don't think Granny Adeline—"

But Augie was already nodding. "Adeline did it. Or, rather, had it done. Probably one of those goons she keeps around the house. I'm going to burn her ass down, just like she burned my orchard."

Ray turned the lighter over in his pocket. The lighter which may or may not be evidence in a criminal act. "That's a hefty accusation, Augie. Your name may be good in Ashford County, but Granny's is solid gold."

"Our name isn't what it used to be," Augie said, "unless we're serving up complimentary Christmas brunch."

"If you're going to accuse Adeline, you better have some proof," Ray warned. "I'm serious. If you take her to court and she's found innocent, your name really won't be worth toilet paper."

"Who said anything about court?" Augie asked.

Ray goggled at his friend, who had never done anything but the right way. The lawful way. "What do you mean, exactly?"

"Think about it. With Fahrlander in her pocketbook, do you sincerely think she'd ever be charged, much less see the inside of a jail cell?"

Ray considered a moment, then said, "Augie, there's something else I got to tell you."

"What is it?" Augie asked.

Ray told him about the threatening telephone call he'd received at the Country Store. "Someone knew I was in there. I think you're right. It had to be one of Granny's guys. Someone nearby saw me go in."

Augie slammed a fist into his palm and swore under his breath.

"What do you mean to do?" Ray asked.

"I've got an idea, a way, maybe, to turn this tragedy into something good while I work out how I mean to attack Adeline. Been thinking about it a long time, actually, and it kind of crystalized on my drive back from Michigan," Augie said, looking his friend in the eyes. "But I'm going to need your help getting it off the ground."

"Sure, Augie. Anything."

"Don't be so quick to jump on board until you hear what it is. If you decide you want no part of it, I won't hold it against you."

"What is it?" Ray asked.

Augie told him.

CHAPTER EIGHTY-FOUR

Rachel waited in her bedroom. She figured if Dennis had any reason to return, she would be it. In the days she'd been harboring him in the hayloft of her father's hog barn, they had grown closer. She thought so, anyway. Sometimes they held hands while they talked.

He'd confessed everything he'd done and she had not judged. It had been, of course, in self-defense and he'd taken appropriate action. She never even questioned the idea the chief of police had been in business with Mr. Stone and Mr. Lang— Rachel sensed corruption even if she did not fully understand the meaning of the word.

She sensed something else as well. She thought she'd determined the true identity of her father. Her mother's words during the harshest of Rachel's punishments had stung her deeply, even if part of her had always known Ray was not her biological father. That didn't matter to her. He would always be Daddy to her and she loved him with a blinding ferocity even if her mother didn't anymore.

The wind gusted through her screen, bringing with it the sound of crickets and the smell of rain. Good. It had been ages since they'd had a decent rainfall, nothing more than a few spring showers up until now. Hopefully this front would bring a deluge with it. Ashford County could use a good cleansing, Rachel figured. And, of course, the corn could use the rain as well.

She stared out into fields, praying to see the double-blip of Dennis's flashlight—their signal to meet. But the fields remained obstinately dark, the cornstalks seeming to stretch to infinity. Their leaves whispered secretly, telling ancient green tales.

"I'll never see him again," she whispered aloud, unknowingly echoing his father's sentiment. That wasn't true, though. She *would* see him again, she had to. Because she loved Dennis Milliard more than any other human being in the world. She loved him with the same intensity that her mother loved God.

The telephone rang and Rachel hoped it would be Dennis, but it wound up being Susie. It was good to hear from her because Susie's calls came less frequently these days. In fact, the girls rarely spoke at all. Rachel couldn't recall the last time she'd seen her friend outside of her home other than the time she'd delivered Dennis's note, and wondered if Susie would truly be all right in the long run.

After the girls hung up, Rachel returned to her room to find Caleb there. He was flipping through the cardboard box of rock albums she thought she'd thoroughly hidden from the world, but which seemed to be a secret to no one.

"Hi, sis," he said absently, selecting her copy of *Led Zeppelin II* and theatrically blowing non-existent dust off its face. "Mind if I spin some tunes?"

"Yes, I mind," she said, snatching the record away from him.

He stood there tall, gaunt, pale with dead eyes. Like a scarecrow. "That's not very sisterly."

"I'm not your sister," she spat.

"Oh, but you are," he said. "No matter how much you wish the truth away, you and I are forever linked in blood."

Rachel turned away and shoved the album back in the box. She hated the way he looked at her.

"Dear Ruth is our mother, to be sure," he said.

"How do you know? Nothing in this godforsaken county is as it seems."

"How do I know? I remember you being born," he said. "And I remember *me* being born."

Rachel faced him, checking for some kind of trick but detected no guile.

"It's the truth," he said. "And you can't have truth without 'Ruth.' Isn't that funny, sis?"

Rachel said, "Get out of my room."

"And if I refuse?"

"Then I'll tell Mom."

"Tell her. She likes me better anyway."

"Then I'll tell Dad."

Caleb snorted at that, a wild, porcine sound and said, as though he'd read her thoughts from moments ago, "You still call him 'Dad'?"

"He *is* our dad."

"You're not nearly as sharp as you look, sis."

She crossed her arms and tried to sound nonchalant. "Fine, then who is?"

"Your father is your business. My father is mine. And my business with him is blessedly through."

A wave of exhaustion and confusion flooded her. She needed time to be alone, time to think. So much had happened in such a short time—could it have only been nine months ago that she'd entered the Milliard Country store to buy donuts from Dennis? Everything seemed to have fallen apart after that.

Rachel opened her mouth to order her brother out of her bedroom again, but he had already turned away. She shut the door behind him and would have locked it if her mother hadn't removed the lock. Then she sat on her bed and wondered who her father could be if it couldn't be Ray Safford.

CHAPTER EIGHTY-FIVE

Ray went to the fridge, dug around until he found a Hamm's, cracked it, and drank long while leaning on the open door. Cold air wafted out, a fine sensation on such a warm evening. He had heard Augie's plan and thought it might work out. Of course, contingent on the insurance company paying out for the ruined orchard. Couldn't get a project like this off the ground without major moolah.

Ray mulled that over. Insurance would only pay out if certain criteria were met. The agent would need to determine the cause of the fire and make sure it wasn't set deliberately by the payee.

When he was thirteen, Ray's father, Roger, had set fire to one of the Safford farm's dilapidated outbuildings which had gone unused for years. The damnable thing had taken on a definite tilt which could only be corrected by jamming a pair of sawed-off telephone poles against its leeward side. It presented nothing more useful than a deathtrap to the Safford brood, so the old man had set it ablaze one thundery June night. He'd claimed lightning got it, but the state fire marshal, who'd driven all the way out from Springfield, had seen things differently and had called it arson. Self-set arson, more specifically, which had earned Roger a three-month stay in the brig. That had been when Ray had truly taken over the farm. Roger lived only ten months after his release, dropping over from an embolism while feeding his beloved hogs. Wham-bam-on-the-tram. Ray hoped to go that very same way when his time came.

But before it did, he had work to do. Augie wanted to get started right away, and Ray's part would be particularly important.

"Do you plan on cooling the entire house?" Ruth asked from the doorway. Ray jumped and nearly spilled his beer. He hadn't heard her come up behind him.

"Sorry, love. I was just thinking," he said.

"And you needed the light in the refrigerator to help with that?"

Ray mumbled another apology and shut the door. Now they stood in sheer darkness, with only the light from the corridor to outline the shape of his wife. He still loved her even if she no longer loved him. Maybe she never had. Their arrangement had never required such, though Ray had hoped she'd grow into it.

"Where's Sammy?" he asked because he hadn't seen the tyke in some time and he felt that something ought to be said in all that dark silence.

"He's in bed. Where you ought to be."

"I'll get there."

Ruth crossed her arms and said nothing more. Ray excused himself, stepped around her, and carried his beer into his small den off the main hallway. He closed the door, set his beer down on his desk, dropped into the cracked-leather chair his father had used, found some paper and a pencil, and began sketching. Yes, Augie's idea just might work. It could be exactly what Ashford County needed. And Ray would be part of it. Heck, he might even one day be famous if this all panned out the way Augie thought it would. And Augie, Ray knew, was rarely wrong.

Ray sketched until his hand cramped, then reviewed his work. Excitement fluttered in his gut. They would need the proper materials and the proper licenses and permissions, but something like this ... well, it could inject a lot of bread into their little local economy. Something that would be sorely amiss with no Apple Fest to look forward to this fall. The notion depressed Ray and he settled back in his chair and closed his eyes.

In a semi-dreamlike state, he thought about his old man and he thought about Augie. He thought about the lighter he'd found on the ground at the orchard. Had Augie gone the same route Roger Safford had? Even considering such seemed absurd. Why would Augie destroy all the work three generations of his family had put in place? It made no sense.

As he drifted deeper, he dreamed of a shadow standing in the doorway. He couldn't see the face, but it looked like Ruthie. As he watched, though, the shape changed and became the size of Augie. It held for a moment, then morphed into what he took to be his father. Ray grunted. He didn't like this dream.

He snapped awake, unsure of what had roused him. A sound, he thought. Had someone knocked on the den's door? Ray peered into the perimeter of shadows cast by the desk lamp and could identify nothing discernible. What had it been?

The answer came immediately. The sky lit up like noonday, held its breath, then boomed. A storm brewed in the west, the first of many that Bicentennial summer. Good. The crop needed the rain.

CHAPTER EIGHTY-SIX

Over the next week, the Safford family's phone rang exactly three times. Once for Ray, once for Ruth, and once for Rachel.

Ray's call came from Augie early Monday morning, who informed him he'd received approval from the Village Hall. The news sent a quiver through Ray's belly. He hadn't actually thought the project would ever get past the stuffy council and certainly not so quickly; Augie had clearly pulled many of the considerable strings he held.

Ray cleared his throat, spat into the kitchen sink, and ran the water. "So when do we begin?"

"No time like the present. I've already got most of the stumps cleared. First material shipment drops Thursday."

"Augie, something's been bugging me," Ray conceded.

"What's that?"

"How are you paying for all this? Insurance couldn't have paid off already."

"You let me worry about financing. I need you to worry about being my project foreman. Can I still count on you?"

Only a hint of hesitation. "Of course, Augie. Right after I get the hogs to market. Should be no later'n Wednesday."

"Good man," Augie said and hung up.

Ruth's call came from Father Scudder, who simply asked her if she was ready to move forward.

"Is it time already?" she asked him, her heart kicking up a gear.

"It is," Scudder confirmed. "Are you ready to do the Lord's work?"

"Every hour of every day."

"You are a humble and faithful servant to Him," the priest said and hung up.

Rachel's call came late Thursday evening, after Ray had put in a full day sorting materials on the Milliard property. He'd come home sunburned and exhausted and his wife had given him nothing more than a disgusted glance as he tromped off to shower.

Then the phone rang.

"It's for you, sis," Caleb said. "A *boy*."

The world seemed to glow momentarily too bright and she rushed to the receiver lying on the table like something dead. "Dennis?"

Only the caller wasn't Dennis and certainly was no boy. "It's Lorelai, Rachel."

Rachel's heart stopped. "What do you want?"

"I need to speak with Dennis. It's important."

"So speak with him."

"I don't know where he is. But I heard you do."

"I haven't seen him in a week."

"But you know where he is."

"No, I don't. And I wouldn't tell you even if I did."

A considering pause. "I need to talk to you, then. In person."

"I have nothing to say to you."

"But I have something to say to you and I can't do it over the phone," Lorelai said. "Meet me tonight at the Country Store."

Rachel glanced around to ensure no one else in earshot. Then she said, "Go to hell," and hung up.

CHAPTER EIGHTY-SEVEN

On the morning of the third day of labor, Ray dropped a bundle of wooden stakes, put his hands on his hips, and looked around.

"Say, where's your family, anyway?" he asked Augie. "Still at the cabin?"

Augie didn't look up from where he'd been riveting steel girders together. The crew had finished pulling stumps from the orchard and had set about filling the holes.

"They're staying in East Lansing for a spell," Augie said. "We got family there."

Ray didn't care for the response. "Nothing's happened, I hope?"

"Let's just say Tree doesn't much care for my idea."

Ray tipped his straw hat back and wiped his forehead. "I got to admit, she may have a point."

Augie stood. "Ray, if you want out, now's the time. Don't make me wish I'd hired someone else."

"Don't get me wrong, I'm happy for the extra work. And I love the idea. But I mean, it just all seems so sudden. So out of the blue."

Augie shrugged a shoulder. "I've always wanted to open an amusement park. Nothing so grand as Disney or even that Great America they're building up north. Just something simple. Something more than a corn maze, you know? A few rides, a few concessions, an agricultural museum, maybe a mascot in a pig suit handing out balloons. It'll be a three-season attraction that will shutter in winter so we can all take a much-needed break over the holidays. I figure I might as well turn this tragedy with my orchards into a blessing. What better way to commemorate the memory of this county with the opening of an agriculture-based theme park?"

"I guess you're right," Ray said doubtfully. "Maybe this is what Ashford County needs."

"Of course it is," Augie said. "You'll see. I figure if we really bust our tails, we can hold Farmland's Grand Opening the first week of fall. Then you and Tree and everyone can see how much fun it will be. How good for the local economy."

Ray relaxed some. Augie had never steered him wrong before. "That sounds real good," he said.

Augie clapped his hands once, sharp, and loosed a grin. "Then let's bust some tail, buddy ol' pal."

By Independence Day of that Bicentennial year, an enormous archway had been erected over the parking lot. FARMLAND, it read in eight-foot-high characters outlined in tinted light bulbs, like something you'd see in Times Square instead of smack in the middle of corn country. Ray had painted it himself and felt quite proud of his work. He'd also assisted a crew in constructing the frame of what Augie said would become a Ferris wheel (with each car painted with various agricultural icons such as smiling pigs, dancing milk bottles, happy apples, and singing ears of corn). It stood against the sky like the skeleton of some long-forgotten monster. The Country Store had been converted into "Ashford County's One and Only Museum of Agriculture," though aside from a few personal relics from the first August Milliard's regime, it remained empty.

"You got anything you'd like to donate, feel free," Augie told Ray that morning. "Going to take a lot to fill her."

"I'll see what I can dig up in the crawlspace. Say, are you heading to the fireworks tonight? Supposed to be quite the display, what with the Bicentennial and all."

"Weatherman says it's supposed to rain. Besides, you wouldn't catch me dead at Lang's Corn Fest. Damn rip-off artist, is what he is."

Ray kicked a rock. Rain on the Fourth didn't seem fair, especially not on the nation's 200th birthday, but saw no point in fussing over it so he changed gears. "You hear from Dennis again?"

Augie set down the crate he'd been carrying and shook his head. "I don't want to talk about Dennis. He's a man now. He made his bed and now he must lie in it."

Ray blinked. He couldn't fathom taking such an indifferent attitude with any one of his kids were they in Dennis's position (and he found it hard to swallow Caleb hadn't been in trouble with the law yet). He loved all three with everything he had. Even the ones who weren't biologically his.

They worked on Farmland until late afternoon, when another storm did indeed blow in and chased them all home. There would be no fireworks display that night. Too bad, too, Ray thought. The Bicentennial of their great nation ought to be celebrated loud and proud, in his estimation.

That night in bed, with rain raving on the roof, Ruth asked him how much he was getting paid for helping Augie. Ray tried to shrug off the question because he was dead tired, but she kept after him.

"Hunnert a week," he said. Thunder grumbled.

"That's to be his foreman?" she asked, her voice riding a hint of scorn and disgust. "How much is he paying those other men?"

"That ain't none of my concern, Ruthie."

"Meanwhile your farm is languishing and your children miss you." Scorn and disgust had moved on to open contempt.

"Ruthie, we can use the extra money. And I've got Caleb slopping the hogs each day now that school's out."

"How much did you get when you took the last truckload to market?"

"Aw, Ruthie, you know where I keep the passbook. I can't recall off the top of my head."

His wife climbed out of bed, cinched her bathrobe about her, and stalked toward the stairs.

"Where you going?" he called after her.

She turned back wearing an ugly, taunting leer. "To fix Ray-Ray a midnight snack. Would you like two cookies or three with your glass of warm milk?"

Ray listened to her footsteps on the stairs and slumped back against his pillows. When had Ruthie grown so hateful toward him? So hateful in general? The only thing that gave her pleasure anymore was attending church and reading the Bible. God, Jesus, and Mary. All that made Ray's head spin. If he could see that the stuff in the Good Book should be taken metaphorically, why couldn't Ruthie? No, she actually believed a man built an ark large enough to hold two critters of every last species on the planet. Couldn't she grasp the logistical impossibility of such a vessel?

The storm groaned outside and sent Ray spiraling toward sleep where only jangled and jagged dreams of smiling pigs and dancing corn awaited. When a particularly loud peal of thunder startled him awake, he saw the clock hands stood just shy of three a.m. Ruth's side of the bed remained cold and empty so Ray hauled himself up, stepped into his slippers, and went downstairs.

He found her in the parlor, asleep in her chair, her Bible open on her thighs. A candle burned nearby. As quietly as he could, Ray closed the book and placed it on the side table, covered Ruth with an afghan, and blew out the candle. This time when he returned to bed, the dreams that came had their way with him and he muttered and moaned until morning.

CHAPTER EIGHTY-EIGHT

Rachel sat at the edge of the remains of the orchard, watching the men work. She had begun making ham sandwiches at home and bringing them over for their lunch, which her mother despised but the laborers appreciated. Her father seemed to enjoy his tasks and went about them whistling snatches of unknown tunes from times long gone. The place had truly started to take shape and she couldn't believe the pace at which Mr. Milliard had done it. He drove on like a man possessed. She wondered when Susie and the rest would come home, but thought it imprudent to ask. She wondered, too, whether Dennis might turn up here. It seemed as likely a place as any, if he ever decided to turn up again anywhere at all.

But she had another reason to be there as well. She wanted to see if Lorelai would show up. An interaction with the eldest Lang daughter stood at about number 18,000 on the list of things she wanted to do, but the girl had sounded so desperate on the phone. The least Rachel could do, she supposed, would be to hear her out. It was the Christian thing to do.

But Lorelai never showed up. In fact, she never showed up anywhere again, at least to Rachel's knowledge. She disappeared from Ashford County as if she'd never existed. From what Rachel could piece together over the years, nothing from her room appeared to be missing and the savings account her father had set up for her college tuition remained untouched. Her yellow Mustang sat in the driveway of her aunt Delia's house for better than a year before her mother Dinah sold it.

Lorelai Lang simply vanished, like a ghost.

The fireworks had been rescheduled for Monday, July 5th and

Rachel rode to Murdoch's Corn Fest with her father and brothers. The entire county seemed to have turned out for the event and all seemed to have forgiven God the slight postponement in celebrating their great nation. Ruth had not gone with them. She'd said she had some work to do at St. Joseph's. None of the other Saffords protested. Ruth's presence had become practically unbearable. Even Ray could hardly stand being around her now.

"Come on, kids. Let's go find some popcorn for the show," he said, trying to sound amiable, but Rachel could sense a deep sadness in him stemming from the changes in his wife. Rachel cursed her mother silently for her mistreatment of them.

Grant had spared no expense in celebrating the Bicentennial. Patriotic bunting hung from the grandstands and adorned the bleachers. Clowns juggled bowling pins and tied balloon animals. Merchandise booths sold paper stars and stripes stovepipe hats for two bits apiece alongside sparklers for a dime. A local band played mostly contemporary country hits, along with a passable cover of Mungo Jerry's "In the Summertime," which got the crowd amped, before butchering a rendition of the national anthem, over the braying protests of the audience. Someone threw a cup of beer at the bass player, who barely dodged a dousing, when they clearly should have targeted the lead guitarist who'd proven beyond a doubt he would never be mistaken for the second coming of Jimi Hendrix. Yes, the place outdid the Milliard Apple Festival in every way, even Ray had to admit.

They found a concession stand and ordered a large popcorn and a round of Cokes, but Samuel demanded a corn dog instead.

"Sammy, those cost a buck apiece and I don't see no ketchup nowhere," Ray said.

"You can afford a dog," Caleb said. "You're making all that extra bread over at the Milliards' place."

"Ain't all that much extra, son," Ray said with a sigh. "Come on, let's find seats 'fore they're all sucked up. Sun's already set and the show will be starting soon."

Grant Lang himself approached them and shook Ray's hand. Rachel noted how his fingers trembled slightly, though the corn farmer appeared to have made a full recovery otherwise.

"Raymond, it's been a spell," Grant said. "How's that ag park Augie's got you slaving on going over?"

"It's fine, I guess."

"Adeline been by to see it up close yet?"

Ray shook his head. That had been something he had been wondering about. Augie had not cleared the project with the Queen of Ashford County, but the old lady hadn't shown a single silver hair down the valley. Neither had her hired men. "Not that I know of, anyway."

"Shame what happened to the trees," Grant said. "But seems like you and August have the matter well in hand."

"We'll see how it pans out."

Grant turned to Ray's children. "Your boys are growing up fast now, aren't they?"

"Like July corn."

Grant looked Rachel over and she caught a glimmer of something in his eyes. "And, my gracious, young miss. You are like a picture postcard, aren't you?"

That line of talk would have made Rachel uncomfortable on any other day, but on this one she realized something. She had Grant's eyes. No two ways about it. Same shape, same shade. Even more similar than her mother's. This revelation startled her into speechlessness, and Grant all but confirmed it for her when he patted her cheek and said, "You be sure to say hello to your mother for me now, okay?"

Then he strode off through the throng. Ray watched after him a spell, looking as though he'd like to chase the man down and throttle him, but then he shook his head and ushered his brood on.

When they passed a beer vendor, someone standing on the windward side touched Rachel's arm. A guy in full Uncle Sam regalia stood there. Rachel started, but it would take more than a phony beard for her not to recognize Dennis Milliard. His pale blue eyes regarded her with some emotion she could not identify.

"Dennis?" she whispered, unnecessarily. He held a white-gloved finger to his lips.

"Can you come with me?"

"Rachel?" her father called. "You coming?"

"I'll catch up, Dad. Just ran into a school friend."

Ray regarded the man dressed as Uncle Sam and nodded. The disguise had, at least, cowed him. "Okay, then. We'll try to find seats near the front."

Rachel waited until he led the boys away, Caleb glaring back over his shoulder. Then she let Dennis take her hand and lead her to the empty space beneath the bleachers.

"Where have you been?" she asked when they confirmed no one else in the vicinity.

"Doesn't matter," he said, yanking the stupid beard off. "What matters is where I'm going."

She listened to him, lost in his voice and eyes, and confirmed she understood his plan.

"Will I ever see you again?" she asked.

"You can bet the farm on it," he said. He kissed her then, just as the first rockets exploded in the sky, raining pink and green and gold.

They were nothing compared to the fireworks exploding in Rachel's head as she kissed Dennis Milliard for the first and final time.

CHAPTER EIGHTY-NINE

Ruth met Father Scudder in the office of St. Joseph's that night, far from any Bicentennial celebration. After they'd finished conducting their weekly devotional, with Ruth bent over his desk as she had been every week for the past two months, they parted and adjusted their clothes. The time, Father Francis Scudder declared as he patted sweat from his bald scalp, had come.

"Is our holy receptacle ready, my dear?" he asked.

Ruth nodded solemnly. "She is ready, Father."

"Then we shall proceed next week and our savior shall be reborn."

Ruth bowed her head, silent, and buttoned her blouse. Scudder touched her shoulder.

"I wish it could have been you, of course. You know that, don't you?"

Ruth nodded and said nothing. She fought off tears. This should have been her rite, no one else's. *She* should have been the receptacle. Alas, her womb had simply worn out.

"We agreed, though, that if Our Lord could not find his way back to Earth through you, it would have to be through another."

"I know, Father. She'll be ready to do her part."

Scudder grinned, a ghastly jack-o-lantern leer that made Ruth feel like shrieking. "We'll be remembered for all time, Ruth. You especially. Your part is of utmost importance."

"Yes, Father."

He patted her shoulder companionably, then tweaked her nipple through her blouse. She jerked away from his touch.

On a Saturday in late July, with the temperature climbing toward ninety by noon, Acting Chief Pernell pulled up to the Farmland site and got out of his cruiser. Rachel had found her place at the edge of the orchard and had just finished unloading sandwiches for the workers.

"Mr. Milliard?" she called.

Augie stood shirtless with a riveting gun in hand and sweat sheening his skin. He set his tool aside and went to shake the cop's hand. "Scott, what can I do for you today?"

Pernell said, "Is there someplace private we can talk?"

"Dennis okay?" Augie asked, pulling on a T-shirt.

"I think we ought to—"

"Christ, just spit it out," Augie said. "Is my son alive?"

"He's alive," Pernell said. "DeKalb County picked him up early this morning. Found him asleep in a barn."

"DeKalb County, Illinois?"

"DeKalb County, Georgia."

Augie nodded as if expecting nothing less. "But he's okay?"

"A little malnourished and dehydrated, but he'll be fine."

Rachel became aware that all the other workers, including her father, had quit toiling and stood listening along with her. She did not care for the idea of Dennis behind bars, but it sure as hell beat the alternative. She sent a little moth of a prayer skyward. He'd told her his plan had been to make it to the East Coast and hopefully stow away on a ship bound for Europe. It hadn't worked out, but at least he still had breath in his body. Maybe one day they could still be together. She held out hope.

"What's he been charged with?"

"Right now, only aiding and abetting a fugitive," Pernell said. He wiped an errant bead of sweat from his brow.

"That a felony or misdemeanor?"

"Can be up to a class four felony, depending on his level of involvement."

"How stiff a penalty that carry?"

Pernell shrugged a shoulder. "Two years in prison, maybe a hefty fine thrown in. We can get that reduced if he testifies against Zeb in court. Maybe get down to time served, no fine."

"Christ," Augie muttered, swiping a hand through his damp hair. He shifted his weight. "They gonna extradite him?"

"Paperwork's already been submitted. My guess is he'll be back in-state by middle of next week." The reluctant Acting Chief shifted his weight from one foot to the other. "There's something else, though."

Augie waited. Rachel marveled at his calm demeanor. She saw where Dennis got it.

"There're some folks who think it may have been Zeb or Dennis or both who shot Al Engel and clubbed Mike Stone."

"You think my boy murdered those men? You think that gentle kid is capable of something like that?" Oh, he was good. He could've won an Academy Award with his performance.

"Now, I didn't say anyone was charging him with anything. But we know Al had been putting all his resources into locating those two. Could be he caught them, brought them into the jail, and then somehow Zeb or Dennis got the drop on them."

"Where's the arrest report?" Augie asked. "If Al arrested someone, there ought to be documentation somewhere."

Pernell shrugged that shoulder again. "Could be the killer—or killers—took it with them."

"Or it could be Al didn't want the arrest recorded. Everyone knows he was crooked as a creek bed. Everyone knows how close he was with Grant and may have taken Grant's shooting personally. Maybe he didn't want anyone to know he'd caught his prime suspects so they could do a little country justice and skip the kangaroo court routine altogether."

"That's a lot of speculation, Augie," Pernell said, tugging an ear.

"Well, it's a lot of speculation in even pretending to think my kid could do that."

"I just wanted you to be aware. The FBI is involved now and they're collecting evidence—"

"You know your former boss was part of a drug racket with Grant and Mike, don't you?"

Pernell shut his mouth. Rachel heard an audible click as his teeth came together.

A strange grin had crept onto Augie's face, humorless and

feral. It looked so alien that Rachel took a step back. "Oh yeah. They tried to bring me in on it way back and when I refused, that's when all the shit started running downhill for my family. The dead kid, the maze, the attack at the parade. Think that's a coincidence? Why don't you have your FBI friends investigate that?"

Pernell also took a step back, toward his cruiser. "I'll call you when he's in Ashford County custody. I'm sorry to have to break the news." He climbed into the car, but Augie hindered him from closing the door with a hand on the frame.

"Any word on Zeb Tuel?"

"Not a whisper," Pernell said.

"Good," Augie said, still wearing that awful goblin's grin. "That's good."

"Is it?" Pernell asked.

"It is," Augie said, turning away. "Grant Lang had that coming to him for a long time. Figure he got off light with what Zeb dished out."

Rachel went home that evening with a flush on her skin that had nothing to do with sunburn. Dennis would be home again, back where he belonged. He didn't belong on any cattle boat bound for Europe. But how long would he sit in jail? Would there be a big trial, like when the cops caught Harry Durst embezzling from his father's used car business? That had landed Harry behind bars for better than three years and what Dennis had been accused of might carry a steeper sentence.

If he confessed to it. He must have, though, or else the police would have nothing on him. They wouldn't even be able to pin aiding and abetting unless they caught Zeb and he confessed.

"Oh, Dennis, what did you do?" she whispered as she came through the mudroom and into the kitchen.

"Talking to yourself?" Caleb asked. "Crazy people talk to themselves."

"Then you must give yourself entire state of the union addresses," she said, shouldering past him and opening the Frigidaire.

Caleb opened his mouth to retort, but their mother entered

the room and ordered him out. When Ruth used such a tone, you dare not ignore it. Even Caleb. He left.

Rachel went about scrounging an apple, trying not to show fear. Her mother could smell fear the way you could smell the Safford farm downwind in summertime five miles away. And her mother's behavior had grown increasingly erratic.

"I want you to come with me tonight," she said.

"Where to?" Rachel asked.

"Church."

"Mom, it's Saturday. I wanted to go to a movie with my friends."

Ruth glared her down. "You fool about with your friends another time. It's important you accompany me tonight. Be ready in an hour. Wear a dress."

"Okay, okay."

Mercifully, Ruth left the room and Rachel sat at the table wondering what could possibly be so important they go to church tonight. Maybe they were rehearsing a new hymn for choir. Singing was the one reason she still enjoyed going to church—she thought she could make a career of it one day, like Joni Mitchell or Dusty Springfield, and often fantasized about it while in her crawlspace hideaway. When she finished her apple, she tossed the core in the trash and went to pick out a dress for the evening. White or purple? White, probably. Her mother would think purple too brazen.

A white dress for church, then. She'd made up her mind before she'd even made it to the stairs.

CHAPTER NINETY

Caleb stood in the shadows of the parlor at half past two on Sunday morning when his mother led his sister back into the house. Rachel walked unsteadily, like a wobbly calf freshly dropped from the cow's womb. Ruth remained utterly silent and did not turn on the light to aid her daughter's passage.

What did you do, Mother? What did you make your daughter do?

He'd been standing in the same spot for longer than three hours awaiting their return. He had initially considered following, but Ruth had a radar on her when it came to being pursued. Caleb figured she'd had plenty of practice on the matter during her youth.

Rachel disappeared upstairs, taking the stairs like a toddler: one foot up, two feet up, one foot, two, each riser a miniature mountain range. Only when her bedroom door closed high overhead, did Ruth release a shuddering breath and turn on the hallway light.

She caught sight of her eldest child standing in the crook where the parlor walls met. Caleb had hoped to startle her, perhaps elicit a gasp and a hand clutching her throat, but Ruth merely looked incensed at his presence, as she had for a decade or longer.

"Go to bed, boy," she said.

"I'm not tired yet, Mother."

"It doesn't matter if you're tired. You can lie awake until your father stumbles off to help that man on his fool's errand come dawn for all I care. So long as you're not up and creeping around."

Caleb ignored this. His father was dead. "Where did you take her?" he asked instead.

"That's none of your concern. Go to bed."

"What happens at church on Saturday night in the heat of summer? It can't be anything good. It can't be anything … godly."

"Don't speak to me about godliness, you heretic. You're as bad as your father. Or your sister, the whore of Babylon."

Caleb stiffened. "What did you make her do? If you hurt that girl, so help me—"

"We didn't hurt her, boy, we helped her," Ruth said. "Tonight, we helped the world."

She went into the kitchen without awaiting a response.

Caleb knocked on his half-sister's door. Rachel did not reply. He knew what she'd undergone, or thought he did, but needed confirmation. He knocked again, worried she had killed herself, and opened the door.

Rachel lay beneath layers of blankets despite the night's heat. Her eyes were open, staring at the ceiling, and her lips moved.

"What did she do to you?" Caleb asked.

Rachel's head turned toward him, lips still moving. Her eyes did not perceive him, at least not wholly. She had been swept up on the wings of her own private Rapture.

"What did she make you do?"

But Rachel did not reply. Caleb closed the door and stepped down the hall, with red thoughts chasing each other through his mind.

CHAPTER NINETY-ONE

Judge Fahrlander set Dennis's bail at $100,000, a figure Augie found ludicrous when you considered the charge. He only needed to come up with ten percent of that amount, but didn't see how that would be feasible, given what he'd spent on materials for his Farmland project.

Teresa had left the twins with her aunt in East Lansing and had come home with the older kids to visit Dennis. She and Augie had not spoken more than a hatful of words since he'd concocted the idea of opening an agricultural-based theme park. She stayed at the house, but in a spare bedroom. When she found herself in the same room with her husband, she quickly picked someplace else to be.

All this Rachel knew because Susie told her over the phone, in whispered conversations as they tested the limits of their phone cords hiding in closets or around corners. Rachel listened with something close to sympathy, but nothing affecting the Milliard household came close to what had affected her. She still had told no one about it, but found herself on the verge of spitting it into Susie's ear through three miles of phone line. If anyone could commiserate, it would be Susie, who had been through a similar ordeal.

"I have to tell you something, a secret," Rachel said when Susie had gotten her familial woes off her chest. "But I can't over the phone."

"Meet me at the Country Store in half an hour," Susie told her. "Or what used to be the Country Store. I don't know what possessed my dad to do what he's doing, but he's not out there tonight. I'll pinch they key. No one will bother us."

Rachel agreed and they hung up.

Alone in the confines of the new agricultural museum, Rachel
spilled everything. Her mother ordering her to church two
Saturdays previous. The lights low, candles lit. Father Scudder
waiting for them at the altar. Her mother ordering her to remove
her clothes. Rachel at first refusing, before Ruth threatened to
do it for her. She'd tried to run, but her mother had snatched her
by the hair with surprising strength and thrown her toward the
altar. Rachel's head had connected with it and stars exploded
before her eyes. She said she'd felt as if part of her went away,
but that the part of her still present could feel Father Scudder
working her underpants down over her shoes.

"And then, my God, he was trying to squeeze inside me,
Suze. It felt like he was ramming a pole around down there. It
seemed like it must be happening to someone else, like I was far
away, but all the time, I could smell his breath. Like cloves and
canned ham. And he just kept whispering, telling me I was the
vessel. The receptacle for the Second Coming of Christ. That
I would be the Mother to the Savior Reborn. The new Blessed
Virgin for our new age. He told me history would forever know
my name. But I had to loosen up and let him in."

Susan listened, a hand over her mouth as if to stop herself
from gagging. "But he couldn't get it inside you?"

Rachel shook her head. "No, thank God. That would've
been so much worse."

"And your mom just stood there? She let him?"

Rachel's face drew into a snarl. "She's the one who took me
to him. She believes his bullshit. Or pretends she does."

"When that man took me, it could have been so much worse.
Mr. Lang stopped him though. I wish he'd been there to stop
Father Scudder."

Rachel kept quiet at that. She wasn't altogether sure what
she felt about Mr. Lang, outside of some indefinable misplaced
emotion.

"You have to tell someone. He raped you. The police. Rachel,
he needs to go to jail."

But Rachel shook her head. "No. No police. They'd be on
his side. I know how this works. No one would ever believe me.

He's a well-respected man in this county. I'm just the daughter of the village idiot and the town whore-turned-Bible-thumper. And he didn't rape me. He never got inside."

Susie looked appalled but did not argue. Rumors spread like herpes in Ashford County and she'd heard her share about Ruth Safford. Everyone had, even if they kept quiet about it. Ruth was, after all, a member in good standing of St. Joe's congregation.

"I can't believe he just … what a total disgusting creep."

Rachel studied her the toes of her shoes.

"So what are you going to do?" Susie asked.

Rachel told her closest friend that she had no idea what she'd do about it.

CHAPTER NINETY-TWO

Rachel made sure to be present at the Farmland site when Augie took the morning of July 23rd off to bail his oldest son out of Ashford County Jail. He put Ray in charge and Ray thought he did a pretty good job delegating tasks to the laborers, though in truth, they already knew what to do and how to do it. The first phase of Farmland was nearly complete and in Ray's opinion it looked even better than he'd imagined. Augie just might be a genius. And if Augie's schedule held up, Farmland would open its gates the same weekend the Apple Festival had run, the perfect finishing touch. Only this would be so much more. So much *better*. Ray couldn't wait.

He had just finished his lunch break when Augie pulled up with Dennis riding shotgun. Through the windshield, the boy looked drawn and haggard, like he hadn't slept in a week. Ray figured Augie must have given the kid what-for the whole drive home. But when Dennis saw Farmland, his face changed. It ballooned with delight. That's what Ray thought, anyway.

Really, though, his face changed when he saw Rachel. Rachel knew it at once and her heart thumped so hard she thought it might burst. She had not managed to get out of her head the betrayal her priest had perpetrated on her, not to mention that of her mother, and doubted she ever would, but at that moment neither of them were anywhere near her mind. Only Dennis. She had to restrain herself from running to the car.

He got out, slowly, hesitant, as if wondering if she'd still feel the way she felt that Thanksgiving night that now seemed somehow half a century ago. Rachel didn't think she'd ever feel the way she had with his hand in hers beneath the pungent decaying leaves, but she knew she wanted to find out. She wanted to be Dennis's forever and ever. It didn't matter if he harbored a thousand fugitives or murdered a million men. She wanted—no, needed—him by her side. The two of them, together, always.

Augie must have noticed the connection because he said, "Why don't you and Rachel go on in and see what we've done inside. You two probably have some catching up to do. But don't you go far, Denny. I'm not done with you yet."

"Yes, sir," Dennis said.

The pair walked side by side, silent as shadows, into the new agricultural museum, not daring to touch or speak. When the door shut behind them, only then did Rachel throw her arms around his neck and lay her face against the cotton of his T-shirt.

"I probably smell a mess," Dennis said. "Haven't showered in two days."

Rachel didn't care if he hadn't showered in two months. Dennis had come back. He hadn't gone to Europe on a cattle boat. He probably wouldn't be going to jail, at least not for very long. Maybe not at all if he told Judge Fahrlander what he knew about Zebulon. He could stay here in Derby until they were grown, then they could move away together. Maybe start their own farm somewhere far away from Ashford County. He could protect her and she could protect him.

But she couldn't tell him about what Father Scudder and her mother had done to her. Her shame had consumed her and Susan was the only person in whom she could ever confide such an atrocity. Something sparked inside her, an impulse far too powerful to ignore.

"Let's run away," she said, face flushing with the passion of the thought. "Let's go, right now. Somewhere no one will ever find us. Europe, like you said. Take a cattle boat. Or maybe Canada. It's closer. Mexico is warmer, though, and—"

"Slow down," Dennis said, taking a step back. "I can't go anywhere. Not with the hearing coming up."

"That's the point," Rachel said, her plan solidifying even as it manifested. "There wouldn't be any hearing. You wouldn't have to go to jail. Oh, Dennis, let's run away right now before anyone knows we're gone."

"Where's all this coming from?" Dennis asked, the color rising in his own cheeks.

"This town is bad," Rachel said. "This whole county is rotten to the core. Can't you feel it? Haven't you always felt it? It looks shiny and pretty on the outside, like one of your apples, but inside its glutted with worms."

Dennis nodded. "Yeah. I've known it pretty much all my life. Bad things happened here and still happen. Probably always will. My grandfather called it cursed country."

Rachel knew enough about that to last her a lifetime. "I can't stay here, Dennis. Won't you go with me?"

"What about our folks?"

"We can call them from wherever we find ourselves, let them know we're okay."

Dennis's eyes hardened with resolve. She could see it calcify on his face like a death mask. "Let me pack a bag. I've got some money squirreled away, too. Meet me back here in an hour."

Rachel shook her head. "I don't need anything. I'm never going home again. Let's go."

"Did something happen?"

"I don't want to talk about it. Not now. Let's go, can't we?"

Without further discourse, they rushed out the back door, up the ridge, and toward the Milliard house. There would be a stretch of open road where anyone looking would be able to see them, but no one did.

CHAPTER NINETY-THREE

A ugie sauntered up to the County Store-turned-ag museum and pounded on the door.

"Denny, let's head home. We still have some things to discuss."

The door opened, but instead of his eldest child coming out, he found Ray Safford, wide-eyed and slack-jawed. "They ain't in here, Augie. Place is empty."

"What're you talking about, empty?" Augie said, pushing past his makeshift foreman. He came out again a minute later.

"They took off together, didn't they?" Ray asked, his voice afloat with raw wonder. "Rachel and Dennis? They ran away together, just like a couple of kids in a fairy tale."

"We don't know that," Augie said. "For all we know, they went down to Gert's for hot fudge sundaes."

Ray did know, though. He might not have understood the nature of the rift between his daughter and his wife, but he understood it existed and had grown larger. So large, in fact, someone was bound to fall into it and be lost forever. He thought Rachel might have been the one to do so and had maybe taken Dennis with her.

"They ain't at Gert's," Ray said. "They ran."

Augie rounded on him. "Now how can you possibly know that, Ray, goddammit?"

Ray shrugged a hock of a shoulder. "I 'unno, Augie. I just know. Like how a horse knows a storm's coming, maybe. My girl's gone and she took your boy with her."

"You can hang around here with your storms and your feelings all you want. I'm going up and check the house. Probably went up for a cold Coke and some friendly conversation, that's all."

"Yeah," Ray said, his voice sounding in his ears as if from a great distance. "You do that, Augie. I'm going home, tell Ruthie Rachel took off."

"Don't you go worrying Ruth about this just yet," Augie called as Ray climbed behind the wheel of his pickup.

Ray didn't answer. He keyed the engine and drove home.

"What do you mean, she's *gone*?" Ruth cried.

"I mean she ain't here no more," Ray said. "Her and Dennis Milliard took off."

"Took off? Took off *where*?"

"I can't promise we'll ever know that, Ruthie," Ray said. "You seen how distant she's been lately. Like she's someone else altogether."

"She's going to ruin everything," Ruth said. "The little jezebel is going to ruin all our plans."

That hit Ray like a slap across the face and he fixed his wife with a glare. "What plans? What on God's green earth are you talking about, plans?"

Ruth's lips peeled back. "Church business, dear *husband*. Nothing you'd understand."

Something inside Ray that he'd long suppressed like a corpse weighed down with rocks bubbled, stinking, to the surface. Heat raced to his face and he raised a thick finger in the air.

"Now you listen here, woman. I may not know much, but I know I took you in when no one else would, not even your precious church. I raised them children as if they was my own and love them the same way. I turned the other cheek when I heard whispers of your past around town because I loved you once upon a time, or thought I did."

Ruth opened her mouth to offer some tart retort, but Ray would not be stopped.

"No, you don't get to speak now," he said. "Now it's my turn and you will hear every last goddamned word I have to say."

Ruth's jaw snapped shut. She listened.

Rachel and Dennis made it to the Milliard garage with the intention of taking to the road via bicycle—she could borrow Susie's until they got the chance to return it—because Dennis figured a missing car would be easier to spot. They would stick to back roads until they made it to Murdoch, where he had a buddy who could loan them a car, or else drive them over the border into Wisconsin.

"So once we make it to Wisconsin, what do we do?"

"Then we'll catch a bus to Canada."

"Why not just take a bus from Murdoch?"

Dennis shook his head. "Once they realize we're gone, they'll call the cops. The cops'll set up roadblocks, but the radius will only be so far. They'll be looking for us on bikes, on account of two being missing from our garage, and by then we'll be long gone, outside their perimeter."

God, he was smart. Rachel studied his profile as he dragged Susie's bike out into the drive. Smart and handsome as the devil. And he was hers. All hers. No Lorelai Lang sashaying around in front of him anymore.

"Stay here a second. I'll be right back," Dennis said and stepped into the house. He seemed to be gone a long time, but when he came out, he had changed into a long-sleeved shirt and was stuffing a wad of cash into his wallet.

A long, tan Pontiac sedan pulled into the drive behind them and Rachel's heart sank.

"Who is that?"

"I don't know, but play it cool," Dennis said, pushing the wallet deep into his front pocket.

The passenger door opened and a big guy Rachel recognized from Adeline's Thanksgiving party stepped out. The other guy waited behind the steering wheel.

"Get in," the first guy barked at Dennis, yanking open the rear passenger door.

"Don't do it," Rachel said.

"Get in," the guy repeated. "I won't ask a third time."

"What for?" Rachel asked.

"Adeline needs to speak with the boy, now that he's been

located. You're free to go about your business, young miss."

"What does she need to talk about?" Rachel asked.

"That's a matter for them to discuss."

"Where he goes, I go," Rachel said.

The guy glanced her over. "Fine. You both get in before I stuff you in."

Dennis let the bike drop. "Rachel, you go on ahead. I'll catch up with you. Meet me at Arch's Market in Murdoch, okay?"

She wound her fingers through his. "Where you go, I go," she said and settled the matter by climbing into the backseat. Dennis followed her.

CHAPTER NINETY-FOUR

Scudder said, "What do you mean, she's gone?"

Ruth glowered at him across his desk. "Ray says she's gone. Run off with the Milliard boy."

"But our work isn't done yet, not by a long shot," the priest said. "We have to get her back."

Ruth stared him down, said nothing.

"Do you have any idea where they might have gone?"

She shook her head.

"What about Ray? Would he know?"

"Ray doesn't know how to flush the john half the time."

Scudder slumped. He inhaled through his nose, held it, released. "I would hate to have to find another vessel ..."

This rocked Ruth back on her heels. "We don't need another. We need Rachel. You said it yourself, she's the one."

"Oh, she is, she is," Scudder said. He spread his hands out on the polished surface of his vast desk. "But if she's absent too long or damaged in any way, say the Milliard boy defiles her, our hands would be forced, wouldn't they?"

Ruth could actually feel the color drain from her face. "I'll make some calls," she said. "I'll find her."

The priest smiled. "I hoped you might say that."

Ruth gave him a long look, then left the church to find her daughter.

No one spoke during the short ride to Adeline Gable's farm mansion. Halfway there Dennis reached out and took Rachel's hand. They were in this together. They would protect one another. Now and always.

When the boat of a car rocked to a stop at the top of the

Gable house's long drive, the passenger got out and opened the rear door. The driver made no move.

"Follow," the passenger said and the kids did as commanded. They wound their way through the warren of passages Rachel remembered from the Thanksgiving party, though she knew without a guide she would soon become lost. At last they stopped outside a tall, heavy door and the man rapped sharply, once.

From within, Granny Adeline bid them enter. When their escort opened the door, Rachel became aware of two things at once. First, the lady of the house appeared in remarkably similar appearance to Marlon Brando's titular character in *The Godfather*. She sat signpost straight behind an enormous desk constructed of some dark polished wood. She wore a dress of black velvet with a white collar, almost priestly, and she stroked her ratty little dog who appeared to be deeply asleep or maybe dead in her lap.

"My children," she said by way of greeting, her lips peeling back to reveal ancient discolored false teeth. "Do you know why I've invited you to my home today?"

"I wouldn't call that an invitation so much as a kidnapping," Dennis said.

"Watch your mouth, boy," the goon said, giving his shoulder a shove, but Adeline waved him off.

"I've caught wind that someone recently burned down a cabin. Do you happen to know of which cabin I speak?"

Understanding dawned in Dennis's eyes. Rachel could see it plainly on his face. For her part, she had no idea what the old crone was talking about, but she had an idea finding out would happen sooner than later.

"Yes," Dennis said.

"Yes what, child?"

"Yes, I know what you're talking about."

Adeline cocked her head. The hand stroking the dog stopped and the creature stirred. So, not dead yet. Rachel took small comfort in that.

"And do you happen to know who might be responsible for such an action?" the old woman asked.

"Maybe," Dennis said. "But why do you care?"

Adeline became very still. The dog squirmed in her lap and then jumped down to find a more comfortable position of repose. The lady of the house made only a slight gesture with her head, no more than an imperceptible nod, and the goon stepped forward and clouted the boy on the side of the head. The force almost knocked him off the chair to the Oriental rug. Rachel shrieked and moved to help him.

"Leave him, girl," Adeline said. "We'll see if he's man enough yet to take care of himself."

Dennis recovered slowly, using the back of the chair to haul himself up. His hair had come disheveled and the flesh around his left eye burned fiery red.

"I care, dear, sweet, stupid boy, because I had much of my own money invested in that operation."

Dennis looked her in the eye. He cleared his throat. "I know who is responsible for burning down the shack."

Adeline's papery grin returned. "Was it you? You and that drunk darkie friend?"

Dennis's face pinched. "It was us. We burned all your goddamn grass. And you can burn with it, for all I care, preferably in hell."

"Dennis, don't—" Rachel whined.

But the boy would not be stopped. He resumed as if he hadn't heard. "And you just killed yourself, you old bitch. No one disrespects my friend Zeb."

The goon came forward again and said, "Why you little—"

But he never got a chance to finish because Dennis yanked Mike Stone's Smith & Wesson Airweight from the back of his pants and shot him in the throat. The guy clapped a hand to his larynx and staggered back into one of the room's many bookcases.

Adeline tried to gain her feet, perhaps forgetting she'd been wheelchair-bound for the better part of a decade, and slouched down again, face slackening in shock, eyes shimmering.

"You didn't search them?" she screeched at the expiring manservant. Rachel could barely hear her over the ringing in her ears from the sound of the report, but she was aware enough of what would happen next to clap her hands to her ears. Granny Addie still had not fully processed what Dennis had done. "Milo, you didn't *search* them?"

They turned out to be Adeline Gable's last words because Dennis shot her through her discolored dentures.

CHAPTER NINETY-FIVE

Augie heard the pair of shots from driveway of his house, where he stood puzzling over his son and daughter's fallen bicycles. Gunshots weren't an uncommon occurrence in Ashford County, so he gave them no more thought than a cursory hope that some hunter had gotten lucky and would have a couple of roast squirrels for dinner tonight.

But when the third shot sounded a few minutes later, he turned toward the origin of the sound, which appeared to be the Gable house, and waited. Nothing moved, aside from a flock of sparrows displaced by the report. Had the shots come from there? He started up the lane toward the property, fear blossoming in his chest.

By the time he sprinted up the long driveway, his shirt soaked through from the effort, he watched his fear come to life. Dennis and Rachel stood over the body of one of Adeline's henchmen, who appeared to have been making his way up the front porch steps. A gun lay on the gravel between the body and the children. Blood spotted their clothes.

"What in God's name did you do?" Augie bellowed, rushing up on them. They both jumped like kids caught playing doctor.

The tone Dennis used to answer his very reasonable query came out dead and hollow, the voice of a seasoned criminal. "I killed them, Dad. All three. Granny and her guys."

Augie couldn't decide what scared him more: his son's deed or the change that had overtaken the boy. No longer his sweet ruffian second-string football player, Dennis Milliard had become something else entirely. The first thing that shot through Augie's head was: *What on earth is his mother going to think?*

"They were going to kill us, Mr. Milliard," Rachel said. "Or torture us. Or something."

"What in God's name makes you think a fool thing like that?"

"Because I stole her grass, Dad," Dennis said, still employing that zombie tone. "And then I burned the cabin flat."

"Granny was a drug dealer," Rachel said. "And Mr. Stone and Mr. Lang were her partners."

On the ground, Curley's left little finger twitched and fell still again. Augie nearly puked then, but he somehow held it together. He didn't let on that he'd once been asked to invest in the grass business and had declined.

"Okay, look. We can fix this," he said. "But we need to get you out of here right now."

"No," Dennis said. Rachel looked at him.

Augie's jaw worked. "What?"

"I said no, Dad. I'm done running. I killed these three monsters, and Chief Engel and Mike Stone, and I aim to own up to it."

"You can't," Augie said when he found his tongue. "Son, they'll send you away for the rest of your life."

"I don't care anymore," Dennis said.

"You will," Augie said. "What you see in the pictures, that's not what jail's like. You don't get to play football in the yard like Burt Reynolds. The guards don't sneak in pretty ladies for conjugal visits."

Dennis finally met his father's eyes and spoke in measured clips, each word its own sentence. "I. Don't. Care. Anymore."

"Dennis," Rachel said and Augie realized she would be the only key to his son seeing reason. The only key that could keep him out of jail. They needed to get away from the Gable farm and somewhere they could talk.

"Let's take a drive," Augie said.

Dennis opened his mouth, undoubtedly to protest, but Rachel slid her hand into his and he closed it again. The three of them marched back to the house and got into Augie's pickup. He had no idea where to go, but he keyed the ignition and drove out onto the highway.

CHAPTER NINETY-SIX

The gunshots woke Ray from an uneasy doze (arguing with his wife always wore him out and this one had been a doozy). They sounded distant, perhaps in the woods beyond the Gable property. Or the Gable property itself. He sat up and rubbed his eyes. In the other room came the sound of Samuel sobbing and Ruth's voice, indiscernible but sharp as sulfur beneath it. Probably the tyke had spilled his juice on the rug again.

"Ruthie, you hear them shots?" Ray called, but when he came around the corner saw the culprit behind the crying was no spilled juice.

Ruth had a suitcase packed and set of sunglasses on her nose. She never wore sunglasses.

"Where you going?" Ray asked.

"I'm leaving for a while," she said. "I need time alone to pray."

"You can pray here, where you belong."

"I don't belong here. I don't belong anywhere, much less with you or these misbegotten kids."

"Mama," Samuel said before the tears overtook him again.

Ray's face darkened and a dull ache began pulsing in his temples. "Like hell you're leaving. I love these kids like they're my own, but I ain't got it in me to raise them up alone."

"Try and stop me, Ray," Ruth said. "If you're lucky, I'll be back in a week or two. If you're not, I hope you're happy in hell."

Ruth was not a large woman, but she bulled by Ray with as little effort as a Mack truck through a railroad gate. Ray stood there, tongue working, hands balling and unballing. When he found it in him, he ran to the door and shouted after her.

"You light out of here, Ruthie, you just figure on not comin' back, you hear? The kids'n I'll be just fine on our own." He knew before the words even left him that they would make zero impact and he didn't mean them anyway. Ray took his wedding vows seriously, even if his partner did not.

Ruth never looked back. She climbed behind the wheel of her Chrysler and rattled down the drive.

"Papa," Samuel said, sobbing harder.

"That's all right, son," Ray said. "You go on and cry. You cry for the both of us, just as hard as you please."

When the boy still had not quieted five minutes later, Ray, defeated, took the boy on his knee and cradled him, the way Ray's mama Julia had done for him. After a time, he took up a song he remembered used to comfort him when his ma sang it, something about sunrise and sunset and quickly pass the years, but gave it up after the first verse because he'd forgotten the words to time's stealthy sleight of hand.

Caleb sauntered into the family room, doubtless to discover the cause of the ruckus, but Ray only shook his head at the teen: Please do not disturb. Ray watched the boy watch him with those storm-dark eyes and wondered not for the first time nor the last what black magic brewed behind them. Ray hoped he never found out firsthand.

Finally Caleb said, "Where's Mother?"

"I don't rightly know," Ray said.

"Is she coming back? She's not, is she?"

"I don't rightly know that neither." Tears burned the edges of his eyes.

Caleb went out onto the porch, letting the door bang behind him. Ray watched out the window until the boy had swaggered off up the road and then he let the tears fall. He cried so hard Samuel stopped to watch.

"Papa?" he squeaked.

"It's going to be okay, son," he said. "Somehow, I know it will be okay. Not through the Good Book, like your mama thinks, but somehow it will."

"I miss Mama," Samuel said. "Not the Mama who walked out that door, but the one I knew before."

"I do too," Ray said. "Boy, don't I ever."

Light leaked beneath the door of Father Scudder's office and voices issued from within. She opened the door without knocking. Scudder looked up through his gold-rimmed glasses, the overhead light reflecting off his bald scalp.

"Ruth? You know better than to come barging in without knocking," he said. His guests turned to look over their shoulders at the woman intruding on their meeting.

Ruth recognized the people seated in the priests office as Tina and Tanya Burgess, two of St. Joseph's congregants. Tanya was in Rachel's class and Tina, well, Ruth may have once been the town harlot, but Tina had replaced her long ago. Ruth had heard rumors. Everyone had. At least Ruth had given up her wild ways and had prayed to God for forgiveness, while Tina practically flaunted her indiscretions. Why, right here, in Father Scudder's office, she dared to wear a low-cut blouse bearing a deep divide of cleavage. And the daughter, well, she looked primed to follow in her mother's whorish high-heeled footsteps.

"What are *they* doing here?" Ruth demanded, taking a tone she'd not taken with a member of the clergy before. Because she didn't need an answer. She knew what the Burgess ladies were doing here. "No, you're not replacing Rachel. Not with this little slut."

Scudder stood up so fast his chair wheeled back and clattered into the wall behind him and his face flushed as purple as the Communion wine he doled out Sundays. "Ruth, that is quite enough."

"They're unclean," she pleaded, a whine creeping into her voice. "This little bitch is not worthy of being a vessel for the holy lord's return."

Tanya Burgess burst into tears and her mother's face turned into a troll's scowl. "*What* did you call my daughter?"

Before Ruth knew it, the hussy leapt up and snatched a handful of her hair in a tight talon. Ruth shrieked and batted a fist around, but Tina evaded and bore down with all her might. Ruth hit the floor face first and felt a tooth snap off. Maybe more than one. She couldn't tell through the pain.

Tina straddled Ruth like a rodeo rider and slammed her

head into the tile twice before the priest pulled her off. Ruth could hear him bellowing something, but couldn't seem to make sense of the words. Her vision had gone all red and gummy and a star seemed to be strobing at the edge of her perception. From a distance she heard what sounded like a far distant train whistle before realizing it came from her. She tried to make it quit, but couldn't seem to get the command to transmit from the brain to her mouth.

Then the redness clouding her vision faded to black and the strobing star winked out.

Ruth woke up someplace dark. Her head felt like a bell someone had struck with a hammer, heavy and hollow and shimmery. The pain in her mouth made her wince, which sent a shockwave through her. The side of her head where the Burgess bitch had yanked her hair felt as though it had been burned. She moaned.

When she found the means to sit up sometime later, a cold cloth that had been placed over her forehead dropped into her lap. A clock ticked in the darkness and rain plinked on glass. Her life had completely collapsed in the span of mere hours.

Rachel had run off. Ray had been right about that much at least. She'd run off with the Milliard boy everyone said was a drug dealer and was currently charged with aiding a murdering Black man. Her daughter, who had been pure enough to become a holy vessel, even with her hidden rock and roll and her skin-slicing. She had still been pure enough, Father Scudder had promised. And by now, no doubt, the criminal had sunk his filthy criminal self into her daughter. Something occurred to her then and her head ached anew.

What if the Milliard boy was sharing her with the Negro? Oh, the Lord would never deem fit for her to become holy then.

Ruth made her way out of Father Scudder's private chambers and into the office area. It stood vacant, so she opened the door to the chancel.

Father Scudder stood at the altar, preparing for Sunday's Mass. He turned at the sound of the door.

"Ruth, I must say I'm shocked by your behavior. And you look an absolute mess. Really, what has gotten into you?"

"You can't replace Rachel. She's the one."

Father Scudder glanced at the likeness of Christ hanging from the giant crucifix above them and whispered, "You would do well not to mention such things here, in broad daylight."

Despite everything, Ruth grinned. It felt stretched and misplaced on her face. "Why not? Isn't it His will, Father?"

Scudder looked as conflicted as a pig trying to decide if it wanted to bathe in mud or shit. He cleared his throat. "Of course it is."

"What were you talking to the Burgesses about?"

"That is church business."

"You were trying to persuade them to replace Rachel."

"I think you'd better leave, Ruth. Take a couple of weeks, come back to Mass after the school year starts."

"Maybe I won't come back at all," Ruth said, heading for the door.

"Come now, don't say that."

She turned at the vestibule and favored him with a sour stare. "Did you know that until I joined this church, I thought all of this … all of it was horseshit? But in my wild days, I longed to be a part of something larger than myself. I was lost, wanton. Lustful. I came here because I had nowhere else to go. And the congregation took me in, showed me how wonderful unity could feel. And I bought into it. Drank it up. Allowed myself to be showered in the light of God."

Scudder swallowed and waited for her to resume. Sweat sparkled on his pallid pate.

"But even though I loved feeling connected, I never fully believed it. What we planned for my daughter, I told myself it would be my last chance to feel that full, final connection with God. Instead, I helped the devil. I sacrificed Rachel's innocence to you, of all people. You, nothing more than a charlatan. A charmer who promises guidance and enlightenment but serves up only shit." The grin widened. "Have fun in hell whenever you find your way there, Father."

"Ruth, wait," Scudder called, but she didn't and she made it as far as the vestibule when the figure stepped out of the shadows.

At first she noticed only the red galoshes and bright yellow of the raincoat it wore, familiar items in her closet, and she opened her mouth to say her son's name. Then she saw the head of the pig, yellowed stubs of teeth poking out through peeling lips, and she shrieked. Her son had been possessed by the devil, she now understood. And the devil had come for her.

"Ruth?" Scudder called, rushing forward. "Ruth, what is it, what's wrong?"

She backed into the nave, still shrieking, and watched as her possessed son raised her husband's wood-chopping ax over its head. Behind her, the priest had seen the same thing and his voice joined hers in hollering. The ax sliced first one into silence, then the other.

CHAPTER NINETY-SEVEN

Augie drove them well into the evening. Fireflies flickered over the fields and they spied a family of deer scampering into the corn. On the way, Dennis had broken down and confessed everything, from the moment Kodi had convinced him to sell grass for him. Rachel sat quiet, listening. Not yet sixteen and she felt she'd lived a hundred lives already.

"I just don't know what the hell you were thinking," Augie said for perhaps the tenth time.

Dennis, weary: "About which part, Dad?"

"About any of it. What were you thinking, getting mixed up in that bad business? You had a bright future. You could still, if you do as I say."

Dennis hung his head. "I want to do what's right, even if I don't really know what right is in this situation."

"You're going to do exactly what I tell you to do. I'm still your father and you're still my boy."

When Dennis looked up, his eyes were dry but red-rimmed. "Dad, whatever happens, don't tell Ma, okay?"

Augie seized on that. "If you're thinking about turning yourself in, you better damn well know your mother is going to find out about all of it. She'll know. And if it doesn't kill her outright, it will do the job slowly, drawn out over years. I'm not sure which would be worse."

That did it. Dennis broke down, sobbing into his hands like a child spurned by his schoolmates. Rachel put her arm around his shoulders and he leaned into her. She kissed him gently on the head.

"And then there's this young lady to think of," Augie said, hoping to catalyze his point. "If you go off to jail, I have a feeling she might miss you something awful."

"He's right, I would," Rachel whispered.

"Now you may have to face a charge of abetting a fugitive or some such nonsense when it comes to what you did to help Zeb, but that sentence won't be as steep as quintuple homicides."

Without raising his head, he said, "Dad, I never wanted to kill anyone. It's just they didn't give me a choice, you know? Mr. Stone? Chief Engel? They planned to do me and Zebbo in. They had us locked up and, I swear to God, they were going to take us out into the corn somewhere and shoot us and bury us."

"You did what you had to do, son," Augie said. "You saved your skin and Zeb's. Now Zeb is a grown man and can take care of himself. But you did what you had to and you need some help. I aim to provide it."

"But who will take the blame for Granny and her guys?"

Augie paused, flicked his eyes to the rearview mirror, thought it through again before speaking. "Well, I suppose whoever they'll blame for Mike and Al. Mike never did come around well enough to tell who did it before he passed, so he took your identity to the grave. I figure the case may stay open a spell before it goes cold. They may look at ol' Zebbo, but they'll never have an eye on you. Not a good boy from a respected family."

"But Zebbo didn't do it. I did."

"Well, now, think about it, son. Zeb started the rock rolling down the hill when he shot Grant."

Dennis finally raised his head. "No, Dad. Grant started that when he pushed Zeb about his old man being lynched. That's nothing that ought to ever be brought up. And he called Zeb the N-word."

Augie grunted, a dismissal of his son's core argument. "That's just a word."

"Not to Black folk it isn't."

"Words never killed anyone. Bullets have. What I'm trying to say is shooting Grant is not an appropriate response to anything Grant may or may not have said to him. And that includes that particular vulgarity."

"We don't get to choose that, Dad," Dennis said, watching

his father in the rearview. "We're white. We're born into what we get, and most often what we got is a sight better than what Black folk get. Zeb, hell, you been to that shack where he lives."

"Zeb lives in a shack because he drinks up all his earnings."

"Zeb drinks up all his earnings because he lives in a shack. Dad, you're the smartest man I ever met. Can't you see the difference?"

Augie stayed quiet a long time. Gravel ticked along the truck's undercarriage. Somewhere overhead an owl howled. Finally he said, "I guess I do see the difference, but I can't tell what difference that difference will make. Zeb's my friend, but he still did wrong. In this country, it's still illegal to put a bullet in a man, no matter what he calls you. He's got to go away, either to prison or far away where he'll never be seen by anyone from Ashford County again. And he's damn well smart enough to know that much."

"What if we help him?"

Augie turned and looked at his oldest child. "We turn him in, that is helping him. The way I see it, the best course of action is to let Zeb take the fall for Granny and Mike and the others. He's already on the hook for Grant Lang because that tough old bastard had enough gusto left in him to live through two shots."

"Are you saying what I think you're saying?" Dennis asked.

"What I'm saying is Zeb is already looking at life, being a Black drunkard who attempted murder on a prominent white citizen of this county. What's five more life sentences going to mean to him?"

"Dad—"

"Whereas you, a kid with his whole life ahead of him—" He glanced over his son's head at Rachel. "—with marriage and a family and a good career and a strong inheritance awaiting him? There isn't much of a choice that I can see."

"Dad, we can't let Zebbo take the blame for what I did. He would never do it, anyway, even if we could."

"Yes he would," Augie said.

"How do you figure that?"

"I figure it like this. Out here, unless Zeb runs far and wide away from Ashford County, and I'm not talking to Chicago or

New York or even Los Angeles, I'm talking into the wilds of Alaska or all the way down to goddam Guatemala, his life is forfeit. Grant Lang will not stop until he finds and murders that man. I'm sure I don't have to spell that out to you. Lang is a stout spider with his webs cast everywhere. He'll find Zeb before long."

"Unless Zeb finds him first," Dennis whispered.

"Don't even go down that path," Augie said. "Now that Grant knows Zeb's gunning for him, he'll have Zeb flushed out into the open before long. Grant commands an army; Zeb is one man."

Augie failed to mention that Grant's army was pretty well in tatters and not nearly what it was even five years ago, but his son didn't pick up on that.

Dennis said: "So what are you thinking?"

"We convince Zeb to take the fall, send him to prison far downstate. He lives out his remaining days with three hots and a cot, and best of all, he's protected from Lang's long reach. And I can arrange for him to get a monthly stipend for his commissary account. He'd do all right in Pinckneyville or Big Muddy River. Those places'll be a damn sight better than that rotten old hovel he calls home, anyway. Be practically a hotel suite by comparison."

Dennis sat quietly while Rachel stroked the back of his hand.

"Do you think that will actually work?" he asked at last.

"Well, first we need to find Zeb, talk it through with him. You got any idea where he is?"

"No. The last time I saw him—"

Rachel said, "I might have an idea where to find him."

The Milliard men looked at her. She told them where to go.

She led them straight to her family's farm. Ray saw them drive up and came out of the house with a beer in his hand. His daughter had absconded with a boy not much her senior and his wife had walked out on them all. He was thrilled to see that at least Augie had found Rachel and appeared to have talked some sense into her. A body could always count on Augie to do that much.

"Rachel, thank God," he said when the three of them climbed out of the pickup.

"Hi, Daddy," she said and gave him a squeeze around the waist.

"I'm glad you decided to come home. The place is emptying out pretty quick," Ray said and explained Ruth's departure.

"I'm glad she's gone," Rachel said.

Ray heaved a sigh as if wondering how his wobbly little world had abruptly dumped completely over on its axis. "I guess you have a right to. I know that woman could be cruel to you."

"You don't know the half of it," Rachel said. The men looked at her.

Ray said, "Come again?"

"Not now," Rachel said. "Maybe someday, if she ever has the nerve to come crawling back here." She strode over to the hog barn, hauled the door open, and called into the darkness: "Mr. Tuel? You still here?"

"Zebbo stole my idea," Dennis said.

"He borrowed it," Rachel corrected, then stood back from the gap in the door and they waited.

Before long the man in question stepped out. "Miss Rachel? It safe to come out?"

"It's safe, Zeb," Augie said.

"Mr. Milliard, my Lord it's good to see you," Zeb said. The men embraced.

"How long you been living out here in my barn?" Ray asked.

"Not but three days, I swear it. I move around a lot."

"That true what they say about you blasting away at Grant Lang?" Ray asked.

Zebulon looked around. "I guess that cat's fled the bag."

Ray shook Zeb's hand. "That mean bastard's had it coming for a piece now. I only wished you'd finished the job."

Zeb curled a lip. "That makes two of us."

"I heard gunshots earlier," Ray said. "I don't suppose you got itchy and decided to take out Granny, did you?"

It came out sounding a joke, but no one laughed. Rachel and Dennis looked at one another.

Augie said, "Look, why don't we leave Rachel in the care of her father and the rest of us go find a place to talk. I'm sure if we put our heads together we can figure a way to wiggle out of this web."

Ray said, "Why don't we all go inside? I've got pork roast in the oven and a case of Hamm's in the icebox. Come on, there's enough for everyone."

"I don't suppose your kids ought to hear some of what we need to discuss. Or you either, for that matter, Ray. There are some things you're better off not knowing."

"Come on, Augie. Don't leave me out of the loop. I'm not as dull as some people seem to think. I can help. I got good ideas in my head, time to time."

Augie inhaled and released it. "I guess you do. Couldn't have gotten Farmland off the ground without you, truth be told. But you have to promise something, okay? You have to promise nothing we discuss ever leaves your property. We got some bad business we need to sort through."

Ray ran an X across his chest with a farm-hardened finger. "Cross my heart, hope to die."

"I sure could use some home cooking, too," Zeb said, "and maybe a place to clean up."

"You got it, my friend," Ray said and led the troop inside.

Over pork, potatoes, fresh peas swimming in butter, and applesauce pressed from Milliard apples, Augie laid out his plan step by step. Rachel thought if the man ever decided to quit this Farmland business, he could go sell sand to beach resorts. Or maybe run for President. He could be downright convincing when he needed to be.

When he finally quit talking and the plates of seconds (and, in Zeb's case, thirds—the man had been subsisting on some scant fare Rachel had smuggled to the barn), everyone sat in quiet contemplation. The subject matter had had no effect on Zeb's appetite and he sat chewing through a plate of peach cobbler as he considered what he'd heard.

"So what you're saying," he said at last, "is that I turn myself in and take the blame for everyone? Including Mr. Stone, the police chief, and Granny? As well as her guys?"

"You see the logic in it, don't you?" Augie asked. "Because you're already in the frying pan for Lang."

"But I didn't do the others."

"Right, but you'd be safe in prison," Augie said.

"I figure no one's safe in prison," Zeb said.

"You'll be safer in there than out here, at least until Grant expires."

"Maybe I ought to make that my mission, see that he does."

"Look, Zeb, I think of you as my friend and equal," Augie said. "And if you don't go to prison, you've got to go somewhere. You stick around here, they're going to catch you sooner or later. Either Lang or the law, one of them will. And you'll want it to be the law, I assure you, because to injure Grant Lang the way you did and have him catch you … let's just say I would imagine you'd wish you were dead long before you were."

Zeb shoved the plate away. The fork clattered onto the table. "You don't seem to get it, Mr. Milliard," he said. "You'll never get it. You're white. You think you can just talk your way into and out of situations that don't suit you. Maybe pay your way out. Truth is, you white folk don't get to skip atonement. You think you do, but you don't. Your actions have consequences, just as colored folks have. You need to answer for them, own up, see? You don't get to just ship the Black boy off to jail so the clean white kid can go play football at state, get married to a pretty girl, live happily ever after."

"Zeb, you got it figured wrong," Augie said, holding up a deferential hand.

"No, I think I got it figured pretty rightly. And goddam if I didn't think you were better than most white folk, Mr. Milliard. I did think of you as a friend, but now I just don't know."

Ray stood and started gathering the plates to take to the kitchen sink and ordered Rachel to help him wash and Dennis to wipe. They left with their arms heaping with porcelain and silverware.

Augie leaned over the table and lowered his voice. "My boy has his whole life ahead of him. I aim for it to be a good life for him, with a family and a fortune. Maybe even with that girl who just cleared your plate. What have you got to look forward to, even if you're absolved of everything against you? Huh? Sipping gin in your one-room hovel? Working odd jobs in some other county because you been run out on a rail in this one? I want you to think on that very carefully, Zeb. Okay? Just think on it a minute. I'm going to use the john."

Augie got up and left the room in full knowledge he'd laid all his cards on the table. All but one, which he planned to play now. He hated himself for it, but he hoped it would trump anything Zeb held.

Instead of going to the bathroom, he stepped into Ray's bedroom, closed the door, picked up the phone extension, and dialed a number. When the line went live, he said, "Yeah, Nathan? Augie Milliard over here at Ray Safford's place. Look, we got Zebulon Tuel here and he's just confessed to multiple homicides and the attempted murder of Grant Lang. I need you and your boss out here right away."

CHAPTER NINETY-EIGHT

When Augie returned to the dining room, he half-expected to find Zebulon absconded from the property, but the man still sat in place, a scowl of contemplation hard on his face as if chiseled there.

"Can I get you a fresh beer?" Augie asked.

"I don't think I ought to. Sometimes I say things I regret when I have too many."

Augie sat and placed his palms flat on the tablecloth. "Look, Zeb. You're a good friend, okay? That's never going to change. And anyone who knows me as well as you knows I would never willingly put a friend in danger. I really think this is the best course of action we can possibly take."

"I know you do," Zeb said. "You and every other white man with money and power. Way I see it, you're not far off the horse from Grant Lang. Not anymore."

"Zeb, do you know how much that pains me to hear? I'm nothing like the man you shot. Not like any of them. I'm especially not like the lady you ended, you get me? Granny Adeline, Grant Lang, Mike Stone, Al Engel? They're the bad guys here. You did us all a service by putting them down. Hell, you'll be a hero once this goes to trial. Everyone I just named had an army of enemies."

"An army of friends too who'll be none too happy a colored man killed so many white folks."

Augie waved this away, stalling now. He had mere minutes to seal the deal, though he knew it likely wouldn't matter one way or the other. This was going to go only one way, because it was five white voices against one Black. He'd never been a man motivated by racial prejudice, but when it came to his family, he'd also never been a man to take risks.

"On the inside, you'll not only be protected, you'll be on *top*. Your people hear you killed five rich white folk and tried to hit a sixth? You'll be elected president in there, you understand me? Hell, forget president—they'll crown you king inside a week."

The kitchen door creaked open. Augie heard water running and a light clatter as Rachel and his son scrubbed the dishes. If everything went according to plan, that would be a nightly ritual for decades to come—at least until their kids had grown old enough to take over the chore.

"Augie?" Ray asked.

"What is it?"

"Chief Pernell just pulled up with Nate Berryman riding shotgun."

Zeb jumped up, knocking his chair over, any spell Augie might have weaved over him broken. "Goddamn you," he spat. "I won't forgive you this, Mr. Milliard, no matter how long I live."

He rushed toward the back door, yanked it open, and ran straight into Berryman. Nate might have been slow, but he was large, and he wrestled Zebulon to the ground.

"I got him, Chief!" the big boy called as he clamped the cuffs on his prisoner's wrists. Pernell came around the house and helped haul Zeb to his feet.

"I didn't do it," Zeb said. "I didn't."

By this time, everyone had crowded out onto the back stoop. Tears stood in Dennis's eyes. He still clutched the dishtowel he'd been using to dry, a navy and white checked cloth with the baby powder blue silhouette of a pig embroidered onto it. Augie would never, until his dying day, forget that detail of this last terrible night as an intact family.

"You can tell that shit to Judge Fahrlander," Pernell said. Then he drew back a fist and launched it full-bore into Zeb's belly.

"Stop it, goddam you!" Dennis bellowed. "He's telling the truth."

Everyone looked at around at him. Augie whispered, "Son,

what the hell do you think you're doing?"

"I did it," Dennis said. "I shot them all, starting with Grant Lang."

CHAPTER NINETY-NINE

It took until the end of summer to sort through all the miles of legal red tape surrounding the Dennis Milliard case. The entire family turned out to support him, and Augie hired an attorney from the Chicago suburbs to represent his boy. By then the Farmland project had been put on indefinite hold.

With the confession, there wouldn't have to be weeks spent in a courtroom, the lawyer advised, but more than one person contested the confession. The boy's father, of course, though that meant about as much legally as a passport drawn in crayon.

Grant Lang, though, refused to allow the boy to take the fall for shooting him. He was quoted as saying: "Dennis Milliard may have gunned down Adeline Gable in cold blood, that's up to you to determine, but that boy was home by the fire with a bellyful of egg nog and Christmas cookies when Zebulon Tuel drew on me in American Pastime. I saw him clear as summer showers."

Zebulon, who had been locked up right alongside Dennis until everything could get sorted, admitted his deed. He couldn't, he said, let Dennis take the blame for something he did and maybe get another forty years tacked on to his sentence.

Of course, by then the decapitated bodies of Ruth Safford and Father Francis Scudder had been found stacked neatly on the back pews of St. Joseph's Catholic Church, but it took only a cursory investigation to understand Dennis had not been responsible for their murders. No, this *modus operandi*, the lead FBI agent working the case, made clear was of a different ilk altogether. Even so, the ME's report established the time of death as occurring during or just prior to the arrests made at the Safford property, which eliminated both Dennis and Zeb as suspects.

In the end, with Dennis's eighteenth birthday looming a slim three weeks away, Judge Linda Mathis (the pinko liberal who regularly drew Grant Lang's ire) sentenced him as an adult to life in prison with the possibility of parole in the year 2021. The year Dennis turned 63. She'd shown him that slight mercy because, after hearing all the testimony, she claimed to believe Dennis had acted in self-defense on both occasions. Had Dennis drawn Judge Fahrlander in this case, he would have gone in for life without possibility of parole, no doubt about it.

Teresa Milliard nearly fainted in the courtroom when the judge read the ruling and so did her husband, who had sprouted a generous cropping of white hair since his son's reckless confession.

For his part, Dennis took the sentencing stoically, quietly standing and staring at the American flag looming behind the bench. He was to be transferred via the Illinois Department of Corrections to Bosco Correctional Center roughly three hours from Derby. Less than a year later, Illinois would reinstate the death penalty; over time, as Dennis served out his sentence, he would be forever grateful his transgressions took place when they did. Prison he could handle. Facing the Almighty he was certain he could not. Not, at least, until he atoned.

Atonement, though, was something his family, especially his father, continuously informed him he did not need. He had acted in self-defense. He had tried to help a family friend, who'd started the ball rolling. He *this*. He *that*. Dennis didn't care. He knew he had a long and careful peace to make with his Creator and he meant to do just that with his remaining time on Earth.

Zebulon was not so lucky when it came to judges. Fahrlander tried his case and when the jury found him guilty, sentenced the man to the maximum for attempted murder. The attorney representing him, paid for by the Milliard family, was able to successfully convince the jurors that his client's act had been a crime of passion and not premeditated, which dropped the sentence from potential life imprisonment to 15 years. With good behavior, Zebulon Tuel might be out before the end of the 1980s. He went quietly when the officers led him away, though he stared down the man he'd shot all the way out of the courtroom, and when that man found it impossible to hold his gaze, Zebulon smiled.

The morning they transferred Dennis from Ashford County to Bosco CC, damn near the entire county turned out. Two factions formed—those who shouted curses and death threats, and those who came to support the youngster. As a detachment of guards led him from the jail to the IDOC bus, someone threw an ear of corn and someone else—surprise, surprise—an apple. Neither struck their intended target, but rather folks in the opposing crowd and a melee ensued as the bus rattled off down the road.

Before authorities could separate the throng, a dozen people had sustained injuries, one of them life-threatening. Augie had kept his family clear of the fracas and they'd all gotten one last look at Dennis before his change of residence became official. The boy stared out at them through the grimy mesh-covered glass and raised a hand in farewell. Raised them both, actually, as they'd been cuffed together. It was an image August Milliard III never dreamed he'd see if he lived a thousand lifetimes.

Afterward, as the weeks churned on and things settled down, the Milliards strived to return to normalcy. A fine idea, perhaps, but one that would never come to fruition. Augie, understandably, lost interest in his Farmland project and by the time the school year rolled around production had been completely abandoned. Arguments with Teresa grew more frequent and ferocious. The kids became sullen and withdrawn, except for the twins who didn't seem to fully grasp their new reality or had already found the resiliency to adapt to it. They tried desperately to cheer their remaining family up, to no avail.

Facing a mountain of debt and a swiftly fracturing family, Augie packed a bag one early morning and drove away. Rachel was there at the time, having stayed the night with Susie (who needed a friend now more than ever), and happened to be in the kitchen getting a drink of water and watching lightning on the horizon through the window when Augie crept in carrying a suitcase at three a.m. with Timber pacing at his side.

"Rachel? Everything all right?" he asked.

"Yes, Mr. Milliard. Are you going somewhere?"

"I have to go away for a little while." He watched her, biting a lip as he came to a decision. "Will you do something for me?"

"Of course, sure."

Augie set the suitcase on the breakfast island where the family had made so many wonderful memories in their white cocoon of privilege. Rain pattered the kitchen window and thunder grumbled.

"Could you to look after Susie for me? Make sure you be as gentle as possible with her. What she needs now is someone she can talk to, confide in. And so do you. Cry together, you and Susan, if necessary. You girls have been through too much too young and you'll need one another in the coming years. Understand?"

Tears stung Rachel's eyes. "Yes, Mr. Milliard. I understand. I'll be Susie's friend as long as she'll have me." She paused, unsure whether to ask what came to mind, but decided it couldn't hurt at this point. "Are you coming back? Or are you going away forever, like Dennis?"

Augie breathed deep. "I don't know. That's an honest answer. But if I don't come back for a while, tell your father I said farewell. He's a good man. You're lucky to have him. And he's lucky to have you."

"I will, Mr. Milliard." Then, before she could stop herself, she rushed across the tiles and hugged him. He squeezed back briefly, then patted her shoulder to cue her release.

"Take care of yourself, darlin'. It may not seem like it now, but life's going to go on. You're going to finish growing up and lead a spectacular life. I may not know much, but I know that."

Then, without another word, Augie snatched up the suitcase and walked out the door into the weather. Rachel watched him drive down the lane and out of sight. When she could no longer see his taillights, she crept back upstairs and climbed into bed beside Susie and listened to her friend breathing in the darkness with Timber huddled between them. Thunder bowled and Rachel rolled over, tucked an arm beneath her head, and closed her eyes.

CHAPTER ONE HUNDRED

September 20, 1976
Dear Rachel,

Hello from the dungeon! Have I mentioned how much I love it here? They have a chocolate fountain in the cafeteria, an open bar on D Block, and a water park in the exercise yard. We get weekly massages and once a month a magician performs for the entire prison!

Just kidding, this place sucks eggs. But it's not as bad as I imagined. At least not yet. They have a great automotive class that I signed up for, so that's fun. I've even managed to make a few friends, or as close to friends as you can have in a place like this. I wish Zebbo would've come here instead of being sent downstate. Anyway, I guess I better get used to it because this is my new reality.

How are you holding up? How's your old man? Is my lil sis being nice? Oops, lights out so I have to wrap this up. Give my love to everyone back home.

Yours,
Dennis

September 30, 1976
Dear Rachel,

Got my ass kicked for the first time the other day. Up till then, I'd done a good job of steering clear of trouble. This guy, I don't know his Christian name, but they call him Steelhead in here. Well, he just up and blindsides me in the cafeteria. Dropped my tray of scrambled eggs (if that's what you call the watery slop they serve) and found myself eye to eye with the mess. This guy drops a knee on me and tells me to start licking it up. Says, "Slurp on it, pretty boy, and then I'll give you something else to slurp on." The guards? They just laugh.

So while Steelhead is laughing along with them, I throw an elbow into his eye. Heard the bone around it crack, like a baseball hit out of Tiger Park. Guy screams and falls over. Then his friends are on me, like four at once. I still got my football muscle, but what am I going to do against four hardened prisoners? They beat me six ways from Sunday and I spent three days in the infirmary. I'm better now, but I'll need to watch my back. Damn, do I wish Zebbo had come here with me. More later.

Yours,
Dennis

P.S. Got word the Johansens moved out of the state. Ohio, I guess? Randy never said good-bye to me. I miss my friends. I miss you.

January 2, 1977
Dear Rachel,

Finally made a few friends. Not friends, really. Allies, I guess. Hate to say it, but they're Aryans. I know Zeb wouldn't like that, but I bet it would make Grant Lang's day.

I had to, though. The beatings had become a regular thing. You know? And it's not like I buy any of the bullshit they sell. It's like wearing a Halloween mask year round.

They made me "prove my loyalty," through a pretty rough initiation, which I'll spare you the details on. Had to shave my head and let them tattoo me too, but I figure it's all part of the costume, you know? Now I have protection, at least, though I get some pretty hard looks from the Brothers and Hispanics. One day this place is going to explode, but for now each group keeps to itself and I'm content with that.

I live for nights. Night is my time now. With no cellmate (currently, fingers crossed it lasts forever!), I can have some peace. I can think clearly. I can atone for what needs atoning. It's a blessing, really. Lights out. Bye.

Yours,

D

P.S. You heard my folks sold the farm? They're moving back to Michigan to try and start over, I guess. They went through a rough patch for a while. Sold my Firebird, too. I can't blame them.

September 12, 1978
Dear Rachel,

Been some time, huh? Sorry about that. I got a lot on my mind these days. I'm sure you can relate.

My folks came to visit the other day and, as always, my mother broke down. She can't stand the way I look now, I don't think. The skinhead vibe and all. I can't say I blame her. My dad, he can barely keep it together either. They look like they've aged five years. They won't let my brothers and sisters come, not anymore. Not since I joined up with the Aryans.

But guess what? I'm moving up in the ranks! See, I got an idea and I ran it past Bulldog (he's our leader). And he loved it!

With everything that's been going on over the past couple years, I almost forgot about what Zeb and I took out of the cabin. You know what I mean, right? And I thought, with Bulldog's connections outside, he might be able to get to it. So when I told him about it, his face just lights up and he says, "Oh, hell yeah I got someone who can get to it. How much are we talkin', Big D?" (Big D is my new name here. Kind of cool, yeah?)

And I tell him, "Bulldog, we're talking at least twenty pounds."

And his jaw just drops! And he says, "Big D, if this is a fuckin' joke I'm going to feed you to the n***ers in pieces."

With Bulldog, you never know if he's joking, so I tell him, "I swear to God, Bulldog. I can tell you exactly where it's at and your man can get it and distribute it and send you some proceeds."

So that's our plan. We'll see how it winds up. Ok, lights out. Yours,

Big D

P.S. I love that signature!!

March 25, 1982
Dear Rachel,

I heard the news about Susan. Mom and Dad haven't visited in better than a year, but Suze came alone to tell me in person. I cannot believe she plans on marrying that man. What the hell is she thinking?

Rachel, I know I haven't written in some time (the operation I outlined in my last letter has occupied much of my time as Bulldog has put me in charge of it). But I have a favor to ask you. If you still talk to Susie, could you please PLEASE try and talk some sense into her? I understand her motivations, I guess, but I cannot condone them. I'm sure Mom and Dad have tried to talk her out of it, but you know Susie—she's always been bullheaded.

Of course, I tried to talk to her myself while she was here, but it did no good. Come June, I fear she'll make the biggest mistake of her life … one that might drop my father right into his grave, assuming she goes through with it. He didn't work this hard in life to deserve an end like that.

Anyway. Sorry to dump this on you. I hope you're well. Susan said you graduated from Derby High third in your class, which kind of puts me behind the times in terms of current events. For what it's worth now, congratulations! I'll write again soon.

Forever Yours,
Big D

P.S. Did you hear Tommy is going to Michigan on a football scholarship?! I'm so proud of that kid. He'll make a hell of a QB for the Wolverines, I just know it. Football, I think, kept his head on straight through everything. I wish it would have kept mine on.

October 2, 1984
Dear Rachel,

I heard you moved to New England recently. Suze visited for
the first time in a while and had some news, that being the first
piece she shared with me. After that she broke it to me gentle that
you got married. A shrink, I guess? That's a good choice. And so
is New England. I've never been, but I read about it sometimes in
the library here and think of you. And that means you missed all
of the craziness that's going on back home, huh? That poor girl
getting kidnapped and some kind of crazy commune brewing
right in our own Ashford County? I'm guessing the events are
related. The hicks aren't going to go for any hippie kidnappers for
long, I can tell you that. It always seems like something is going
on there nowadays; remember before the corn maze incident how
boring our county was? Far out, as we used to say back when.

Did you hear about Tommy's trouble in Ann Arbor? They
cut him from the team and I can't say I blame them. Did you
watch his games? I caught them sometimes; they have a TV
in the day room we get to watch for a few hours a week. Kid
is heading home to finish college, I guess. He'll play for NCU
because they're about the only school that would take him
after what happened. At least he avoided any legal issues, he
wouldn't do well in prison.

Still haven't seen the twins since I left town. That makes me
sad, but my folks tell me they're doing well.

Oh, did you hear about Grant? Lost everything in what
the news is calling a "grain crisis." They say the Soviets are
retaliating against Carter's embargo and are "diversifying"
their agricultural suppliers. In other words, they're no longer
buying American corn. And Reagan's subsidies aren't cutting
it, according to Cronkite. I think I should feel happier about
Grant's ruin than I do, but I don't. And you know why that is.
I guess they're planning on moving to Iowa, where taxes are
cheaper. So much for his beloved Corn Fest now, huh? I wonder
if the county will set up anything to take its place—our people
need some kind of fun way out there in the boonies.

Oh, well. What can I do from in here? Not a damn thing is what. But at least things are going well from an operational standpoint. The Brotherhood has never been so prosperous, and Bulldog has made me his right hand man! I guess that's all for now. I wish you had come to visit before you moved, but I understand why you didn't. And I don't blame you.

Forever Yours,

Big D

P.S. Mom and Dad came to visit again, finally, and brought Hannah. God, it was good to see them again. We had a great time, or at least as great a time as we can have with a wall of glass between us. I keep hoping their joint visits will spark them to get back together, but it seems like Mom and Dad are done for good.

P.P.S. Did you hear they found Old Dad's body buried in a field up near the county line? ID'd by dental records, from what I hear. They don't know for sure, not 100%, but my sources on the outside tell me they think he had his throat cut from behind. They don't know who did it, though.

March 12, 1987
Dear Rachel,

I just learned Candace has been accepted into Loyola School of Law and Richard into the U of I's architecture program!! I'm so happy I could break into song.

Of course, I have to temper that happiness with what happened to Tommy. I'm sure you heard about him blowing out his knee in the bowl game a while back? The kid's devastated, and rightly so. He could have gone pro. He NEEDED to go pro. Docs say he'll walk again, but probably always with a limp. Feel SO bad for him. It's just no damn fair.

Anyway, hope all is well with you and your family. I guess you've got a little girl now? I'm happy for you, too, you know.

Forever Yours,

Big D

February 14, 1991
Dear Rachel,

Happy Valentine's Day.
I love you.
Dennis Milliard

June 7, 1992
Dear Susan,

First off, Happy Anniversary. You made it 10 years and I'm very happy for you. It sounds like you've shaken off much of what happened from back home and are doing well for yourself. Congratulations. Listen, if you think about it, next time you talk to Mom or Dad, could you please ask them to come see me? I miss them terribly. Tell them to bring everyone. Please. You're the only one who still speaks to me, and even that's only once every few years. Thanks.
    Love you, sis.
    Your Big Brother,

Dennis

September 18, 1996
Dear Rachel,

I have now officially been in custody of the Illinois Department of Corrections for 20 years. Two decades. It feels like I've lived here forever, like time has stood still and there's nothing on the other side of these walls. On the other hand, I've done all right for myself inside. Bulldog died last year and now I run the show. I do it better than he ever did, too, and that's not bragging. Sure, I've been in my fair share of brawls and have taken a shiv twice, but all in all, I manage to keep the peace.
    See, the leaders of the Brothers and the Hispanics and I made a secret pact. A truce. No one wants bloodshed, but sometimes their soldiers (or mine) get antsy and we have to allow them a

small skirmish. But once that's over, and no one is too seriously injured, we return to peace. Snap, just like that. And it WORKS. There hasn't been all-out war since I took over. Pretty brilliant, if I do say so myself. (I think I'm allowed to toot my own horn sometimes, right?)

Also, our Ashford County operation has moved from grass to meth. Call it an upgrade: a better high and more dough for me and my crew. Manufacturing end of it is perfect, because the ingredients are all things you can find right there in Farmland. Give it a decade and it'll all be regulated up the wazoo, you'll need a passport, a state ID, and a thumbprint to buy Sudafed, but for now we're raking it in hand over fist. (And, in case you're wondering, no I'm not concerned about the warden reading this letter and adding another decade for drug peddling; he's on my payroll now.)

Hope you're doing all right. I miss you.

Yours Forever,

Dennis

P.S. Did you hear Zebbo got out? He's AS FREE AS A BIRD NOW! (Get the Skynyrd reference, hah!) He bought a house in one of those picturesque old neighborhoods in Murdoch, you know the ones with the shade trees and windchimes? And he's working full-time at Arch's Market—he's out of the business for good and living legit. I'm happy for him. I had a couple of my trusted guys keep an eye on him for a while to make sure Grant Lang attempted no retaliation, but I don't think the old farmer has it in him anymore; he lost all of his muscle when he lost his farm.

April 11, 2002
Dear Rachel,

I heard about Caleb, that he was charged with those four murders from back when. Forensic science is going to close a whole lot more cold cases in the coming years. Have you heard from him at all? I'm guessing not. It seems he wound up like

Lorelai Lang, simply vanished into the wind.

If that's the case, it must be difficult not to have some closure. I only know part of the story, but I know he had a reason for what he did. He wasn't the psycho people said he was. Believe me, I've met my fair share of psychos in here, and your brother wasn't one of them. Well, maybe he was. To do what he did, I guess you'd have to be, at least a little. But he didn't do it out of evil. He did it out of good. Protection. I'm sure you know that. Same with those farmhands up at the Stone place. I read the case file on them (yes, I can get pretty much any police report in here; my crew keeps me in the loop), what Ursula reported they tried to do to her a few nights before the hands were killed. I'm guessing she must have told Caleb, or else he found out some other way. They got what they had coming. Justice isn't always pretty when it's served. Sometimes it takes on another level of ugly. I guess your mother and the priest found that out, didn't they?

Anyways, I'll let you go. This is getting morbid.

Yours,

Dennis

July 23, 2013

Dear Rachel!

Have you heard! They found evidence of a criminal drug conspiracy in Ashford County. Judge Fahrlander, who I'm sure you heard died in '04, well whoever bought his estate, they found a bunch of stuff tying him to a marijuana manufacturing and distribution operation way back in the 70s. Mike Stone and Chief of the Village of Derby Police Alvin Engel were also involved.

Between you and me, I may have had a hand in orchestrating that find. See, my guys on the outside, I had them start snooping around, figuring there had to be something to prove all those guys were in it together AND THERE WAS! My boys found it.

All I can say is I hope to GOD Grant Lang goes away for the rest of his miserable life. He's the only one left out of that bunch, but someone ought to pay for it. And if we can get a posthumous smirch on the rest of their records, well, I guess that wouldn't hurt either.

Anyways, hope all is well. Keep cool this summer.

Yours,

Dennis M.

January 15, 2014
Dear Rachel,

Looks like Grant's going to weasel out of it somehow. Hard for me to get the optics on it from in here, but from what my boys tell me, Grant's Teflon.

The others, not so much. Stone, Engel, and Fahrlander were all found posthumously guilty of criminal conspiracy.

Grant always was the smart one, though. If anyone knew how to keep his name out of the mud, it was that old snake. Hard to believe he's still alive, but I'm sure Susie's thankful. He did save her, after all, I guess. And I guess I ought to be thankful for him too for that. Maybe I've been too hard on him all these years. I don't know what to think anymore. I better cut this short so I don't drive myself nuts.

Happy New Year, Rachel.

Yours,

Dennis M.

July 4, 2021
Dear Mom,

Tomorrow I go before the parole board to find out if they see fit to turn me loose. I can hardly think, and my pulse isn't quite steady. I've read that book and seen the movie version of that prisoner who gets institutionalized and can't make it on the outside. I'm not sure I can either, but I'm grateful for the folks who'll be there to help and support me. I love you all, and if I don't make it out this time, I hope you all have a wonderful Independence Day.

All of my love forever and ever,

Dennis

July 6, 2021
Dear Rachel,

They're letting me out end of September. I don't know how to feel about that. I don't know much of anything anymore. It's like my brain can't calm down and I feel all itchy and jittery. Is that normal? I suppose it is.

They're throwing me a parole party on October 13. I don't know if you'll be able to make it, but I hope you can. I would love to see you. And meet your family, of course.

Yours Always and Forever,

Dennis Milliard

P.S. Time's a slippery fish, isn't it? It doesn't hardly make sense when you think about it. When you think about it, nothing does. Jeez Louise. Strange thing, this life. I hope the next one's better. For all of us.

POSTLUDE

They pulled into the parking lot of the newly constructed (well, newish—a plaque bolted to the wall claimed construction had been completed in 2015) Village of Derby Dale Civic Center and Don dropped the car into PARK and made a move toward the ignition. Rachel stilled his hand.

"Can we just sit a moment?" she asked.

"Of course, hon. Take all the time you need."

The session in the hotel room had served to calm her squalling nerves, but now they twanged again like a detuned banjo. The lot had already filled most of the way up, the party having been scheduled to start an hour ago.

"Is fashionably late still fashionable?" Rachel asked with a nervous titter.

"I suppose it always will be," Don said and, after a pause: "We don't have to go in, you know. We can turn around and drive back to the hotel and have a repeat of that tender lovin'."

Rachel knotted her fingers in her lap. "No, I need to do this. Some circles need to be closed." Then she added (perhaps unnecessarily): "Forever."

A car pulled into the lot and Rachel craned to see who it might be, shading her eyes against the sun. Her pulse did a quiet little hiccup, but it was no one she recognized; probably an extended family member from out of town.

"Okay," she said, releasing shaky breath. "I'm as ready as I'll ever be."

Don reached over and gave her hand a squeeze and they opened their doors together.

Rachel would never quite be able to remember the walk up to the Civic Center. It happened as if in a dream. One moment she'd been climbing out of the car and the next Don had been hauling the big glass-paneled door open and ushering her inside. A sign with a bright yellow arrow seemed to jump out at her, bearing the legend: MILLIARD PARTY RM 110. That was a detail that would stick in her brain the rest of her days: that arrow and that legend. She followed the sign to the gymnasium-sized space and paused at the door, taking in the sight.

Better than a hundred people milled about, sipping from Styrofoam cups or dipping veggies into onion dip. She had a spell where the room seemed to get too bright and she thought she might faint, but it passed and she breathed and summoned her poise. This would be okay. Everything would turn out fine, just as Mr. Milliard had promised all those years ago on the morning he left his family. Rachel wondered if he'd put in an appearance tonight. She hoped so; his presence had always been one of tranquility and peace.

"Rachel Safford? Is that you?" a voice nearby called and before she could even turn someone swept her into a tight embrace that smelled of Musk perfume.

"Well, it was. I'm Rachel Healy now," she said, patting the strange shoulder, "but who the hell are you?"

The woman laughed and released her, stepping back. "I'm sorry I bum-rushed you like that. It's just been so darn *long*."

Rachel studied the woman's face and at last put together she was looking at Hannah Milliard. Now Hannah Something-or-other; she couldn't recall her married name. "It has been quite a while," she said, beaming, knowing—truly *knowing*—everything would be okay despite the flutterings in her belly that seemed to portend otherwise.

"Well, come on in. Susie is going to be so happy you made it. So is Dennis, of course, but he's not much in a party mood right now, as you can probably imagine," Hannah said and swooped Rachel inside.

"I don't suppose my husband could tag along?" Rachel asked and Hannah practically screamed laughter.

"Oh my, I'm sorry." When Don stepped forward, grinning, and offered his hand, she said: "This must be the lucky fellow."

Don said his name and added, in a very un-Don-like fashion:

"She's the lucky one in this relationship. I'm quite the catch."

Hannah cawed again, too loud, and said, "I bet you are, handsome. Now come on. So much catching up to do. Oh, Susie! Susan Lynn Lang, come over here at once."

A slight woman with short silver hair turned at the sound of her name, a smile etched from ear to ear. When she saw Rachel, it slipped for a moment before returning full force. "Rachel," she said. A moment of paralysis elongated between them and then they rushed into one another's arms.

When they parted, their fingers remained locked and they looked one another over with sparkling eyes. "Thank you for coming. It means the world to me. And to that old thick-headed brother of mine."

"Where is he, anyway?" Rachel asked, peering around. She had no idea what to expect when it came to Dennis. It had been nearly half a century since she'd seen him.

"He's taking a break from all of this," Susan said, waving her hand. "After all that time, I think it's a little overwhelming for him. We probably should have planned a smaller gathering, but so many people couldn't wait to see him."

Rachel introduced her husband and the three of them found drinks and chatted about how the last few decades had treated them. At various points, others would sneak up to greet Rachel. The Milliard twins, Candace and Richard, sidled up first and introduced their families. Candace had graduated from Loyola law and opened a practice in Chicago, which Rachel had read about at some point, while Richard had earned his Master's in architecture and had designed the very Civic Center in which they now stood.

"An F-5 twister couldn't tear this place down," he said, kicking a wall with one wingtip, while his wife and his sisters took turns berating his varnished ego.

Rachel asked if their middle brother, Thomas, had made the trip.

Susan frowned. "Tommy said he couldn't make it because he had too much work, but we know that's simply not true. He's always blamed Dennis for the family falling apart. And with the injury that sidelined his football career and what happened before, well, he kind of just sticks to himself these days."

"Oh. I'm sorry to hear that. Tell him I wish him the best next time you speak to him, will you?"

Susan promised she would.

Rachel asked, "What about your folks? Are they here?"

"Mom's been stuck talking to the Burgess clan for damn near an hour now. I suppose I ought to rescue her. Come on, she'll be thrilled to see you again."

They made their way through the throng and Susan tapped her mother's shoulder. When Teresa turned, no hint of recognition showed in her eyes until Susan offered the name of their guest.

"Rachel?" Teresa said. "Oh my. Thank you for coming. Dennis will be *thrilled*. If anyone can put a smile on his face today, you can. Let me go get him, you wait right here."

As she hurried off, a fresh flock of fireflies erupted through Rachel's core and she had to make a conscious effort not to wring her hands. To pass the time, she said, "What about your father? Is he here?"

Susan's face puckered some. "I'm sorry, sweetie. I thought you might have heard. Dad had a stroke about a year ago. It dropped him like a bolt of lightning."

This news startled Rachel more than she imagined. Of course, she had long acknowledged the possibility Augie Milliard might be no longer among the living, but she had never really accepted it. The man had seemed somehow immortal to her, unlike her own father, who had been felled by a heart attack in 1989. Oh, she knew Ray wasn't her real father. She'd suspected it for years, even before she knew for sure, but that had not stopped her from mourning him like he was. Blood does not make a man a father, after all: love does.

"I'm very sorry to hear that, Susan."

Susan shrugged a slender shoulder. "The death bug is gonna bite us all sooner or later. Dad lived a long and eventful life. We just have to enjoy what time we have and with whom we have it, right?"

Rachel confirmed this sentiment. She turned to find her husband and found he'd struck up a conversation with another scholarly looking fellow whom she did not recognize. Good for him. She was happy he wouldn't feel like a third wheel.

At the same time, an ancient husk of a man in an electric wheelchair buzzed up beside Susan. Most of his thin white hair, what little of it was left, lay plastered to a liver-spotted scalp. Ears the size of prawns dangled damn near to his scrawny shoulders. Deep lines creased his face and his eyes held little of life's light in them. One palsied hand shook its way toward Rachel and he said something in a voice so choked with age she couldn't understand it, but she took the hand anyway.

Susie said, "Rachel, you remember my husband, don't you? Grant?"

Of course, Rachel had heard of the wedding of Susan Milliard and the Lang patriarch when it happened in the early 1980s, and it had been one of the reasons she'd drifted apart from her longtime best friend. But to see Grant here, like this, still alive but barely living, shocked her more than learning of Augie's passing. Grant had survived two gunshots and had lived long enough to marry the child he had once rescued from a psychotic farmhand. That God had seen fit to let him live, but had struck Augie and her father down like cattle seemed somehow disgraceful. Then again, at least Augie and Ray would be in heaven while Grant lingered here on earth, stuck in a chair and pissing himself, if the odor emanating from him was any indication. Maybe Augie and Ray had gotten the better deal after all. They still had their dignities and their legacies.

"Hello, Mr. Lang. It's been a long time."

Grant croaked something else and withdrew his papery hand.

"Okay, dear, why don't we get you a plate of barbeque?" Susan said and waved someone over to help her.

"Are any of your, um, stepdaughters here today?" Rachel asked, hoping she wasn't overstepping.

That sour face Susan appeared to have mastered sometime in the intervening years returned. "They're not my stepdaughters. Their mother moved them out of state ages ago. The youngest, anyway. No one's heard from Lorelai since everything went south. Figure her for dead. None of the others have come to see their father or even called in all the years we've been married. Grant doesn't seem to care. He did early on, I could tell, but I think that time of his life burned out of him long ago."

"I'm surprised your … your husband came, what with his and Dennis's past."

"Oh, they called a truce years ago. Grant went to visit my big brother in the pen and they worked something out between them. I doubt they'll ever sit down to watch a Super Bowl together, but they're at least on better terms now."

The person Susan had hailed, someone Rachel didn't know—a hired aide, perhaps—helped Grant with a plate of food, which he wound up spilling in his lap. Rachel looked away from the scene, embarrassed.

"Did your daughter come?" Susan asked.

Rachel smiled. "Jasmine is busy researching her next book and couldn't make it."

"Oh, that's a shame," Susan said. "I read her first one about the legends of the Midwest—it was a fun read and to learn some history of our little neck of the woods was fascinating."

"Rachel?" a voice whispered from behind her and her heart seized like an engine drained of oil. She closed her eyes and gathered herself before she brought herself to turn.

Dennis Milliard had changed little over the years. He'd put on maybe 20 pounds, mostly muscle (even at his age). His hair—short, but not shaved—had turned shock white and a long pink scar adorned one cheek, but mostly he looked the same. The biggest change had come to his eyes, which, like Grant Lang's, held no spark of life in their dark depths. Someone, the penitentiary perhaps, had gotten him in an ill-fitting suit to stand in. None of his white supremacist jailhouse tattoos were visible, and Rachel was thankful for that.

She breathed his name and took a step toward him, hands out, not wanting to startle him. He stood staring at her a moment, looking her over, drinking her in, and then a smile brightened his face like sunrise. Something sparked in his dead eyes and she realized they were tears. He opened his arms and she collapsed into him. God, he even smelled the same as he had on that Thanksgiving night in 1975. How could that be possible with all the time he'd spent caged up? Some things never change, though, Rachel knew, and for the briefest of moments she felt at home for the first time in decades.

"I'm surprised you came," he said, his voice a diesel rumble in her ear.

"I wouldn't have missed it," she said. "Welcome back."

"I wrote you. Probably a hundred letters over the years."

"I know. I saved them all in a cigar box that was my father's."

"You never wrote back."

Rachel, already flushed, felt her face flame anew. "I did. I tried, anyway. I tore them up afterward."

"Jeez Louise, why?"

"None of them ever felt authentic enough to send. I always felt like that little girl you knew back when."

"Can we go somewhere and talk? Alone?" He glanced at Don, who he'd clearly pegged as belonging to Rachel.

"I'd like that," Rachel said, beaming and wiping her eyes. She looked at her man and he made a shooing gesture with one hand. There might have been a sparkle in his eyes as well. He was a good husband.

"Come with me," he said. "I know the perfect place."

She let him lead her out the Civic Center's back door where a grounds crew had meticulously maintained the lawn for outdoor events like Easter Egg Hunts and Independence Day extravaganzas and parole parties. Except for the pile of fallen leaves that would likely be ushered to the curb come morning.

For now, though, they had it to themselves. Dennis held her hand while she toed off her shoes and climbed into the rich, aromatic epicenter. It wasn't nearly as large as the one Dennis had made of apple leaves those years ago, but it was big enough for both of them. It was big enough for *now*. Together, in the autumn sunshine, they found each other's fingers, and locked them tight for a long, long time.

MEET THE AUTHOR

Aaron Gudmunson is the author of *Snow Globe, The Slingerman*, and *Emma Tremendous*, as well as the collection *From the Dusklands*. His short fiction, essays, columns, interviews, and articles have appeared in numerous publications.

Follow him on Twitter @ADGudmun.

Curious about other Crossroad Press books?
Stop by our site:
http://store.crossroadpress.com
We offer quality writing
in digital, audio, and print formats.

www.ingramcontent.com/pod-product-compliance
Lightning Source LLC
Chambersburg PA
CBHW020458020726
47493CB00001B/87